32 VOTES BEFORE BREAK- FAST

Books by Jesse Stuart

MAN WITH A BULL-TONGUE PLOW

HEAD O' W-HOLLOW

TREES OF HEAVEN

MEN OF THE MOUNTAINS

TAPS FOR PRIVATE TUSSIE

MONGREL METTLE

ALBUM OF DESTINY

FORETASTE OF GLORY

TALES FROM THE PLUM GROVE HILLS

THE THREAD THAT RUNS SO TRUE

HIE TO THE HUNTERS

CLEARING IN THE SKY

KENTUCKY IS MY LAND

THE GOOD SPIRIT OF LAUREL RIDGE

THE YEAR OF MY REBIRTH

32 VOTES BEFORE BREAK-FAST

Politics at the grass roots,
as seen in short stories by

JESSE STUART

McGraw-Hill Book Company

New York   St. Louis   San Francisco
Düsseldorf   London   Mexico   Sydney   Toronto

Book Designed by Marcy J. Katz

123456789BPBP7987654

Library of Congress Cataloging in Publication Data

Stuart, Jesse, date
  32 votes before breakfast.

    CONTENTS: Uncle Casper.—A little piece of striped
candy-colored string.—Rothwell Periwinkle was my
teacher. [etc.]

    I. Title.
PZ3.S9306Th [PS3537.T92516]   813'.5'2   73–18049
ISBN 0–07–062299–X

To the winners and losers, Republicans and Democrats (called, in this book, Little Party and Big Party and Greenoughs and Dinwiddies)—the most colorful, intriguing and fascinating men of any profession, who battled with no holds barred to win public offices in county, state and national elections

Contents

CONTENTS

Uncle Casper

Uncle Casper comes to town on Saturday. He is running for state senator. His eyes are two, black, sparkling slits. His mustache is a tuft of dead bull grass, neatly pruned, and his nose is the sawed-off root of an oak tree. His hair is two spoiled waves of sickled timothy parted in the middle—the east wind blew a swath west and the west wind blew a swath east. There is a cricket ravine between the swaths.

If you could see Uncle Casper. There are white milk-weed stems among the dead-timothy hair. If you could see the long arms and the age-spotted hands like the spots on the body of an aged sassafras. His black suit fits his body like the winter bark on an oak tree. The toes of his black shoes have fought the rocks and stumps on

I

Kenney Ridge. His socks fall over the tops of his shoes to hide the scars.

Here comes Uncle Casper on the courthouse square. His black eyes dance, his arms swing like a willow wand waving in a swift wind of spring. "What is your name, son," says Uncle Casper, "and are you old enough to vote, my son?"

"Press Freeman is my name, I have had the seven-year 'each' three times. I'd be over twenty-one on Election Day all right."

"Which ticket do you vote, my son?"

"I vote on the side of the Lord."

"That is the ticket I belong to," says Uncle Casper, "and, my son, I am runnin' for state senator. I aim to give the poor people a chance since I am a poor man. My family has broke me up. Sent a boy to college—borrowed the money—mortgaged my home. Found him on the bank of a river in Michigan a-fishin'. Sent another boy out to college and he didn't do no good, took to a pack of cards and a bottle. I went to the eighth grade, son, in the old school and I've teached for fifty-nine years. Now, I'm a broke-up man. Set out of a house and home. Can't get a school any more since we ain't got school trustees. I used to run my trustees and get my schools. I could a got four or five. Things has changed. Not like they used to be. Vote for me in November and I'll make them like they used to be."

Uncle Casper's eyes blink. His hands talk.

"A vote for me means better roads, better schools, better schoolhouses, feather beds for men when they get drunk instead of ditches, homes for the widows and the orphans, no totin' pistols nor bowie knives. I'll put two pieces of bread in your safe where you ain't got but one. Pensions for the old broke-down men like myself and your pap, and I'll put the school trustees back—three to every deestrict. A vote for me means a help to you, son, I am a poor man and I'll help the poor people."

"I'll be there, Uncle Casper, to vote on the ticket the Lord and me and you is on. I'll be there and I'll finish the third spell of the seven-year 'each' by then."

Uncle Casper goes down the courthouse square. He talks with his hands. He talks to this one. He talks to that one. Men gather around Uncle Casper to hear him talk. "I lived on corn bread and onions to get my education, and wore shorts made out'n coffee sacks and muslin and calico. My boys has broke me up. I've preached the word of God and teached school for fifty-nine year. Brothers, I ask you in the name of the Lord to help me in November and I'll guarantee you every vote you cast for me will mean two slices of bread in your safe where you ain't got but one, and one slice of bread in your safe where you ain't got any. Two hams of meat in your smokehouse where you ain't got but one, and one ham of meat in your smokehouse if you ain't got any."

Then Uncle Casper goes down square and he meets Press Freeman. Uncle Casper says, "And what might your name be, my son?"

"You just met me awhile ago," says Press, "I am Press Freeman. Don't you remember me? Remember we talked about who was on the Lord's side and who wasn't?"

3

"Yes, I remember you now, son. We talked about the old times. I just want you to remember me in November. Did I ever tell you the story about the snake?"

"No, you ain't never," says Press.

"Set down in this bandstand," says Uncle Casper.

"Okie-dough," says Press.

"I was sittin' in the yard," says Uncle Casper, "with my feet propped up on the side of the house when I saw it. I was smokin' my pipe and lookin' toward my potato patch to see if I couldn't just about see my potatoes grow. When all of a sudden, I saw a big black snake's head bobbin' up and down out of the ragweed patch beside the potato rows. That snake, bigger than a baby's leg, went tearin' right out of that ragweed patch and took down across the potato ridges fast as a horse could run. I thinks to myself, 'What now!'

"The snake sorty halted in the garden between two rows of cabbage heads. I saw him bob his head up and down. He looked like a scared rabbit. I kept my eye on him. There was a little patch of briars beside the cabbage patch—in the old fence row beside the garden. That black snake, big around as a baby's leg and long as a rail-fence rider, made a headlong dive into that briar patch like a cat divin' for a mouse. It acted like a cat that smelled a mouse and jumped to get it. And then I saw what I saw. I stopped smokin' my pipe and forgot about my leg bein' left lame from that bullet I got on Brush Creek at that Revival Meetin'.

"That black snake wropped around that big rattler so quick it would make your head swim. I saw it all right there in that briar patch. That black snake wropped that big rattler up like a love vine wrops a ragweed. Then the black snake started to slampin' down with all its strength and bitin' the rattler's throat. Then he squeezed. I let them fight. The old rattler was squeezed so tight he couldn't rattle. Think about me a-sittin' that close to a rattler and not knowin' it!

"That black snake worked hard—squeezin', bitin', beatin' with its head. Then it uncoiled a wrop at a time until it got down to the last wrop—then it uncoiled the last wrop and sprung way out in the cabbage patch. It bobbed its head up and looked back. It saw the rattler was still movin'. Then it took right back into that briar patch. It wropped that rattler up tighter than ever. It bit it harder than ever. It whipped it with its tail like it was a buggy whip. The old rattler couldn't take the last beatin'. It give up the ghost and turned over on its back and died. Its belly was turned up to the sun. The black snake took out of there and run out and bit him off a little chew of a weed. Munched it in his flat jaws like a rabbit munches clover.

"I hopped up on my lame leg and parted the briars with my cane. I pulled that dead rattler and took it in and showed it to Liz, my wife. It had twenty-seven rattlers and nine buttons. W'y Liz wouldn't believe what I told her about that fight and the black snake killin' the rattler. I skinned the rattler and made me a belt out of its hide and Liz a pair of garters."

"I'll be dogged," says Press.

5

II

"Somethin' kept catchin' our chickens. Every mornin' we would go out to the barn and count the hens. There would be one missin'. So I looked under the roost and found a lot of loose feathers and part of a old white hen. Chuck Winters said to me: 'W'y Casper, that is one of them little chicken owls doin' all this. They can hold more chicken than a fox. I'll show you how to trap him.' So I took Chuck at his word.

"We took a dozen steel traps down to where the white hen was layin' on the ground. Her head was eaten off and some of the meat was gouged out from under her wing.

"Chuck said: 'Now dig a little ditch around the hen. Throw the loose dirt away. Set the traps in a circle around the hen. Put feathers over the traps. Drive a stake down through the body of the hen so when the owl pulls he can't move her. And in the mornin' we'll have the bird that caught that hen. When a owl eats no more of a hen than this he always comes back for the second mess.' And we set the traps, covered them with feathers and staked the steel-trap chains to the ground with little wooden pegs. We staked the hen down.

"Behold the next mornin' if there wasn't one of them old barred hoot owls bigger 'n a turkey gobbler a-settin' right on the hen with his neck feathers all bowed up like a rooster ready to fight. He was caught by one toe. But we had the chicken thief that had caught over thirty hens.

"And I said to Chuck, 'Chuck, what kind of punish-

6

ment are we going to give this bird?' Chuck studied for a minute and he said, 'W'y Casper, let's saturate him with coal oil, set his tail feathers on fire and turn him back into the elements.' Chuck has always been quick to think of things like that. So, I went to the kitchen, got the coal-oil can and a match and went back to the owl under the chicken roost. I throwed the coal oil on him. We could not get very close to him. Chuck got broom sage and tied it to the end of a stick and set fire to it. I pulled the peg out of the ground that held the trap and Chuck set the fire to his tail.

"Gentlemen, right up into the elements with that steel trap janglin' from his toe—that fire to his tail—he soared a red stream of blaze through the elements. Fire from that owl fell onto my meadow. It was in late March when the wind was blowin' steady and everythin' was so dry. Fire popped up all over the meadow at once. It looked like the red flames of hell and the wind was a-ragin'. That owl went right on through the elements.

"I hollered to Chuck to shoot him with a pistol before he fired the whole country. Chuck put seven hot balls of lead at that owl. But it soared right on through the elements. It went right over Mart Haley's timber. The blaze shot up like flames from hell. Flames lapped right up through the dead saw briars and leaves. 'All my timber is gone,' shouted Chuck—'timber land jines Haley's timber lands. My rail fences are all gone. That owl will set the world on fire if somebody don't shoot him from the elements or the fire don't consume him.' I tell you, gentlemen, that owl set fire to the whole country. My land was ruined. My timber was burned to death. That fire burnt up one thousand panels of rail fence for me. It ruined my meadows. It ruined my neighbors. We had to get together and have workins and put the fence back. We had to put some barns back and two houses. It ruined the whole country. If I hadn't a had good Baptis' neighbors, I would a been sued over that owl and would be a broke-up man today."

"Well I'll be dogged," says Press. "Grandma said to burn owl feathers you'd have bad luck among your chickens for seven years."

"Not so, I ain't had a bit of bad luck since then," says Uncle Casper.

III

"One day Chuck and me was out diggin' ginsang. Chuck and me used to run together a good deal and this is the way we made a little spendin' money. We had our sacks nearly filled with two-prongs, three-prongs, and four-prongs. Chuck looked down in the weeds and saw a big rattlesnake. 'Come here, Casper,' he said to me. I went over where Chuck was and by the eternal God I never saw such a rattlesnake in my life. It was big as a cow's leg. 'I can handle that snake,' says Chuck. 'I never was afraid of a snake—not the meanest snake that ever growed.' Chuck was drinkin' some brandy—some persimmon brandy. So he jumps right in a-straddle of the rattlesnake and brakes it down in the back with his fist. Then he begins to choke.

8

"It scared me to see Chuck a-straddle of that rattle-snake. So, I says: 'Chuck, get off that rattler's back. It will bite you shore as God made little apples.' Chuck just looked up and grinned at me. Then he said: 'You hold it down and I'll pull its teeth and we'll take it home and show it to Ike Wampler. He'll never believe we captured a snake this big.' So I gets down a-straddle of this rattler's neck. 'Choke it,' says Chuck. I choked it till I was black in the face. Chuck says: 'I see its fangs and a little gall bladder of pizen back in there. Wait till I twist a withe and I'll yank them teeth out'n there before you can say Jack Robinson.' My grip kept givin' out. My hands got so tired a-hold of that big rattler's neck. And when my grip was goin' Chuck hollered out that it had shot a stream of the pizen from the gall bladder through the fang into his eye. He said: 'I'm stingin' in the eye like a barrel of red pepper had been dumped into my eye. I'm pizened in the eye by that rattlesnake.' I jumped off'n the rattlesnake's back and got hold of Chuck and drug him down among the nettles and the pea vine.

"The first thing I thought of when Chuck was glombin' and clawin' at this eye, was my twist of taste-bud tobacco. It is that old-time tobacco that used to be growin' around the barn on old manure piles. Well, that is where I got this. The twist was bigger'n my forearm. So I bit me off a big chew and I chawed it. I got Chuck down, for he was smartin' a right smart by now. I put my feet on his chest and held each one of his hands in a hand of mine and I chawed that chew up and squirted every bit of it in his eye. He squalled a little, but I knowed it was a case of life or death. Then I took off another chaw and chewed it and squirted that in Chuck's eye. I kept on till I chewed up the whole thing and squirted it into Chuck's eye. And when I let Chuck up Chuck says to me, 'I'd rather have the disease as to have that remedy.' "

"Well, I'll be dogged," says Press.

"I went upon the hill one day to cut a pole of stove wood. I saw a dead sourwood pole and I took my ax and thought I would cut it. It looked dry, hard and seasoned. I saw a knothole upon the side and the sour gnats were comin' out and goin' in. Before I got to the pole a racer snake sprung at my throat and I struck at it with the double-bitted ax. It saw I was going to put up a fight so it started to scramble. I took after it with the ax. It went straight to the pole and wropped right around it—right up that pole like a black movin' corkscrew. Then it ducked down in the hole where the sour gnats was. It stuck its head out and licked out its tongue at me. I thought, 'Old Boy, I'll fix you.' So I climbs up the pole with a wooden glut in my hand and drove it down in the hole with a stick. 'I'll let you stay in this tree awhile,' I says.

"Well, I went on and cut some dry locust poles for stove wood. I took them into the wood yard and cut them up. One year after that I was back on this same hill gettin' stove wood and I happened to see this sourwood pole with that glut stickin' in the hole. So, I remembered the snake. I went up and whacked down the sourwood pole. The tree was hollow down to the roots, and when I cut into the hollow, out popped that snake poor as

Job's turkey. I could a-counted its ribs if I'd had time. But that racer remembered me. It coiled around my leg like it was a rope around a well windlass. It grabbed me by the ankle. I took off the hill hollerin'. I just couldn't help it. Its sharp pin teeth stuck into my ankle bone.

"I run to the wood yard hard as I could go. That snake tightened down on my leg and cut off the blood from circulation. I'd about give up the ghost when Liz come out and she said, 'Casper, what is the matter with you? You are white as a piece of flour poke.' And I says, 'See what has me by the leg, don't you?' And Liz went in and got a butcher knife. That snake still held me by the ankle. It tightened its holts. It bit me harder. Liz just reached down with that butcher knife and she cut that snake into ten pieces. It was wropped around my leg five times if I am right. Its head still held to my leg. Its teeth held right into my ankle bone. Then Liz pulled at its head and she yanked its teeth out, but they brought a hunk of meat.

"When our baby boy Frons was born he had the prints of the prettiest little racer black snake right over his heart."

"I'll be dogged," says Press, spitting at a knothole on the bandstand. Uncle Casper spits at it. "Center as a die," says Uncle Casper. "That's a sign I'm goin' to get elected senator."

IV

"Chuck took a notion to run for representative of Greenbriar County. Chuck preaches some, you know, and one Sunday afternoon when he was preachin' Abraham Fox's funeral he said to the people, 'Did you know, folks, that you was a-lookin' square at Greenbriar County's next representative? If you don't know it, I'll tell you that you are lookin' square at him.' And Chuck Haley goes out and tells the people that he is goin' to pass a law that the people will get a bounty for every fox hide they bring in to the county-seat town of Green-briar. He told the people that if they didn't clean out the foxes that they was a-goin' to clean out the chickens and there wouldn't be enough yaller-legged pullets left for a Baptis' preacher a mess. Well, as you know, Greenbriar County has a lot of Baptis' and they elected Chuck, though he was on the wrong party. They went for their religion before they did their party. Chuck was elected, but not by the fox hunters. They stuck by their foxes.

"Chuck told me all about goin' to Frankfort. He said they let him talk in a little thing that looked like a fryin' pan. He said it was over behind the pianer. He told them about his bill on the bounty of fox hides. Some said they fooled old Chuck about talkin' over the air—said he talked over a old broke-down telephone without any wires to it. Then he did talk over the air. But he give his speech about foxes. I knowed Chuck was goin' to get into it with the fox hunters. When he come back from Frankfort and the news got into the Greenbriar Gazette about his big speech over the air on foxes and him actin' like that and belongin' to the wrong party too, w'y the fox hunters had done had their meetin' and they was a-layin' for him. Chuck hired a hack and started home smokin' a cigar he'd rolled out'n twist-bud tobacco and plump went a hole through his black Stetson hat. Chuck whipped the horses fast and got away from that bunch of rocks up on the Winsor place. That is where they waylaid Chuck.

"Some said it was old Tiger MacMeans that waylaid Chuck. Old Tiger is a big fox hunter. One time he run a young fox around one pint and up over another pint and into a dirt hole and he dug it out with a stick. Another time one of his Bluetick hounds got hung up in a rock cliff and he blasted rock down with dynamite for eight days and hired everybody in the neighborhood to help him get old Queen. And old Tiger got her too. She was so nigh gone she couldn't stand up, but when they found her she had the fox right by the tail. He took Queen home and fed her goat's milk, and she got all right. Well, he is the fellow we thought put the bullet through Chuck's Stetson hat.

"Gentlemen, by the eternal God, them fox hunters, I guess it was, got after the Baptis' and we had a regular war in Greenbriar County. Barns filled with tobacco burnt all over Finish Creek and Laurel Creek. Cattle barns was burnt to the ground with all the livestock in them. It was a time. I never heard tell of anythin' like it. And out on the hills a body could find Irish taters with rat pizen on them—fried taters and dead hound dogs along the ridges. They was dead along the creeks where they had tried to get water when the pizen struck them and their insides went to burnin'. Chuck couldn't get to church. People looked for him—men that had had their hound dogs pizened. The fox hunters waited for him when they tooted their horns for dogs that never come home. Of course, Chuck never put the pizen out. But friends of Chuck's put it out when Chuck's Stetson was plugged from a rock cliff.

"And Tid Redfern picked up a coffee sack full of pizened biscuits put out to get the dogs. We don't know who put them out. It might a been the shepherds on the hillsides that had been losin' sheep, and when the Baptis' and fox hunters got into it they put their noses into it, for the time was right for them to get the dogs. They wasn't a hound dog left in that country big enough to run a fox or to teach the young pups how to start a cold trail. They said old Tiger could get down and smell where a fox had been and put the young hounds on a cold trail. They wasn't a barn left on Tiger Creek or Laurel Creek big enough to house a yearlin' calf. Bloodhounds were used to track men that done the burnin', but they used red pepper on their shoe soles and when the bloodhounds sniffed that they didn't sniff anymore. So, no one was caught. And people just cooled down in three or four years themselves.

"Bert Flannery said he never could get over it when his milk cows burned in his barn. His barn doors were left open, but the cows would not come out of their stalls. He said he heard the cows bawl so pitifully that it made him cry. He said he couldn't forget that dreadful night and it would stay with him as long as there was wind in his body. Bert Flannery is a good man. He is a good prayin' man and he tends to his own business, but he was just drawed into the fracas like a lot of us innocent men. Fudas Pimbroke said he could never forget seein' his old Fleet turned on her back on the ridge road where she had been leadin' a fox when the pizen got her down. He said she was stretched there bloated with wind. He said he could never forget the look on that dead hound dog's face.

"When the next session of time come around for Chuck to go back to Frankfort, they hauled him to the station one night under a load of fodder. He took the train straight for Frankfort to get his law about bounty on foxes repealed. And Chuck told them about the dogs pizened and the barns and church houses and homes burnt in Greenbriar County and about the war still ragin' there—and they wiped that law right out. Got rid of it root, leaf and branch. But that got all the Baptis' mad at Chuck. Now they was all mad at him—the Baptis' *and* the fox hunters. He didn't have a side to cling to. So, he went home to stay and one mornin' when he was milkin' the cow, flop went another bullet through his hat. So he got under another load of fodder and went to Greenbriar. He caught a train for West Virginia. He never come back to Greenbriar. I was readin' the paper where he had been killed givin' a West Virginia hound arsenic. The fox hunter hit him in the head with a coal pick. He wasn't any count for a representative anyway, for he couldn't read nor write nor cipher. And besides, he didn't belong to the right party. When a man goes out of the bounds of his party to elect a man of the wrong

party, then you can take care. Things are a-goin' to pop.
People in Greenbriar County has kindly come back together agin after a time."

"I'll be dogged," says Press, "I'll be right there to vote
for you, Uncle Casper, in November." Press spits at the
knothole. He misses. Uncle Casper spits from his wad
of homemade taste-bud. "Center as a die," says Uncle
Casper, "sign I'll be your next senator of Kentucky."

A Little Piece of Striped Candy-Colored String

Willie Battles flicked a speck of lint from his coat lapel while his wife Sarah arranged his bow tie so the bow would be parallel with his shoulders. While Willie looked on she arranged the white handkerchief in his coat pocket until half an inch would show. She smoothed out the wrinkles in the handkerchief. Then, she stepped back three paces in their comfortable living room and looked her husband over.

"Willie, I'm proud of you," she said, beaming shyly. "After all these years of using an air hammer and riveting hot rivets to make railway cars for our state and country you are still a fine-looking husband and you have amounted to something in life!"

She stood silently for a moment looking at Willie, admiring his handsomeness in his new suit. Willie looked at Sarah with a new light in his eyes. He was happy to have this flattery from his wife.

"Yes, Willie, I'm proud I married you," she said. "I'm proud of our two sons. It does me good to tell people we have two sons in Morehead College! And now," she sighed softly, "How happy I am to tell people my husband is a member of the Rosten City Council."

"But I hope you didn't tell them, Mother"—he spoke proudly—"that the third time was the charm for your Willie. Yes, Mother, I had a time getting on the Rosten City Council, but I finally made it."

Then he laughed loudly as a thought came into his mind.

"You can tell them, Mother, tell all our friends, tell everybody, that your husband is an honest man," he said. "You can tell them everybody who voted for me was eighteen years old or over. Explain, if you're talking to someone from Ohio, that we allow our youngsters in Kentucky to vote at eighteen. But you can't tell them that when I looked at that tombstone up there on Lonesome Hill the night I was up there electioneering I found Wyant Abraham's name on that stone, checked the dates of his birth and death, and when I counted his time on this earth—and he was a real Rostenian, born, lived, and died here—he lacked eighteen days of being old enough to vote. So I said to myself as I put my flashlight in my pocket, 'No, no, Wyant, you're not old enough to vote for me. I know you'd like to, but you can't. You didn't get old enough to vote. If you'd 've lived another eighteen days you might have voted for sixty years or more. You might have voted for me when I run for governor of Kentucky!' Ah, Mother, I did a lot of electioneering up there on Lonesome Hill, and the voters up there had no choice, whether they were Democrat or Republican in their natural lives, but to vote for me."

"Oh, Willie, I'll never tell that, and you mustn't tell it either," Sarah sighed softly. "You mustn't tell that to anyone! And when you become governor of Kentucky and I become the First Lady, don't you think I'll be proud! And don't you think Timmie and Don, who will be through Morehead College and be educated men, won't be proud too! They'll be proud of a father who didn't finish the Elementary!"

"Mother, do you think I'm crazy?" he asked. "No man gives away the secrets of his road to success until he has gone all the way. It's 160 miles from Rosten to Frankfort. That's a long 160 miles, but I've got ten years. I'm now forty-five, and I'll be in the governor's seat at fifty-five! And my secret, Mama ... you know, there are a lot of Lonesome Hills in Kentucky! They say Kentuckians are the damndest when it comes to politics—I'd like to change that and say, 'Kentuckians are the smartest when it comes to politics.' Mother, the emblem of our party is wrong. It should be a Kentucky thoroughbred so we can win all the races! And I'll be the jockey in the saddle on that thoroughbred ten years from now and my opposition won't be able to see me for the dust. So, I won't tell that story about how honest I was on Lonesome Hill when I told Wyant Abraham he lacked eighteen days being old enough to vote for me! That's honesty, Mother! Say it is!"

"No, let's don't talk about that," she said. "Turn around and walk to the door, then turn around and come back and stand before me. I want to see how you look. I don't want you to go to a Rosten City Council meeting and not be the best-dressed man there!"

Willie, who was caught by the first draft in World War II, had served during the war in the United States. But he still knew how to do an about-face. He did an about-face and walked to the door as his wife had suggested; there, he came to a snappy halt, bringing the left foot up and placing it by his right foot with a loud stomp. Quickly he about-faced again, marched up in front of his wife, halted and stood at attention with his chest full of wind. He looked "eyes straight ahead" at the wall while Sarah readjusted the white handkerchief in his coat pocket.

"You're a fine-looking man, Willie!" she exclaimed, beaming. "You're downright handsome. In ten more years when you get a little frost in your hair, you will make the most dignified-looking governor Kentucky has had in its long history of great governors! Now, Willie, no more of this army stuff. I know you were a brave soldier and defended your country as much as those who went overseas, for you were needed here. But be yourself, relax and talk to me before you go to the meeting. It's going to be a rough meeting, isn't it?"

"Yes, Mother," Willie replied. His beaming face turned serious instantly. "Yes, our great congressman brought home the bacon from Washington! You know, Mother, a half-million for a sewerage disposal plant! Now our big task is dividing this bacon. It will be a thankless task. Yet somebody has to do it. We are going to use Rosten labor, Rosten trucks, Rosten everything we can! A half-million in good bacon for Rosten! When Congressman Clayton wants a promotion, we'll urge him to run for state senator. We'll keep him out of the race for governor!"

"Willie, you are a smart man!"

"Well, Mother, it pays to look ahead."

"I can't understand why you never went beyond the Elementary."

"Ah, you know, young and trifling then," he answered with a sigh. "Sorry about it now. We lived within two blocks of Rosten High School too. Now, I can see where I missed it. But I have always believed there are shortcuts. "And"—he laughed loudly—"I believe the Houndshells know there are shorter cuts too! They'd like to know where I got that majority! Mother, don't you ever get mad at me and spill the beans. Lonesome Hill, that silent city, elected me! The Lonesome Hills of Kentucky will elect me for a state office. See, the voters of those silent cities don't talk. They don't tell tales."

"Ah, but those Houndshells do, and . . ."

"Don't worry about them," Willie interrupted. He looked at his wristwatch, which reflected an eerie light from a sunbeam entering through a windowpane. "Generation ago we battled with Houndshells up the Big Sandy! They've been on one side of the fence and we've

been on the other. We never agreed with them on anything! They ride the workhorse and we ride the thoroughbred. That's the difference, Mother. They don't know
about Lonesome Hill."

"Yes, but never underrate a Houndshell," Sarah said.
"I've been in the Battles family twenty-five years and I
know the stories about them!"

"We know not to underrate them," Willie said. "But
every time they got one of us up on Big Sandy in those
turbulent years, we got two of them. Remember, an eye
for an eye and a tooth for a tooth! Well, we always got
good measure—two eyes for one, six teeth for a tooth,
and two or more Houndshells for one Battles. They soon
learned the Battleses didn't play a losing game. Why they
ever followed us to Rosten and settled here I don't
know. My father, Uncle Jake, and Uncle Kim thought
they were shaking them off when they moved here. They
hadn't been here a year until six of Seymore Houndshell's
sons moved here. And they got railroad jobs."

"I won't hold you any longer, darling," Sarah said. "I
don't want you to be late."

"I've got plenty of time, Mother," he said. "You
brought up those awful Houndshells. Did you know all
six Houndshells have sons the right age to be in Morehead College and there's not a Houndshell there, or in
any other college? They don't have it in the head."

"Yes, but as I've said, Willie, we must never take them
for granted," she said.

Willie walked out onto his front porch with Sarah
still holding his arm. He breathed deeply and exhaled
slowly.

"Good October air," he said. He breathed deeply again, this time standing on his tiptoes. Then he exhaled slowly. "Breathing air of the pioneers," he said with a smile. Then he looked up the street toward Rosten Town Hall. "I see Old 'Rabbit' English going in. Maybe I'd better get up there. I don't have anything in common with him, for he's about a fifth cousin to the Houndshells. But I want to be there the minute the meeting starts so I can see that my living friends, those who worked for me in the Rosten City Council election, get just a little more than their share of the bacon when it's divided. And you know the old trick of the majority of three getting there early and conducting business before the others arrive! Well, I want to be there when the meeting starts!"

Willie Battles took Sarah's arm loose from his own, planted a casual kiss on her cheek and hurried down the steps. When he walked out to the street, he turned to look back at his wife who was now his age, very buxom, her hair sprayed with silver, her eyes blue and soft. She was watching him walk toward the Rosten Town Hall.

"Oh, how good you look, Willie," she said. "You're my handsome husband. I want to stand here and watch you go all the way to City Hall!"

"I'll go all the way in more ways than one, Mother," he said proudly. "I'll see how the bacon is divided. It will be a task, you know." He winked and smiled again at her and did an about-face, which he liked to do on the street ever since he had served in the army. Then he walked stiffly up the street with clipped steps in a military gait. Sarah gazed after him admiringly. She watched him cross the street, almost goose-stepping, to the other side, where he walked up to the Rosten Town Hall. Just before he started up the steps of the small, squat, block building with a plain front and three windows on each side, he stopped to stare at something. Sarah could see it from where she stood. He was looking at a string on the doorstep. She had watched Old "Rabbit" English, who had gone in just before Willie, step over the string. But Old "Rabbit," sixty-five or seventy, was a stiff old man who walked with a cane and wore the old-fashioned celluloid collars, broad neckties and a stickpin. He was the kind, she had often thought, who was too stiff to stoop even if he were a sixth cousin to the Houndshells. But the Houndshells, she thought, would stoop for anything.

She watched her handsome Willie, all of his six-feet-two, 220 pounds, pink cheeks, wavy black hair that opponents in the Rosten City Council race had accused him of going out of Rosten to have curled before the election so he would attract more women voters, as he stood there admiring that little piece of string. It looked like a striped piece of candy. Willie, she knew, had always been more attracted to colors than most men. He often had teased her about how much better looking were the cockbirds, wild or domestic, with their brilliant gay plumage and sharp spurs than their plain-looking mates the hens. So there wasn't any reason why he shouldn't be attracted by this striped candy-colored string, which was about as large around the middle as a stick of candy. She watched Willie bend over to pick up the string. A quick thought flashed through her mind that she hoped he wouldn't get his bow tie twisted or the white handkerchief in his coat pocket disheveled.

The thought left her as suddenly as it had been conceived. There was a crack like thunder, a stack of fire with brilliant little multicolored flames going in all directions.

"I'm blown up!" Willie shouted. "I'm killed!"

First, Sarah was so shocked she had to hold to a porch post for support. Then she left the porch with her hands high in the air shouting, "My Willie has been blown up!"

When Sarah ran up the street over the dry leaves that had fallen from the elms and oaks, they went out from her feet in all directions making strange sounds. A few people who heard the explosion and Willie's shout were coming up and down the street. Willie was running in a circle around the smoking string. When the string exploded it had jumped from his hand or he had let it loose.

"The Houndshells've got me this time!" Willie shouted.

Old "Rabbit" English, who had heard the commotion, came slowly and stiffly from the inside of Rosten City Hall.

"What's the excitement about?" he asked.

"Can't you see," Roy Gilliam, who was the third councilman to arrive, said loudly above the din of loud talking and shouting, "that Willie Battles picked up a piece of string and he was blown up!"

"Yes, I stepped over that string," Old "Rabbit" said. "I have made it a policy not to pick up discarded dirty things from the street. I have always bought new things and practiced my philosophy of looking up and not down."

"But Willie Battles is hurt," Roy said. "Look at him!"

"Yes, but he's not blown up," Old "Rabbit" said.

"When the smoke clears away he will have only a scorched hand!"

Sarah came panting and screaming and threw her arms around her husband's neck. He was prancing in pain trying to free himself so he could give his wounded hand movement so the October air would cool it.

"Oh, my Willie!" Sarah wept. "Who is trying to kill you?"

"Mrs. Battles, no one is trying to kill Willie," Old "Rabbit" told her. "He just stopped when he shouldn't have to pick up a piece of string."

"But who put the string there?" she asked. She was sobbing hysterically. "Why was it put here today when the council had such an important meeting?"

"Oh, it might have been a prank by a Hallowe'ener," Ephraim Goldsmith said. He was a Rosten city councilman who was just arriving. "I can't believe anybody would want to hurt Mr. Battles, one of the most talented of our councilmen!"

"My Willie, my Willie," Sarah sobbed, holding on with her arms around her husband's neck. "It's not a prank either. Somebody is trying to kill 'im."

"Mrs. Battles, by chance I saw the string there on the step, but its gaudy colors didn't entice me," Old "Rabbit" explained. "I even stepped over and not on it, or I would have received the same treatment as your husband. My injuries probably would have been worse, since I am much older and not as strong as he is. Hallowe'en isn't but two weeks away. Already the tricksters and treaters move over our streets each night. I suggest

26

at this meeting we bring up a motion for a curfew and that we leave the business of dividing the sewerage-disposal spoils over to another meeting. We are going to need Mr. Battles' special talent when we divide!"

"Sarah, I must get to Doc Henson," Willie said. "You must turn loose of my neck. My hand is burning! It's a painful burn!"

"You're not killed, Willie, as you shouted you were," Old "Rabbit" said. "I suggest you go to Doc Hensen and get your hand dressed. It's only a minor accident."

Sarah took her arms from around his neck very slowly. Then she took hold of her husband's arm with both hands, the arm that had the well hand. Willie began moving his burned hand briskly through the October wind to feel the soothing coolness against the heat of the burn.

"Come, darling," she said, "we won't know about this ten years from today except the political scars it will leave on your hand. You can show them to the public when you run for a bigger office. These scars, if you get good ones, will get you an extra one hundred thousand of the living votes."

"Be careful, Sarah," Willie interrupted as they walked down the street toward Doc Henson's office.

"Now just what did Mrs. Battles mean by the living votes?" Roy Gilliam asked.

"I wouldn't know about that," Old "Rabbit" replied. "I know I must get back to my duty inside. We must pass on a curfew at this meeting before some of our members are blown up over this sewerage-disposal gift from our benevolent government. A half-million dollars is something for our sixteen hundred Rostenians to fight over. Railroading isn't very good right now, you know!"

"That's the stinkingest smoke I ever smelled," said Bob Perkins. He slapped with his big hand at a small cloud still hanging before his face. "I believe it was some kind of a bomb planted there for one of us councilmen. Surely no child would be allowed to play with a Hallowe'en gadget as dangerous as that! Besides, I never saw a piece of string colored like that one before."

"Yes, where there's five hundred-thousand dollars to be spent for the benefit of sixteen hundred people there are bound to be explosions," Dale Bradley said. He was the last of the councilmen to arrive. "There will be other kinds of explosions. That's a lot of green leaves shaken from that tall and mighty government tree that's got its branches up there in the sky! While we attend to our fair city's affairs, I suggest that you disperse and go back to your little shops and shake the green leaves from your little trees."

"My philosophy for you, my fellow Rostenians, before you depart to shake your trees," said Old "Rabbit," who had been listening to the conversation before entering the Town Hall, "is to look upward to the green leaves on your little trees instead of looking down at a little piece of striped candy-colored string on the ground."

The Moonshine War

You don't know me and you never will. But I was born in Argill in Greenwood County in Kentucky. Now, you've never been in Argill—a store, post office, two filling stations and a Methodist Church where, maybe, two dozen people attend every Sunday.

Now, Argill is a place with a reputation for moonshine whiskey. It used to be many people made moonshine here and sold it by the gallon jug and the horse quart. My father was one. And I used to help him. Many a night, I was a lookout for the Law, county, state, and feds! When they made raids. Pop, now long dead and gone, was smart. He had our still up a dark hollow near an old deserted coal mine. There was only one road leading in. When I heard the Law coming, I blew three toots on a foxhorn and this was a signal for Pop and my older brothers Charlie and Zeke to take off to the old coal mine to leave the still and hide from the Law. The Law would confiscate our still and have a big rigmarrow in the *Greenwood County Gazette* about this. But, they never got the operator, Chris Caudell (my father) and my brothers—Charlie and Zeke. And when I blew that foxhorn I took up the hill and hid behind a tree in the dark woods. There were many trees for me to hide behind.

Now, my name is Little Chris Caudell. I was named for my father. Pop was often called Big Chris by a lot of people. And big he was with a short bull neck and shoulders as broad as a corncrib door. He had arms like small fence posts and legs as large as young saplings. He had hands bigger than small fire shovels. And Pop had sharp hawk eyes. My Pop was more man than any of his sons. We took after Ma, who was a Matlick, and the Matlicks are not big people.

Pop was never caught by the Law as many of the other moonshiners were around Argill, the center of Greenwood County's moonshining industry. And this is what that brought on so much trouble among our neighbors in the years to come. Pop moonshined for twenty years, before Ma, a righteous woman, persuaded him to lay his sins upon the Mourner's Bench in the Argill Methodist Church. Here Pop confessed breaking the law and moonshining. Well, it wasn't ever again moonshining for Big Chris Caudell and his sons.

After Pop got us out of "the business," the county, state and feds began to close in on Fonse Whaley and his sons Bill and Tarwin. The Law sent Fonse up for a couple of years but freed his sons. They were seventeen and sixteen years old.

Then, the feds moved in, with the aid of the state and the Greenwood County Sheriff, Bill Darby, and his deputies, on old Abner Fortner, who had bragged if the Law got him, they'd have to take him dead. They got him alive and tried him and his son, Willie. They gave Old Abner five years and his Willie two years. All other moonshiners and the people were glad they were gone. The Fortners, Old Abner and son Willie, were considered dangerous people.

"Old Abner said Fonse Whaley's boy Tarwin spied on him," Pop told us at the supper table. "Young Willie said when he got back from the pen he'd get Tarwin. Dangerous people. I'm glad I'm saved and sanctified and the Lord has taken me out of that dangerous business."

"Yes, Pop, I'm glad too," brother Charlie said. "There's getting to be bad blood among the people around Argill."

"It's the way of sin," Ma said.

"Somebody might get hurt before this thing is over," Brother Zeke said. "The Caudells, Whaleys, Fortners and the Luttrells, called the Big Four in Moonshining all gone but one family. Old Mark Luttrell and his boys, Roy, Jonse and Al, is the only family still in business."

"Better get out while they can," Pop said. "I've talked to Old Mark about his sins. I told him he'd better lay them on the Mourner's Bench, walk in the light of the Lord and be able to lay down and sleep at night without the fear of the Law. I told him he'd better have the Lord on his side."

"Amen, Chris," Ma said.

Now we were a happy family. We were not afraid any more of the Law. But due to tippling Pop's good warm whiskey at the still, I'd got a little hankering for the stuff—and so had my brother Zeke. Pop and Ma found out about this and prayed for us at home and down at the little Methodist Church.

But how right my big father was about Mark Luttrell. Somebody must have tipped the Law off for old Mark had moved his still several times. He was up on the Right Fork of Sand Suck, two miles from Argill. He had a coal mine close beside his still to hide in, too. But County Sheriff Bill Darby, his deputies, the state and federal officers were already there and hidden around the still when old Mark and his boys went to start a night's run. They let them start and then moved in from their hiding places and caught them red-handed. They couldn't do anything but confess and be sentenced. Old Mark got five years and son Roy twenty years. Al got two years and Jonse, eighteen, got one year. Al, only sixteen, was talked to by the judge but he let him go scot free. The Luttrells, not a mean family, was the last of the Big Four Families in The Business. The Lord and the Law had captured all four families.

"I warned Old Mark to quit fooling with the stuff and change his ways," Pop said at the supper table. At the supper table is where Pop and Ma always talked with their three sons. "Now, Mark away in the pen with two of his sons there with him! Look what will happen to his wife and six children at home."

"Only the Lord knows what will happen to the Whaley, Fortner and Luttrell mothers and their youngins," Ma said. "But not one of the mothers walks in the light of the Lord."

Because of Willie Fortner's age, nineteen, he served only one year in the pen. He was the first of the men from the families of the Big Four Families in The Business at Argill to get home from the pen.

Brother Zeke and I had taken our little farm truck to Greenwood, six miles north of Argill. Here we could buy moonshine by the pint, quart, horse quart, half or gallon. We always liked to see the people who came in from all over Greenwood County on Saturdays. We liked to loaf on the Courthouse Square. Here there were eight benches over the courthouse yard and these were always filled by old men who liked to come see one another, talk of the times as they sat, chewing tobacco or smoking and each one trying to whittle the longest shavings.

Brother Zeke and I got our pints in the men's room in the courthouse. This was the safe place to buy it. We bought from Pegleg Joe Radner. Pegleg Joe had a hard time living since he couldn't plow on a pegleg on the hillside. We allus patronized Pegleg Joe. He did a thriving business selling only half pints which he carried in a hunting coat that he wore the summer, as well as winter. After we got our pints, Zeke and I swigged, then walked out onto the square to mix and mingle with old friends.

"Look," I said to Zeke. "There's Willie Fortner out

there. Let's go greet him, shake his hand and welcome him home from the pen!"

Well, it was good to see Willie again, even if the Fortners were considered dangerous people. We'd never been very neighborly with them. I walked in front of Brother Zeke with my hand out to shake Willie's hand. Brother Zeke was a couple of steps behind me.

"Willie," I said, "glad to see you home, old boy!"

But Willie snarled. A cold of frowns came over his face. He reached into his pocket and came out with his knife.

"Dam ye Caudells, ye damn spies," he said opening his knife.

Well, I turned and started running with Brother Zeke at my side. But Willie followed only a few steps.

"I'll get you and some others," he shouted to us as we turned into the courthouse corridor—ran past the men's room and out at the other side.

Now, the Caudells aren't cowards, mind you. I'm one hundred ninety pounds. Brother Zeke is nigh two hundred. But we're small beside of Pap. And Brother Zeke and I have good fists. But what that scared us was that long hawk-billed knife that Willie Fortner pulled on me. We went home and told Pop about what had happened.

"It's trouble," Pop said. "The sin of moonshining has brought bad blood amongst us and we are a dangerous people! The best thing to do is lay your sins on the Mourner's Bench and walk in the light of the Lord."

Zeke and I talked this over. We didn't go all the way with Pop. We loved our father but we knew we were in

34

danger. Zeke and I bought pistols at the Lawton Hardware in Greenwood. We knew we didn't want to be knifed to death. And the Fortners, wherever one was found, were known as knifers.

Two weeks later, Tarwin Whaley, whose father Fonse was still in the pen, was found near his home, beside the road, sliced to death. The ground beneath him was red with his blood. Earth had soaked up his blood. And Willie Fortner was the last man seen by Thorken Spears on this road.

Willie Fortner was arrested by Sheriff Bill Darby. Tarwin's father was let come home from the pen for his son's funeral. I'll bet a thousand people attended that funeral. It was too big for the Argill Methodist Church to hold. It was conducted out in the Whaley apple orchard for now it was spring and the apple trees were snow white with blossoms.

"It's strange," Fonse told Pop. "Look out for there will be others killed around Argill if that Willie isn't put back where he belongs!"

"He tried to knife me on the courthouse square," I told Fonse.

"The Fortners are dangerous people," Fonse said. "They're knifers! But proving that he killed my son is something else."

After Tarwin's funeral, Bill Darby took Fonse back to the pen to finish serving his second year.

"I worry about my wife and my son Bill," Fonse told Pop just before he left to finish serving his sentence. "Everyone here is in danger, Chris, You'd better arm!"

35

"I am armed," Pop said. "I'm armed with the Spirit of the Lord!"

"But Willie Fortner is the killer, I believe," Fonse said. "He doesn't know or respect the Spirit of the Lord!"

Fonse Whaley went back to LeGrange Penitentiary. And Willie Fortner was tried in the Greenwood County High Court on circumstantial evidence and he came clear.

Zeke and I never told Pop that we had armed. But we told Brother Charlie and he armed too!

Down at one-armed Cliff Webb's filling station, I saw Willie Fortner and four of his friends pull up and get gas for the car. I was across the road at Kenton's store. I was sitting on the porch on some feed sacks enjoying the warm May breeze. I knew all four of the men with Willie. They were Tobie Radner, son of Pegleg, Morris Skinner, Bully Short and Tobias Winters. All these young men were tough. All had sold moonshine. All drank it. All had served sentences in the Greenwood County jail. All were lawbreakers. These were the roughest young men in Greenwood County. I was glad I was armed. I sat there with my hand on my .38. And how I wished Brother Zeke was with me. If there had been a shoot-out I would have had some help. Both Zeke and I could really handle our firearms. We are fast with our guns. I was glad when they got their gasoline from one-armed Cliff Webb and moved on down the road.

Well, the knifer struck again. This time it was Lucretia Luttrell, twenty-one-year-old daughter of Mark Luttrell who was on her way back home, on a half-mile walk from Kenton's store in Argill. She was found sliced to death. And the earth beneath her was red and blood soaked. Her small sack of groceries was beside her. Mark and his sons, Roy and Jonse were allowed to come home from LeGrange for the funeral. There must have been two thousand people at Lucretia's funeral.

"Why would our daughter be stabbed," Mark said weeping. "She never did any evil to anybody. She was beautiful! And she was to be married next month to Bill Whaley!"

There were no clues to this murder. There were no arrests. There was only suspicion among the people that Willie Fortner might have done this. Yet, people wondered if Willie, as mean as he was, would stab a young woman to death! And many reasoned a moonshine war in the hills of Kentucky was a dangerous thing. Many wondered when the killing would stop—if it ever would. Many thought because of the sins of the fathers it might go on for generations.

"We have to go to the Methodist Church—all in the Light of the Lord and pray for the Lord to give us a sign." Pop said at our supper table.

"Amen, Chris," Ma said.

"What kind of sign?" I asked.

"The Lord has devious ways," Pop said.

"Amen," Ma said.

I looked across the table at Brother Zeke. He looked at me. It was hard for us to surpress our laughter. Even Brother Charlie, the son most like our father, almost smiled.

37

But Pop and Ma did go to the Methodist Church and pray for the Lord to send a sign so the killer could be found. While they were doing this we brothers were holding onto our hardware ready to shoot it out if we were ever attacked.

Al Luttrell, the only one left at home (for his father and brother were taken back to serve their sentences), armed himself to protect his mother and five more sisters. Bill Whaley armed. Many of the people around Argill, who had never made moonshine whiskey, armed.

When Brother Charlie didn't bring the team in at noon, Pop, Brother Zeke and I went to the bottom where he was plowing to see why he hadn't come. We'd been setting tobacco in a fertile bottom near our barn. Brother Charlie was plowing a large bottom on our farm we called Sycamore Bottom for sycamore trees lined the bank along the side near the Sandy River. This bottom wasn't a quarter mile from our house.

"I think something has happened to Charlie," Pop said. "He's always on time. He's my son who doesn't drink."

My father hurried in front of us. When we reached Sycamore bottom we saw our span of horses over near the Sandy River bank, eating the tall horseweeds. They'd dragged the plow across the bottom.

"I told you, I told you," Pop said.

At the end of the field we found Brother Charlie laying in a pool of his own blood. He'd been stabbed to death. He'd been plowing, armed with his pistol. His pistol was laying on his chest. He was flat of his back on the ground. It was an awful sight.

Well, all of us cried. I thought my father was going to fall over. He shook all over but he didn't go down.

"My son, Charlie," Pop said. "Look for tracks in this soft plowed ground! Don't step on one!"

Well, we found the tracks. And it was a big shoe. We measured the tracks with sticks, length and breadth.

Talk about a time in Argill—when the news spread— Blake Henderson saw us in the field and he came over. And when he came and saw Brother Charlie sliced to death and in a pool of blood, he ran down to Argill and narrated the news.

"I'll get that Willie," Brother Zeke said.

"No, it will be my pleasure," I said.

"No, no, no," Pop said. "The Lord will handle this! We've prayed! We've prayed honestly and hard and we believe we're going to get an answer. But we will take this to man's court! Willie Fortner will be tried!"

Talk about a funeral at Argill! When Brother Charlie was buried people came from all over Greenwood County. I'd say there were three thousand people. And this nearly killed Pop and Ma. Brother Zeke and I talked together about shooting Willie Fortner on sight.

"If there's no law to protect us," Brother Zeke said, "there's none to condemn us. Damn this circumstantial evidence stuff! We've got to take the law into our own hands!"

Willie Fortner was arrested again. All the evidence we had were the tracks in the field. And Willie's shoes were much smaller than the tracks we'd measured in the soft ground in Sycamore Bottom. Willie sat in the courtroom and smiled. He knew he'd come "clear." And he did come clear.

But I remembered how he'd rushed at me with his hawk-bill knife on the Greenwood County courthouse square. I couldn't believe anything else but what he was the killer of Tarwin Whaley, Lucretia Luttrell and Brother Charlie. All had been killed the same way. They'd been stabbed to death. And I thought he'd figured out how to get Brother Charlie by hiding in the horse-weeds at the end of the field and when Charlie turned the horses and started back he'd come in from behind. And he knew he'd leave tracks in the soft ground, as the only clue, and he'd worn a pair of larger shoes to do his evil deed.

About every man in Argill was armed now. This moon-shine competition among men—their being caught by the law and sent to the pen (all but Pop who had the good sense to get out of it)—had caused these killings. Brother Zeke and I had sworn to each other never to drink moon-shine again. Yes, after we'd lost brother Charlie who now slept in the Argill cemetery with his blood soaked up in our Sycamore Tree Bottom.

Almost every man in Argill feared for his life and members of his family. The Lawton Hardware in Greenwood had had a big sale of handguns. And men carried them, too. So had Brother Charlie. We knew the killer was still loose.

But two weeks after brother Charlie was buried a strange thing happened. I thought it strange. But my father didn't think it was.

Bully Short was driving the car. Tobie Radner was in the front seat beside him. Morris Skinner and Tobias Winter were in the rear seat with Willie Fortner between them. They were coming at a high speed down State Route One. Bully missed the Argill Bridge—sailed through the air and landed on a large, flat rock down in knee-deep water in the Sandy River. They had plunged more than one hundred feet.

More than a hundred people gathered at the Argill Bridge. The state police, Sheriff Darby and his three deputies came. Dr. C. Hensley Conroy, the coroner, came. Both Jason Winiston and Alvin Rigsley, rival undertakers in Greenwood arrived with their ambulances. Doc Conroy waded out to the car and climbed upon the rock. There wasn't any water in the car. Jason Winiston and Alvin Rigsley waded over and upon the rock with their helpers and stretchers to carry the bodies out. Brother Zeke and I went, too, while Pop and Ma waited among our Argill neighbors gathered on the Sandy River bank.

"Can anyone identify these men?" Doctor Conroy asked.

"Yes, I can," I said.

"The driver?" Doc said. "He's very much alive."

"He's Bully Short," I said.

"I'll take him," Jason Winiston said. "Come on, Don, with the stretcher." They put Bully on the stretcher, waded the water and up the bank to their ambulance.

"Man here in the front seat beside him?"

"Doc, he's Tobie Radner," Brother Zeke said.

"He's alive, too," Doc Conroy said. "He's in shock. He's in a stupor."

"Maybe drunk," Zeke said.

"We'll take him," Alvin Rigsley said. "Come on, Eddie, with the stretchers."

"Now to the rear seat," Doc Conroy said. "Who's this man?"

"Morris Skinner," I said.

"He's alive but I don't know how he is, to look at this wrecked car," Doc Conroy said.

"We're ready for him," Jason Winiston said.

Jason and Don with the help of Doc Conroy, Brother Zeke and I loaded him on the stretcher. They went in a hurry to their ambulance. The undertakers were in a hurry to get the bodies.

"All right, this one," Doc Conroy said. "This man in between in the back seat."

When Doctor Conroy laid his hand on him he fell over in the seat.

"He's Willie Fortner," I said. "I thought everybody knew him."

"I don't," Doc Conroy said. "I don't know any of these men."

Doc Conroy put his hand on his heart.

"No heart," he said. "I believe he's dead."

Just then Alvin Rigsley and Eddie, his helper, came.

"Dead, huh," Alvin smiled. "I didn't get the first one, but I've got a dead one."

"Willie Fortner dead," was echoed in unison among our Argill neighbors on the Sandy River bank.

Willie Fortner was dead. Alvin Rigsley and his helper Eddie got the body.

"I'm not dead, Doc," said the fifth man. "I'm half drunk but I ain't dead and my name is Tobias Winters."

"But you're going to Kingston Hospital in Auckland," Doc Conroy said.

"We'll take him, Doc," Jason Winiston said.

Jason Winiston and his helper Don with Brother Zeke's and my help put Tobias Winters on a stretcher. He kicked and cursed but Brother Zeke and I helped them carry him up the bank and put him in their ambulance.

When Zeke and I walked back among our Argill neighbors gathered on the river bank there wasn't any crying or tears shed. There were not exactly smiles upon their faces, but there didn't seem to be any fear written on them either.

"It's strange how Willie was the only one killed when he had the best place in the car," I said to Pop and Ma.

"There will be no more killings here, son," my father said. "You will see! I'm glad you and Zeke didn't use your guns! Now, you see!"

The ambulances hurried away, one after the other, with sirens screaming and revolving lights flashing. Down in Sandy River, on the only big, flat rock there, set the demolished car. Four men had come out alive. One, Willie Fortner, had been killed.

We walked back with our neighbors, some talking about how strange it was the only man suspicioned of murder three times and tried twice in court and had

43

come "clear" had been the only one killed. Pop and Ma talked about the death of Brother Charlie.

"But, you'll see we'll have peace," Pa said. "The knife killings are over!"

Pop was right. All the moonshiners convicted are back from the pen with their families. The moonshine war is over. Ten years have passed and there's not been another killing. There is peace again in Argill.

Rothwell Periwinkle
Was My Teacher

Rothwell Periwinkle had been my teacher in Greenwood High School before he decided to get into politics and help run this nation. We thought Mr. Periwinkle was a fine teacher. But nearly all of the last year he taught us history he said if our country was a man he'd be a cripple. Early in the year he said he'd be so crippled that he'd be walking with a cane. Before the year was over and we got our grades he said if our country was a man at that present time he'd be so crippled he'd have to have braces on his legs and be hobbling and scooting a step at a time on crutches. He told us he planned to do something about our country's situation—that he was going to run for Congress.

Now Mr. Periwinkle was in the Big Party and I was in the Little Party. But the boys and girls in our history class in Greenwood High School whose parents were in the Little Party agreed with Mr. Periwinkle because we wanted good grades in history. And, of course, boys and girls whose parents were in the Big Party agreed with Mr. Periwinkle that the reason our country was walking on a cane and then crutches was that infernal Little Party whose members were always lying about what was going on—since they couldn't get very many congressmen and senators elected—and hardly ever a President. But still, in this Little Party were the trouble-makers and the Little Party should be blamed for crippling our country.

"Pa, you know Mr. Periwinkle, our history teacher in Greenwood High School, is goin' to quit teaching and run for Congress," I said.

"What ticket is he on?" Pa asked.

"The Big Party ticket," I replied.

"I'm against that jasper," Pa said. "First, I belong to the Little Party as my father before me. He voted for the first President ever to run on the Little Party ticket. I was born a Little Party man. I'll continue to be a Little Party man until I die."

"But Mr. Periwinkle is such a good teacher," I said. "I hate for him to leave Greenwood County High School."

"I'll do my best to defeat him so you can keep him," Pa said. "I know that man! He walks slow. He talks slow. He's a lazy easy-going man. I can't help it if he is your teacher, you will see! If elected, our old Eleventh Congressional District won't be well represented."

I didn't tell my father, but if I had been old enough, I

would have registered so my vote would have counted. My father had voted in every election since I could remember. He'd always get there to cast his vote for the people on the Little Party. And very few times in his life had he been a winner. Now I wasn't old enough to vote. So I couldn't change my vote to vote for my teacher Rothwell Periwinkle.

Now, Rothwell Periwinkle announced in his political speeches against two men—Alvin Spruce and Tom Sperry, seeking the nomination in the Big Party—that they were badly scarred men! He even hinted they were filled with blemishes and colored with taint. He said if he defeated them and got the nomination, his own Big Party would send him to Washington, D.C. But he told the people, for I attended three of his political rallies, Farlington, Rosten and Auckland, where he traveled in a sedan, covered with slogans and pictures of himself—and a ladder up one side to the top for him to climb up and down and speak from the top through a loud speaker. This way he could stand up and be seen by everybody below him. He looked much bigger above them. And they looked smaller to him down below.

The three speeches I heard were all the same. He told the people he was the best-qualified man in his party to do the job in Washington, D.C. And now was the time for the voters to help him discard the braces on crippled Uncle Sam's legs and to throw away his cane and crutches. I had heard him say everything in our history class in Greenwood High School that he was saying in his speeches.

Now, as my father said, he was slow in action. I watched him slowly climb up the ladder on the side of the sedan. But he was a big man. Rothwell Periwinkle was about five ten, two hundred pounds, with a face as round as a plate. And he had round, soft pink cheeks like halves of red apples. His nose was short—almost a pug nose. His eyes were little saucers of watery blue that sloshed like slow-moving turtles in their sockets. His handshake wasn't of great strength because his short hands and stubby fingers were ripe-grape soft. And there were little pones of fat on the back of his hands. He wore glasses, a broad-brimmed hat, conservative business suits and wore his brown hair parted on the side.

When I heard him speak in Farlington, Rosten and Auckland I heard many comments from men in the crowd.

"Old Roth might be a school teacher but he's a common man—one of the people—just like me!" So many of his followers could see themselves in Mr. Periwinkle, my teacher.

Alvin Spruce and Tom Sperry were defeated so badly in that primary in the Big Party they hardly knew they'd been in a political race. Rothwell Periwinkle had spoken in every town in our Eleventh District. He'd spoken in every village. He had attended dozens of funerals, Baptist Foot Washings. (Although not one of the Old Regular Baptists, he washed feet on the riverbanks with them.) Rothwell Periwinkle said he believed he had kissed three hundred babies, too.

"I never saw anybody like him," Pa said. "He's bound

to beat Joe Chaffins who got our Little Party nomination with our primary opposition by seven to one. That's about the way the registration runs here. And old Rothwell might beat our Joe ten to one. He's liable to cut in on our Little Party vote."

Pa's prophecy was nearly right. Rothwell Periwinkle did cut in on our Little Party vote. He carried the Eleventh Congressional District by a majority of nine to one. Now began the longest tenure of any Big Party Congressman in the history of the Eleventh District. Not anyone had ever prophecied that Rothwell Periwinkle would be elected to fourteen successive terms in Congress, that I would finish high school, college, be married, have a family and be a grandfather before something happened to Congressman Periwinkle.

As soon as he was elected to Congress he moved from his Blakesburg home with his wife and four children to Washington, D.C. There he purchased another home. He maintained a home in Washington and one in Blakesburg.

"Old Roth's in the money now," Uglybird Skinner said. "When a man can have a winter home in Washington and a summer home in Blakesburg he's in the money. That Congress job pays awful big they tell me! That's why 'Old Roth' and his family can live so high on the hog!"

Old Uglybird Skinner of Blakesburg was one of Rothwell Periwinkle's strongest supporters. Uglybird couldn't read and write but he knew early in the Big Party primaries when men of the Big Party tried to defeat Rothwell Periwinkle in the primary he'd get a paper with

Rothwell Periwinkle's picture in it, carry the paper over town and then he'd stop his friends on the street and say:

"See where 'Old Roth' is running again." He would show his friend he'd stopped on the street our local weekly paper which carried a picture of Rothwell Periwinkle on the front page each primary and final election he was in. Uglybird carried the paper in his hip pocket. He tried to pretend to the people he could read. He said 'Old Roth' was a common man just like he was. Thousands of men in the Eleventh District must have seen themselves in Rothwell Periwinkle. He really got the votes.

Now Rothwell Periwinkle did something unusual. He had two offices. He had one in Washington, D.C., and one in Blakesburg, not the largest city in the Eleventh District, but it was in the town in which he lived and about the center of the Eleventh District. He arranged a bulletin board which he put up in his office window in Blakesburg showing the days he would be in his hometown office. Since Blakesburg was the center of Greenwood County and the courthouse was the center of Blakesburg there were always people milling about in the courthouse paying the office holders friendly visits and reading the signs. Often many of these people came for handouts and to get his favorite office holder to sign a note for him so he could borrow money at the bank.

Now our Congressman Rothwell Periwinkle had a sign painter to paint a lot of signs on his outside and inside the courthouse windows. Here are some of the outside signs that people walking the Blakesburg street below could look up and read: Don't Forget Your Congressman Rothwell Periwinkle; Run In and Have a Friendly Chat with Old Roth; Rothwell Periwinkle Is Never Too Busy to See His Constituents; This Is Your Office for Congressman Periwinkle Has Prepared It for His People.

Then there were signs on the windows of Congressman Periwinkle's office in the corridor: Run In For Coffee or Tea with Roth; Be Befriended by Your Friendly Congressman; Toddle In and Talk with Roth; Your Congressman Periwinkle Is Your Servant and Here *to Serve You!*

His office in the Greenwood County courthouse consisted of two rooms. Space was scarce in our courthouse but Congressman Periwinkle could get it. He had power. He could get what he wanted. He could do magic things —things beyond all belief of the people. In his front office he met the people. In the second room was where he had consultations with them about their problems. When he moved in with one who had a problem to discuss, his secretary, Nancy Hill, moved in to the front office to meet and talk with the visitors. Congressman Periwinkle's office was often filled to overflowing. We had seen lines in the courthouse corridor up to his door waiting to get in. His office, when he was home, was the busiest office in our courthouse. There was never another office as busy as Congressman Periwinkle's.

And from his beginning year as a congressman just about everybody in the Big Party and the Little Party got free flower seed sent to them. And they got little booklets distributed to them free, of course, on how to milk a cow, how to use a hoe, time of year best to repair fences, how to spray apple trees, how to care for lawns— just about every week my father got something and said he never had and never would vote for him. He said he'd vote for his candidate in the Little Party who ran against him, but there wasn't any use. My father said with a sigh that Rothwell Periwinkle would hold the office as long as he lived.

We knew that Rothwell Periwinkle had sent his children to colleges and universities "up East" for we read in the *Greenwood County News* when each finished. We also read when his two sons and two daughters married.

My memory goes back to his eighth election when the Big Party didn't have anybody running against him in the primary. And from this eighth election until the fourteenth he never had opposition in his primaries. No one ever dared run in the last six primaries against Rothwell Periwinkle.

And everyone knew Congressman Rothwell Periwinkle had to be a man of great wealth. He maintained a home, automobile and chauffeur for Mrs. Periwinkle and himself in Washington after his children were educated, married and left home. And in Blakesburg, he had the nicest new home in the town. Although Mr. Periwinkle could drive a car, now our congressman's being a much older man, he preferred that neither he nor his wife drive the car. He paid a man a regular fee just to drive their car for them. This man didn't wear a chauffeur's uniform but he was always dressed spick-and-span in a nice suit of clothes, shirt, necktie and hat. He always sat alone in the front seat of their extremely large and expensive car while Congressman and Mrs. Rothwell Periwinkle sat in the rear seat.

"Old Roth has really come up in the world," Uglybird Skinner said to me once on a Blakesburg street when their chauffeur Redwell Testerman drove by with the Periwinkles. "Must be a millionaire too to do all the things!"

"Yes, the Rothwell Periwinkles have had an interesting life," I said. "They're well known and important people! He's known all over the United States!"

"Old Roth has helped a lot of people," Uglybird said. "But he can afford to help them! See, he's got it! A lot of big men like 'Old Roth' get the dollar signs before their eyes! They have the money! They have so much—they don't know what to do with it! Now, you take me! How do I make mine? I clean out septic tanks! I go down in them! I am a water-witch too. I can find water and dig wells and springs! But I don't have the dollar signs before my eyes!"

We watched the big limousine bearing our congressman and his wife move slowly down the street as people stopped on the street when they recognized them, to wave as they passed.

"He's going to his Blakesburg office now," Uglybird said. "Old Redwell his driver will take "Berth" Periwinkle back to their mansion. Yes, they've got it. Worth a million if they're worth one cent! Man, 'Old Roth' has helped a lot of people around here. He's helped some good people and he's accommodated some deadbeats!

He's signed notes at the First National Bank in Blakesburg for good honest men who will pay their obligations. And he's signed a lot of notes for men who never expect to pay—but just be able to get the money because his signature is on their notes and the bankers know he's got the money and he will pay."

"Why would he do that?" I asked.

"Oh, maybe, for past favors," Uglybird sighed. "Maybe, to get their votes and their families' votes! You know, that's one way to get the votes—well, most of them in this Eleventh Congressional District—you buy them! I know what I'm talking about! I've worked in every election for 'Old Roth' from the first one until now. You know I handle a lot of money for 'Old Roth.' But I make his dollars pay. I get the vote with them. One thing that pleased me more than anything that's ever happened to me—'Old Roth' thinks as much of me and I of him, he said if he went first he wanted me to be one of his pallbearers. And I've requested of him if I go first, and he has promised me, he will be one of my pallbearers. We're just about like brothers—more like identical twins in our thinking in the Big Party only we don't look alike."

After Rothwell Periwinkle's thirteenth election, my oldest daughter was married and had a son and I became a grandfather. I will never forget this. Rothwell Periwinkle sent our daughter a little book. This showed he didn't forget. My being a grandparent now was one way to measure time. Rothwell Periwinkle's thirteenth election and, of course, he was a winner for Congress! How great and durable he was! Was Rothwell Periwinkle an indispensable Congressman? Many in old Eleventh District thought he was! All the people knew he was a millionaire—some thought twice a millionaire and a few thought he was a multimillionaire. Uglybird Skinner was one who thought he might be the way he signed notes for people and had to pay them off and how he spent money in elections. And Uglybird Skinner was as close to Rothwell Periwinkle, so he told me, as any of his constituents in the Eleventh Congressional District. And I believed Uglybird was telling me the truth.

Now, in Congressman Rothwell Periwinkle's thirteenth term as a Congressman—and thirteen being a bad luck number must have been bad luck for him—he lost Bertha Bush Periwinkle, his beloved wife, who had been, so he told women in the Big Party in every speech he made to them, by his side in all his life and all his decisions. Her loss was a big blow to our Congressman.

Said Old Uglybird Skinner who claimed he didn't have dollar marks before his own eyes but he kept a close watch on the dollar: "Now if poor 'Old Roth' goes, that big Congressional pension won't do either of them any good. You know 'Old Roth' will run again."

Well, 'Old Roth' did run again as Uglybird had predicted. Uglybird went around with a copy of the *Greenwood County News,* which had a picture of Congressman Rothwell Periwinkle on the entire front page and an article about his seeking the unprecedented fourteenth term in Congress from the Eleventh District. He didn't have any opposition from his Big Party in the primary and for the first time, in his fourteenth race, he didn't have any opposition from the Little Party. He was given the office by the voters. He was what we call here a "shoo in." He really owned the office. He didn't have to run for it. He was the indispensable congressman of our Eleventh District.

We had heard through Uglybird Skinner that Congressman Periwinkle, after the loss of his wife, had sold his property in Washington, D.C. He said he had sold his car too and divided his furniture among his children. Now, I had heard talk—maybe, it was gossip—on the Blakesburg streets that Congressman Periwinkle was so badly in debt that his Blakesburg home, even his furniture and car, were mortgaged beyond what they would bring at a public auction.

Now something happened! Man can really hardly own anything upon this earth—especially a public office. Rothwell Periwinkle had to go to the hospital for a minor operation. But he got a blood clot which stopped his heart and he died. He didn't finish all of his fourteenth term. He lacked only two months and two days. And, according to my friend Uglybird Skinner, he was making preparations for his fifteenth election.

Now here is where the strange story comes in. Uglybird Skinner was one of the pallbearers as well as five others of Congressman Rothwell Periwinkle's real close political friends. My friend, the septic-tank cleaner, the water-witch, spring and well digger, Uglybird Skinner, knew all the pallbearers. And I had always before and I would always in the future believe my friend Uglybird

Skinner that when they carried Congressman Rothwell Periwinkle's coffin from the church, they carried an empty coffin. You can ask Uglybird about this or any of the other five pallbearers. They were sure of what they were saying when they said there was no body in that casket hauled to Sunset Burial Grounds.

What had happened, so Uglybird and other pallbearers learned later, was that Congressman Rothwell Periwinkle, who was so badly in debt that his assets in bankruptcy law could never pay his liabilities, had sold his body, for a fabulous price, to science. Uglybird said with the price he received for his body, plus his assets, he might break even. Uglybird told me scientific medical men were particularly interested in his brain—a brain that had held the voters of the Eleventh District in the palm of his hand for fourteen terms as a congressman. Uglybird said they were under the impression that it took an unusual brain, one worthy of scientific investigation to do this.

The Senator Is Dead

"The Senator is dead," said Mae Marberry. "Senator Foulfoot has kicked the bucket. He has gone to the great beyond." She drove her needle in and out of the crazy-quilt top and it clicked tin-tin each time on the battered thimble.

"Senator Foulfoot was a good man to the poor people too," said Dave Marberry as he spit in the fire and it sizzled in the yellow flame. "Oh, they was a few things against the Senator. No man could trust him around where the women folks was. He was a bad 'n that way. He's got children planted all over the county. His seed will never die. There will be more smart children springin' from these hills than there ever was before."

The wind whipped down among the February dead

grasses that stood back of the smokehouse with a lonesome sound. The clapboards flapped on the roof. The smokehouse door creaked on the rusty hinges. The glass jars slithered on the paling ends. The dry, dead grass caught between the slats of palings sighed in the wind.

"This is a bad night to have a settin'-up with the Senator. It is such a lonesome time out. We ought to go over and show our last respects to the dead. I never did vote for the Senator because he was not on my ticket, but he was a good man. I believe in payin' last respects to the dead. Get your shawl and coat, Mae. Drop that needle. Let's go over the hill to the settin'-up. Martha will be glad to have us in a time like this even if we didn't vote for her man. She knows we are not on that ticket."

The moon is a yellow ribbon cut short. The stars are blotches of white silver in the sky. There is a handful of dishrag clouds that whips down among the spicewood twigs. The rabbits play in the moonlight. There are many rocks and roots in the cow path that leads to where the Senator lies now a corpse.

"What killed Senator Foulfoot, Dave, do you know?"

"I don't exactly know, but I have heard."

"What was it?"

"I heard it was his belly got too big."

"He got awful big before he died, all right."

"How much did he weigh?"

"Three hundred and forty pounds."

"You remember when he got up and made that talk back in 1930, don't you, down at Hangtown? He told the people that they would have to use a corn knife and cut these government expenses to the bone. Somebody in the crowd that didn't vote his ticket said: 'Couldn't cut you to the bone, Senator, with a corn knife. It wouldn't reach one of your bones for the fat.' And the Senator's big jowls just flopped when he laughed and he went right on talkin'. Didn't stop for nary a thing the people said to him."

"And his belly got him at last."

"Yes!"

"It was his own fault. It was the way he et."

"Yes."

"W'y, I've heard about him stoppin' at a restaurant and orderin' up a beef stew. The waiter knew it was the Senator. He stacked his dish up high with big white potatoes and chunks of beef—and the gravy would just be floatin' the potatoes. He'd eat that stew. 'Anything else?' the waiter would say. 'Yes,' the Senator would say, 'duplicate that order please.' He would hold up two fingers and the waiter would know what he meant. He'd eat that. The waiter would say, 'Anything more, Senator?' The Senator would say, 'Triplicate that order, please.' He would hold up three fingers and the waiter would know what he meant. Then on top of that he would eat a whole pie, drink a couple of bottles of pop and a quart of buttermilk."

"No wonder the Senator is dead. He et too much for his own good. He was a good man. He got that road from Hampton to Jericho or we wouldn't a had a road that we could have rid a horse over. He got that schoolhouse upon Plum Branch. We wouldn't had a house to had a school in if it hadn't been for the Senator."

"I believe in payin' last respects to the Senator even if we are out of place. We don't belong to his ticket. We'll be there after a while anyway and we will see how Martha and the Senator's children treat us."

"The Senator loved children, didn't he?"

"Yes, the Senator loved children. He kissed enough of them when he was runnin' for office. He come to Tackett's once when a bunch of women was up there with their little dirty-nosed brats and the Senator kissed all them dirty-mouthed, dirty-nosed children and give them a nickel apiece and told them he'd get them a school. And they took to the store with the nickels. The Senator got all the women votes there but nine, for they belonged to his ticket. They liked the Senator. They said they'd heard little things on him but he was a good man. He got Curt Hix's boy out of the pen for cuttin' the Jones boy with intent to kill. He was sent for twenty years, but the Senator pulled the right ropes and got him out. Curt is a free boy today."

Here is where the Senator lives. See. The house is white. It is a big house at the foot of the mountain. It is weatherboarded. Here is the well in the front yard. Here hangs the bucket on the well sweep. It is blown by the wind. The pole suspended to the sweep swings like the pendulum of a clock and hits the limbs of a tan-barked peach tree at the well. This is the home of Senator Foulfoot.

"Howdy-do, Dave. Howdy-do, Mae. Come right in by the fire and take off your wraps. Get you some chears up closer to the fire."

"No, thank you, Martha. We ain't a bit cold."

"That February wind blows pretty cold and mighty lonesome here tonight. It's awful lonesome the way old Shep howls tonight by the winder and the corpse in the back room. Mighty glad you come, Mae—you and Dave. Ain't a soul come in yet. Just me and the children here and the Senator's corpse is in the back room."

"Where is Thad and Dawson—Jack, Seymore, Bill and Lum—ain't they got here yet? They was always good friends to the Senator, wasn't they?"

"They appeared to be. They were good friends to the Senator when he was alive makin' speeches and gettin' things done. Now he is dead, they are not here. No. They have not come."

"They voted his ticket, too."

"Yes."

"And they don't come!"

"No."

"Well, I didn't vote his ticket. I'll come and pay my last respects to the dead. I never did vote the Senator's ticket. I never will unless I do it in the grave when I don't know anythin' about it. I don't have a child that will ever vote his ticket either. If one of my children does and I'm in the grave, I'll turn over in my coffin with my face down. I don't believe in the Senator's ticket. I forget that tonight. I am here to pay my last respects to the dead. We don't live forever and just to think I'll be right down there in the same graveyard with the Senator. I'll not be far from him and when Resurrection mornin' comes, I'll be one of the first to shake his hand. Not in Heaven will I vote his ticket if he hasn't changed it by then."

"Shep! Shep! You get away from that winder. I can't stand to hear you howl like that. Funny a dog understands when his master is dead. Shep knows the Senator is dead."

"Has anybody offered to lay the Senator out?"

"No."

"Get me a razor, soap, mug and hot water. I'll shave the Senator and lay him out in his coffin if you women will help me do the liftin'."

"We'll do our best."

"No. It is not right for you to have to help, Martha. It is not right for you to help lay out your dead husband. Not the kin shall put away the dead. But the dead's friends shall bury the dead. We'll get him ready and put him away. Somethin' might happen to you if you have a thing to do with it. You stay out of this. Let Mae and me do the whole works."

"Give that dog some milk to lick from the cat's pan. Stop his barkin'. His barks are more lonesome than the howlin' of the wind tonight. Just everything seems to say: 'The Senator is dead! The Senator is dead.' I can hear it in the wind tonight. I can hear them words among the fruit jars on the palings. I can hear them in the dead grass in the yard and in the peach-tree limbs by the well box. I can hear: 'The Senator is dead. The Senator is dead!' Oh my God! Have mercy on me! What am I to do? The Senator is dead! And his friends don't come! The Senator is dead. They don't come. Men from his ticket don't think enough of him to come! A man from another ticket has come to lay him out. The Senator is dead and his friends don't come after all he has done for them! Got 'em out of the pen. Got 'em all the roads they've got. Got 'em a schoolhouse. Give 'em money and broke his own self and his family up. They don't come when he lays a corpse and help lay him out for burial."

"Be steady, Martha, and brace yourself up. Get me the hot water, the mug, soap and razor. I am ready to begin. Light the lamp. Turn the wick up so there'll be plenty of light and I can see in that room. I don't want to shave the Senator in a dark room."

The razor is not sharp, but it will do by stropping it on his pants' leg. The Senator's beard is a reddish saw-briar color. It is tough as blackberry vines for a razor to cut. Martha brings the hot water in a wash pan, the shaving brush, the mug and razor that the Senator always used. "Here they are," she said.

The dim lamp throws a yellow light on the Senator's white-clay cheek. There he lies in the bed with a sheet spread over him. He looks like a pile of white dirt that is big in the middle and tapers at both ends. There lies the Senator—with his face sandy with reddish beard.

Dave said: "Martha, you go out of the room. You are not supposed to lay out your own dead. Somethin' might happen to you. I'll take care of the Senator."

Martha walks out of the house—out into the wind—out into the moonlight.

"Shep-Shep-Shep—you stop that barkin'," she said. "I can't stand it. That barkin' is lonesome as the wind."

Dead fat flesh is wobbly like flour dough and hard to shave. The lather is hot, for the water was just poured from the tea kettle. The lather softens the beard as rain softens the willows in the spring. White lather on the face of a dead fat man in the yellow lamplighted room. The black sheets of night without, a little yellow moon lodged up in the sky. The night is lonesome and the wind whips lonely through the garden palings. The Senator is dead. Senator Foulfoot is dead.

"It makes me have cold chills to run up and down my spine to think Dave has to come in and lay the Senator out," said Martha. "He got them roads. He got them schoolhouses. He got them out of the pen. He kissed their dirty-nosed babies. They forsake him in death. Dave has to come in and lay him out. Man of another ticket has to come in and lay out the Senator."

"Take it easy, Martha," said Mae, "take it easy. Death has come and there is not anything a body can do about Death. Death comes to men like the Senator as it comes to men like my man Dave."

"But the night and the way old Shep barks—it makes me lonely here. I cannot stand to ever eat from this table again. I can't stand to draw water from that well or carry meat through that smokehouse door. The Senator sleepin' up there on that hill. W'y, I'm afraid I'll meet his speret out here on some dark night. I just can't stand to stay here. I'll go stay with my married children is what I'll do. I'll have to break up housekeepin'. I can't even stand to see that wash kettle out there in the front yard. Just to think about the way the Senator used to come up there when I was makin' lye soap from wood ashes. He'd come there and stand and watch me and tell me about his race —how he was makin' big talks and gettin' on with the people. He'd say: 'Now Martha, you watch that lye soap and don't let it get on your hands too long. It will eat your hands up. It will make them rough as a gritter.' And I can see him walkin' out to the wash kettle right now. I just can't stand to ever look at that kettle again.'"

"The Senator is dressed, Martha. He made one of the prettiest corpses a body ever looked at. I put his speech-makin' suit on him. He looks as natural as anybody I ever saw. He looks like he is standin' up ready to say, 'Now ladies and Gentlemen, if you want good roads, vote for me.' That is just the way he looks. His lips are curved like he was sayin' them very words. I never put him in the coffin. I left him under the sheet. He is big as a skinned ox to lift—too much for me and you women folks to tug our daylights out tryin' to lift. Besides, you should never help bury your own dead."

"Now Martha, me and Dave are goin' to have to leave you, for we left the children at home by themselves and we are afraid of fire, you know. We got burnt out once this way. We don't want to get burnt out again. If there is anythin' more we can help you do, let us know. We don't vote your ticket, but we're glad to help you in a time of distress."

From the weatherboarded house—out past the well box and the peach-tree limbs whistling in the night wind —Mae and Dave walk toward home. Dave sings:

> When you get married
> And live over the hill,
> Send me a kiss
> By the whippoorwill.

The wind howls loudly and lonesome through the brush. This is the mountain cow path Mae and Dave walked across. It is steep. There are rocks in it. There are stumps and roots. The moon is getting low and red. It rides low over the dark hills. The moon is like a copper penny set in a bowl lined with dirty dishrags.

"And the Senator is dead," said Dave, "come to the ground at last. I had the awfulest time layin' that man out. His beard was hard to cut. He was dirty to wash even if he was a Senator. It was like puttin' clothes on a barrel tryin' to put that silk suit on the Senator. I rolled and tusseled and finally made it while you was out talkin' to Martha. It was a job, I'm tellin' you. The Senator is like a piece of lead to lift. I rolled him into his clothes. I know it was his belly that killed him. It is as big as a small doodle of cane hay."

At the top of the mountain the lonesome February wind blows through the dead grasses in the graveyard and through the bare branches of the wild-cherry trees. One can see the white headstones gleam in the moon-lighted night. One can see white pieces of paper caught onto the graveyard saw briars and holding there.

"It is here where they'll haul the Senator tomorrow," said Mae.

"Yes, Mae, it is here," said Dave.

"And this is such a lonesome place here. I wouldn't be buried here at all if it wasn't for my mother and my grandmother being buried here. Your Pap and Ma are buried here too. You and me will be buried here some-day. Just think way up here in this lonesome place. We'll

67

not be buried very far away from the Senator, will we?"

"No. I have just said that I'll greet the Senator on Resurrection morn. I'll tell him there that I won't vote his ticket if he's still runnin' for Senator on the same ticket. I'll just be glad to talk things over with the Senator."

"Do you think the Senator will be in Heaven?"

"I haven't thought about it."

"I have thought about it, but I haven't said what I thought."

"The Senator was a good man."

"Yes."

"I never heard of him wrongin' anybody."

"No."

"The Senator done a whole lot for these people."

"Yes."

"I hate to pass a grave yard at night. Let's hurry up and get past. Listen to that fodder blade rattlin' in the wind. See it hangin' to that greenbrier! Look at them tombstones. See how they gleam in the moonlight. It will be lonesome for Senator Foulfoot upon this mountaintop. They'll haul him here day after tomorrow with that big span of black horses they use for to take places the hearse can't go."

"Yes."

"I felt so sorry for Martha there by herself and the way that shepherd dog howled and the way the wind blowed. It was enough to make anybody cry. And just to think, none of the Senator's friends come in to lay him out. That beat anythin' I ever heard tell of."

"And Martha, the way she talked about the Senator

comin' out to the wash kettle when she was makin' lye soap. She said she never could get over that. Said she could never stand to see that wash kettle out by the wood yard again."

The path is rough going down the mountain. The moon hangs low. The wind whips through the saw briars and the mountain-tea stems. The dog barks at the house below. It is old Lead barking. The house is empty and silent as a black autumn leaf weighted by rain to the wet earth. The night is black as a new leather shoe.

"The Senator is dead," said Mae, "and it is a good thing that daisies won't tell."

The Governor of Kentucky

"Are you ready?" Mose said to me.

"Not quite," I said to Mose.

"Hurry it up then. Don't you know the bus is out there waitin' on you and me? I'm out huntin' you up. It's time we's on our way to Chicago."

I grabbed my hat. I said to Mose, "I got a little bit of Kentucky herbs to take along if you'll give me time to run home and get them."

"Get on the bus. Never mind about the herbs. And never mind about your wife if you've got one. We got herbs on the bus. We got a-plenty. This trip is on me. I'm throwin' this party for all my good Ohio herb customers. Get right down there to that bus."

Well, there was the bus. The engine was warmin' up. I never saw such a well-dressed party. It was Mose Win-

throp's party. Not a hoodlum among his herb customers.
I saw old Jake Spradling on the bus. He was from
Kentucky. I said hello to Jake. He said hello to me. I
passed and repassed with everybody. But there was a
lot of strangers on the bus. I saw four women. Eighteen
men besides me and Mose. It was a big Greyhound bus
that Mose had rented for the trip. There set the driver
all dolled up in a gray, clean uniform. The whole thing
was tip-top. Everybody was laughin' and talkin'. Everybody seemed happy.

I took my seat. I looked down beside me. There was a
gallon of herbs right by my seat. It was a white jug with
a brown neck. That's the kind Mose Winthrop uses to
deliver his herbs in. We know old Mose. Drunk a many
a gallon of the herbs Mose delivers across the river into
Crummit, Ohio. I am a Kentuckian, but I work in
Crummit, you see. I live just over the river on the Kentucky side in Flickers, Kentucky. It is cheaper to live in
Kentucky and row a johnboat over to my work. Mose
doesn't have to work. He buys the sugar and the corn and
runs a herb distillery. He has the post office and the store
on Deer Creek and buys a few cattle on the side. He
has a pull with the Law and gets the boys out of trouble
when the Law catches them makin' herbs. He just tells
the Law to keep hands off and the Law does it. That is
Mose. He takes care of his herb makers. He lets one get
in the county jail sometimes. But never lets one go to the
pen. Mose is a big boy about helpin' electin' the Law.
He's got the Republicans and Democrats organized on
Deer Creek. They stick together. They have to if they
make herbs and sell them. Their votes usually decide

the election. They decide for the fellow who decides with them.

"Well, what's holdin' things up?" said Mose. "We'd better be on our way."

"You left your sign in the bus station," said the bus driver.

"Run and get the sign," Mose said to me. "We need that sign."

I ran in the bus station. I asked the clerk, "Did Mose Winthrop leave a sign in here?"

"Yes," the pale clerk said, "right over there is the sign Mose left in here. Goin' to have a good trip, aren't you?"

"I hope so."

"Well, you will with the Herb King of Kentucky. You fellows are bound to have a glorious trip out of it."

I could tell that clerk envied my trip. I could tell the way he looked at me. I looked at the sign on the run back to the bus. It said:

> Hurrah for the Wildcats!
> Hurrah for the Wildcats!
> Wildcats beat the Bears!
> Crummit Wildcats Beat Bears!

"Driver, put that up on the front of the bus," said Mose. "That's where it belongs. We want people to know that we are goin' to follow our football team to Chicago. We are right with them."

"Are we goin' to Chicago sure enough, Mose?" I said.

"We are right now headin' for Chicago. You've got enough herbs, haven't you, for the trip? If you haven't we can get them. We'll go down here and fill up at the reserve herbs tank I've got in Crummit."

"Yes, I've got enough herbs."

"That's all I wanted to hear. The trip is all on me. I make the money. The people on the bus are my best herb buyers. They can tell you I put out good stuff and once a customer, always a customer is the way they deal with me."

"You're right," said the woman up front. She wore a black hat. She had blue laughin' eyes. She was smilin'. "When you once take a drink of Mose Winthrop's herbs you'll never buy 'em any place else. He makes the best herbs I ever put my tongue to, gentlemen. I don't know all the women I've told about his herbs. They're so much in demand among the women here in Crummit that half the time the reserve tank is empty and they can't get them."

"That is only when they catch a couple of my workers and lodge them over night in the county jail and I got to go after them. That don't happen often. You know that, Jenny Lovelace. Sometimes I can't get sugar. You know, I buy sugar here and there. I don't buy too much in one place. I have eleven men workin' for me. Nine makes. Two delivers. I run the business. I don't care for you people knowin'. When I buy sugar I put it in the expense row right then and there. Later when I sell I deduct this amount. I know I am hopin' to sell and just how much I am goin' to get. That's the way we work things out on Deer Creek. I am worth more money than a man holdin' office in my county. They have tried to get me to run so I could throw some money in the ring—something besides my hat. I never wanted to get tied up with the Law.

73

I don't want the Law to work me for a livin'. I want to work the Law for a livin'."

Everybody talks on the bus. Everybody gets acquainted. Men shakes hands. They say: "Old Mose is honest as the day. What he tells you about his herbs you can depend on it. He makes good herbs. You just can't beat them. I'd ruther have his herbs as any government herbs I ever tasted. He makes good herbs."

"Old Mose is a good sport. Ever been out to his house? Got a nice farm out there. The nicest on Deer Creek. He's got the store and the post office. He's got a lot of cattle. He buys and sells cattle. He makes money right and left. Big hunter. He invites his best customers out to hunt with him. Treats them right too. You just got to eat with him. He has plenty to eat too. I never saw as much grub in any one home in my life as I saw out there."

"When Old Mose and me knocked down them eighty birds that day he had it on me. He was so tall he could just walk through the fields and step over the five-wire fences and shoot at the same time. He beats any man with a gun I ever saw. He gets more shots in than any man I ever saw."

"You wouldn't take Mose Winthrop for what he is. You'd take him for the governor of a state. Don't he remind you of a governor? A lot of people call him governor. They say he can make as fine a speech as a body ever heard out at the Sheriff races over in Greenbriar County. I heard one fellow say he met with the Republicans out on a hilltop one night. Mose was there. And they said he got up and made the best talk that was made that night and they had a senator from the deestrict there.

They said Mose talked rings around him. He don't have to be no herb maker. That man can do anythin' he wants to do. W'y, he used to go to college. He went to the University of Kentucky."

The bus sped over the hard road. It was in front of us like a cow snake—a cow-snake-colored ribbon of road leadin' us from Crummit to Cincinnnati. The farmhouses where the Ohio River barns showed the people had plenty by their fat sides bulgin' out with hay, ears of white and yellow corn showin' heaped in the latticed corncribs in the hallways. We saw clean meadows. Sheep standin' around the haystacks and cattle feedin' from haymows fixed in the fields in hayracks. But what did we care for the horns of plenty? We were goin' to Chicago. Mose was givin' us a party. We were speedin' right along.

"A little faster, driver," said Mose. "We are just makin' sixty. I can do this with my old Ford. Around seventy. We got to be in Chicago for the game by tomorrow at noon. Step on it. We got to go."

The driver stepped on the gas. We whirled past farmhouses fast enough to make you dizzy headed if you looked at the sheep and cattle on the farms, and God knows I liked to look at fat barns and pretty cattle. I liked to see the clean-cut meadows and sheep eatin' around a doodle of straw.

"Time for herbs, gentlemen and ladies," said Mose.

"You are right," said Jenny Mae Lovelace. "It is time for herbs. Let's every man and every woman to his own jug and try our capacities."

Everybody lifted the jug to his lips. Everybody supped.

Everybody said: "A-a-ham. Good stuff." Everybody talked. Everybody laughed. Everybody was merry. We'd talked to each other, but we didn't know one another very well. We had to get acquainted yet. Anybody knows that if there is anything in the world that will bring on a quick acquaintance it is herbs. Drink herbs together and if you belong to one feud family and your partner belongs to another, you'll be friends long as the herbs last. After the herbs are gone you'll wonder why you two have been friends and get mad at yourself for bein' so friendly and tellin' your mind to your enemy and he'll be in the same boat and wonder why he's been so durn friendly with you. But herbs was the thing that put the old friendship there. If we didn't have herbs on this bus there'd a been a lot of grouches along. But everybody smiled. Everybody was happy.

"Comin' to the big town, boys. Ain't this Cincinnati, Ohio?"

"Yes, Jake Spradling, this is Cincinnati. Have you ever been here before?"

"No. But I've heard of Cincinnati all my life. This is the first time I have ever been here."

"How'd you know it was Cincinnati then?"

"I've heard so much talk about how big it was. I just allowed we'd come to it. See the big house. See the smoke from the mills. A body can tell it is a big town. I purt nigh knowed it was Cincinnati."

Cincinnati is a big town when a person is in a hurry. Stoplights all the time red. Traffic in the way. Hard for us to plow through. People pointin' to the sign Mose had printed and put in front of his bus. People laughin' at the sign. What did we care. We'd not see Cincinnati for a couple of days. We'd never see these same people again. We had the bus and the herbs. They could have the laugh.

Out of Cincinnati. And was I glad to get through that town and get on the highway where we could move again. Soon we were on the ribbon of highway headin' for Indiana. Mose said: "When you come to a pretty nice lookin' restaurant, Mr. Driver, throw on your brakes. We want to stop. We need grub. We need to stop."

Well, I never can forget Mose. The way he rode in that bus. Pon my honor, he did look like a governor. He is a tall man. He is about six feet five. He has a keen, dark eye. He wears them little ribbon bow ties like a oldtime speaker at the old-fashion barbecues like we used to have up on Beaver. He just set back there and puffed on a cigar like he owned the world. His eyes twinkled and his face was red. He was all rared back. In his coat lapel was a red rose Jenny Mae Lovelace had brought him from the hothouse. He just commanded the whole bus. We listened to him doin' the talkin'. He would say: "I was cut out to be the Governor of Kentucky. They lost the pattern they cut me out by when they got the governor they got. They need old Mose down there at Frankfort. I'd show them how to run this state. I'm not jokin'. Don't you think I couldn't run it better than it is run. I could just set there and do nothin' and it would go on better than it is goin'. You know you can do too much when you are the Governor of Kentucky.

77

I've been on Deer Creek too long now, though, to be Governor of Kentucky."

"W'y, you are the Governor of Kentucky," said Ollie Spry. "We have the Governor of Kentucky right on this bus with us, gentlemen and ladies. We have Gov. Randall Spoon. He is right with us goin' to see a ball game in Chicago. This is the Governor's party and we are his guests. Lady Jenny Mae Lovelace, you are Tessie La-More, his secretary. You are pretty enough to be a governor's secretary."

"Oh, thank you, Ollie Spry," said Jenny Mae Lovelace. "I accept the position right now. I accept the compliments. May I say, Ollie, that you are Lt. Gov. S. M. Radnor."

"Smart woman," said Ollie and he continued, "Bill Dugan here is Sec. of State Hammonds Sizemore. Fred Kemp here is Att. Gen. Caley C. Rooten. That's about as big a party of state officials as we need. Sorry we can't make you all public officials. Who's a good Kentucky Colonel among you? Anybody got chin whiskers?"

"Fred Land here. He's got a nice set of chin whiskers."

"Make him Colonel Whitt then, famous drinkin' Kentucky Colonel."

"Suits me."

"All right. We are all set," said Ollie.

"Do you reckon we're ever goin' to find that restaurant, Mister Driver?" said Mary Snider. "My stomach's feelin' hollow as a gourd. We got to find a place to eat."

"Comin' into Indiana," said the driver. "See the car license. Won't be long until we'll be in Richmond, Indiana. We can find the good restaurants there. I used

78

to work in Richmond. I'll take you to a good one."

"Okay. Just so we get to a restaurant."

Well, we pulled into Richmond. The party was gettin' livelier now. The car was filled with tobacco smoke. Everybody had sampled his gallon of herbs. People on our bus were feelin' just a little friendlier than when we left Crummit. People looked at our sign as we passed and pointed to our bus. We didn't care. The driver was takin' us to his favorite restaurant. We pulled up and came to a halt in front of the restaurant.

"Here's the best restaurant in Richmond, gentlemen and ladies. Here is the place I used to eat when I drove bus through here."

"Do they know you in here?" said Ollie Spry.

"Yes, they do," said the driver.

"Do they believe you in here?" said Ollie.

"I'd think they would," said the driver.

"Well, you tell the manager that we have the Governor of Kentucky on this bus and part of his staff. You be damn sure you tell him that. Tell him to give us service. We got to have service. We got to be treated royal. We are the Royal House of our state not for two more years but for two days. We are the Governor's party."

"You are quite right," said Mose. "I want one more drink of herbs to act like the governor and make speeches. I am already the governor. Secretary, you work for the Ford Motor Company in Crummit. You know shorthand surely. You be ready to take down my speech if I make one along the road. Maybe one in this restaurant if I am called on. I may just get up and talk if I am not called on. I am the Governor of Kentucky."

Well, we got out. The driver pulled down the windows, fastened them and locked the doors. We didn't want any-body in Indiana to know the Governor of Kentucky had herbs on his party. We didn't care about the tobacco smoke. Anybody knows that's respectable and decent and expected that the governor of any state smokes long cigars. It might be expected of the Kentucky governor to take a little drink. But we weren't takin' any chances. We didn't want the people of Indiana to smell whiskey on our governor's breath.

The proprietor was standin' back of the counter. He was a short man with a black handlebar mustache. He was wipin' a plate when we went in. He looked at our crowd and kindly smiled. Of course we didn't look very fresh after gettin' off the bus for nearly a hundred-and-fifty-mile ride or maybe more. The women needed to powder their noses and redden their lips a little. We needed to step out and wash our hands and faces and comb our heads. We made it straight for the washrooms. Our driver went over and shook hands with the pro-prietor. We saw him whisper somethin' to him.

We got brushed up a little and walked back into the room. The proprietor had a serious look on his face. He was hurryin' here and there. All the waiters were runnin'. "The Governor wants the best dinner you serve for twenty-four people of his party and the bus driver," said Ollie. The Governor came out, tall and stately with his eyes twinklin'. His conversation was fast and intelligent. The waitresses looked at him. I heard one whisper: "That is Gov. Randall Spoon of Kentucky."

I wondered what we were doin stoppin' in a restaurant

quite so small. No wonder the proprietor was mortally shocked. Just think of the Governor and his party stoppin' at a restaurant unknown as one havin' class for the royalty of any state. But the royalty of Deer Creek and Crummit was right there. The Governor of Kentucky and part of his staff, the rest his friends. "Gettin' up there, aren't you, boy," I heard the proprietor whisper to the bus driver, "drivin' the Governor of Kentucky around? Is he a football fan too? I know how all Kentuckians are about their horses. I know how the Governor likes horse racin'. He must be some sport to like football the way he does."

"Our Governor is a sport. He's about the best sport you ever saw. He likes prize fightin' and wrestlin'. He likes shootin' matches, baseball, pool, spittin' at cracks and chicken fightin'. Of course we don't put that out every place. But he's a sport. He's a big bird hunter too. He's a crack shot, that man is. He's another King Arthur when it comes to bravery and fightin'. He's a Von Hindenburg when it comes to huntin'. He's a Henry VIII when it comes to women. He's another George Washington when it comes to statesmanship for his state. Of course that's his limits you know, within the bounds of his state. Would you like to meet him?"

"I'd be tickled to death!"

"Gov. Randall Spoon, I'd like to introduce John Farmer to you. He runs this restaurant and I've known him for years. He wants to meet you."

"I am glad to have the pleasure of meetin' you," said the Governor. "Won't you be seated a minute?"

"No, Governor, I must hurry along with these plates. I

wished I'd a knowed you was comin'. You caught us not prepared for so many dignitaries. Just to think I've seen your picture in the paper so much, but I never dreamed about you ever stoppin' here."

"Well you can't tell about the turn of things. No one knows just what fruit that time will bear. You just can't tell. I never knew that I'd ever stop here either. We are en route to Chicago to a ball game—a pleasure trip combined with business."

"But you don't look like your picture. You are a much better-lookin' man."

"Oh, thank you," said the Governor, "you are quite liberal with your remarks when you say I am a good-lookin' man. The picture you see of mine in the papers is made from an old picture I had made after the worries of a hard campaign. You perhaps remember readin' about that campaign. It was a bitter struggle. That Republican came nigh as a pea gettin' it. They put out on me in Kentucky that I was against racin' and good whiskey. That nearly wrecked me. But we overcome all the propaganda. I got the election by a fairly conservative margin."

The proprietor went back to help with the plates of food. "That is where he belongs," said the Governor. "I like the common man, but I'm durn tired. I want coffee and grub. I am in a hurry.

"Well," said the Governor, "the smell of this food is just wonderful. The sight of it is appetizin'. See that everybody is well fed. See that all the men that will smoke them get a good cigar after the meal. I must eat. I am hungry."

"The Governor of Kentucky," said one of the waitresses, "watch him eat. He is a hearty eater. He can put the food away. I've heard it said that about all big people head of the country are gluttonous eaters. I've heard it said there was a novelist come through Indiana once and he stopped at Halleck's Restaurant here in town. That he ordered a whole stewed hen. And when he took a piece of that hen he just run it through his mouth and threw the naked bone on the floor. He never stopped eatin' like that till he finished that stewed hen and the rest of the grub and got up in a hurry—had to be asked to pay. He said, 'I'm sorry, I was about to forget.' The movies was makin' a picture of one of his novels."

"This is good grub," said the Governor, "you bring me some more coffee, please. I like your mutton chops. I like the sauce that goes with the chops. I like everything that you have. The food tastes fine. I was a very hungry man. I am not now, however, after all this food. Bring me a San Felice cigar, please."

Well, we put the grub away. Girls ran this way and that. They waited on us in a royal manner. It pays to be in company with the governor of a state or some big name. Then you get service. But I wasn't asked to autograph any napkins. Thank goodness! They kept the governor busy autographin' napkins until he could hardly smoke his cigar. I felt sorry for the governor. But he took his popularity with a smile. He said: "All this comes with bein' a big man in affairs of the state. I am a big man and I expect all this. It sometimes takes a little of the joy out of life. But I don't mind. You pay for all you get out of this life anyway whether you are a big man in affairs of the state or a man diggin' in the ditch.

"Secretary, find out how much the bill is, please," said the Governor. "Add in five dollars for service. I'll not write a check. I'll pay off in money right from my pocket."

"Twenty-five dollars even. The cigars go with the dollar meals."

"No sales tax," said the Governor. "They ought to have the sales tax. It takes the sales tax to turn the wheels of finance. Let a dollar turn over thirty-four times and it makes a dollar for the state. Not foolin me'. Right here is the money."

Our driver said to the Governor: "Say, Mr. Farmer wants you to speak a few words while you are here. See, they's a little crowd gathered in here. Word is out in Richmond that the Governor is passin' through here. Said he could have newspaper reporters in here in just a few minutes if it would be all right with the Governor."

"Yes, but you tell him that I'll speak a few words, but I don't want any newspaper reporters in here. This is not a publicity trip. This is a pleasure trip. Go right over there now and tell him what I said. I'll give them a little talk. I'll get up right now and give it to them and we've got to be movin' on toward Chicago."

The driver walked over to the proprietor. He whispered somethin'. The Governor got up from his chair, brushed the gray ashes off the end of his cigar. He laid it down on the edge of his plate: "Ladies and gentlemen and fellow citizens: I am just passin' through your beautiful state, I've come up from a sister state of yours as you well know, the state of Kentucky. And I want to say even on this trip of pleasure, it is a part of this pleasure trip to speak a few words to you of Indiana. I have looked your people over in Indiana and you are so much like us Kentuckians that I can't tell you apart. There is not any way of knowin'. (Laughter.)

"In our state we have a few things you do not have. But we are about the same people after all. We have our horses down there and we love them. We have our hills and our bluegrass and our mountains. We have our little specks of trouble as any state will have. As Indiana will have, Ohio will have and West Virginia will have. And we have some things that other states don't have. The pioneer spirit of this nation still exists in the people of Kentucky. People have to be guarded at the polls on election day with soldiers. We take our religion and our politics seriously. And why not? Aren't they both vital pillars in this Constitution of ours? Aren't they strong pillars to hold Old Glory up to flutter in the breeze over the land, over America?"

The Governor of Kentucky spoke for twenty minutes. He let the words fly. People stood with their mouths open. Our secretary took down the Governor's speech. When the Governor closed he said: "Ladies and gentlemen, I beseech you, one and all, to stand as pillars—to stand as mountain rocks under this government of ours for support. Let us stand as oak-tree sentinels for democracy and keep Old Glory free to wave from coast to coast, over the Land of the Free and the Home of the Brave. I thank you." (Applause.) (More applause.)

But Governor Randall picked up his cigar and walked out. He said, "Good-by, Indiana. We 'll meet you at the Kentucky Derby. Good-by, Mr. Farmer. Hope to eat another good meal with you sometime."

The driver unlocked the door. We got back on the bus. We took our old seats. The motor hummed. We started through Richmond on our way to Chicago. We felt much better. The Governor was a success speakin' to the Indiana people. "I'll speak again when we stop," said the Governor. "I like it. I like to be Governor. Every man now and every woman to his own jug. Help thyself to the herbs. We are out of the city now. Drink and be merry. You don't know about tomorrow. You don't know what tomorrow holds for you."

Well, we helped ourselves to the herbs. Now when one man starts on a gallon of honest-to-goodness, mule-kickin' herbs it takes a long time to kill it if one drinks moderately. We tried to take our herbs moderately goin'. Comin' back didn't matter so much long as the driver didn't get any herbs. We didn't intend to give him any herbs. We intended to keep his hand on the throttle and his eye on the rail.

We passed through Muncie, Marion, Logansport and into Hammond. We had been jostled down. We were ready to eat again. It was dark. We were gettin' tired. It was in the evenin'. "What do you say, gentlemen and ladies, we stop and eat and relax before we get into Chicago?"

"Suits me," said Ollie Spry. "I'm feelin' like it's bean time again. I am ready to eat. I am a hungry man. What do you say, Governor, that when we get in front of a nice-lookin' restaurant that you let me go in and ask the Whole-Cheese what he would take to fix a steak dinner for the Governor of Kentucky and his party which includes several of his staff?"

"Suits me fine," said the Governor. "It lets them know in advance who to expect. That is a bright idea. I'll be thinkin' of another speech to give at partin'."

"What shall it be, Governor?"

"Fair Women, Fast Horses, Honorable Herbs!"

"What a talk! What a talk! Can you handle that subject?"

"Can Rubinoff play his violin?"

"Here is a nice-lookin' soup house," said the driver. "You want me to stop here, Governor?"

"Why not?"

"Let me out, you people. Get your feet up square around until I get out and make arrangements for a meal for the Governor of Kentucky and his party."

Ollie walked down the aisle. He went out the bus door. We saw him enter the restaurant. We saw him talkin' to the head cheese. We saw him motion, "Bring 'em on." They all wanted the honor of havin' the Governor of Kentucky. No one would turn us down. They really couldn't turn us down. It puts them on the spot. Not us.

"Come on, all of you," said Ollie, "he said it was a pleasure for him to have the honor of feedin' the governor of the state. That it would increase business for him. That he would name the restaurant Spoon Restaurant for the honor of havin' fed the Governor of Kentucky.

He wants the Governor's picture to put up in the window. He wants his autograph. He wants his napkin autographed. When he runs his ad in the paper next week he is goin' to say: 'We feed many notable celebrities. The Governor of Kentucky and the majority of his staff dined with us Saturday evening last.' Boy, he really wants you, Governor of Kentucky."

"Well, he can have twenty-five hungry people just in the minute. Herbs in place. The door locked and the windows down, driver. Let's eat. Come on, everybody. Come on with your Governor!"

We walked into the restaurant. Waiters ran quickly. The proprietor came out and said: "This is the Hon. Randall Spoon of Kentucky, isn't it?"

"Yes, this is he," said Mose. "Yes. I am the Governor of Kentucky."

"I am glad to welcome you and your party into my restaurant. I hope we can serve you to your satisfaction."

"I think you can, all right," said the Governor.

"If I had just had word that you were comin' and could have fixed for you. You caught me unexpectedly. I never dreamed of seein' a governor here today. We'll do our best by you."

"That's all a mule can do," said the Governor laughin'. "Just take it easy. We are not hard to please. We are very tired, hungry and in a hurry. We are en route to Chicago and we have been delayed by motor troubles or we would be in Chicago now."

"May I call a newspaper reporter in and give him this story? Let him interview you? I'd like to."

"Yes, but don't do it. This is a pleasure trip. We are on our way to see a football game between the Bears and the Wildcats tomorrow. And I have a little business in Chicago to fix up tonight. I don't have time to be interviewed."

"I am sorry then, Governor."

"That's quite all right. I appreciate your thoughtfulness. I hope you understand my position. You know the affairs of state are many and large. It is not often the governor of a state can slip out like I did this mornin' early. Not a paper reporter got that I was takin' this trip. Just to think every time you go out even to see a neighbor it is told in all the papers. You've seen my name in your papers here many times. You have seen my picture. Thank heavens I'm out tonight just with my staff members and my friends. No reporters askin' me questions and sendin' it out to all parts of the country."

We went to the washrooms and got ready for dinner. The Governor was delayed talkin' to the proprietor. But the Governor just walked away to the washroom. They were carryin' hot dishes of steak dinners to our tables white-clothed and big enough for four. The Governor, Attorney General, Secretary of State and Lieutenant Governor ate at the same table. I was at the table with the Governor's Secretary, the Kentucky Colonel Whitt and another not of the Royal House but just a friend of the Governor. His name was Ely Hunt. Did they carry the grub to us! We started carvin' the tender steak. The Governor's table got the most attention. Our table was the second to be recognized.

The waiters nearly fell over each other carryin' food to our table. "More coffee," Mose would say. They went in a run to get coffee for the Governor. He would sit back, his red face beamin' like a winesap in the autumn sun. His eyes would twinkle like two liquid stars set against a sky of red. He would eat and his shoulders would twitch. He was serious.

"How is the food?" asked the proprietor.

"Couldn't be any better," said the Governor. "You have real food here. We are enjoyin' it."

"Write that down with your name here on this napkin, Governor. I'm glad to hear you say that."

"I don't very often do this. But I'll do it for you. Secretary, ask for the bill, please," said the Governor. "Include smokes for all and ten bucks for service. Now," said the Governor, "I'm ready to say a few words and we got to be goin'. I hope he asks me to speak."

"We'll see that you get to speak, Governor," said Lt. Gov. S. M. Radnor. "You must speak before you leave here, Governor. You can't miss givin' that three-point publicity speech on your state. Remember what you said in the bus."

"Bill is nothin'. Not a thing," said Sec. Tessie LaMore.

"I won't have that," said the Governor. "He must take his pay."

"No," said the proprietor, "I won't have it. I won't have it. I won't have a thing. No use to insult me by askin' me to take it. I just won't do it. You have helped me more than all the ads I could put in the paper. Your presence here has helped me. Your signature will help me. Do you have a picture of yourself with you?"

"Sorry, but I do not have."

"Quite all right. Do you reckon you could send me one?"

"Surely."

"Do you have somethin' to say before you leave? You see some people have gathered in here. They heard you was in here and they've heard so much about the Governor of Kentucky. They want to see him in person and hear him. How about a few words, Governor?"

"Citizens of Indiana," said the Governor of Kentucky, "It is a pleasure to speak a few words to you while passin' through your most beautiful state and sister state of Kentucky. It is a pleasure indeed to note the progress your state is makin'. I could go on and on and speak to you of your own State. I have kept a close observation on the state of Indiana for years. Her people are so much like our own people. Just crossin' the river one can't tell a Hoosier from a Corncracker. (Applause.) God has been good to Indiana by the looks of the fat barns over the countryside. (Applause.) Now if I make a talk here this evenin', my new Indiana friends, citizens of one of these great states of America, I choose to call that talk, 'Fair Women, Fast Horses, Honorable Herbs.' (Laughter and applause.)

"You know we got the prettiest women in the world. We got them in the mountains and we got them in the bluegrass. Our state is shaped like a plow point. We got fair women all over the old plow point. Check any place you please. They are tall in the bluegrass. It is the lime in the food products from the soil that makes the bones grow in the women same as in the horses and men.

They got the stock in them too. I have been warned about the importation of so many canned goods into this fertile section of our state. That practice, ladies and gentlemen, must be discontinued. If you want fine-lookin' women, fair women, come to Kentucky. (Laughter and applause.)

"There is no need for me to tell you about our horses. There is but little left to say after all that has been said. The world knows about our horses. We love a horse, us men do, better than we do our wives. (Shouts and applause.) Our women, though, ladies and gentlemen, love the horses better than they do their husbands. (Shouts and louder applause.) We bury our horses with ceremony. We name our churches for our horses. We put up marble tombstones at their graves. Let me tell you about a scrub horse once. He came from a farm back in the hills. He won every race he was put in—just a old scrub horse. He wouldn't work at nothin'. People thought he was a workhorse. The truth was found out about his mother's breedin'. She'd jumped the fence and got to Satan, that famous horse of the turf. Satan was the father of this plug that swept the race track and focused the eyes of the nation upon Kentucky. That just goes to show you we got the horses with the blood in them.

"Now, ladies and gentlemen, last but not the least thing in our state we are very proud of. That is herbs. (Laughter and whispering.) You may not know what we call herbs. You may have another name for herbs. You, perhaps, up in this section of the United States call it 'moon' or 'white mule.' But the real name of it is 'herbs.' (Laughter and applause.) We call it herbs for it is good herb medicine for snakebites, chills and fevers and a lot of things I could go on here and enumerate until mornin.' That would be useless, my good Indiana friends. When one of our citizens has made herbs that is no more than his duty. Our fathers have made them for generations. You know, about all of us like our herbs. When I was a judge I never sentenced a man for makin' herbs. Now I have the chance to go one further. When he is put behind the dark walls—all it takes is my name to fetch him out into the light and make him a free man. Honorable herbs, ladies and gentlemen! W'y, do you think I'd degrade a reputable man's reputation by puttin' him in a buggy jail? No! I'd take him home with me if I could to the Governor's mansion and give him a decent feather bed! I feel for humanity! God turned the water into wine! Didn't he do it? Then what is wrong with Honorable Herbs! When you come to our state don't forget our herbs. (Applause. Applause. More Applause.) So, good night, ladies and gentlemen, and may God bless you." (Applause. Applause. Applause.)

The Governor of Kentucky walked out the door. We followed him to the bus. He made a stirrin' talk. People ran up with napkins, papers, whiskey-bottle labels and asked for the Governor's autograph. He hurriedly scribbled, "The Governor of Kentucky" and so on. He was tall and stately as a pine tree on a Kentucky hillside. He had the military bearin' of a knight in search of the Holy Grail. He smoked a cigar and blew the smoke out into the cool Indiana air. We loaded in the bus as the motor hummed. We roared away to Chicago.

"I'll take some Honorable Herbs, boys," said the

Governor liftin' the jug to his mouth: "How about you, gentlemen and ladies?"

"Suits us," said Ollie. "I love my herbs. Chicago is not far away. Better take them now. Dry country, you know. Maybe the time will come when the people will crave herbs and vote them back. But government herbs don't come up to these herbs."

The bus went by leaps and bounds. Ollie gave the driver a swig of herbs. That had been what was wrong all the time. He just started drivin' now. We were just a matter of minutes from Chicago. Each person took a little dram of herbs. The bus roared on. We passed everythin' on the road. Our driver would say: "Lay over, road hog. Lay over before I knock you off the road." And we droned right into the Chicago Loop.

"Are we goin' into the Big City, boys?" said the Governor. "Looks like a lot of town here. Seems like we've come over Hell and half of Georgia. Hurrah for the Wildcats! Hurrah for the Wildcats. Wildcats scratch the Bears! Paw them Bears! Scratch their eyes out! Hurrah for the Wildcats!"

Boom-boom-zzzrrr—motorcycle cops whizzing past us.

Clop-clop-clop—mounted police!

Zzzzzzzzzzzzzzzz—police cars.

"STOP!" One pulled in front of us with a growl.

Uniformed men stepped forth from all sides. Our bus had been stopped! What was wrong? Herbs? Surely not.

"Open the door, driver," said the Governor.

The driver opened the door. A uniformed policeman

stuck his head in at the door. He said, "Consider your-self under arrest."

"What for?" said Ollie Spry.

"You are goin' in the wrong way on the Loop. That's what for. You know better than this, driver."

"You can't do this," said Ollie. "We got the Governor of Kentucky on here and part of the House of Representa-tives. We got part of the staff. We are already due in Chicago at the Mortfield Hotel!"

"Pardon me, gentlemen," said the policeman, "if your governor is on that bus. Go right on. Go right on. Go right in on this side the Loop!"

"Thank you."

"Say, officer, don't you want to meet the Governor!"

"I'll be delighted."

Our Governor from Kentucky stepped out where the police could see him.

"Yes, I am the Governor of Kentucky. I am glad to meet you, gentlemen. I am sorry my chauffeur made this mistake. Verry sorry. Gentlemen, you know I am a law-abidin' man. I assure you nothin' like this will happen again and if you gentlemen will be so kind I'd be happier if you wouldn't mention it. You understand! Well, good-by, gentlemen, and good luck."

"Good-by, Governor, and good luck to you."

One said: "My lands, but isn't the governor of Ken-tucky a big scamp? He's a good-lookin' man too. Sur-prised me. I thought from his picture he wasn't so hot-goin' from his looks. W'y, he's a fine-lookin' man!"

We drove in on the wrong side of the Loop. People

dodged us and razzed us. We were tired out. We were
goin' to the Mortfield Hotel. I don't know whether it
was because we were on the wrong side of the Loop the
reason why people razzed us or the sign on the front of
our bus.

"Just soon as we get in front of the hotel, women and
men, get your herbs in your luggage. You know people
are on the lookout these days for good herbs. Put your
herbs away. Get your reservations. The Governor pays
for your rooms and your meals while you are here. Remember, driver, take that sign off soon as we light in
front of the hotel."

The porters ran out. A whole swarm of them, blue
uniformed with rows of brass buttons up the sides. "Say,
what's the sign doin' up there! Comin' up to beat us, are
you?"

"That's what we've come for. Just a friendly match
in sports," said the Governor. "We have come to give
you a tussle if we don't give you a sound beatin'."

"Uh," said the porter.

"Say," said Ollie, nudgin' the porter with his elbow,
"you don't know who you are arguin' with. You should
know better than this long as you've been a porter. You
are arguin' with the Governor of Kentucky. Ain't you
never heard of him? Stand there with your mouth open!
Don't drop my grip."

Then it was whispered: "Governor of Kentucky is on
that bus. He's the big, tall, fine-looking man. See him
there. Look at him!"

Each porter tried to get his leather bag. One nabbed

it. The Governor didn't pay any attention to them fightin' for his leather bag. He had the affairs of state at heart, and the affairs of Chicago at heart presently. We had to get rooms for the night. It was late. We were tired.

"The hotel manager met us: "Is the Governor of Kentucky here?"

"Yes. This is he."

"My name is James Hampton. Glad to know you, Governor. Welcome you to our hotel."

"Glad to know you, Mr. Hampton. Glad to be a guest in your hotel for tonight."

"We'll have your rooms just in a few minutes. I know you must be tired."

"We are," said our Governor of Kentucky, "we're tired out. We started out early this morning. It's late now. I've made two talks on the way. The only thing, Mr. Hampton, I ask of you, is not let it be known we are here. I don't want any newspaper reporters here. I want rest. Hear me!"

"I do, Governor Spoon. I'll see you are not disturbed."

"I don't know who stayed with the Governor. I know he went to bed. He didn't stay up and discuss affairs of state. I went to bed. I roomed with the Lieutenant Governor. I don't remember much else. I needed sleep. Look what a place we were in. Chicago hotel with the Governor of Kentucky. Only this mornin' we started as just ordinary folks. We were goin' fast up that ladder of celebrities. You become a celebrity overnight when you get into affairs of state.

It was nine o'clock Sunday morning. The telephone brought me out of bed.

"The Governor wants you downstairs in the dinin' room to breakfast, sir."

I dressed and went downstairs. The Governor was at the table already with nearly all of our party. We just had Ollie to wait on before we started breakfast. Table was dressed the best it had been for a long time. It was dressed for company. "Ladies and gentlemen," said our Governor, "here's each of you a complimentary ticket to the game between the Bears and the Wildcats."

"Thank you, Governor."

"Yes, thank you, Governor."

"That's nice of you, Governor."

"Can't thank you enough, Governor."

"Waiter," said the Governor, "bring us two-for-a-quarter cigars, please. Good as you got and that's the best you have for I got one this mornin'. It's the Pince-Pete Cigar. It's a jim-dandy."

We had breakfast. We smoked. The women took to cigarettes. They held them properly in their fingers and pointed them beautifully when they weren't between their bought-red lips. We had a crowd of dignitaries, all right. I felt proud to be with the Governor of Kentucky. I'd remembered old dates with him, the prize fights, the bird hunts, the fox hunts, the square dances, the political rallies, at the herb reservoir, at the chicken fights. The Governor was at home any place you put him. He had dignity. He could make a speech. He could buy cattle, farm, hand out your letters at the post office out on Deer

Creek. He could get men out of jail. Demand them of the Law. Why couldn't he make a good governor?

Well, we got a section of seats—box seats where we could see the Wildcat-Bear football game. If ever the Governor enjoyed himself it was here. He pounded my hat in once when the Wildcats scratched the Bears for a long run up the muddy field. He hit Ollie on the ear with a quirt and made it bleed when the Wildcats intercepted a Bear pass and made a fifty-yard run. It was a hard game. Just a few minutes to play after the long struggle when neither side had scored. One of the Bears kicked a field goal and then the whistle. We lost. The game was over. We made for the gate, and to our bus. We had to return to the hotel to get our luggage and settle our bill.

Our rooms were four dollars for each of us. The Governor's room was a little more. "But the bill was light," the Governor said. "One good reservoir of Honorable Herbs will pay that little bill of $142 plus tips."

We loaded on the bus. The motor hummed. The Governor was delayed. We were waitin'. He ran down the steps: "Step on the gas, driver. Newspaper men wantin' to interview me. I don't have the time. We must be gettin' back to the affairs of state. Be damn sure you go out the right way on the Loop. Our trip has been a success. We've got a few herbs left, haven't we? All right. Help yourselves to the herbs. When you run out we have a reserve amount of herbs on this bus. If you get by with a gallon to the man and a gallon to the woman, why not? Remember, we'll have our herbs."

We smoked. We sang songs. We talked about affairs of state. We breezed over the ribbon of white road. Back into Indiana. Back to Hammond. Back through Marion, Muncie, Richmond. We stopped at a new restaurant. It was night. Darkness had covered the level Indiana countryside. "Now," said Hattie Ogles, "I'll make a speech here. I want to talk."

"Don't let the herbs be too much your guide," said our Governor of Kentucky, "but speak from the heart if you say anythin' and not from the herbs."

We stopped at a midnight restaurant. "Lunch for twenty-five soon as you can fix it," said the Governor. "We are in a hurry. Do it quickly as you can."

Our driver slipped over and said somethin' to the little restaurant keeper. "What," said the restaurant keeper, "this time of night?"

He hurried about. His waitresses hurried. We didn't have to wait twenty minutes for a midnight meal. We were tired out. We were hungry. We needed food. The owner came over. He said: "I heard the Governor of Kentucky was here among you. Is this the Governor of Kentucky?"

"Yes," said Mose, "I'm the Governor of Kentucky. How did you know I was the Governor?"

"You look like some great man," the fellow said foldin' his thin hands and squintin' his eyes.

"Thank you," said the Governor. "It is very nice of you to hand me such complimentary remarks. I appreciate them to the depths of my heart. I am the Governor of Kentucky and a few of my friends and I have been to

Chicago on a combined business and pleasure trip. We are gettin' back late. I must be servin' my state tomorrow. I am in a hurry."

"Just a minute, Governor, and we'll be ready for you."

Food never tasted any better to me in my life. It was a midnight lunch. We got buttermilk and sauerkraut with lunch. I ordered that. Some got coffee. I took buttermilk. My stomach was in an uproar. It was now near midnight. We had to get in before daylight. The Governor had to be on Deer Creek by that time. He must get in before daylight.

We finished the food. It was fine. We lighted our cigars and started to push back from the table. "Ladies and Gentlemen and Our Most Honorable Governor of Kentucky," said Hattie Ogles, "I have a few words I'd like to say before we move on where our party will disband, each to go to our respective duties, the Governor go to his affairs of state and his staff members go with him—I want to say that as an outsider, not a native Kentuckian, but one from a sister state, that I have never been with a more loyal group of people nor better sports than with this group of Kentuckians. I have had the most memorable trip in my life. (Applause.)

"Kentucky has one of the greatest governors of all the governors in these United States of America. He is a sport above all. He is a man of the common people— the governor for the man of the street you people have heard so much talk about. Kentucky has produced her Breckenridges, her Clays, her Lincoln, and ladies and gentlemen, she has produced her Randall Spoon, our most worthy Governor of Kentucky with you at this minute." (Applause. Applause.) ("Full of Honorable Herbs," whispered Ollie. "Get her down if you can.") "He has come to the people of Kentucky in a time of need. We were goin' in debt by degrees. He has given us a tax that is honorable for all men alike. He will bring our state to the front. It is comin' there already, after his services to his state and then to the world. He is a man for the country. He is bigger than his state. Ladies and gentlemen, this is all I have to say and for the privilege of sayin' these words, I most heartily thank you."

Our Governor stood and knocked the gray ashes from his cigar tip with his long index finger. He was the man of the hour. He bowed to the crowd in the restaurant. He walked out. "Good night, gentlemen," he said.

We walked out into the cold air. The moon was racin' through some big, cold, gray clouds. "I believe I am the Governor of Kentucky," said Mose. "If I'm not, I'd make a good one. I could be the Governor of Kentucky. Now. Just think, tomorrow, I won't be anything but a post-master, a storekeeper, a cattle buyer, a good sport, a handler of good Honorable Herbs. It's hard to fall to that after this trip. Get in the bus, my friends. Get in the bus and us move on toward Crummit. You know my wife has left me once over stuff like this. You remember that trip to Columbus that filled all the papers that time that I had such hard time gettin' out of. I couldn't handle the Ohio Law like I did the Kentucky Law. You know I'm rooted in Kentucky and it's a pretty damn good dirt for the roots to grow in too."

We loaded in the bus. We got our seats. "The herbs are gettin' low, Mr. Governor," said Fliam Flannery, "mighty low. Mighty low. Mine is down to the very dregs. But here's to you all!" He turned the jug to his lips and emptied it stone dry, dregs and all went down.

"I love my herbs," said Mose, "and here's the last. My jug is emptied. My herbs are gone. All gone. My friends are all here. We have had a good time together. Sing 'The Old Ship of Zion.' Sing. Sing. Sing."

We sang "The Old Ship of Zion." The bus plunged on through the darkness. The stars were bright balls of fire glued in the blue above us. We could see the bright lights boom past us on the highway. We overtook and passed each car we got sight of. We moved. We gave our driver herbs and told him to step on the gas. He did his best. We made seventy. We made all the bus would do. We made top speed around the curves. Three o'clock Monday mornin' and Crummit!

We shook hands. We parted. Men shed tears. Spirits in us were high. We had finished our Honorable Herbs. Those of us who had not finished, Mose told to take the jugs home but be damn sure and save the jugs for he needed them. It was a sad partin'.

I went with Mose to get his car and ride to Kentucky. He had left it parked in Crummit. The Crummit policemen had picked it up. It was in their custody. We were informed by a policeman we asked to search for a stolen car and gave him our number. We had to go to the police station.

"Yes, Mr. Winthrop, we have your car. We thought

we would take care of it for you. Next time don't leave it out in the street."

"What's the bill of fare to get it?" said Mose.

"Not a thing but your good will. You understand."

"I do," said Mose.

"Good night, Cap."

"Good night."

We got in the car and breezed across the bridge. The toll collector was asleep. We needed the time more than he did the money anyway. I lived near Deer Creek.

"Now if I can just get by the old woman good as I got out of that, w'y I'll be on top of the world. My worst is yet to come. And I got a date with a woman at four o'clock in our barn this mornin'. It's goin' to be just one more trial. Pray for the Governor of Kentucky. Don't let his spirits fall."

I left Mose. I got out near home. I'd have to slip in at the window to keep from wakin' my wife. I heard a chicken a-crowin'. Soon would be day. What a night! What a trip! What a party!

"When I got home," said Mose, "I put my car away and run down to the barn. I was supposed to see that sweet little Claire County widow down there at four o'clock. Well, she was in by the manger. I pulled her up in my arms. I kissed her. I called her honey. And she answered and say, 'W'y, Mose. You do love me, don't you?' And I'll declare, if it wasn't my wife, I'm a liar by the clock. She had come to the barn early to see about some young chickens. And I said, 'W'y yes, honey, I love you. I've always loved you!' And we hadn't spoken to each other in two months. We made up right there."

Love beyond the Law

As we rode down the muddy White Oak jolt-wagon road, I looked across the valley toward the White Oak Freewill Baptist Church. From in the saddle where I sat, I could see every little turn in the road that led to the church. And I took a good look at the covered bridge that spanned the creek and the willows whose long leafless fingers clawed at the raw wind. It was here that I had stood in the moonlight on my way from church with Subrina Williams. We had stood beneath these weeping willows when the moon was like a ripe September pumpkin in the blue sky. And we'd have our arms around each other and look down from the bridge into the blue still waters of White Oak Creek, and there we'd see the moon too.

Then I'd take my arms from around Subrina and I'd pull my pet from my pocket and I'd shoot six times, so fast you couldn't hear the shots, at the moon in the water, and Subrina would laugh and I would laugh. And I'd reload my pet and let Subrina shoot him at the moon in the water. It was great fun. Somewhere up the road we'd hear other pistols barking at the moon in the sky while mine barked at the moon in the water. And there'd never be a word said about it. That was the natural thing to do.

The only thing that ever bothered me was old Percy Cadle. He nearly pestered Subrina and me to death. He had always wanted to go with Subrina. And since she would rather be with me and stand beneath the weeping willows at the bridge and shoot at the moon in the water, old Percy would walk along on the other side of me and pretend to be my friend while he slipped things into my pockets, a live mouse, frog, lizard, crawdad, bumblebee, wasp or water dog. About the time I'd get ready to shoot, something would move in my pocket and tickle or sting me; and I'd have to let Subrina hold my pistol while I cleaned out my pockets. And about that time we'd hear old Percy going down the road laughing to himself.

Now I looked at the road, the bridge and the church until our mules were around the bend. For this was my little world, a world that I had never been away from, any farther than Greenwood where I was now going. And I hated to leave this little world. That's why I had never listened to Sheriff Larkin explaining the new laws to Pa. New laws or old laws didn't bother me. I'd never intentionally broken one in my life. I was thinking about what I was leaving while Pa and Sheriff Larkin talked. I was thinking about Subrina Williams and how I hated to leave her. I was remembering now, more than any time in my life, the good times we had had together. And now I knew that when I was sent to the penitentiary I would be forgotten at home and that Percy would be with the girl I loved. I hoped, as my mule followed the mule Pa was riding, that some other boy would walk along beside Percy when he was walking beside Subrina and slip a frog, lizard, wasp, bumblebee, water dog, crawdad or mouse into old Percy's pocket and let him know how aggravating it was to have someone to do him like he had always done me. All of this was behind me now. We were down White Oak and far out of sight of this little world of mine that I had known and loved all my life.

Subrina, I thought; what will she think when she hears about all that has happened to me?

"No, sheriff," Pa said. "I'm not worth enough to go Adger's bond. Henry Gamble is a man of our Party and he is a jailer that feeds our people well. I know men that have spent the winter with him wouldn't leave the jail because they were so well fed and so well cared for. It won't hurt Adger to spend a few days with Henry until the date for his trial is set. It's not the stain of his being in jail that I worry about. Many good men are at sometime or the other in their lives lodged in jail. But the penitentiary is something different."

"That's right, Jarvis," Sheriff Larkin agreed. "Old Henry will take good care of Adger. And if he got bond and got to come home," Sheriff Larkin explained, "I'd have to make this two-day trip again to notify him. Jail is better for Adger until the trial is over. Who knows, it might be moved up or postponed for a few days. Henry will feed him and take care of him."

"And I can't spend any time in Greenwood right now," Pa said. "My tobacco's in case, and I'll have to strip it and hand it with Adger gone. Don't know how I'll get it done unless Cindy helps me."

"Henry and I together will look after Adger the best we can," Sheriff Larkin said. "Don't worry too much about him, Jarvis. We'll take good care of him in his time of trouble same as if you were there."

We passed the big, two-story, white frame house where the Cadles lived. They had one of the good farms in the White Oak Valley and they raised tobacco. I saw Percy standing at the tobacco barn, and when he saw me he threw up his hand and waved to me. I knew that he wondered why I was going down the road on a mule with Pa and Sheriff Larkin. But I wondered if he wasn't glad to see me going, for now he would be first with Subrina. He watched us until we were out of sight down the road.

When we reached the mouth of White Oak Creek, where the waters of this stream poured into the Tiber River, we came to Sheriff Larkin's car. It was parked in front of Hal Mennix's store and post office.

"Here's where I get off my horse," Sheriff Larkin said. "I'll turn him back over to Hal."

"And here is where I turn back," Pa said.

Then Pa looked at me. For I didn't say anything. I got down from my saddle with my suitcase in my hand. It was light and easy to handle.

"Adger," Pa said, and his voice was nervous, "you tell the jury you never heard tell of that darned law. You'll be tellin' them the truth. A law like that," Pa talked on, "burns me up. It takes the last of a man's freedom!"

While Sheriff Larkin turned the horse back to Hal Mennix and paid him for his night's lodging, I put my suitcase in his car; and then I unsnapped old Dick's bridle rein to give it more length so Pa could lead him. I gave the unsnapped rein to Pa.

"I wonder who could have indicted you," Pa said, shaking his head sadly.

"I don't have any idea," I said.

"But you will know," Pa said. "He'll have to be a witness for the state in your trial. Remember, I'll be at the trial. I'll get the news by the grapevine and I'll be there."

"All right, Pa," I said. "I'll be lookin' for you."

Just then Sheriff Larkin came from the store.

"We're ready, Adger," he said.

"Good-by, Pa," I said.

"Good-by, Jarvis," Sheriff Larkin said as he got in the car. I followed him. I looked back as we moved down the graveled road, and I saw Pa sitting on Dinah and holding Dick's rein. He was watching the car. He was still sitting there watching us when we turned the Tiber River bend and was moving toward Greenwood. "These things happen," Sheriff Larkin said, as we drove along. "Don't be too nervous. Take it easy."

"I'm not as nervous now as I was this mornin', sheriff," I said. "You know how it is in the hills of Greenwood County when we see the sheriff comin'. Nearly everybody takes to the hills. I might have done that," I told him, "if you hadn't caught me in the barn door. I've heard old men say you've never been arrested until you're arrested by a Greenwood County High Sheriff."

Sheriff Larkin laughed and laughed.

"Since there's no one to go your bond," he said after he was through laughing, "I'll just take you down and let Henry keep you until we set a day for your trial?"

"That'll be all right with me," I said, for I knew I couldn't do anything else.

"Oh, you'll get a good bed and three square meals a day," Sheriff Larkin said. "There might be a few in Henry's family that you won't like. You know he's got about forty there now."

"I'll get along all right," I said.

We drove down the Tiber turnpike, and then we turned up Hinton Creek and crossed the Benton Hill. Then we went down into another valley and crossed Hinton Creek, climbed another hill and went down Raccoon until we came to the Sandy River road that followed the curves of the river to Greenwood. It was a good ride with the sheriff, but all along the road when we met people in cars or walking, on horseback or in wagons, they tried to look into Sheriff Larkin's car to see who he had. Everybody knew his car.

"Now, Adger, I'll run you down to Henry's," Sheriff Larkin said soon as we drove across the railroad tracks into the town.

We drove across Greenwood and turned down a street near the courthouse. We came to a big brick building with iron bars across the windows, and twenty-five or thirty beardy faces were pressed against the windowpanes to see who the sheriff was bringing.

"Look who the sheriff is bringin'," I heard one say. "Look how he's all trigged up!"

"Welcome to the Greenwood Lodge," another shouted.

"Shut up your jabberin' around," we heard a gruff voice say as we entered the jail.

"Henry, here's Jarvis Prince's boy, Adger," Sheriff Larkin said to the gruff-voiced man that had been yelling to quiet the prisoners. "You remember old Jarvis, don't you?"

"Sure do," Henry said. "He helped me in the election."

"And, boy," he said to me, "don't you worry while you're with old Henry. You'll get three good meals a day and a good bed to sleep in. If you have any complaints, make them to me. Old Henry takes care of his family. You'll see."

Sheriff Larkin left me in jailer Henry's hands. He walked from the jail toward his car. And Henry unlocked a big steel door and I followed him into the jail. All this over my carrying a pistol, I thought. Here I am in jail.

Henry Gamble took me upstairs and showed me my bed. Nice clean sheets and pillows on it. Then he introduced me to a few of the fellows.

"They can introduce you to the rest," Henry said. "Don't know all the members of my family. They keep comin' and goin' so fast, I can't keep track of all their names."

Then Henry went back downstairs. I talked to the

fellows and watched a few card games going on where they were playing for big stakes, but I didn't see any money. "I'll owe you over a million dollars when I get out of this jail," I heard a man say; then everybody laughed.

I would have rather been home in my own bed than to have been in jail. I would rather have been there milking the cows, feeding the hogs and mules, and cutting wood, and working beneath the sun and stars. I missed Subrina, Ma and Pa, and the livestock at home so much it hurt after I'd been away for a day. As night came on, I got homesick. But when Henry shoved our suppers through the window on a big tray, I knew he told the truth when he said that he fed and cared for his family. We had plenty to eat. That night I went to sleep thinking about home.

We had just finished breakfast next morning, and I was watching the card games start when jailer Henry came upstairs and said: "Adger, I've got to take you up to the courthouse and let Judge Bailey set the time for your trial."

"You're lucky," one of the fellows said to me. "You got here just in time to have your trial in a hurry. I've been waitin' two months."

I didn't know that men in jail wanted to have their trials and get them over with before until after I'd been in jail for one night. They talked about lawyers, prosecuting attorneys and judges. They talked about sentences and freedom. And many talked about home, their mothers, wives and children, as they sat playing cards.

But I didn't answer him. I didn't know whether I was lucky or not. I followed Henry downstairs and he unlocked the big steel door and let me through and then he fastened the door and turned the key behind us. I walked with him up to the big courthouse and we went up a long pair of steps and into a big room filled with people. I'd never seen this room before, for I'd never been upstairs in the courthouse where they had their trials. Then I followed jailer Henry up the aisle where many well-dressed and poorly dressed people were sitting. We passed a little fenced-off place where twelve men and women were sitting. We walked up to a platform where two well-dressed men were arguing something before an old man who was sitting up higher than anybody in the courtroom. Many big books were around him. He looked over the courthouse as if he were the father of everybody sitting inside. He had a bright eye and a kind wrinkled face.

"Your Honor," jailer Henry said, "I have a young man, Adger Prince, indicted by the last Grand Jury for carrying a deadly concealed weapon. Sheriff Larkin brought him down to the jail yesterday."

"Nobody to go your bond?" Judge Bailey asked me.

"No, sir," I said.

"Then we'll have your trial tomorrow," he said. "Do you have an attorney?"

"I do not have," I said.

"Then the Court will appoint an attorney for you," he said. "You must and will get a fair trial in this court."

"Thank you, Your Honor," jailer Henry said as the

two men, who had stopped arguing while Judge Bailey talked to us, started again. I followed jailer Henry back the way we had come until we reached the jail.

"You're lucky to get a trial this soon," jailer Henry said. "You don't know how lucky you are."

Then he unlocked the door and I went back inside the jail. I heard his key turn the lock behind me when I went upstairs, and it gave me a funny feeling to think I was locked up over something I didn't know was wrong. And I had always known as much freedom as the wild fox among the hills, and it hurt me just to think that I couldn't get up and go where I wanted to go and when I pleased. And just to think I am guilty, I thought. I am as guilty as can be. And I will have to go to the penitentiary. Now I felt as weak and trembly as I did when I met Sheriff Larkin face to face at the break of day in our barn door. All day I thought about leaving my good home and the little roads, trees, rock cliffs, bridges and fields and streams in the little world I knew on White Oak. I thought about the Freewill Baptist Church and the good times I had had going there with Subrina and bringing her home, and how we shot at the blowing wind and at the leaves on the trees and the moon in the water. And now, for all of this, I must pay with years of my life behind locked doors and iron bars in the penitentiary.

That night I could hardly eat my supper. For I thought of Subrina. I wondered if old Percy was seeing her now that I was away.

But there wasn't anything I could do about it. For I was in jail. And my trial was tomorrow. I wondered who would be the witnesses that would appear against me. I hoped they wouldn't appear and that they would let me out of jail and let me go home once more. For I was homesick. And I wondered if Pa would get the news and be to Greenwood in time for my trial. He said that he would be there, but I thought the trial might be scheduled sooner than he had expected. I did want Pa to be there for the trial. So many things raced through my mind. I could hardly go to sleep. But I did go to sleep, and I dreamed I was at church with Subrina and that we stood at the bridge and shot my pistol at the quarter moon that looked like a golden fish swimming in the still blue waters of White Oak Creek. I thought I missed the moon and Subrina laughed and I hugged her and kissed her because old Percy wasn't close. Then I felt something move in my pocket, and I screamed as I pulled out a water dog.

"Shut up over there, so we can go to sleep," somebody yelled. Then a pillow hit me and I woke up.

"I'm glad, young fellow, you have your trial tomorrow," Beardy Bert said. "Then we can get some sleep in this jail. Dreamin' of that gal every night and a-talkin' to 'er like she was with you! Makes us all homesick."

Then I heard several men laugh. I didn't say a word. But I lay awake a long time, thinking I wouldn't go back to sleep and talk in my sleep and wake everybody. But I went back to sleep and dreamed I wasn't asleep. Next morning I awoke and shaved and washed my face and put on a clean shirt for my trial. After breakfast, several of the fellows called me a lucky devil. And I wondered if

I were lucky or not. Jailer Henry came up about eight forty-five and I went with him to the courthouse. The house was filled with people.

The Court had appointed lawyer Ossie Purnell to defend me. He was a young lawyer and he seemed to like me and I did like him. I knew my fate depended on him. As I stood before my lawyer and near Circuit Judge Bailey, I saw people shaking hands and talking as if this were a big revival meeting. Everybody was very friendly with everybody else. And the longer they talked, the louder they got, until Judge Bailey had to pound on his desk with a wooden mallet for order. I looked back at the sea of faces, and they all seemed to be looking in my direction. Then I didn't search the crowd any more for Pa. I knew he hadn't been notified by the grapevine, for my trial had been called sooner than he had expected and he wouldn't be here. But I didn't see anybody I knew in the sea of faces except Sheriff Larkin, Judge Bailey, jailer Henry Gamble and my lawyer.

Then Ossie Purnell told me that he wanted to talk things over with me while the jury was selected. So I followed him into a little room. There he asked me if I had carried a pistol. I told him I had. He asked me how long. And I told him since I'd been about fourteen years old. He asked me if I knew the law about carrying a concealed weapon. I told him I didn't. He asked me about my home, my Ma and Pa, and if I'd ever been away from home and how far I had been. I told him the truth. Then he asked me if I was going with a girl on Big White Oak

and what her name was and if I loved her and a lot of
things I'd never think a lawyer would ask a body. But
I told him the truth. He asked me if I planned to marry
Subrina, and I told him I did, but I didn't guess I would
now . . . not if I had to go to the penitentiary for carrying a deadly concealed weapon; for when I came home,
she was such a pretty girl that I knew she'd be married
to somebody else. We talked until some man came to the
door, knocked and said it was time to start the trial.

When I walked out and took my seat, I looked behind
the jury box and there sat Pa. I felt like shouting. I felt
so good that he had been grapevined and had reached
the trial on time. He looked at me and his black eyes
danced. I nodded to him. He was the only one I saw that
I knew in the sea of faces. Then the judge called lawyer
Ossie and me over where a group of men were gathered
around. The judge said to my lawyer: "Do you enter a
plea of guilty?"

Lawyer Ossie said to Judge Bailey: "Your Honor, we
want a trial. I suppose you'd call it not guilty."

"Then we shall proceed with the trial," Judge Bailey
said.

After circuit-court clerk Mannie Bocook had repeated
the oath to the jurors while they stood there with their
right hands raised and had repeated "I will" after the
oath, then prosecuting attorney Lester Lancaster stood
up and read the indictment to the jury and the court.

"Percy Cadle, will you take the witness stand?" he
said.

I could have fallen from my chair when I saw old Percy jump up like a scared rabbit and run to the chair and drop down.

"Hold up your hand and be sworn," prosecutor Lancaster said.

While Mannie Bocook gave old Percy the oath, I looked back to see what Pa was doing. He was as restless as a leaf in the wind. I knew just about what he was thinking. I felt like Pa and I was thinking the same way.

Then prosecutor Lancaster asked old Percy his name and where he lived and if he knew me and a lot of things like that. He brought on the questions that didn't mean a lot, and old Percy answered them just like they had had a secret meeting somewhere like my lawyer and I had had to talk things over.

"Now, on what night was it that you were coming from the Freewill Baptist Church with Adger Prince and you saw him display a deadly weapon?"

"October twelfth," Percy said.

"Just who was in that crowd?" prosecutor Lancaster asked.

"Adger Prince, Subrina Williams and myself," he said.

"Did Adger Prince do any shooting?"

"Yessir," old Percy said.

"What did he shoot at?"

"The moon in the water."

Then everybody in the courthouse laughed until Judge Bailey pounded with his gavel on his desk for order. I looked up and Judge Bailey was trying to keep from laughing.

"Will you repeat that statement to the jury, Percy Cadle?" Judge Bailey said.

"He shot six times at the moon in the water faster than a snake could bat its eye," he said.

"But a snake can't bat its eye, Percy Cadle," I said, jumping up from my chair. "A snake doesn't have any eyelids!"

Then everybody laughed louder than ever. Judge Bailey pulled the white handkerchief from his pocket and wiped his eyes as he pounded with his gavel for order. The eight men and four women jurors laughed until they bent over. They wiped their eyes with handkerchiefs and the back of their hands. Everybody laughed, even to prosecutor Lancaster, and Ossie Purnell laughed. The laughing caught on like the measles. At first Pa didn't laugh, and when I looked at him the second time he was shaking all over. But one person didn't laugh. That was old Percy. His face got red as a turkey's snout. He thought everybody was laughing at him. Once he started to rise from the witness chair but prosecutor Lancaster motioned for him to stay put. Old Percy was scared too. And while he fidgeted in the witness chair, I looked over on the front row and there sat Subrina Williams.

Is she a witness against me? I thought. Then I wondered how I had missed seeing her. I wondered if they'd get her for shooting my pistol with me. For Subrina had shot my little toy many times at the moon in the water at White Oak bridge; and she had shot many times at the moon in the sky, and at the leaves on the weeping willows and at the laughing of the wind.

"Order, or we shall have to discontinue court," Judge Bailey said.

Several people were jerking as they tried to keep from laughing.

"Tell this jury what you know about Adger Prince's pistol packing," prosecutor Lancaster said. "How many times have you seen him with a pistol?"

"Hundreds of times," old Percy said. "I've knowed Adger five years. I've never seen him without his old pistol that he calls 'his pet.' "

"That's all," prosecutor Lancaster said, and old Percy thought he was through and started to leave the witness stand.

"Just a minute, Mr. Cadle," Ossie Purnell said. "You said you'd seen Adger's pistol hundreds of times. You must be with Adger quite a lot, aren't you?"

"Yes, quite a bit," old Percy said.

"When are you with him most?" he asked.

"We come from church together two and three times a week," he said.

"Anybody else with you?"

"I object," prosecutor Lancaster said.

"Objection overruled," Judge Bailey said as he looked down at the witness from his bench, his bald head shining like a wan moon in the White Oak waters.

"Subrina Williams is usually along," he admitted.

"That's all," Ossie Purnell said.

Then old Percy jumped up from the chair like he had been shot at. He ran like a rabbit back to his seat and everybody laughed. For they knew he was glad to get away.

Then prosecutor Lancaster called Subrina Williams to the witness stand and red-faced and fat-cheeked Mannie Bocook gave her the oath. The prosecutor asked her a lot of questions like he had old Percy. But she wasn't scared like him. She sat there, beautiful as the picture of a queen. She looked everybody in the face with her pretty blue eyes that held two patches of the White Oak skies in them.

"You know Adger Prince?" prosecutor Lancaster asked.

"I do."

"Were you with him on the night of October twelfth when he pulled his pistol at the White Oak bridge and shot six times at the moon in the water?"

"I was."

"Did you see his pistol?"

"I did."

"How long have you known him?"

"Since I can remember."

"How long has he carried a pistol?"

"Since he was about fourteen."

"That's all."

"Miss Williams, in what ways do you know Adger Prince?" Ossie asked her. "Just tell it to the jury."

"I object," prosecutor Lancaster said. "That has nothin' to do with this case. That's a foolish question."

"Objection overruled," Judge Bailey said, as he was

beginning to get more interested as the trial went on.

"I played with him when we were babies," she said. "I went to White Oak School with him. And," she added thoughtfully, "I have had dates with him for the last two years."

"That's all," Ossie said.

Then Ossie called my name and I went to the witness stand. I didn't run like Percy either. I wasn't going to get scared. But I walked up to the chair and sat down just like I would at home. I raised my right hand and took oath that I would swear the truth.

"Were you at the Freewill Baptist Church on the night of October twelfth?" Ossie asked me.

"I was," I said.

"Did you bring Subrina Williams home from church?"

"I did," I said.

"Who else was along with you?"

"Percy Cadle," I said.

"Did you pull a deadly concealed weapon from your pocket and shoot six times at the moon's reflection in White Oak waters?"

"I did."

"What was Percy Cadle doing along with you and your girl?"

"I object, Your Honor," prosecutor Lancaster said.

"Objection overruled," Judge Bailey said. "This has something to do with the trial and I want to know the facts. I want to get at the bottom of his trouble."

"Percy's been tryin' to beat my time with Subrina," I said. "He's followed us from church almost every night that I've brought Subrina home for the last three years. Percy walks along on the other side of me and he slips a live mouse, bumblebee, wasp, water dog or a lizard into my pocket. And when I start to get it out he laughs fit to die."

Then everybody started laughing again. They looked at Percy while they laughed, and Judge Bailey had to pound his gavel against his desk to restore order.

"Did you know it was a felony to carry a concealed deadly weapon?" Ossie asked me.

"I did not," I said. "I didn't know it was until Sheriff Larkin met me in the barn door at daylight two mornings ago and served a bench warrant on me. He explained to me what I'd been indicted for."

"Do you take a newspaper in your home?"

"No, sir."

"And you will swear under oath you didn't know it was a law."

"I object, Your Honor," prosecutor Lancaster said. "Ignorance is no excuse when you disobey the law."

"Objection overruled," Judge Bailey said. "I want the facts in this case."

"I'll swear under oath I didn't know it was a law. If I had known, I would have left my pistol at home."

"How far do you live from Greenwood?"

"Thirty-six miles."

"How do you get to your home?" Ossie asked.

"Go to Mennix's store and post office at the mouth of White Oak in a car," I said. "The rest of the way up White Oak on foot or mule's back."

"Where were you born?"

"In the house where I live now," I said. "I've lived there all my life."

"How many times have you been to Greenwood in your life?"

"Don't exactly know," I said, "but about six or seven times."

"That's all."

Ossie Purnell and prosecutor Lancaster agreed that they would not argue the case. They agreed to leave it to the jury to decide my fate. Then Judge Bailey straightened back in his chair and read the instructions to the jury while everybody listened. I looked at Pa and he was still nervous as a white-oak leaf in the November wind. I looked at Subrina and her face was red. She wasn't looking toward old Percy. Though she was a state's witness same as he, she was sitting with her back to him.

"By the defendant's own testimony," the judge read, "you will find the defendant guilty as charged in indictment and fix his penalty as described by law by confinement in the penitentiary not less than two and not more than five years."

I knew I was guilty. I had told the truth. And now I knew what my punishment would be. I didn't know how long it would be. I looked at Pa. He was sitting with his head down looking at the floor. I looked at Subrina and she was sitting with her hand over her eyes.

Sheriff Larkin followed the jurors to the jury room. Then he came back. There were many whispers in the courtroom. But there wasn't any laughter now. The old judge sat and twirled his gavel in his hand. This was the longest short wait I had ever known. The jurors were not away more than five minutes, but it seemed to me like five hours. Then they returned. And one man stepped up front of the other jurors.

"As foreman of the Greenwood County Jury," he said, "we find the defendant guilty, and we fix his sentence at the minimum of two years to serve in the penitentiary."

Subrina cried like her heart would break. And Pa tried to cry but he couldn't. I looked first at Subrina then at Pa. I knew that I would be leaving now. Then the judge hit the desk with his gavel.

"For twenty-three years I have been your circuit judge in Greenwood and Holcomb counties," he said. "I have tried to be honest and fair and in accordance with the law on all decisions. Due to this young man's honest testimony and due to a few other circumstances that I see, feel and know, by the testimonies I have heard in this trial, I am giving him another chance. I am," he spoke firmly, "suspending his sentence. I am giving him another chance."

I never heard such applause come from a group of people in my life. Everybody was pleased. The jurors tried to beat me to Judge Bailey, but I was there first and shook his hand and thanked him and told him I would never carry another concealed deadly weapon. Then the jurors swarmed around him and thanked him, and then they shook my hand and said they were glad.

Pa pushed through the crowd to see Judge Bailey and thanked him with tears in his eyes. Pa was so happy that he was crying now. And Subrina tried to push through the crowd around Judge Bailey and me but she could not push her way. So I went to her. I looked for old Percy, and I saw him getting out of the courtroom as fast as he could. "The judge saw through it," Subrina whispered in my ear, for the noise in the courtroom was enough to drown all words. "Percy's little trick didn't work. It wouldn't have worked even if you had gone to prison." That was all I wanted to hear now as the happy voices of hundreds of people were agreed for once, and the judge's gavel failed this time to restore order.

As the People Choose

I saw a streak of dust rise like white soup beans toward the sky. The streak of dust was comin' toward me. It followed the Tiger River road. "Who could that be," I thought, "comin' that fast down that crooked road?"

I wasn't long findin' out. I saw two black horses, slim as racer blacksnakes, lopin' in front of the storm clouds of dust. I heard them gettin' their breath long before they reached me. I saw a little driver sittin' on the front seat of the two-horse surrey. I heard a voice cry out from the back seat: "Pewee, stop the horses." Then I heard a big laugh like low thunder from the back seat of the surrey.

Pewee pulled up beside of me and stopped. The horses' sides were working in and out like a bee smoker. Their tongues were out where the bridle bits go in their mouths. Flakes of white foam dropped from their mouths to the dusty road. Their sleek black skins were covered with patches of foamy sweat that looked like patches of snow the sun didn't melt on the dark winter hills.

"Dog my hide if it ain't old Dusty Boone," says a big husky voice from the back seat. "Where you goin', Dusty?"

"I'm out to skeer me up a few votes," I says. "You ain't seen any up the river, have you?"

"You don't mean to tell me you're out tryin' to beat me," says Jason Mennix, "if that's what you're doin', you'd as well go home and smoke your pipe. I've done skeered all the votes out'n the brush. They're goin' to vote for old Jason. They call me 'Suits the People' Jason Mennix." Jason bent over as far as his stomach would let him. He laughed and laughed and hit his knees with his big fat hands. He puffed big clouds of smoke from his long black cigar that he held between two rows of gold-covered teeth.

"Jason, I'm out to beat you," I says. "I'll tell you what I'll do. If you beat me, I'll let you roll me off'n Town Hill in a barrel. If I beat you, you let me roll you off'n Town Hill in a barrel. We'll invite the people out to watch one of us roll."

"I hate to roll you off'n that high hill in a barrel," says Jason, "but I guess I'll haf to do it."

"You hear the bargin, Pewee," says Jason. "Now remember it to me when I get into office."

"Yes-sir, Mr. Mennix," says Pewee holdin' to the

leather checklines and lookin' straight ahead at the road. "I'll remind you of it, Mr. Mennix."

"I've got the Boone Mountain precinct in the bag," says Jason. "I've got all that Boone tribe. You know when I get them I've got a big vote. I've got most all the Reffitt vote over on Reffitt Mountain. I'd get 'em all but they think the Boones are fur me. They won't vote for a man the Boones vote fur."

"It looks like you have the election in the bag," I says, "when you get the Boones. They are my kinfolks."

"You ain't akin to the Boones are you, Dusty?" says Jason. "It's too fur back fur the blood to count."

"I'm akin to 'em today," I says. "You never got back on the ridges and in the heads of the hollows with that rig. You are too big to walk over the cow paths and shake their hands and ast them how their crops are gettin' along. I'm goin' back and visit among my people today."

Jason bends over and laughs and laughs. He throws his cigar stub down on the dusty road. He takes another cigar from his coat's front pocket. He takes a match from his big black hat band, strikes it on his blue serge pant leg and lights another cigar. He puffs out a big blue cloud of smoke. "Go amongst all of 'em, Dusty," he says. "Remember I was in the American-Spanish War. See my medals pinned here on my coat! People like medals pinned on a brave man!"

"My scars will mean more than your medals," I says, "if I take my shirt off and show my scars. There's not a place on my body big enough to lay a pin down but what there is a scar. I ain't been in just one war. I ain't never been out of a war, Jason. I've been fightin' ever since I could remember! Look what the Boone tribe has been through among these hills! Fightin' the Reffitts ever since I could remember!"

"Sorry you come out agin me," says Jason. "I'll haf to be movin' along. Pewee, tack up one of my pictures on that locust tree over there. It's a good place to catch the eyes of the people when they make this bend in the road."

"All right, Mr. Mennix," says Pewee. "Yes-sir, Mr. Mennix."

Jason reaches him the picture, the hammer and tacks.

"You ain't got a picture tacked up anyplace," says Jason. "What's the matter? Don't you know people want to see your mug along the turnpike? You might get a lot of wimmen votes. If it wasn't fur my picture, you would." Jason laughs and blows smoke to the hot July wind. Pewee tacks up Jason's picture on the locust tree. He walks back to the surrey, steps on the stirrup and unwraps the lines from the whip holster.

"You'd better take care of your team," I says. "If you don't quit runnin' 'em so hard this hot weather, you'll give 'em the thumps."

"Won't matter," says Jason. "I've got to canvass the county with this team. When I go back into office, I'll buy me a better team and a rubber-tired surrey. Here, Dusty, take one of my pictures as a partin' gift before I roll you over Town Hill in a barrel." Jason laughed and laughed—I heard him long after the surrey had disappeared behind the clouds of rollin' dust.

"I'll beat him," I says. "I'll beat 'Suits the People' Jason Mennix. He's had the office six years. I'll have it the next six years, durned my hide if I don't. He's never been back amongst the Boones. He's just rid along the turnpikes and stopped at the houses. I'll go back among them."

I looked at Jason's picture. A big man with three chins and a big cigar in his mouth. Medals pinned all over the front of his coat. A half-dozen cigars and a fountain pen in the front pocket by his coat lapel. A row of matches behind the band of his big black hat. Down below the picture it said in big black letters: "Vote for 'Suits the People' Jason Mennix. I am for good roads, churches, schools and the farms. I am a veteran of the American-Spanish War. If elected, I will faithfully fulfill the duties of my office, subject to your approval, August 8th."

"He's got a good speel here," I thought. "I'll haf to go over to Uncle Tobias Boone's. I'll haf to see Cousin Subrinea Boone. I know that she's one of the Boones that loves a Reffitt—too bad but she loves Roosevelt Reffitt."

I rode Nell up to the Spruce Pine Gap. I turned to my left. I followed the little path under the dark fir trees that led me to the home of Uncle Tobias Boone. I was in the land of the Boones—a land of log shacks, ter-backer patches and cornfields. I saw Uncle Tobias hoein' 'taters on the bluff back of the barn.

"Howdy, Uncle Tobias," I says. "Do you need an extra hand to help you with your 'taters?"

"Shore do, Dusty," says Uncle Tobias, looking up at the sun and stroking his long red beard with one hand, holding to his hoe handle with the other. "I need another Boone down here. Fetch that hoe from the fur end of the 'tater patch and come along."

I got the hoe and walked down the bluff. I started diggin' in a row right above Uncle Tobias. I hadn't been in the 'tater patch a minute until Uncle Tobias says: "How's the election goin', Dusty? Gettin' purty warm, ain't she?"

"It all depends on you, Uncle Tobias," I says. "If the Boones stand by, I'll have a chance."

"I planned to vote fer Jason Mennix," says Uncle Tobias, "if you didn't get around to see your kinfolks. We're akin, Dusty. The same blood flows in your veins flows in my veins. It's a way back yander where we branched off and I could explain it to you if I had time. I've got to get my 'taters out'n the weeds!"

"I'll help you with the 'taters," I says. "I know we are akin. The reason I ain't got to see you before now, I've had to canvass the whole county. I've come here last for I know how you stand. I know blood is thicker than water. Whatever you say, Uncle Tobias, the Boones will do. If you fight for me, all of the Boones will fight for me. I just want to show you the picture Jason gave me over on the Tiger River Turnpike a few minutes ago." I took the picture from under my coat.

"Look, Uncle Tobias," I says. "See the medals on his coat! Says he's a brave man in the American-Spanish War. I'll show you what a brave man really is. Wait until I strip my coat and shirt off." I took them right off in the 'tater patch.

"Look at the scars on me," I says. "How do you think I got these?"

"I don't know," says Uncle Tobias, "fightin', I 'spect, like the other Boones."

"You're right," I says. "I got them fightin' Reffitts."

"Lord he'p me," says Uncle Tobias, "I'll let the weeds take the 'taters, I'll ride a mule among the Boones day and night until the election. I'll see you get every Boone of the name. Put your shirt and coat back on and go to work."

"Jason told me he'd carry the Reffitt vote," I says. "Said he'd carry the Boones' vote too. I ask him how he expected to take my blood and kin vote. I thought if you all turned agin me, I wouldn't have a chance."

"We ain't turnin' agin you, son," says Uncle Tobias as he sticks his hoe in the ground. "I'm saddlin' my mule and ridin' and ridin' right now until I see every Boone of the name old enough to vote and a lot of 'em not old enough to vote. We'll show Jason who'll be the next prosecutin' attorney. He's had it six years anyhow. Dad-durned if I don't beat that Jason! Goin' over there and cavortin' around with that bunch of Reffitts! Then he comes over here and talks wild honey to me. His words were sweeter than wild honey. You've got to be on one side or t'other. I'm standin' by a Boone first, last and always when he thinks enough of his kinfolks to visit them."

"I'm trustin' you, Uncle Tobias," I says. "I'm dependin' on you. I'll see Cousin Subrinea. Then I'll be on my way."

"I'll go to the barn lot and get my mule and I'll be

on my way," says Uncle Tobias. He hopped over the 'tater ridges toward the barn lot like a sparrow bird. I put my shirt on and carried my coat under my arm. I took Jason's picture with me. I clim into the saddle, waves good-by to Uncle Tobias as he clim on his mule and rode away—up a rocky path under the dark spruce pines.

The mule galloped away and his red beard was bent back by the wind against his body. I rode toward the log house under the pines.

"Howdy, Subrinea," I says—"Looks like you're puttin' out a pretty good-sized washin' there."

"Howdy, Cousin Dusty," says Cousin Subrinea.

Subrinea stood straight behind the washtub she had placed on a stool under a spruce pine. I thought she was the purtiest woman I'd ever seen. She was tall and fair. Her hair was golden as the moonbeams when a harvest moon shines over a ripe wheat field. Her sleeves were rolled halfway up her lily-white arms and the soapsuds clung to her long slim fingers. He teeth were two rows of agate-white marbles.

"You're the purtiest woman that ever wore the name of Boone, Subrinea," I says, "if you don't mind my tellin' you."

"Any woman loves to hear that," says Subrinea. Her lips curved in smile and her teeth beamed in the sunlight that filtered through the dark fingers on the spruce pine.

"If you weren't my sixth cousin," I says, "and I wasn't a married man, I could love you, Subrinea. And you love Roosevelt Reffitt! You love him, don't you Subrinea?"

"Shhhhh," says Subrinea. She flings the suds from her hands. She walks over to the fence. "I don't want Grandma to hear you. You know how they feel about the Reffitts. I'll tell you, Dusty, this fight has gone on long enough. It's dangerous fur a Boone to go beyond that Gap where you turned away from the turnpike. That's where the Boone territory ends and the Reffitt territory begins. We've been fightin' 'em for seventy-five years. They've killed us and we've killed them. I guess we'll keep on killin' one another if something doesn't happen to bring us together. The last time the Reffitts and the Boones met, two Reffitts were killed, and two Boones. Uncle Charlie and Fonse were killed. Grandpa will never git over it."

"But you love a Reffitt more than words can tell," I says. "I know you love a man when you hide out to see him."

"Yes," says Subrinea. "There's no use of this killin' goin' on forever and forever. A Reffitt is afraid to poke his head over on Boone territory. He's even afraid to squirrel hunt over here. He can't own land on this side of the turnpike. He can't fish on our side of the river. There's been gun battles across the river when we fished down there."

"Subrinea," I says. "I don't blame a Reffitt for lovin' a girl purty as you are. I don't blame you for lovin' a Reffitt handsome as Roosevelt Reffitt. It you'll git the wimmen vote out among the Boone wimmen for me, and I am elected prosecutin' attorney, I'll get the Reffitts and the Boones together. You'll never regret all you've done for me. You won't haf to meet Roosevelt Reffitt where neither Boone nor Reffitt eyes must see you. I'll fix everything. These murder trials never come to court, did they, while Jason Mennix was prosecutin' attorney?"

"No, they didn't," says Subrinea—"but you know, Dusty, they can't come to court. They must never come to court. It would take thirty years to try all the trials betwixt our families. Our killings are even now on both sides. We just don't want any more. And I'll tell you, Cousin Dusty, it would take all of Kentucky's National Guards stationed at the courthouse the thirty years it took to try the cases. Long as there is a Reffitt left and a Boone left, they'll fight at the trial. If you can do anything about it, I'll wear my shoes out over these hills to get the wimmen out to vote for you."

"Get 'em out, Subrinea," I says, "but don't let Uncle Tobias know what I am doin'. You love Roosevelt Reffitt and I'll see that you get him. I'll see that this killin' stops."

"It's an awful hard promise for you to keep, Cousin Dusty," says Subrinea, "but I'm goin' to work for you soon as I finish my washin'! I'll go from house to house."

"I'll be ridin' on, Subrinea," I says. "Just a few more days, you know, and I've got a lot of work to do. Good-by, Cousin Subrinea."

"Good-by, Cousin Dusty," she says. "You can depend on my gettin' the wimmen to the polls."

I reined Nell away from the palin' fence. I left the purtiest girl I'd ever seen standin' like an angel under the tall spruce pine with her sleeves rolled up, her golden hair frizzled by the wind. I rode out the path and down over the big mountain to the Spruce Pine Gap. "How can I win the Reffitt vote?" I thought, as Nell stepped over the big rocks layin' along the mountain path. I rocked from one side of my saddle to the other.

"The Reffitts are great moonshiners," I thought. "Last year was a dry season. The corn crop was light on the mountain slopes. The Reffitts need corn to feed their moonshine stills. I'll see Uncle Roosevelt Reffitt, the head of the Reffitt family. I'll send him a carload of cracked corn to feed his moonshine stills if he'll line up the votes just right."

I reined Nell to my right after I'd gone one mile from Spruce Pine Gap down the turnpike. I went up a rough mountain path under tough-butted white oaks, tall chestnut oaks and black oaks. "Funny," I thought—"even the timber changes when a body rides across that valley. Over here are the Reffitts under the oaks—over there are the Boones under the Spruce pines. They are about as much alike as their timber is alike." And then I thought: "What if Uncle Tobias ever finds out I run into a barb-wire fence huntin' one night and got my scars where barb-wire cut me?" Another thought come to me as I rode along up the narrow path—over the big rocks, under the shade of the tall oaks.

I reached the top of the mountain, rode along and watched the squirrels jumpin' from oak to oak over my head. Soon I saw the log shack under the oaks where Roosevelt Reffitt lived. I rode down before the house. I hollered, "Hello! Anybody home!"

"Yes, young man," says Roosevelt Reffitt. He walked

in a dogtrot from the house with a Bible in his hand. "What might your name be and what do you want?" He stroked his long, white beard with his hand.

"I want a drink of cold water," I says. "I've been ridin' hard and I'm dry as a bone!"

"Get down off'n that nag," he says, "and go over to the well under that oak yander and hep yourself. There's a well bucket there and gourd hangin' on the well gum. What might your name be?"

"Dusty Boone," I says.

"Boone," he says—"you ain't welcome to drink of water here. You're on the wrong mountain! The quicker you can get off, the better it will be fer you, young man."

"I'm not akin to the Boones on yan side of the mountain," I says. "I'm another Boone. I'm runnin' for prosecutin' attorney. I met Jason Mennix down yander on the turnpike and he told me he'd get every Boone vote of the name. He's got all the Boones lined up for him. If he gets the Boones, I ought to get the Reffitts. Here's a picture, Uncle Roosevelt, I want you to see, then I want to show you something."

I got off the mule. I walked over to the dogtrot. Uncle Roosevelt took the picture of Jason Mennix's. "Here's the fellar," I says, "that told me he had the election in the bag. He said he had all the Boone vote. He's not a common man like I am. Look at the big cigars in his coat pocket! Look at the medals pinned on his coat! Read the words where he calls hisself 'Suits the People' Jason Mennix."

"Uh-huh," says Uncle Roosevelt Reffitt—"a betrayer. He may suit the Boones but he don't suit us Reffitts. Anybody that suits them can't suit us. There's as many Reffitts, young man, as there are Boones. If the vote ain't here, we'll get it anyhow. I'll call the Reffitts together and let them know what's goin' on. I'll get the Gullets, Rayburns and Ratcliffs too. They've married into the Reffitts in so many places. We'll show the Boones."

"You see them medals, Uncle Roosevelt," I says— "Jason said he got them for bravery in the American-Spanish War. Let me show you something. I ain't never been out'n a war since I was a little shaver. Wait until I haul off my coat and shirt. I'll show you." I pulled my shirt and coat off. "See these scars!"

"Uh-huh," says Uncle Roosevelt Reffitt, strokin' his long white beard with one hand and holdin' the Bible with the other. He walks up close and looks at the long white scars across my body. "How did you get 'em, young man?"

"Fightin' Boones," I says. "They knifed me there but I used a club. A club was all that saved me."

"Young man, put up your nag in my barn," he says, "and stay the night with us. You'll find a little feed out there. You air welcome to all the feed we got."

"Had a bad corn crop last year?"

"Yes," says Uncle Roosevelt. "Everything purt nigh burnt up on this mountain last year. This year has been a golly-whopper on poor people."

I took Nell to the barn, let her drink from the trough, put oats in her manger and corn in her box. I took the saddle off and hung it up by a stirrup to a spike nail on the barn post. I walked back toward the house.

"I ain't got but one boy at home," says Uncle Roosevelt. "He bears my name. He's my baby boy and he tries to marry a Boone gal. He's plum wild about her. I ain't had a youngin to ever look at a Boone but him. He's wild about old Tobias Boone's granddaughter. I think her name's Subrinea."

"Too bad," I says. "Maybe I can help you a little. Let me talk to him tonight."

"It's a funny thing," he says, "out'n seventeen youngins my last one—and the one that bears his Pap's name— wants to marry a Boone. Went hog-wild about her at a pie supper. That was the night he lost two brothers. Her uncles kilt 'em. I can't understand it fer the life o' me. Th' only good Boones I know air dead Boones—sleepin' on that mountain over yander under the spruce pines. Roosevelt's comin' now. He's comin' dog-tired from th' terbacker patch."

"Roosevelt," says Uncle Roosevelt Reffitt, "this is a Boone—the first one that will ever sleep in this house. I want you to meet 'im. He ain't no kin to the Boones on yan side of the mountain."

"Glad to meet you," he says reachin' me his hard brown hand. His eagle eyes looked straight at me. His black wavy hair was mangled by the wind on the mountain. "It's funny to see a Boone in this house. I guess you're the first one in seventy-five years."

"Let me have that Jason Mennix's picture again," says Uncle Roosevelt. I handed him the picture. He held it before him. "A Reffitt betrayer," he says. He spit a bright sluice of amber in one eye. He waddled his cud behind his jaw. He spit a bright sluice of amber into the other eye. He tore the picture in two, threw the pieces on the dogtrot floor and stomped them. "Reffitt betrayer—that's old 'Suits the People' Jason Mennix. That pot-bellied hellion! He'll never get a Reffitt vote if I can hep it. I'll show 'im who the people's choice is. You fellars dabble in the pan and git ready to eat. It's on the table now."

I never set down to better grub.

"My spouse Manda, Dusty Boone," says Uncle Roosevelt Reffitt. "Mother of seventeen and gettin' younger every day."

"I'm glad to know you," I says.

"Glad to know you," she says, "but I don't like your name."

"Forget about the Boones, Ma," says young Roosevelt.

"You would say that," she says. "Young man, don't ever bring one in under the Reffitt roof." Her black eyes danced when she said these words.

"I can see her," says young Roosevelt Reffitt. "I can see her golden hair and her blue eyes. I can remember how tall she was. I can remember the dress she wore. I couldn't believe she was a woman. She looked like an angel to me. I wanted to see her again—and again."

"If I thought you meant that, young man," says Uncle Roosevelt, "I'd take a five-year-old club to you. You ain't too big fer me to whip. You might be six feet and four inches tall—but I can limb you yet. Git to eatin' the grub before you—"

"Moonshine, milk 'r water to drink, Mr. Boone?" says Mrs. Reffitt.

"Moonshine, if you please, ma'am," I says. "I'm a man

of mountain ways and I can't git high-kaflutin' and go back on what I was raised on, like Jason Mennix. He used sich big words today I couldn't understand what he was talkin' about."

Then I reached for my glass. It looked clear as water but there were beads in it clear as crystals. I put it to my lips. I couldn't take it away until I drained it dry. "Lord, this is the best I have ever tasted," I says. "Another glass, ma'am, if you please."

"Go a little light, son," says Uncle Roosevelt—"it will lift your heels on an empty stummick. I've got a little heady in my time but never once has it lifted my heels. I never let it defile the temple of clay!"

I don't know how much grub I put away. It was before me. I know I helped myself. I remember leavin' the table. I remember takin' Uncle Roosevelt Reffitt by the arm. I remember sayin', "We are brothers, ain't we, Uncle Roosevelt?"

"Yes, we are brothers," he says. "We Reffitts will stand by you. We will give you every vote there is in our family and then some."

"And you need corn," I says—"you need cracked corn. You need what we call 'chop.' You need a carload of it and I will send it to the foot of the mountain. I will put it in that rock cliff for you. You will have chop to make good corn licker. You have had a bad season and you'll have corn for your stills. It is because of that good drink I had for my supper."

"And young man, you need not fear," he says. "You will git your votes. You must go upstairs to bed now. You don't mind sleepin' with young Roosevelt, do you?"

"Of course not," I says—"I want to talk to him. I want to have a talk with him. I'll tell him about the Boones. I'll tell him about the girl he thinks he loves. The boy is tired out but I'll wake him and I'll tell him."

Uncle Roosevelt took me to the door. He lit the lamp and showed me to the bed. He left the lamp on the dresser—I undressed, blew out the lamp and crawled in beside of young Roosevelt Reffitt. The moonlight fell across the bed.

"Young Roosevelt, wake up," I says—"don't be a sleepy head. I've got a message for you—"

"Huh," he says.

"Wake up," I says. "I've got a message of love from Subrinea for you."

"Oh, what is it?" he asks—"When did you see her?"

"Today."

"What did she say?"

"That she loved you. Said all this trouble betwixt your families was all foolishness. Said she loved you and always would. That is why I am here. If you'll git all the young vote out and help put me over—I'll help you get her. Maybe we can stop all this fightin' between your people and her people. Her grandpa—Uncle Tobias—hates your pap as much as your pap hates him."

"That's a shame. We ought to let bygones be bygones. We ought to lay our rifles down and put our knives away. Jist because they live under the spruce pines on yan mountain and we live under the oaks on this mountain— ain't no sign we should go on and hate each other eternally."

"That's the way I feel. Honest, I think Subrinea is the

143

purtiest woman I ever saw. She was washin' clothes under a spruce pine. She looked like an angel to me. I could love her."

"Don't talk like that. If I knowed you loved her, you'd never get out'n this bed. I'd slit your throat from ear to ear."

"I'm her cousin. I couldn't marry her. Don't tell your pa I'm her cousin. She is workin' in the election for me. She said for you to. She sent me to you. I am a married man. I don't want to leave my wife nohow. I want to be your next prosecutin' attorney. If I am elected, I'll surprise you. I'll get all of you people back together, that is if you'll help me."

"I'll work my toenails off for you."

"Thank you, young Roosevelt Reffitt."

We went to sleep. I heard young Roosevelt say "Subrinea" throughout the night. He talked in his sleep. "I love you," he said. He flung his arms out and tried to grab me. He would hug his pillow. I could see him in the moonlight that fell across my bed.

"This election is mine," I thought. "I'll run neck and neck all over the county with Jason. I'll carry the Reffitts and the Boones—something no man has done for seventy-five years. I'll beat Jason two to one when all the votes are counted."

We got up at five o'clock. Breakfast was waitin' for us. I et my breakfast with young Roosevelt. He had a big grin on his face. He would look at me and he would eat. When breakfast was over Uncle Roosevelt Reffitt stroked his long white beard and says: "I've fed your horse. I don't want you to run off but I'm takin' young Roosevelt and we're goin' on mules amongst all our people. You won't need to go with us. You go amongst others. We'll take care of this mountain. We'll soon be startin'."

"I'm ready, Pap," says young Roosevelt. "I want to help Dusty. He's a good man. I listened to him last night. He told me a lot I didn't know."

"I thought he could," says Uncle Roosevelt—"I thought he could give you a little light on the boogers on t'other side of the mountain."

"He give me a lot," says young Roosevelt. "I'm a new man this mornin'. I feel like one of the flock that has strayed away and just come home."

I thanked Manda Reffitt for the good grub. I ask her for a vial of drink to take along. She fixed it for me. I put it in my pocket, went to the barn and saddled Nell. I climbed in the saddle and waved good-by. I saw Uncle Roosevelt and young Roosevelt ridin' their mules out the ridge road—both waved good-by to me. "No need for me to do anymore but send the carload of chop to Roosevelt Reffitt," I thought—"just lay low and wait a few days." I rode over the mountain and down the river turnpike to town.

On August 4th the carload of chop was set off on the switch. I started four trucks haulin' it to the foot of Reffitt Mountain. "Ast me no questions, fellars," I says, "you just deliver the chop and stack it under the rock cliff on the right-hand side of the road that goes over the mountain. You'll have a little totin' to do. Just get the chop safe from the rain."

August 8th, I saddled Nell and rode to Spruce Pine Gap. I rode up a little drain where the bright water dashed over the rocks. I hitched Nell to a saplin' where people couldn't see her when they passed the road. I had my precinct workers all lined up. I was ready for the election—the biggest primary election ever held in these parts. I wanted to watch the wagons loaded with voters goin' down the turnpike. I wanted to watch them comin' off'n the mountain.

I laid in the shade and smoked my pipe. I saw wagons loaded with Reffitts goin' down the road. I saw wagons loaded with Boones goin' down the road. I never heard the people speak to each other or as much as wave a hand. They looked at each other hard. They were goin' to the polls in great multitudes. Sometimes I saw boys among the Reffitts that didn't look sixteen years old. They were all goin' to vote. It was fun to lay in the shade and think about old Jason.

I wondered where he was goin' and if he was smokin' his big black cigars. I wondered if young Roosevelt saw Subrinea at the polls. I wondered if he thought she was as purty as I thought she was. I wondered what Old Roosevelt Reffitt would do when he saw Jason. I wondered if Uncle Tobias Boone and Uncle Roosevelt Reffitt got into a fight on the election grounds if they would pull each other's beards. I just laid in the shade and had a lot of wild thoughts.

At five o'clock I clim into the saddle. Nell was a-prancin' and rearin' to go. I let her have full rein toward town. By the time I got there the votes would all be in from the precincts and we'd start countin' them.

The Reffitts and the Boones would be there. They'd be there to see if their man winned. I was their man. Nell took me home in a hurry. There weren't any dead this time to count. The vote count started.

It was the primary in our party and we counted the vote fast. Just a gun pulled now and then but Sheriff Holliday took the guns. We were runnin' neck to neck. Jason stood over in the corner. He laughed and puffed a big cigar.

"Just wait until the big vote come in," he says. Then he laughed a big horse laugh and looked at me. I smoked my pipe and waited. I saw Subrinea among the Boones. The Boones were on one side of the courthouse and the Reffitts on the other. I saw young Roosevelt Reffitt among the Reffitts. He looked at Subrinea and she looked at him.

She couldn't go to him and he couldn't go to her.

"Ready for Boone Mountain Precinct," says the Sheriff. "Count 'em boys. Let's git through with this election sometime tonight."

"It's one way," says the tally men. "Ain't but one man gettin' any votes here."

Jason puffed his cigar and laughed and laughed. He handed out boxes of cigars to the men. He thought the vote was goin' his way. He thought he had it in the bag. I saw Subrinea laugh like an angel out among the crowd of Boones.

"Ready for the Reffitt Mountain Precinct," says Sheriff Holliday—"the last precinct. This one will decide who your prosecutin' attorney will be."

The men started to tally the precinct when the sheriff

147

brought the box out and unlocked it. The tally men counted the vote. They looked at the Boones on one side of the courthouse and the Reffitts on the other side. Their eyes got big as they counted the vote. There weren't much talkin' amongst the people. They squirmed and twisted in their seats and waited. Jason smoked his big cigars and laughed. His gold teeth shined brighter than gold dollars under the big lamp in the courthouse.

"The counts is over," says Sheriff Holliday. "Gentlemen, Dusty Boone is your next prosecutin' attorney. He winned by a big vote—Jason Mennix, 1,755 votes. Dusty Boone, 3,456 votes."

A big cheer went up from the Boones. A big cheer went up from the Reffitts. They looked at each other. Uncle Roosevelt Reffitt stroked his long white beard. Uncle Tobias Boone stroked his long red beard. Subrinea Boone walked among the Boones to the middle aisle in the courthouse. Young Roosevelt Reffitt walked amid the Reffitts to the middle aisle and stood beside of Subrinea. The Boones started talkin' among themselves—the Reffitts started talkin' among themselves.

"Just a minute, gentlemen and ladies," I says. "I've got something I want you to witness. I made an agreement with Jason Mennix if he winned this race, he could roll me from the top of Town Hill in a barrel. If I winned this race, I got to roll him off'n Town Hill in a barrel. Uncle Tobias Boone and Uncle Roosevelt Reffitt will roll Jason Mennix in a few minutes from the top of Town Hill in the barrel." The crowd roared. Uncle Tobias looked at Uncle Roosevelt Reffitt. Uncle Roosevelt Reffitt looked at Uncle Tobias.

"Gentlemen and ladies," I says, "I have something else for you to witness. I hope you will excuse me for it but this is the greatest minute of my life. For nearly one century the Boones and the Reffitts have shot at each other across the river and the mountain valley. Tonight, these people have ceased to fight. I, as prosecutin' attorney, dismiss all old indictments. They stop with the same number dead on both sides. There has been a draw. Tonight, they shake hands and renew friendship. The young couple you see standin' in the courthouse aisle will be the first union of the Reffitts and the Boones. I must be on my way with them."

Huckleberry's Diehards

Lawhun Houndshell was a candidate for high sheriff of our Big Party in Greenwood County. Law Houndshell, as all his friends called him, really looked like a high sheriff. And he was "high," too. He was six feet six, straight as a ramrod, had black hair, which he parted on the side, and a black handlebar mustache. He had black, beady, hawk eyes buried deep in narrow slits. He had thin, tight lips that could spread in laughter, enough to show two pearly rows of teeth which were as sound as silver dollars. He didn't have a tooth amiss. He had a hatchet face, long thin sharp nose and for a man of his height, he had a bull neck that held his head onto a strong two-hundred-forty-pound body and a pair of broad shoulders.

At thirty-six Law was as attractive to women as he was attracted by them. Although married to a pretty wife, Myrtle Phelps Houndshell, when a good looking woman passed our Law on the street in Blakesburg he would look her over face to face, then turn to look her over when she walked by him. Many of Law's followers wondered if Law's love of women would hurt him in the primary race in our Big Party. All of us know how natural it was for man to love woman and woman to love man, married, divorced or single. We turned this thing around. We thought our Law would be a great vote getter among the women as attractive as he was to them. We thought this helped to make him a strong candidate.

Our Law had other attractive and noticeable features which we thought would endear him to the voters. He was really a man's man all right and one, we knew, the women loved. And when he came in from working at the Railway Shops he bathed and dressed in a nice suit, polished boots—sometimes with spurs as he had a half dozen pairs. He wore a Kentucky Colonel necktie and a big broad-rimmed hat—black, brown or gray. He had several different colored hats. Then, when his mother's name, Lawhun, was pared down to Law we thought this helped him in his primary. I could see him in my imagination with a broad leather belt around his waist and a strap over his shoulder, carrying his pearl-handled pistol in a leather holster—with his short snub-nosed "autermatic" in his inside coat pocket. These were just a few of the pistols Law had. He loved pistols. He had more than a dozen. He possessed single-barreled, one-shot rifles, rifles with magazines that fired nine times. He had single-barrel, double-barrel and automatic shotguns. He was a gun collector and a lover of guns. And he was the top marksman at the rifle and pistol shoot-outs. He nearly always won the prize turkey. This helped him, we thought, among the voters.

"Yes, I'm good with guns when and if I'd have to use them," he told the voters when he electioneered in our Big Party. "But after I beat Old Huckleberry Wilson in this primary and after I go on to beat Bill "Dodo Bird" Royster who will win his primary in the Little Party two to one—when I'm the real high sheriff of Greenwood County I'll carry my favorite pearl-handle .45 to look more like a sheriff—but I won't have to use it. Not as long as I've got this pair of fists. I don't need a gun."

And this was true about our strong candidate Law Houndshell! The boys over in Toniron, Ohio, where he made the rounds of the bars on Saturday nights, before he got the idea of running for high sheriff of Greenwood County, might remember what a street fighter he was. Only one thing I ever heard people say against Law was his education. Law just about finished the fourth grade. Law could read letters and a newspaper. And he could write a messy letter which a good reader might read. But education couldn't help a Greenwood County high sheriff where his business was to preserve law and order.

I, Sim Creameans, who am telling you this story, finished high school at the bottom of a class of forty-two graduates. None of the other four deputies running with Law went beyond the eighth grade at the one-room county schools. So I had more education than any of our team and I'd get more pay than any deputy. And, I'd carry my pistol as a token but I'd always be away from the shootings and the shoot-outs for I'd be in the Law's office taking care of the books. I never was a brave man. I didn't want to shoot at anybody or be shot at.

In meetings we had at Law's home, we planned our primary strategy. The other deputies were Lin Kidwell, who was fast with a gun, Jim Buckaroo Stephens, a noted fistfighter, Tom Bill James, a prosperous farmer—well-liked by everybody—and Dysard Dials, who was nearly a Sunday School man. With Dysard's being on our team we thought we'd pick up the religious votes. Law thought it best to have a deputy who could pray in public. Law and all his deputies lived in different areas of Greenwood County. This gave balance to our team.

At our first meeting in Law's home we planned how to beat George Huckleberry Wilson—in our Big Party primary. We knew George was a very popular man who had served four years as county judge, then four years as high sheriff and four years again as county judge. Now he was off and running again for high sheriff. A county judge could succeed himself in office but the high sheriff could not. This showed Old Huckleberry liked to be called sheriff more than judge. Some people called him judge. Others called him sheriff. He confused the people.

"I say, we start tales over Greenwood County that Old Huckleberry is a bottle boy," Law suggested to us. "Due to his worries with so many years in public office—so much worry—caused by trials and tribulations that the good contents from the bottle drowned his cares and made him a happy man again."

"I won't go for that or have any part of defaming Huckleberry's character," Dysard Dials said. "He's a dry like I am. He never touches the stuff. That's a tale I won't help start."

"But we've got to get some tales started," Tom Bill James said. "I hear talk that Huckleberry and his four deputies are going to beat us in this primary. Remember, he made a good judge twice and he was a good high sheriff. We're a-runnin' against his good record!"

"Yeah, Old Huckleberry and his deputies look at Law and his deputies as dirt under their feet," Jim Buckaroo Stephens said. "I know, I've heard the talk and the whispers. He feels sure he's got this primary election in the bag. I heard he said: 'We've got the pig in the poke. We don't want to hurt Law and his deputies too much for we'll need part of them, not all, to beat Bill "Dodo Bird" Royster in the final!' Yes, boys that's the kind of talk he's having."

"But we've got to get some little nice thing started about him—something that will take hold among the voters and spread like a forest fire," Dysard Dials said.

"Say something nice?" Law said, his face coloring. "Say, whose side are you on!"

"I have it," Tom Bill James said. "Old Huckleberry is a fine man but at sixty-five he's too old to be high sheriff of Greenwood County. It's a younger man's job—a man Law's age!"

Law's whole face lit up in a smile.

"Why didn't I think of that?" Law said. "That's just wonderful."

Law and all of his deputies, including Dysard Dials, agreed to this. We agreed we'd be telling the truth about Old George Huckleberry Wilson. And we agreed when we spread this word Huckleberry Wilson is a good man but at sixty-five he's too old to be Greenwood County's high sheriff. After this meeting at Law's home we went over Greenwood County to its far corners and we whispered the word.

I know now if we hadn't spread the word, we would have lost this May primary. Huckleberry was sure he had "the pig in the poke" and he did have until what we whispered caught on and spread among our voters like fire whipped by strong winds spreads over a dry autumn forest. We won the primary, which surprised Huckleberry and his deputies.

"Spreading them lies on me that I was too old was the most dangerous thing you could do to me," Huckleberry told Dysard Dials. "You can tell Law and the rest of your deputies I'm sound in body and mind—and I'm as physically fit as I was at forty. I think Lawhun Houndshell is a dangerous man. I think he's trigger happy."

When Law heard this he smiled. His beady hawk eyes beamed.

"It worked all right," Law said.

Dodo Bird Royster, as predicted, won his primary by doubling the vote of his opponent John Stone.

"Well, I'll be the next high sheriff of Greenwood County," Law said. "All we have to do is win over about half of Huckleberry's precinct chairmen. You know the Little Party's not got much strength. It's been a long time since they've had a high sheriff in Greenwood County— twenty years I believe."

When Law went to see Tom Skaggs, chairman of the Allcorn Precinct, to make peace, Tom said: "Law, I'm the same age as George. George made a good high sheriff once and he'd have done it again if it hadn't been for your fellows' lies. Get out of my yard, you liar! You rat!"

"No one calls Greenwood County's next high sheriff a liar and a rat even if I am in your yard," Law shouted looking fiercely at him with his black, beady, hawk eyes. "I won't shoot you. But I'll use my pistol on you in a different way."

Law pulled his pearl-handled .45 from a holster under his coat. And he gave Tom Skaggs a good pistol whipping in his own yard. Then Law went to his car and drove away.

"We don't need Old Tom Skaggs and his little influence," Law told me.

Tom Skaggs went to Blakesburg and had the county judge who was George Huckleberry Wilson—his term wouldn't expire until the end of this election year—to put Law under a "peace bond."

"Gladly will I do it," Huckleberry told him. "He's a dangerous man."

Now this incident got into the *Greenwood County News*.

"That hurts us, boys," Tom Bill James said at Law's home at another strategy meeting.

"Yes, while I'm working with the church people this

should happen," Dysard Dials said. "Still, I don't think Bill Royster of the Little Party will have a chance. We have the Little Party out-registered two to one."

"Yes, but voters might cross party lines in this election," Tom Bill James said. "You know how a little tale can change voters. Look what our story about Huckleberry did to him. It changed the tide of the primary election to us!"

"But all I have to do is stir among the women to get their votes," Law said. "You'll be surprised how many women in the Little Party are going to vote for me."

"Well, I know you're a lady's man," Dysard Dials sighed.

"And I'll tell you something else I'm going to do in this county where voters have staggered up to the polls to vote dry," Law said. "I've already got the permission from the American Legion in the west end and the American Legion in the east end to hold political meetings. And, my future deputies of the Greenwood County's high sheriff's office, I'm going to set up the drinks to the boys. If they like their first drinks, I'll set 'em up again and again."

"Where'll you get your money to do all this?" Jim Buckaroo Stephens asked. "Sounds great to me."

"But not to me," Dysard said. "I'm against it. How'll we arrest drunks later you've treated to drinks three times?"

"I'll answer two questions in one," Law said. "When they get drunk and misbehave, we'll arrest them. The law will be in my hands. And I've got the money to buy the drinks. Why do you think old Law has saved up a tidy five thousand dollars? Well, my wife Myrtle never always got the dress she wanted and a new Easter hat. But I've had this race in mind a long time. I'll spend all the five thousand and sell my two small farms if necessary to be Greenwood County high sheriff."

I was right there and I saw it with my own eyes at both American Legions. Voters came in from all over to Law's political meetings. Law would stand back a tall, handsome man, in his broad-rimmed hat. "Fill 'em up again for the boys. This is on the new high sheriff of Greenwood County."

Law looked like a real sheriff standing up there giving orders.

And the men crowded up to the bar Law had prepared for them in the Legion. And behind each bartender, six in each Legion, thirsty men were in long lines going up

"If this place would be raided, we'd lose the election," I thought. "If Huckleberry had known, he might have tipped the federals off."

But Law was as good as his word. He was successful at both Legions. And I was sure we'd get these hundreds of votes and they'd work on their friends to vote for Law. I was sure Law's strategy would work.

Law went to the Legions in June.

In July he went to the Walnut Hills Precinct to put Jeff Thompson in line. Jeff was a Big Party precinct chairman, who had supported Huckleberry in his unsuccessful primary. Jeff had been talking, so we heard, that Law was a dangerous man to be elected high sheriff of our county. We'd heard that he'd said he might jump over the trace chains and vote for Dodo Bird Royster of the Little Party. We knew this was no way for a Big Party precinct chairman to talk.

I'm sure Law wouldn't have done it if Old Jeff hadn't called Law a real bad name. But Law gave him a real pistol-whipping with his favorite pearl-handled .45. As Law told at a meeting in his home Old Jeff had to be disciplined—that he was a dangerous Big Party man. Law said he couldn't be trusted.

In August, Law pistol-whipped another Big Party chairman of the Honeydell Precinct. He was another Huckleberry diehard. But, I'll tell you by September a lot of talk was going over Greenwood County. And it wasn't favorable for Law and his deputies.

There was a story going on Law that he had a nice wife, Myrtle Phelps Houndshell, at home—and that he had children in three other parts of Greenwood County and soon would have another one—maybe, before the election. Dysard Dials said this would hurt Law among the women voters. Law denied all the charges. Jim Buckaroo Stephens said Law made a mistake denying the charges for women loved a woman's man.

But the charges about Law's having four children in his family and would soon have four by four other women didn't hurt us as much as "Law Houndshell is a trigger happy man. If he's elected high sheriff of Greenwood County and is the big man with law and order he won't pistol-whip then but he'll shoot 'em dead." This was going everywhere like a forest fire, whipped by strong winds in a dry October forest.

Now, we went on the road from house to house, trying to get these tales stopped. I found them among our Big

Party voters. And I'm sure the Little Party voters—men and women—believed them for they wanted to believe them. But the big danger was among our own Big Party voters.

At our last meeting at Law's home, Law raised up out of his big rocker and said: "I've spent my five thousand. I've sold my two farms, one for six thousand and one for seven—thirteen more thousand will go into this election. If we can't persuade them, we can buy them! I'm going to be Greenwood's high sheriff and you're going to be my deputies. And when we get the power there are a few scores I'll be able to settle my way. And it will be legal."

"Two things you said there, I hope don't leave this room," Dysard Dials said. "If you couldn't persuade the voters, you could buy them. You never even know how they'll vote when they go into the booth—even voters you've bought. And what you said about settling a few scores—your way and they'd be legal."

"Dysard, are you a Huckleberry Diehard or are you working with us?" Law asked him.

"I'm working for our team," Dysard said. "But let what you've said get out among the voters and we'll have more tales going! We can't get the tales stopped now after you've pistol-whipped three precinct chairmen of our party. It's going, as you know, you're a dangerous, trigger-happy man. Don't you know the people will be afraid of you for their sheriff?"

"All right, we've got the Little Party out-registered two to one and I've thirteen thousand dollars more to use on election eve and election day," Law said. "It would take a miracle to beat us!"

"But miracles do happen, Law," Dysard spoke softly. "I know there's not much crossing party lines here but one could happen in this election. There's a lot of talk. It might just be loose talk but you know when there's smoke there's bound to be some fire."

"Damn the smoke and fire, tales and loose talk," Law said.

Law had a wild look in his beady black hawk eyes. And the slits that enclosed them narrowed more than I'd ever seen them.

This was our last meeting. One week more and we'd know who the Greenwood County high sheriff and his deputies would be.

On the day before the election our party faithfuls came to get their allotment of one dollar bills and half pints and whole pints of the cheapest whiskey we could buy. As Law said, among thirsty voters, they wouldn't know the difference on election day whether the whiskey was good or bad. Election days in Greenwood County are great days—better than holidays.

At the crack of dawn on election day, we were so organized we had every man at his right place and at the same time. I guess this was the hottest election we ever had in Greenwood County. Fistfights broke out at voting places in all thirty-two precincts. There wasn't a precinct that didn't have from one to a dozen fights. Men were hauled in ambulances to doctors' offices and hospitals— men beaten and knifed—we had six men shot in their legs. And all of this fighting was among Big Party voters. The Huckleberry Diehards fighting us.

I got it from a reliable source, a first cousin of mine,

Don Sims, who was born into the Little Party and he told me that Frank Meenach, Greenwood County's Little Party chairman had started the tales on Law Houndshell. He said Frank had gone to "the right people" all over the county and planted the stories about Law's three children out of wedlock and a fourth one ready to be born any minute. He said Frank had got the "trigger-happy" story going. And he told me that Frank was a cousin to our deputy Dysard Dials.

When the votes were taken from the thirty-two precincts to be counted at the close of this election day, many of our faithful followers followed their precinct ballot boxes to the Greenwood County courthouse. Many of their faces were battered and shirts bloody in front. It was the biggest turnout of voters we'd ever had in a county election. The courthouse was full of people. The courthouse yard was full of people. And all the streets around the courthouse square were jam-packed with people.

Our Big Party wanted to count first the precincts where Law had pistol-whipped our chairmen. The Little Party officials agreed to this.

"Just count any precinct you want to count first," Frank Meenach said. "It won't matter. I predict this time we have the pig in the poke. Not only will our Dodo Bird Royster be Greenwood County high sheriff but we'll carry all the county offices on his strength."

"A lot of hot wind," Law said. "You want to bet, Frank?"

"No, you've not got any money," Frank said. "You've spent it all on this election!"

Law was mad. I was afraid Law might try to pistol-whip the Little Party's Frank Meenach. If he'd heard all my Cousin Don Sims had told me, I know he would have tried to have pistol-whipped Frank, which would have set off a brawl where several would have been killed. Men go around armed in our county election and the Little Party has got some tough boys. They'll shoot first and talk later.

Then the results of the Allcorn Precinct, which had always gone two to one Big Party, were announced over the loud speakers in the courthouse and the courthouse yard: "Bill Royster 206 votes: Lawhun Houndshell 99 votes."

Then, the other candidates' results followed. Little Party candidates carried this precinct and I thought I knew the way the wind was blowing—an evil wind and it was blowing against us. I looked over and saw Frank Meenach whose face was all smiles and I'm sure he wanted to say: "I told you so!"

I turned around and looked back in the crowded courthouse corridor and there stood Old Huckleberry Wilson and his face was beaming with happiness. I felt like going through the crowd and punching him. But he was an old man and I was young enough to be his son. "If I hit him, I'll be destroying party harmony," I thought.

Walnut Hills Precinct was counted second. Old Jeff Thompson, Law had pistol-whipped, showed his power. The vote was even worse.

"Bill Royster 175 votes: Lawhun Houndshell 86 votes."

And the vote for Little Party candidates wasn't as high for them as for their sheriff—but all down the line they carried Walnut Hills Precinct. There were some glum faces among our Big Party faithfuls around me.

When the Honeydell Precinct was counted we lost it three to one. It usually went four to one Big Party. Believe me, I was sick. I thought I'd wait for the results from a precinct where Law hadn't pistol-whipped our chairman. I wanted to see the effects of the stories that had circulated over Greenwood County.

The precinct selected was Rosten No. 1. It was in the eastern part of Greenwood County—and four to one Big Party. This precinct went two to one for Dodo Bird Royster. And Little Party candidates carried it. Since Dodo Bird Royster was stronger in western Greenwood County because he lived there, I knew we were goners. I couldn't take anymore. I eased down the corridor, down the courthouse steps and out into the courthouse yard where the wind was better to breathe. I looked up at the bright stars in a blue sky. I had to forget this day. I knew the stories about Law had done the work. Big tales and loose talk, three pistol-whipped precinct chairmen and Old Huckleberry Wilson and Frank Meenach had defeated us.

I went to my car and drove home. I listened to the late news on Channel Three and I got the results. Frank Meenach was right. Dodo Bird Royster was elected by a fifteen-hundred-vote margin, biggest majority ever recorded up to this time by a Little Party candidate and he carried a full slate of Little Party candidates with him with majorities ranging from seven hundred down to three hundred votes.

Listen, I wept when I read poor old Law's long letter in the *Greenwood County News* the following week, thanking all of his loyal supporters. He also told how he had worn shoes for the same foot back in Edgerton County—how he'd helped his stepfather in the log woods where they pulled saw logs to the mill with cattle. He told how he went to Greenwood County at sixteen, hired out as a helper on a farm for a dollar a day and keeps until he got a job at "The Shops." And bigger wages, he got married, saved money, bought a home and two small farms. And he saved five thousand dollars to run for Greenwood County high sheriff, which was his aim in life. He closed his long letter by saying: "I've lost all. I'll have to build from the start. And I'll never run again for a public office. I've had all I want of politics."

And he did lose all. When his wife Myrtle Phelps Houndshell heard about his "other children" she divorced him and took their four. John Madden, a faithful worker in the Little Party, had lost his wife a year before. He married Myrtle in six months after her divorce. Myrtle changed her registration to the Little Party three days before their marriage.

"Never had any children of my own," John said. "But I've got four now. And I'll be a real father to them. And they'll grow up in our party faith and be members of Our Little Party. We need all the voters we can get.

One of the Lost Tribe

Mick Powderjay is nailing boards on the smokehouse roof. It is the last course of oak clapboards. The autumn air is crisp. The dead oak leaves fly from the brushy-topped scrub black oaks on the yellow bank beside of the house. The leaves drift from the black oaks—down across the path that the children walk from school. Mick drives a nail into the oak board, blows his warm breath on his red knuckles and looks down the path the dead leaves trail over. "It's time Shan was in from school. Wonder what is keepin' him. He's nearly dark a-gettin' in tonight—wood is not in and water is not up."

Mick Powderjay climbs down off the smokehouse. He takes step by step down the short ladder, carefully placing each step like a chicken when it walks up the ladder in the oak tree to roost.

You can see Mick Powderjay as he walks down the dusty autumn road and shuffles the dead leaves with his brogan shoes. He is a little man going through the autumn shadows toward the Collin's Hill. He is looking for Shan. Dusk is coming fast. The tingling sheep bells on the high hills are silenced. The wind blows through the dead leaves and it is a lonesome wind to hear. The wind stirs the dead grass along the path—grass frost-bitten white and dry-sizzling when the October wind blows chilly from the high hills where the sheep are sleeping under the pines. "It's time for Shan. Fightin' again. Fightin' I'll bet."

They have come around the turn in the road beside of the apple tree. There comes Shan. "Shan Powderjay, you stinkin' Republican, I dare you out into your own corn patch."

"A Democrat Sexton never dared me to do nothin.' West Sexton, you and Jim Sexton and no other Sexton can keep me from goin' out into my own cornfield."

Shan walks out through the dead white frostbitten crabgrass—out beside a shock of corn. Mick Powderjay watches from the turn of the road. "Didn't I tell you, Shan, not to go out there?" West says, "You know what I'll do to you—you stinkin' Republican."

West throws a rock that hits Shan in the ribs. "That's cut my wind—my—my breath—" says Shan—"damn you to hell, West Sexton." He comes out of the cornfield crying. He comes toward West.

"I'll tell the teacher on you for cussin', Shan Powderjay," says Jim Sexton. "I'll tell him and he'll tan your hide."

"Tan and be damned. He's a Democrat like the rest of you."

Shan strikes West in the face. "One, two! Left, right—damn you." West is down on the dead grass.

"My Mommie allus said for me to pertect little West. Damn you to hell, Shan Powderjay. You stinkin', flat-nosed Republican you!"

"One, two, three, four—left, right—right—left—left—"

"Enough?"

"No," yelled Shan.

"Enough?"

"No—you can't make me say it."

"Take this coat hanger then over your eye."

Shan is staggered down on the dead grass. He is crying mad. He wipes the tears from his eyes with his bloody hand. "There'll come a time when I'll clean ever' Sexton o' the name. I hate them. I hate both of you."

"Shan—oh, Shan—come on up this road before I come down there and limb the rest of the shirt off'n you. Get on to this house—fightin around agin—" Shan walks ahead of West and Jim. Shan is crying. His eye is closed. He can barely see.

"What are you into it again over?"

"Because I am a Republican, Pop."

"Why are you a Republican?"

"Because you allus told me to be, Pop."

"That's right, son. I did allus tell you that. My Pap allus told me to be. It's hard to be a Republican here, but I stuck it out all my life. I still am a Republican. It don't

mean you boys got to take up politics and fight ever'
time there's a election in this county. No sense in that."

"But you don't know, Pop, what I got to stand out
there at school. They ain't but two Republicans in the
deestrict. I am one. Jack Turner is the other. You know
Jack Turner that stole them geese and carried that pistol.
Well, he is the other Republican."

"They're all Democrats then."

"Yes, all Democrats. Even the teacher and he thinks it
is funny when they call me a stinkin' Republican. Damn
his dirty looks. Hold my hand, Pop, and lead me. I can't
see."

Mick Powderjay leads Shan. They walk up the leaf-
strewn road. The Sexton boys come slowly up the road.
It may be they are afraid of little Mick Powderjay. Mick
stops and holds Shan's hand and waits for them to pass.
"Jim Sexton, don't you know you are twice as big as my
boy? Your brother West there is bigger too. After he
whopped West fair as he could be whopped then you
went over and closed his eyes. I am goin' to school tomorrow and if they ain't somethin' done about this, then
I'm seein' your father and if he don't do somethin', I
warn your father, you and all the Sextons. You tell your
father what I am tellin' you. I mean every word I say."

"Well, I'll tell the old man—but he don't like a stinkin'
Republican no more than I do."

"What's the matter with Shan, Mick?—My Lord, what
is the matter! What is the matter with that youngin's
face?"

"Fit all over the corn patch down yander by that corner

apple tree. I seen it all. He whopped West fair and square and then John Sexton's oldest boy Jim closed both his eyes. My blood biled. If old John had been down there, I'd a landed on him I was so mad. My flesh and blood and your flesh and blood treated that way because he is a Republican."

"Well you know Pap never wanted me to marry you because you was a Republican—"

"Pity your pap couldn't a had his way about it. Look what trouble it has caused me. Your people has been down on me because I was a Republican. My people don't like yours. It's a shame."

"Yes—come on, Shan, and let me hold some camphor to your nose and wash the blood off'n you and you'll feel better. Come in here and let me pour some water from the tea kettle."

"Mom—be easy—oh, that is so sore, Mom. Wash it easier."

"What did he hit you with?"

"Hit me with his big fist. Hit me so fast, Mom, I couldn't count 'em. But I whopped West. I laid it on him. Jim is too big. I'll get him before my dyin day. Mom, I hate a Democrat."

"W'y, Shan, your mother is a full-blooded Democrat. She wants you to be."

"I'll never though—I'll never. I hate 'em all. Mom, you ought'n to be a Democrat. They're so mean, all of them. They've called me everything at school today and the teacher just laughed and laughed. I hate 'em all."

The blood is washed from Shan's face. His flesh is the

color of a young potato plant. It is dark green under his eyes. His face is swollen. His hand is swollen. He cannot see. Mick Powderjay carries in the stovewood and draws water from the well in the two-gallon wooden bucket and puts it on the water bench. He does the work Shan is supposed to do. He comes in and sits before the blazing fore stick. The sap is running out of one end of it and the white-foam slobbers are falling onto the red coals and sizzlin'. Mick sits down on a split-bottom chair. "You know this damned fightin's got to be stopped. I don't aim to stand nary 'nother speck of it. The boy comes in every day with his clothes tore off'n him 'r his eyes blacked. Look at him, won't you! I don't believe in upholdin' my youngins for fightin', but he ought to take a hickory club and brain 'em all. And I hope to see the day that he whops 'em all and outlearns all that bunch out there. I hope to see my boy do it."

The red blazes from the green-oak fore stick lap their tongues up the chimney. It is a wonder they don't dirty their tongues with soot hanging to the rough-stone back walls like pods of green moss. The light flickers over the room.

"Mom, lead me on the outside of the house. Leave me out there. Then come and get me."

"All right, Shan. Reach me your hand." Fronnie leads Shan to the door—out into the dark night that is around the house—that the moon gleams peacefully through enough to show the color of the leaves.

"Leave me now. Then come and get me."

"All right. I'll be back atter you, honey." Shan feels

the wind against his sore eyes. He feels the cool October wind against the sore flesh on his face. He is in a world of blindness. He cannot see. Night is around him. It is the same as day. The world is dark to him. He can feel the wind and hear the dead oak leaves stir above his head.

"Ah, Mom—come and get me."

"I'm right here atter you, Shan."

"You know, Mom, it's awful to be blind—I'd hate to be blind forever."

"I'll bathe your eyes in warm saltwater and work with them tonight so you can go back to school tomorrow. We aim to take you back if we have to put you in the express and haul you plum around the road and get you there."

"Wait till I grow up. I got just a few things I want to do. W'y, Mom, they called me so many names at school today that I got so mad I cried. Then they laughed. They whispered them over the back of the seat to me. They called me a flat-nosed, stinkin' Republican. They called Pop one. I didn't tell him. The teacher laughed when they said smart things to me. I'll get him too. They said Republicans was all cut out of dead horsemeat. A buzzard sailed up over Wheeler's field and they said it was atter me because it smelt me. Jack Turner's the only other Republican out there and they's sixty of them. Jack slipped off from school and said nobody could ever make him go back there and that just leaves me now. I got sick today atter they said all them things. I ast the teacher to go out under the shade of a oak and rest and he laughed and said: "What's the matter, can't you take it?" He let me go. I set out there and watched a little black ant carry a load five times big as it was. The wind hit my face and I felt better. I watched the ants catch the flies and carry big pieces of bread and apples. I watched the jaybirds carry acorns up into the tall oaks and hide them in the tops. I liked it out there a devil o' a sight better than I did in the house."

"Shan, don't you know how it is here? They ain't no Republicans. I used to think a Republican stunk. Pap allus said they did and when I married your pa they nearly took the top the house off over home. Some places here in the mountains you don't find very many Democrats. It was caused by the war between the states way back yander. You ought to read about all that in your primary history. The Republicans here in the mountains are called the Lost Tribe of Israel. They are the only Republicans in these parts to amount to much. I am a Democrat and I wouldn't be anything else. My pap fit back yander in the Rebellion and he hated a Republican worse'n a copperhead. W'y, he turned on his own pap who fit for the Yanks. Grandpap had a regiment of soldiers and fit right here among these hills. And my pap, his own flesh-and-blood boy, fit with Morgan against his own father. And ever since the war we've been Democrats. Your pa's pap fit with the Yanks and that's why your pa is a Republican. That war was awful here. Yanks had Rebels to climb trees. Then they shot 'em out. Rebels had Yanks to climb trees and they shot 'em out. Your pa's people and my people all about got killed in that war. We ain't over it yet. But our children ought to be over it. They ain't no use to talk about it now. You go on and be what you want to be. Go to bed now and get some sleep."

Shan rolls under the heavy quilts. The whole up-stairs is dark. He cannot see the moon throw its rays across the broad planks in the upstairs floor. He cannot see the dead leaves sifting down between the head of his bed and the moon—leaves in the strip of yellow moon-light. He goes into the world of darkness. The wind touches his face and moves the end of his pillowcase—rustles the stiff-starched blue curtains on the upstairs window.

"Just as I thought. Eyes not open. Well, he's goin' back to school today. I'll see that he goes. I'm takin' the mule and the express wagon and takin' him right out there. I just seen the Sexton boys sneak by the house. I'm goin' to see that they all get punished."

"Gear up the mule and hitch him up while I get ready and get Shan ready. I'll have to get Vicey Martin to come over and take care of the rest of the youngins while I go out there. But I'm going too."

Mick gears the mule. He leads him from the barn door—takes him to water. Then he backs him into the shafts. He hitches the traces and fastens the shafts—puts the reins over the hames and the checklines through the harness loops. Fronnie is ready. She has Shan ready. His face is swollen purple as a fire-scorched milkweed pod. He cannot see. They feed him breakfast with a spoon. They lead him to the express and lift him up into the seat. Fronnie climbs in beside of him. Mick takes the reins. "Get up, Barnie. Let's move along now, boy."

The wheels rip-raz the dead leaves. They crush them under the weight of the express. The wind blows. The wind is cool. It touches the white frost that covers every leaf, tree, dead weed, fodder shock, panel of rail fence and briar. The world is white. The crows fly over the white-leafed world. The sun rises through a mist from a red bank of eastern hills. The wind slightly rustles the frosted leaves. Mick sits with his collar up high around his neck and his hands gloved. Fronnie sits with a fur collar up high around her neck.

"I wish I was on the ice this mornin'. That's the way I like to go to school. I like to skate my way there—fall on the ice—break my lookin' glass. Get right up and go again."

Fronnie laughs. Mick is silent. He says, "Move along, Barnie. Move along!" Over the dead leaves—over the ruts. Around the road past the old Keyser house—over the low gap where the sand-briar leaves are red steamin' in the sun. The sun is coming up behind a golden cloud of leaves now—and a white stream of mist goes slowly swirling upwards toward the sky—mist spiraling as dry leaves spiral in a new-ground when the brush is on fire and the wind becomes heated and rises swirling toward the heavens with a load of leaves.

The hoofs of the mule click on the frozen ground. Now Mick says: "Hurry it up, Barnie. Can't you hit a few more mud holes? I believe you do it on purpose. Get up there, Barnie!" They drive past the old McKeans house—down the hill through a leafless apple orchard and out past Perkins' pig lot—turn left—past the old worm-rail fence where the ground squirrels come out and "chee-chee" and dart back in their dirt holes again. The air is so good to breath now. They are passing the Wheeler pawpaw patches.

"I can smell the pawpaw patches, Mom. Smell like ripe pawpaws."

"Yes, Shan. We are passin' them now."

"I can hear the ground squirrels, Mom."

"Yes, they run out on the rails and bark at us, and then they dart back in their holes again."

"Cowards, ain't they? Just like them Sexton boys. They can't take it!"

Now they drive past the Wheeler place. Barns are all over the hill—a big house under the hill with a well in the front yard with a well sweep and water bucket chained to it. "Damned if I'd have my barn upon the hill above my well," says Mick, "I wouldn't drink that water."

The schoolhouse is in sight—just upon the hill past a lane that is lined on both sides with haw bushes. Up the lane. It is rough and rutty where the coal wagons and the crosstie wagons have rolled over heavy loaded. The mule strains at the load and he is now choicy where he places his nimble forefeet. "It takes a mule to pull," says Mick, "they are the sure-footed things for these roads. I have had horses and mules and I know." Up the hill and past the hickory trees into the school yard.

"Get out, Fronnie. Let's help Shan out and you can wait till I tie old Barnie up here to this hickory tree." Mick takes Fronnie's hand. She places her foot on the brake block and he helps her onto the ground. Fronnie takes one of Shan's hands. Mick takes the other. They lift him from the express.

"I am at school now, Mom. Back at school. Old Jim is here. He blinded me, didn't he, Mom. Someday I'll put the cat on him."

"Forget that now. We're going to see the teacher. We'll attend to all of this." Mick has tied the mule to the hickory. The sun is getting up in the heavens now. A golden shower of hickory leaves rustle in the hilltop wind. The jaybirds scold from the black oak treetops where they are laying away a winter supply of acorns.

"Well, come along, Fronnie. Grab his hand. Let's get out to the schoolhouse."

"Good mornin'. This is Mr. Landon, the school teacher of Hickory Grove, ain't it? Well, I'm Shan's pappie and here's his mammie. We're bringin' him back to school this morning."

"Been fightin' again, hasn't he, Mr. Powderjay?"

"Yes."

"Kindly looks that away, don't you think?" says Fronnie.

"Well, I should say so," says schoolmaster John Landon. "He's a bad boy to fight. I've had to correct him several times."

"Well, I ain't come out here to start nothin', but I brought the boy out to show you what kind of a shape he is in and to tell you it's not quite fair for a boy of this size to have to fight two boys at one time the size of my neighbors—the Sexton boys. That's what happened. I was a eyewitness to it all."

177

"Is that right!"

"If it hadn't been, I wouldn't have spoke it. They called the boy a stinkin' Republican and that's what he fights over. I am a Republican and I don't care if God knows it or the Devil knows it or who knows it. He's a Republican because he has heard me say I was. Now that's what all this trouble is over."

"Can't he see a speck?"

"Not a speck. He's blind as a bat. Fronnie's bathed his eyes good last night. We'd a got a doctor, but we's so far away from town and it costs so much. We know the swellin' will go down anyway."

The children turn around in their seats and stare at Shan. He stands holding the desk where the water bucket sets in the back end of the room. Schoolchildren come to get a drink of water just so they can see Shan. They leave the room just so they can see him. There is a piece of a chalk box, fastened by a twine string to a nail, that is marked OUT on one side. When this is turned over and the word OUT is showing it means someone is out and no one is allowed to leave the room until this one returns and turns the board over where the blank side is showing.

"Well, Mr. Powderjay, we'll do something about this. I'll call the boys back here and we'll thresh this thing out right here. Jim Sexton and West Sexton will please come back here for a few minutes."

They rise from their seats—overall-clad, barefooted with big rusty-looking feet, they plod back to the desk where the water bucket sets. The schoolhouse is only one room where eight grades are taught by one teacher. Jim Sexton's big bear-claw hands hang at his side. He is a powerful youth to be in a grammer school. "Jim, did you close this boy's eyes and beat him up like this?"

"I did. He whopped my brother and so I whopped him."

"What started the fight?"

"I called him a Republican and he didn't like it."

"Tell the truth," says Shan, "you called me a stinkin' Republican, and my Pop one, and said they's fit only to eat old dead horsemeat and you know you said it."

Jim Sexton looks at the schoolchildren and smiles. He wants them to think he has done a big piece of work in closing Shan's eyes. Then he says: "I did say somethin like that. I hate a Republican. They are stinkin'. My Pa said they was and you know, Mr. Landon, you told me once goin' across the hill they was."

The color of schoolmaster John Landon's cheeks has flushed to color of a red-oak leaf. He cannot speak. Mick kicks his toe slowly against the wall and looks John Landon in the eye. "I am a Democrat," says Fronnie, "a full-blooded Democrat and not anythin' else. Never voted any other way. But that is my boy. I ain't here to tear up a school and uphold for him, but I hope he cleans house with a few of you around here someday over the abuse he's had to take at this school. He'll not allus be a child, remember."

"No," says John Landon.

"What are you goin' to do about it, Mr. Landon?" says Mick Powderjay.

"I am going to whip all three boys for fighting. Steave Brooker, you go up in the loft and get me a seasoned switch. Better bring three along. Help him put the cedar pole up there, Tiny Literal, so he can get up into the scuddle hole."

Tiny and Steave lift a cedar sapling with branches trimmed off enough to leave a set of steps. They place the top of it in the scuddle hole and the heavy end on the floor. "Steady it, Tiny, and I'll get the switches."

Tiny holds the cedar. Steave scales up it like a cat. Nimble as a cat he darts into the scuddle hole. In less than a minute he is back with three seasoned honey-locust switches. His face is dust dirty. "Here they are, Mr. Landon."

"Thank you, Steave."

The children are silent. Mick Powderjay is silent too. Fronnie says, "Shan, I'll lead you up there and you must take your whoppin' like a man."

"I can take it, Mom. I've been whopped before and I took it."

"Jim Sexton, you come up the platform first."

Jim walks up the aisle between the girls' side and the boys' side of the house. Some of the children snigger at Jim as he goes past. The smile has left his lips. The platform is the place where the teacher has his chair. It is about a foot higher than the rest of the floor. The preacher often holds church in the schoolhouse and he preaches from this little platform. There isn't a church-house close.

"Turn around so they can all see, Jim."

John Landon turns Jim around so his back is to the crowd and his face is to the wall. "Take your hands from back there if you don't want them cut with this switch." Lap—lap—lap. The dust flies. John Landon steps back one more step so he can give more force to the switch. Lap—lap—lap. The dust flies. Lap—lap—

"Oh Lordy, Mr. Landon! Oh Lordy—be merciful, Mr. Landon."

Lap—lap—

"Oh, Mr. Landon, you said the Republicans stunk—o-oooo-oooo——"

"Now go take your seat. Shannon Powderjay next."

Fronnie leads him up to the platform. Shan holds out one hand groping. Jim Sexton is crying at his seat.

"Oh-oh-oh-I'll bet my Poppie'll get you, Mr. Landon."

"Face the wall, Shan."

"Wait till I turn him the right way. He don't know where he is at. He don't know where the dark is or where the light is. He is blind. That boy is blind."

Fronnie turns Shan's back to the wall. Lap—lap—lap—lap—lap. Not a whisper.

"Give me a better switch, Steave. Yes, that one will do."

Lap—lap—lap—lap—lap—lap—lap. Not a whimper. John Landon uses his left hand. Lap—lap—lap—lap. Not a whimper. Now he uses both hands. Lop—lop—lop—lop—lop. The dust flies. Not a whimper.

"All right. Take him to his seat."

Fronnie leads Shan back to the water bucket. As he gets off the platform he says," I'm still a Republican if I have to fight every day in the week and get whopped on Sunday."

"Come up here, West Sexton."

West Sexton walks up crying before he is whipped. "Turn around to the crowd."

"Lap—lap—lap—lap—lap—lap."

"Oh my God, Mr. Landon, that is enough—enough. I can't stand it. I can't stand it. Oh my God, Mr. Landon —oooooooooo-oo-ooo."

"Take your seat. Now I don't want no more fighting around here. Let this be a lesson."

"If you are through, Mr. Landon, I got somethin' I'd like to say before I leave."

"Yes, I am through and you can say anything you'd like to say."

"Well, I am a man to back the school, Mr. Landon. You ain't heard me say nothin' about the school. I ain't got enough education to write my name. But I want my boy to come to this school and get a education, for it is somethin' that no man can take away from him. He ain't but eight years old. Out here fightin' around like this. If he just fights his books like he fights for the Republican party or these other boys would fight their books the way they fight for the Democrat party—then they'd all get some place in life. That's all I got to say."

"I got somethin' to say, Mr. Landon, before I go," said Fronnie. "You know Republicans is scarce as hen's teeth in these parts. I heard my pap talk about the Lost Tribe of Israel and I didn't know what he meant for a long time. I thought it was a church denomination. But I found out he meant the Republicans in these parts.

They's just a little band of them, where I growed up. They never could elect anybody, but they went and voted just the same. They voted the straight ticket. They don't get roads in their deestricts. They don't get public offices. They don't get anythin'. Yet they hold to their party, because their fathers held to it. I married Mick Powderjay. He is a Republican. I know how hard it is to be a Republican here. We can't get any place and our children can't. We have trouble all the time. Have rocks throwed at us. Slurs throwed at us. Just little dirty things. I am not a Republican. I am a Democrat and my people don't like it because I married a Republican. My own father said he'd never darken my door and he never did till he thought I was goin' to die. Then he come to see me. We been Democrats since the Rebellion back yander. Mick Powderjay's people has been Republicans since the Rebellion. Our boy takes atter his pa. That is all right. He has a right to be what he wants to be. I think he ought to be left alone and not have a lot of slurs throwed in his face all time."

"Mrs. Powderjay, I've had to correct Shannon Powderjay quite a lot for fighting. He can tell you. It was just the other day when he hit Henry Lewis in the nose with an apple core and blooded his nose."

"Yes, and Mr. Landon, he called me a stinkin' Republican just what Jim Sexton called me. And the apple didn't hurt him much because I had took a big bite out'n it."

"Well, Shannon, I had to whip you for hitting Denver Wright with a stick."

"Mr. Landon, he throwed my straw hat in a briar patch

goin' over the hill and called me a stinkin' Republican. And I hit him."

"Another evening you crossed the hill with the Crum children. You had a fight with them. I have to correct all of you."

"Dell Crum called me a old horse-eatin' Republican. I hit him with a rock. Then his sister Martha run up and hit me with a old, dead, apple-tree limb. I didn't know any more for a long time. They went on and left me dead on the hill. You know that, Mr. Landon. The time is comin'. I'll get them that's got me and don't you think I won't."

"Let's go, Fronnie."

Fronnie leads Shan by the hand out of the door. Mick Powderjay takes John Landon by the hand, "I wish you a successful school year and soon as Shan can see I'll send him back."

"Thank you, Mr. Powderjay, and good luck to you. I am sorry for all that has happened." Mick walks toward the express shuffling the dead leaves with his brogan shoes.

The sun is up in the sky. The leaves swirl in the bright October wind. The jays scold from their high perches in the oak trees. The children look from the windows as the express wheels screak against the brake blocks going down the hill. Down the rutty lane between the haw trees and out past Wheeler's barns and farmhouse— past the rail fence and the saw briars golden in the sunlight—past the old well and round the turn by the apple tree where the fight started—and back to the log shack.

And Shan says: "Oh, Mom, I can see a little. Oh, I can see the chicken roost and the wash kettle and the smokehouse and the hill. Oh, Mom, my eyes are comin open. Goody. Goody."

Shan Powderjay goes back to school again. He is whipped again by Jim Sexton. He is gotten down in the sand and his mouth poured full of sand. He is held under water at the deep hole by the beech log until the water bubbles. He was pulled out again and rolled on the bank and put in for more. He was thrown in a yellow jacket's nest. He was stung until he was sick. He never whimpered. He was shoved into a hornet's nest. He was unmercifully stung by hornets. He laughed. Jim Sexton would say, "We ain't in school now. No teacher to whop us. Are you still a Republican?"

"I am a Republican," he would say. "I'll show you someday what I am." One time he was put in a box with a groundhog because he would say, "I am a Republican," when they were trying to make him say he was a Democrat. He threw his body on the groundhog, choked it to death with his hands. It scratched into his belly with its sharp claws but not deeply. He choked it to death before it clawed him deeply.

"A groundhog is a dangerous damn thing. Hear about Mick Powderjay's boy fallin' on that one some boys put him in the box with. He fell on it and took his hands and broke its neck. He's the fightin'est boy in this country if he had a chance and they didn't bunch on him."

"Ah, well he'll grow up atter a while and show 'em a few things. I don't like a Republican, but anybody likes a boy or a man that will stand firm. That kid's just about twelve years old now. Growin' up like a bean pole, too. Freckle-faced as a guinea."

"I got the best boy to work in this Hollow," says Mick Powderjay, "he just fights weeds in the corn from daylight till dark. He can take it like a man. He can stand more hot weather and do more work than any man in this Hollow. He's makin' the best grades in his class too. He fights like a bulldog. He won't give up."

"I'm worried all the time about Shan when he is out. He's gettin' up now sort of a man, you know, or thinks he is. He'll fight them Sexton boys to a finish if it ever starts again."

"Did you hear about Shan Powderjay? W'y, he's the craziest boy I ever heard tell of. A blacksnake bit him over there in the strawberry patch and quiled and started to bite him again and he just jumped in and got that snake with his hands. He tore it into pieces with its guts hangin' out. I wish you could a seen it. Snakebite never even stopped him from eatin' strawberries."

"Witnessed one of the hardest fights I ever seed in all my born days a little while ago. It was down there on the sawdust pile. That Shan Powderjay just cleaned that Crum bunch of boys single-handed. He beat Dell till he was blue in the face and choked Oscar's tongue out and kicked Tim plum off the sawdust pile. One of 'em called him a stinkin' Republican. And he says, 'I heard that too much when I was too little, not to do anything about it,' and he bowed up his neck and went at 'em like a bull. I never seed such fightin' in all my born days."

"I saw a funny thing while ago. I saw the pluckiest boy I ever saw in all my life. You know that guinea-freckled-faced Shan Powderjay—ugly and gangly as a half-trimmed bean pole. I saw him get into a yaller jacket's nest. One crawled up his pants' leg and stung him. He went right in and dug out the whole nest and took his hat and club and beat 'em all to death—he got seventeen stings. Cared nary bit for 'em. Fit 'em and the hot sun just a-bilin' right down on his head and the sweat just a-runnin' off'n his face. He didn't care."

A hornet hit Shan once between the eyes and knocked him down and stung him at the same time. He saw not far from him a big hornet's nest, the first one he had ever seen. He saw the hornets climbing all over the nest and preening the long whiskers together and saying something about him. "Plottin' about me, are you. Surely you ain't found out that I am a Republican."

So, Shan gets two long poles, ties a wisp of dead grass to one end, sets the grass on fire and runs the fire up under the nest and burns it to the ground. "I hate to use fire on 'em, but they got the advantage on me—bein' up in the air and so many of them. And they got wings. They can sting and bite all the same time and keep goin'. Have to fight fire with fire."

The children crossed Radnors' pasture to school. That was the only way they had near enough to get there on time. Bill Radnor says: "They tear down my fences. I want them stopped from goin' through here. The law says they're entitled to a way to the school house and they have a right to cross my field. But I got the fightin' bull

John Plummer used to own and put him in there. I've warned them all not to come through my field anymore."

"I'm not afraid of your bull," says Shan. "I'll kill him with a club if he ever makes a pass at me."

"He's paid for when you kill him, you freckled face smartelick, you," says Bill.

"Did you hear about Bill Radnor's bull jumpin' on the schoolchildren the other mornin'? He ought to be sent to the pen doin' a trick like that. Got that bull a purpose to harm schoolchildren. Little Bessie Fials just got through the fence in time. That bull come nigh as a pea gettin' her on his horns. Them kids have to go plum around the road to get to school—five miles around that way and just three across the hill."

"Mick Powderjay's boy killed Bill Radnor's bull. Did you hear about it? He killed him with a four-year-old hickory club. Him and them Sexton boys was crossin' the pasture the other mornin' and here that bull darted out'n the bushes atter 'em and they all took to the trees but Jim and the bull got him on one of his horns in the seat of the pants while he was upon the side of the tree. It got him off and started to pin him to the ground under his horns and that Shan Powderjay nailed him by the horns and put his toes in his nostrils till Jim got up and West got down out of the tree and got a club. Then Shan jumps loose and grabs the club quick as a cat and piles the bull up in a heap. He's layin' over there dead. Bill's goin' to sell him for beef soon as he skins him this mornin'. Lord, but that's a game boy."

Shan sits by the fire on frosty nights now. He sees

the blue flames leap from the forestick—leap up the big-throated chimney and go into nothingness. And he says: "That is madness. It is nothingness. I hate to get mad and have to fight, but I can when I have to. And I fight like the very Devil when I have to fight. No use to go into it slipshod or any old way to get it over with—but go in to win it fair and square. If it's fire a body is fightin', fight it with fire."

Shan hears his father say before the fire when he is studying his geography lesson: "Pap said that war was somethin' awful. He said they was a band of Democrats that heard about a Republican up in Winson County and they started to get him one mornin'. But this fellow was hidin' out in the brush. And he had a muzzle-loadin' rifle with him. He saw them come up to his house and ask his wife where he was. And she said he was gone and she didn't know where he was at and when he'd come in. Then they took all the meal in the house and broke the barrel up into staves and throwed them out the winder. They cut up the feather bedtick and the white feathers just flew in the air. They throwed water buckets and chears out'n the house. They's about ten of 'em and when they got ready to leave they took the man's wife. A rifle cracked on the hill and the man that had tied her wrists with a piece of rope and was leadin' her off against her will, he fell dead as a mackerel with a bullet in his brain. This man was their leader. The rest broke out in a run for the brush. The man come in off the hill, untied his wife. They hauled the dead man down by Little Sandy and buried him in the sand. In about a week a woman come there with a old bony horse hitched to a sled. She was ridin' the horse and reinin' him with the bridle reins. 'Did you kill my man?' she said. 'I killed a man, but I don't know whose man he was and care a damn sight less,' the man of the house said. 'He was tryin' to take my wife. He had her tied with a rope by the wrists.' 'Well where is he now?' 'He's been in Hell for four days now. You'll find him buried down there in the sand with his feet a-stickin' out.' The woman took the old horse and the sled and went down to the sandbank, dug him out and put him on the sled. He was stiff as a board and bobbled up and down on the sled like a pole o' wood. He had sand in his hair and eyes—was a sight too look at, but she said, 'He's my man and I want his remains.' So she got his remains and took 'em back to old Virginia with her."

And Fronnie says: "I remember bands of Rebublicans that used to come to Woodberry County and take the place. They was whole droves of 'em. And they wasn't anythin' the people could do about it. They stole horses and killed and plundered the houses and took the cattle and et 'em. They captured Rebel Harry Meadows and told him if he'd climb to such and such limb on such certain tree that they would turn him loose. Well, he'd climb the sycamore tree up to that limb. Then they told him to go a little higher. He went a little higher. Then they said a little higher yet. Well, he went up just as high as he could get till the top went to saggin' with him and then one up and shoots him out and says, 'Another ring-tailed coon hits the ground.'

"They left him there and his dog tracked him up and would go back to the house and howl. And the dog led his people to where they had left him shot out of the tree. The dog had dug a big enough hole to bury him in. They hauled him out of the woods on a sled and buried him in that thicket on Wellman's pint. I remember the grave when I's a girl. I passed there a many a time. I remember seein' a groundhog hole down into the grave and seein' a lot o' bones work up out of the ground. One time two boys was goin' to dig into the grave and see if he had any money buried with him. One of the awfulest rains fell that night that ever did fall in Woodberry County. It was just a token to leave the dead alone and let them sleep, Pap said. Well, they's a old man by the name of Rebel Bill Withe who said he'd clear the hills of the damned Yankees. So he hid in the brush and got 'em one at a time till he thinned their ranks. And one of Rebel Bill's men spied on him and told the Yanks his hidin' place. So a Yank come one night when old Rebel Bill was in the bed under the kivers. He said, 'You old son-of-a-bitch, I got you now.' And he shot old Bill in bed—walked back down the stairs. He didn't get old Bill. He missed him. And Bill crawled out'n the bed soon as the man got downstairs and Bill shot him. Killed him. I can show you his grave too. No stone there, but a wild cherry grows up through it. Well, no one never got old Bill. He died a natural death, but he died in much misery over killin' so many Yanks. On his deathbed he would say: 'I see him in blue. Take him away. They've come after me. I'm not goin'.' And that is the way old

Rebel Bill died. I wouldn't a been in his socks for his shoes."

"I am a Republican just the same, Mom," says Shan. "I am goin' to whip old Jim Sexton sure as my name is Shan Powderjay. I'm goin' to lay the cat on him as soon as the next trouble starts. My mind is made up. This is the last year we'll be in school together. I'm goin' to whop him before I leave that school. I'm goin' to turn right around then and whop John Landon. He ain't done me nigh right. He's upheld Jim in every move he has made and thought it was funny to call me a stinkin' Republican. I'm goin' to whop 'em if it's the last thing I ever do. That's one reason I kept that bull from killin' Jim. I am savin' him to whop myself. I am a Republican and I don't care if God Almighty and the Devil knows it."

"Well, I got a lot of little tads in school. But I'll soon have one out. Shan finishes in January and I aim to send him to a bigger school summers if I can get the money. He's made the best grades in his class."

"Yes, but Mr. Powderjay, I heard that boy was a wildcat on wheels. I heard he'd fight like a wildcat—just claw and scratch and bite."

"No, Mr. Thombs. They pick on him all the time and they've made him that way. He won't start a fight until they call him a stinkin' Republican here in these parts, but like my own son I have stuck to the faith of my father."

"Did you know that Shan Powderjay said he was goin' to whip Mr. Landon and Jim Sexton tomorrow, the last day of school? He said he was goin' to do it. Jim says he'll close his eyes closer than he did that time before. You remember way back yander when Shan was out of school so long. Jim Sexton closed his eyes then. That was the time old Mick and Fronnie Powderjay come out to school and they whopped all them boys. Lord, that Shan's tough. Can't make him cry. He's whopped all the boys over at Seagrave's watermill playin' lapjack. W'y, they can't make him holler. He's whopped all that's ever hit him."

"And John Long, you must remember that he killed that bull of Bill Radnor's too. He's not so big but he's nervy. He might whop Mr. Landon."

"No, Landon is too much for a boy. He'll eat him up alive."

"Did you hear what happened today at the last day of school? The trouble all popped out soon as Shan Powderjay got his grades. He got the ribbon o' bein' the best scholar in school and his poke of candy for treat. Then he got up and said, 'They's one thing I want to tell this school. First: I am a Republican. Now anyone who wants to call me a stinkin' Republican just step out.' Jim Sexton stepped out with a great big grin on his face. Mr. Landon says, 'Here boys, we don't want no trouble.' But they went right into it. Shan throwed him on the ground and that big tooth of Jim's that pushes out from the rest in front cut plum through his lip. Shan beat him in the face and then he kicked him in the ribs. Mr. Landon run in and said, 'Stop that, Shan, right now.' And Shan says, 'You want some of the same medicine.

I can give it to you.' And Mr. Landon struck at Shan and Shan ducked. Then he come back and hit Mr. Landon in the face and on the nose and the blood just squirted. The children started runnin' home screamin'. I stayed and watched the fight. He got Mr. Landon by the ear with his teeth and one of his fingers in his mouth too and told him he'd bite both ear and finger off if Mr. Landon didn't say he was a Republican and he made him say it. Then he let him up and Mr. Landon was a-bleedin' all over. I was skeered to death. But atter Shan whopped 'em he got his books and says good-by to Hickory Grove forever. He jumped the rail fence and took out through Radnor's pasture for home."

"I ain't got nothin' to say if he whops 'em all. I ruther make a old person mad as a child. It grows on a child. He never forgets. A old person does forget. They used to make Shan's life a misery for him. Now he can take his part."

Shan is sitting before the fire. He is reading. Fronnie is churning milk for supper. She says, "Son, what made you whop Mr. Landon?"

"He ought to a stopped them fights long ago. He didn't do it. Because he was a Democrat he let his feelin's run for that side—the majority. I allus said I'd get even with that crowd. I feel all right tonight. I ain't got nothin' against none o' 'em. I don't even intend to fight one of them again. I've whopped all that old crowd now. They are my friends. I'm a Republican and they are Democrats. We don't mind. I'll be a Republican if they's not but one vote ever cast in this deestrict."

"Boy o' yours, Mick Powderjay, must have some Democrat blood in him the way he's been fightin' around here. All I got to say is I have never voted for a Republican in my life, but if that boy ever runs I'm for him for dogcatcher."

"He's got the Democrat blood in him all right. He gets it from his Ma, but he's a Republican like his Pa. He takes that fightin' atter his pa's people. Pap was allus into it, you know. He was captured twice by the Rebels. They liked Pa so well they wouldn't kill him. He was hung by the Yanks, the fellars he's a-fightin' for. But he got out'n it some way and come back to these parts a-fightin' the Gorillars. He killed 'em like you'd shoot a squirrel. They's the fellars, you know, that plundered the country and killed men, women and children and wouldn't take no side in the War. Shan's like Pap."

"Well, if he ever runs for anything let me know. I'm a full-blooded Democrat, but he's one Republican I'll vote for. I ain't voted for one yet. You can't fool me. It's the good Democrat blood in him."

"You are right, Vim Westbrook. He takes it all atter me, his ma," says Fronnie and she laughs.

"Well, if he's to ever run for anythin' and get the worst lickin' in the world, he'd take it for he's used to enough lickin's. That's about all he's ever got all his life. A groundhog came nigh as a pea tearing his guts out and he never whimpered. Some crazy boys put him in the pen with one because he wouldn't turn over and say he's a Democrat. It backed up in the corner and growled at him and he lit on it and choked it to death. It cut the whole front of his shirt out and he told his ma and me that he got it tore up in the head o' the holler on a swing."

"And he whopped the schoolteacher and a groundhog. Well, I'll be dogged. I'll give him my first Republican vote if he runs for dog catcher of this county and you tell him I said, "I's a stinkin' Democrat.""

Uncle Felix and the
Party Emblem

"You stay home this morning, Hester," Uncle Felix said. He motioned with his hand for me to go back to the house. "I want to be prepared for the big day."

I stood for a few minutes watching Uncle Felix climb the steep slope of a rugged mountain in front of his cabin. He held to sourwood and hickory sprouts along the tiny fox path and pulled himself up the steep slope toward the towering rock cliffs. I wanted to go with him because I went nearly everywhere he went and helped him with his work. I helped him feed his cattle, young mules, hogs, and sheep. But Uncle Felix didn't want me with him now. I didn't understand why he didn't want me to go. It hurt me for him to send me back to the house like I'd seen Pa do when he went to town and his four hound dogs would try to follow him and he'd send them back to the house. After as good as I had been to Uncle Felix and after as good as he'd been to me, he wouldn't let me follow him to the towering cliffs.

While Uncle Felix was gone I went back to his barn and turned the livestock out to get water. And I counted the sheep as Uncle Felix had me to do each morning since the wild dogs in the mountains had been killing them. I thought, maybe, Uncle Felix had gone upon the mountain to look for the wild dogs' den. But when he had done this before, he had always taken me along. And he had always taken a high-powered rifle with him and let me take his single-barrel shotgun to use at close range. But he had gone into the mountains without a gun and he had gone alone. And he had said something about his being "prepared for the big day."

As I walked back home, for we lived on Uncle Felix's big farm and rented land from him to farm and worked for him, I wondered if Uncle Felix went upon the mountain to pray. He was Mom's brother and he had never married. He had lived alone all his life and people didn't know much about him. We were as close to him as anybody and we were not very close. He lived his own life the way he wanted to live, and now that he was getting old I wondered if he was getting prepared to die when he spoke of the "big day."

When I went back that evening to help Uncle Felix feed and milk his eighteen cows, feed his fourteen mules, his twelve horses, seventy-five head of cattle, three hundred and seventy-five sheep and twenty-two hogs, I didn't ask him what he had meant when he spoke of his being "prepared for the big day." I thought if he wanted me to know about it, he would tell me. I watched Uncle Felix work to see if he was getting feeble. But I didn't see anything wrong with him. I'd worked for him eight years ago and he was as active now as he was when I first started working for him.

He was a powerful man on a lift with a pitchfork. And he could sink a double-bitted ax into solid oak to the eye. Uncle Felix had shoulders broad as the corncrib door for he had to turn to one side to squeeze into the crib to get corn. And his arms were bigger than my legs. They were knotted with muscles and his hands looked like small hams. His face was covered with a long white beard for Uncle Felix never shaved from September until April. He didn't look tall since he was so big but Uncle Felix was tall for he had to stoop to walk under any of his barn doors.

Next morning there was a snow on the ground. And while I helped Uncle Felix feed he said, "I can't do any preparing for the big day since there is a snow on the ground."

"What's the snow got to do with it," Uncle Felix?" I asked.

"I don't like to leave my tracks on the snow," he said. "But the sky is clear; the sun will come out and melt the snow and I can go up among the cliffs on that mountain tomorrow."

Uncle Felix pointed to the cliffs on the mountain on the other side of his house, a mountain steeper than the one he had climbed above the barn, a mountain with more jutted cliffs.

"When and where is the big day, Uncle Felix?" I asked him as he carried a barrel of corn out to throw in the pen to his hogs.

"Saturday in Dalton," he said. "I've heard about it. There's going to be a lot a-goin' on. Come Saturday morning early be dressed in your best and go with me."

On Friday there wasn't a speck of snow on the ground. And soon as we'd finished with the feeding, Uncle Felix hurried to the steep mountain behind his house. And I stood watching him scale the rugged cliff where there wasn't even a fox path to walk on. I watched him holding to the little sourwood sprouts that grew from the crevices of rocks. Once he pulled a sprout out by the roots. But he held his other hand to a spur of rock and pulled himself a step higher. When I started for home he had climbed over the first steep bluff and was up among the jagged cliffs where he disappeared like a red fox.

"Early Saturday morning I dressed in my best and when I reached Uncle Felix's cabin it was just daylight. Uncle Felix had already done the feeding by lantern light. And he was dressed in his best clothes, ready to go.

"I've been up since three o'clock," he said. "All the work's done. And I'm ready. We've got a fur piece to walk, Hester. We must be on our way."

Uncle Felix took the lead and I followed him. He took steps twice as long as my legs could reach. I nearly had to run to keep up with him. His big arms with his big

gloveless hands swung like pistons on each side of him
from his shoulders almost to his knees. He wore a gray
suit, with a few dirty spots on it, that bagged at the
knees and seat for Uncle Felix seldom wore his suit and
he had never had it cleaned or pressed. And his big, um-
brella, autumn-oak-leaf-colored hat didn't cover the hair
on his head for his hair was too long and the wind toyed
with the long gray locks beneath. Uncle Felix's rock-
scarred brogan shoes whetted on the frozen clumps of
dirt, frosted leaves and pine needles and made funny
sounds as we hurried along the narrow path, over the
mountains, across the hollows and out the ridge road
toward Dalton.

Once when we reached the ridgetop, Uncle Felix said,
"Let's wind a minute."

We were getting our breaths like tired mules pulling
a sawlog on the ground.

And while we winded, Uncle Felix wiped sweat from
his long white beard with a blue bandana. I wiped sweat
from my face with my handkerchief until it was soaked.
And all the sweat left on my face was soon dried by
the high mountain wind that moaned through the tall
pine trees that grew high on this mountain. Uncle Felix
filled his pipe with burley tobacco leaves that he had
crumpled in his hip pocket.

"Looks like you got a lot o' burley in your pockets,
Uncle Felix," I said. I noticed his bulging coat and pants'
pockets.

"Got more than burley leaves in my pockets," Uncle
Felix said. "There's goin' to be monkey business a-goin'

on in Dalton today. I've heard about it. Cy Pratt climbed over the mountain and told me about it and I'm prepared."

When we went down the mountain path toward Dalton, there was a stream of burley smoke from Uncle Felix's pipe that drifted like a small cloud across his left shoulder, since he held his pipe in the left corner of his mouth, and went down the mountain in his long strides charging against the wind. The stream of smoke nearly strangled me but I managed to keep up with him. Uncle Felix hurried like a man going to a fight. He hurried like he was a needed man in Dalton and that he wasn't goin' to get there on time. It was sixteen miles to Dalton and when we reached the town, Uncle Felix didn't seem to be a bit tired but I was pooped out.

"You'll see a lot of people in Dalton today," Uncle Felix said. "It's a big day."

When we reached the courthouse that stood in the middle of the town, I'd never seen as many people gathered together in one place in my life. And Uncle Felix pushed through the crowd and I followed at his heels for he made a path for me to follow where people were standing thick as sassafras sprouts grow on a deserted, Kentucky-mountain cornfield. They were looking at something that was upon a little platform.

"Here's the monkey business I was a-tellin' you about, Hester," Uncle Felix said. "Look!"

Upon the platform was a little log cabin. It looked something like the picture of the log cabin where Abraham Lincoln was born that I had seen in my Primary

History. But this log cabin also looked like the cabin where Uncle Felix lived. And inside the cabin, I saw one of the meanest-looking, red game roosters I'd ever seen in my life. He had spurs almost three inches long, straight as needles and the ends were sharp as the points of yellow locust thorns. His comb had been trimmed close to his head so other roosters couldn't peck it to pieces in a fight. And when Uncle Felix got up close to look at the cabin, the rooster looked through a crack at him and crowed!

"What do you know about that?" Uncle Felix said.

And there was a piece of paper tacked on the cabin with something written on it. Since Uncle Felix couldn't read, he asked me to read what was on the paper. And I read for Uncle Felix, "Will this bird, the emblem of our Good Party be forced to remain penned up in this log cabin the rest of his life and die of old age and a broken heart? Or will some free-hearted bond buyer of our good party buy more bonds than anyone of our opposing party so that we may free this bird from this log cabin, that he may go out and fight?"

"Ain't that something?" Uncle Felix said. "The bird must stay cooped in that cabin!"

Everybody that had gathered around the rooster in the cabin laughed.

"Listen to that old codger won't you," said a well-dressed man. "If it's up to him, the bird will be freed!"

"That's just what you think," Uncle Felix said, his beardy lips trembling. "If it's in my power that bird will stay in that log cabin and die of old age and a broken heart. You're damned right he will! That's just why I've walked sixteen miles this morning to see that he does stay cooped!"

And while Uncle Felix argued with the well-dressed man who was laughin' as he talked to Uncle Felix, I watched the rooster step proudly up and down the cabin floor. Honest, he stepped more proudly than I have ever seen a turkey gobbler strut. He was the proudest rooster I'd ever seen in a coop. Nearly all of the people were proud of the rooster. They stood looking through the cracks of the cabin at him and their faces beamed with joy. But when Uncle Felix saw him his face grew cloudy with frowns.

"That cocky rooster is in the cabin," Uncle Felix argued with the well-dressed man, "and if it's in my power, I'll keep 'im there!"

"Remember the great Oscar Birchwell is here," the man told Uncle Felix. "Remember he's got the dough!"

I'd heard of Oscar Birchwell, he was the richest man in Caswell County. He'd made his money because he was lucky enough to have good fireclay under the scrubby pines and oaks that grew on his boundless ancestral acres.

"I'm not so sure about Oscar Birchwell," Uncle Felix said.

"Listen to that," the man said as he crowded closer to the cabin. Then he laughed and all the people laughed but a few. I think they were on Uncle Felix's side and wanted the cocky rooster kept in the log cabin. But I would rather watch the rooster strut than to listen to

Uncle Felix argue with the well-dressed stranger. He was a pretty rooster and he wanted out so badly. He would even try to peck the people's faces if they got too close to the cabin cracks. And he would crow and flap his wings and brag and strut. I wondered where on earth they had found such a lively rooster that would get the sympathy of the people. Most anyone would have wanted him out, even I did and he wasn't my party emblem. I hated to see him cooped but I would have been afraid to've told Uncle Felix the thought that were a-goin' through my head as I watched the rooster.

"Just in a few minutes we'll see if the rooster is freed or if he is to remain in that old coop," said a well-dressed woman. She was standing near and heard the arguments goin' on round the cabin.

I saw a man walking up the courthouse steps. He hurried to the top step where he could look over the crowd of milling people. They stood packed on the courthouse square like sardines in a box. And even the streets beyond the courthouse were filled with people.

"Attention people," the man on the courthouse step said. "Please let me have your attention!"

Uncle Felix and the stranger quit their arguing after all of the crowd had become quiet enough until you could hear their breathing and men's wheezing on their pipe-stems.

"We have met here today at this bond rally, to sell bonds for our government," the man said. "We put our country above all of its political parties, but we have the emblem of one great party enclosed in the emblem of the other great party. Now if any man whose political emblem is the rooster buys more dollars worth of bonds than anyone whose political emblem is the log cabin, then the rooster comes out of the cabin. If a man whose political emblem is the log cabin, buys more dollars worth of bonds, then he gets the cabin, rooster and all."

Everybody laughed. Not anybody seemed to be worked up about this like Uncle Felix and the man who had been arguing with him. And I heard people all around me saying, "No use for anybody to try to remove the rooster in the cabin for Oscar Birchwell will get him out." And I know Uncle Felix heard these words too for he was so mad he was trembling like a white-oak leaf in the winter wind. As he stood there, I heard him grit his teeth and whisper, "Maybe, Birchwell will get 'im out! If it's in my power he'll stay in that cabin!"

When the man on the courthouse step started the bidding, many people didn't try to bid. Men and women were lined up at the courthouse doors to go inside and buy bonds and many stayed on the courthouse yard to see what happened to the rooster.

"Who will bid one hundred dollars to see the rooster freed?" the bidder asked.

I looked over the courthouse square and it seemed to me four out of every five men and women held up their hands.

"Who will give two hundred to keep 'im caged?"

Uncle Felix's hand shot up like a bullet from a gun. About one-fifth of all the men and women in the crowd held their hands up.

"Start the bidding at a thousand dollars, Alf," a stranger said.

"That's Oscar Birchwell saying that to eliminate fellows like you," said the well-dressed man to Uncle Felix.

"Start it at five thousand would suit me," Uncle Felix told him.

"All right, one thousand to see 'im freed!"

Not nearly as many hands went up as before.

"Eleven hundred to keep him caged!"

Not nearly so many hands among the small group went up as before. But since Uncle Felix was so tall, his big hand was high above any other man's. I heard people talking about his big ham-of-meat hand with a palm calloused hard as dried groundhog leather.

"Higher biddin', Alf," Oscar Birchwell yelled. "We'll never get through if we keep on biddin' in chicken feed!"

"Two thousand to see him freed!"

Fewer hands went up

"Three thousand to keep him caged!"

Fewer hands went up.

"Higher biddin', Alf," Oscar Birchwell yelled.

"Five thousand to see him freed."

Fewer hands went up.

"Ten thousand to keep him caged!"

Only three hands went up and Uncle Felix's hand was higher than the other two.

"Fifteen thousand to see him freed!"

Only Oscar Birchwell's hand went and that was what Oscar had been wanting to see all the time so the people around us started talking.

"Sixteen thousand to keep him caged!"

Uncle Felix's big hand was up.

"Twenty thousand to see him freed!"

Oscar Birchwell held his hand high.

"Twenty-one thousand to keep him caged!"

"Do you suppose that old beardy man's got that much money?" I heard a woman whisper to a man.

But Uncle Felix's hand was up.

"Twenty-five thousand to see him freed!"

Oscar Birchwell tried to jump high so he could raise his hand as high as Uncle Felix did. A big man grabbed Oscar and put him on his shoulder so everybody could see him fight to free the rooster and there was a great cheering from the crowd. Oscar held his hand high and smiled to the people.

"Twenty-six thousand to keep him caged!"

Uncle Felix's hand went up. And Oscar Birchwell looked a bit worried. Some of the smile left his face.

"Thirty thousand to see him freed!"

Oscar's hand went up more slowly than before.

"Thirty-one thousand to keep him caged!"

Uncle Felix shot his hand up like a bullet from a gun.

"Mister, do you understand this bidding?" Alf asked Uncle Felix. "You are to spend as many dollars for war bonds as you bid here."

"I understand perfectly well, my friend," Uncle Felix said. "I won't bid any higher than I can buy!"

Everyone looked at each other. People started whispering and laughing. And the man that had argued with Uncle Felix looked him over from head to foot and he didn't smile.

"Thirty-five thousand to free the rooster!"

Everybody turned to Oscar to watch him slowly raise his hand.

"Forty thousand to keep him caged!"

Uncle Felix's hand shot high into the air!

Everybody turned toward Uncle Felix. They looked strangely at him. They didn't laugh at him now like they laughed when he first started bidding.

"Forty-five thousand to free 'im!"

Oscar slowly raised his hand and started to say something but a cheer went up from the people that drowned the words he started to say.

Oscar whispered something to the man that held him on his shoulder. Then this man shouted to Alf who was doing the bidding, "Hold the bids down a little, Alf!"

"Forty-six thousand to keep 'im caged!"

Uncle Felix's hand went up and he smiled for the first time.

"Forty-seven thousand to set him free!"

Oscar slowly put his hand up.

"Forty-nine to keep him caged!"

When we looked Oscar Birchwell was not on the man's shoulder and about one-fifth of the people jumped up and down and cheered.

"I'd a-bought more bonds than that just to've got to stuck a fork in that rooster," Uncle Felix said.

When Uncle Felix went inside the courthouse to buy forty-nine thousand dollars worth of bonds, a crowd of people followed him. I knew they didn't think he had the money. I waited beside the log cabin and answered questions people asked me about Uncle Felix. The man he had argued with asked me a lot of questions about Uncle Felix, where he lived, what he worked at, how big a farm and how much livestock he had and even what he ate for breakfast.

Then the crowd started pouring from the courthouse and I heard 'em talking about the thousand dollar bills Uncle Felix had and they were arguing among themselves whether he had had them buried or not. I heard one man say the bills were soft and musty for he had a chance to feel one. Uncle Felix was a happy man when he picked up the cage with the rooster in it to take home. Somebody took his picture with the cabin on his shoulder. Then the man asked him how far he would carry it and Uncle Felix told him sixteen miles. And then he asked Uncle Felix what he planned to do with the rooster.

And before Uncle Felix could speak, I said, "You planned to give 'im to me, didn't you, Uncle Felix, since the hoot owls caught our last rooster?"

"It isn't fair for anybody to dislike this rooster because he's an emblem of a party," I thought. "He can't help it. It's not his fault." And as I looked at this pretty rooster, I thought how happy he'd be with a flock of hens. That was the place where he belonged and I didn't want to see 'im die.

"Hester, I'm not so sure about the stock," Uncle Felix said, laughin'. "I'd planned to stick my fork in 'im at suppertime, but . . ."

And the people laughed until they drowned the words Uncle Felix started to say. Everybody I think followed us but Oscar Birchwell. They were laughing and talking with Uncle Felix, until we reached the outskirts of the town where our path was a dim winding trail up the mountain for a few hundred yards until it disappeared among the pine trees and the high jutted rocks.

The Election

I told Doodle not to put hisself up for school trustee. But Doodle would run for trustee. He run with Brother Hankas. Pee-Pee Littlejohn run with them. You know each deestrict has three trustees. "It takes three trustees to hold a teacher down," says Brother Hankas.

I wanted Brother Hankas to stay out of it. Pee-Pee Littlejohn's not got much reputation. He's bad to fool with licker. He's a gambler too. Bets on roosters. Plays cards for money. Everybody knows it. I told Doodle and Brother Hankas that would go agin him in the election. You know a man has to learn. Brother Hankas and Doodle know by now, I guess.

I'll tell you about that election. It was Clay Creek agin Beech Grove. Clay Creek is in Beech Grove. For fifty years the rest of the Beech Grove deestrict run the school. The Laymores got the school every year. One out of that family taught it. We got tired of it. John Melvin, from Clay Creek, is a young man. We wanted him to have the school. John is a good boy. Raised under a good roof. Doodle, Brother Hankas and Pee-Pee Littlejohn just got together and said they'd make the race agin the Laymores. Clay Creek wanted John Melvin. The rest of Beech Grove wanted Melvina Laymore. I've been at Beech Grove a long time. I've seen them run more than one woman teacher home. Run her through the woods and throw rocks at her.

The night before the election I saw Doodle and Hankas. They were up on the pasture hill. Doodle was layin' it off to Hankas with his hands. He never talks with his hands unless he's had a drink. I knowed that trouble was goin' to brew at the election. I saw the moon come up over the hill. It was big as a wagon wheel. It just looked like it rolled along the ridge top. Then I saw Pee-Pee comin' out of the bushes with a jug in each hand. I could tell something was up. A body can tell Pee-Pee a mile away if he is walking betwixt a body and the light of the moon. Pee-Pee is so yow-necked. He's crooked in more ways than one too.

Doodle came back from the pasture field. He come down to the house. He was struttin' with his hands like a turkey with his wings. He come in the house lickin' his lips. I says to Doodle: "This is a pretty way to win a school election. Out drinkin' and carousin' with Pee-Pee Littlejohn!"

"Done got it winned," says Doodle.

"I'd like to know how," I says.

"I got the old election right over there in a leafpile," says Doodle. "Got it tied up good and tight as you tie a coffee sack with a sea-grass string."

When Doodle said "leaf pile" I knowed what he was drivin' at. Why, Doodle was one of the three Beech Grove trustees for twenty-five years. It just got so they wouldn't put out a man agin Doodle. He'd just fill him up a half-pint bottle for every man that voted for him of the best whiskey made in the deestrict. Seymore County's whiskey. He just took it to the leaf pile below the schoolhouse. He covered the licker bottles over with leaves. Doodle just left it up to them.

Doodle passed through the house. He went to the barn to get the mule. I could tell he's goin' to do a little electioneerin'. I saw Pee-Pee come down the Left-hand Fork of Clay Creek on a sorrel horse. I knowed he was goin' to ride out and see the voters and tell them about the election. I saw Brother Hankas comin' on that old Jack of hissen. Nobody can ride him but Brother Hankas. The boys have to tie him to a pole when they take him out of the stall to water him. The three men met at our house. They rode off down the crick together. Brother Hankas was full of licker as a dog tick or he wouldn't a been on the Jack. He was takin' in both sides of the road. The Jack was after Pee-Pee's sorrel mare. The last I saw of them they turned the bend by the sweet-tater patch. The dust was a-flyin'. Brother Hankas was almost setting straight back to hold the Jack.

The men didn't go to a house on Clay Creek. We had Clay Creek tight as a jug. Doodle, Brother Hankas and Pee-Pee went over into the Laymore territory. They electioneered with the Kitchens, Fraziers and McDonalds. They are our second and third cousins. We thought we'd get them.

The moon rode up over the August hills. I could see it from my winder after I got in bed. I just went to bed and couldn't sleep. I just thought something was goin' to happen. Brother Hankas out on that old Jack a whoopin' and a stavin' around. Drunk as a owl. Mick out on a mean mule that takes spells and runs sideways for a mile. Pee-Pee on his sorrel mare. All drinkin'. God knows when three men are drinkin', two are liable to take sides agin the other.

I just laid in the bed and rolled and tossed. I just laid there and pulled the kivers. August moon above me in the sky; night so pretty; wind comin' in at my winder. Wind stirrin' the leaves on the apple trees out in the yard. I just laid there and thought: "What if Doodle gets killed? He's liable to get into it with Brother Hankas. Liable to get into a knifin' bout over the parties." Then I went to sleep with the wind blowin' across my bed and rufflin' the curtains at the winders.

When I waked up I heard Doodle say to Hankas and Pee-Pee: "Boys, we got them in this election. Clay Creek is goin' to hang together like a leech to a body's leg. The other side is split up. They don't believe a woman ought to teach the school. They believe the Laymore woman's place is in the house. All them bad names been writ on the fences out there for the past twenty years. Time to break it up, boys."

"Funny election though," says Hankas. "Can't hear a thing. Don't know what's goin' to happen."

"Watch that damned Jack," Pee-Pee says, "he's after my mare."

When Doodle come in the house, I just snored away. I wanted him to think I'd been asleep. He come in and pulled off his pants. You know Doodle sleeps in his drawers and shirt. The hounds of Mort Flannery's brought the fox right around on the point back of the house. I never heard such a race in all my life. Joe Dawson's dogs right at their heels. Doodle pulled off his pants and stood at the winder and listened to them take the fox out of hearin'. When Doodle crawled in beside me I could smell that old rotgut on his breath.

Next mornin' I was up at four and got breakfast. I was walkin' on my toes. It was the big day.

At six o'clock the polls opened. You'd a died seein' Doodle and Slim and Hatcher doin' up the work. Both of my boys cut out twenty-ones and put in their shoes. I saw them cut up a page of the calendar so they wouldn't haf to tell a lie. I told Hatcher to take care of Pa and Slim, my youngest boy. I allus send him to the elections with them. Hatcher can knock them out by hittin' them on the chin. Then he drags them off in the weeds till they sober. Better to do that than to get them killed. A man is hard to get. Boys are too hard to raise.

The boys and their pa rode off in the express. Doodle wanted to get polled before seven o'clock. I saw the Clay

Creek people goin' past. Kate Sturgill was barefooted and smokin' her pipe. I saw Pleaze Hackworth and Albert Midshaw goin' down the road on their mules and a wagonload of Bradleys goin' to the election—dogs followin' the wagon. It was a sight to see them! Looked like the whole Creek turned out!

It was just a little while when Hatcher come back to get me. He said Pee-Pee was dog drunk and Brother Hankas was over on the election grounds rippin' and stavin' around on the Jack. It made me so mad I could a bit my pipestem in two. I know Pap and Ma give Hankas better trainin' than that at home.

Brother Hankas is a married man with eight children. Pap has to stop him every now and then when he gets on a big spree. Pap is eighty-seven. Pap makes all his nine boys step. I told Hatcher we'd take Pap with us for we would need his vote before it was over.

"Mom, they ain't nobody even been polled at the election yet but Pa, Uncle Hankas and Pee-Pee Littlejohn," says Hatcher. "Something funny about the whole thing."

"Well," I says, "we'll take Pap anyhow."

When we got to the election ground I was plagued to death to see Brother Hankas on the Jack. The people were gettin' out of his way. It just looked like he was showin' off: He'd ride up the road and holler and whoop as loud as he could. The mares would try to break loose from the saplin's. The Jack would bite at them as he passed. He'd reach out and grab. Once he grabbed Win Bostick by the hip. Of all the hollerin', Win put it up.

It was the quietest election I ever saw. I saw Doodle. He come up through the daisies and he said to me: "Sall, I've just been polled." I could tell Doodle was full as a tick. I can tell when he starts talkin' with his hands. His lips were thick as flour dough.

"Where's them fellows goin' out there in the daisy field?" I says.

"Goin' atter licker," says Doodle. "Never had enough for the boys in the leaf pile this time. Had too many here to vote."

"No use to vote," I says to Doodle, "when they ain't nobody agin you. Nobody's been polled yet. Where are they anyway? What is wrong with this election? You know Melvina Laymore wants the school. They've got something up their sleeves. You're not foolin' this woman."

I went up to the house and voted. There were two judges and three clerks and a man at the door. I just walked in and told them I wanted to vote for the three men that was already polled, Doodle McMeans, Pee-Pee Littlejohn and Hankas Hinton. I just put down a cross there back of each one of their names and walked out. I could see the men comin' out of the daisies. I saw my boy Slim over there.

I could see paths made up among the daisies. I could see men asleep on the hill. Drunk as biled owls. If the Laymore side was here and drunk as our side there would be war. Doodle was down under a persimmon tree. A crowd of boys was around him watchin' him try to stick his knife through the top of his hat. I just went down where Doodle was and I says: "Look here, Doodle

McMeans, if this is all you can do, the best place for you is at home."

"I ain't been polled yet," says Doodle. "Leave me alone, Sall."

"Polled the Devil," I says. "You just don't remember it. You was polled this mornin.' Got ninety-eight votes. You're too drunk to remember you've been polled."

About this time Hankas come tearin' out of the daisy field on the Jack and he whooped out as he passed us. "Old Clay Creek's got them this time. Got them by the heels. Got the old election. Fifteen minutes till four and the polls close at four."

I never heard so much noise in all my life. The people come tearin' out of the woods back of the Beech Grove schoolhouse. It looked like an army of men and wimmen. They come runnin' up to the polls.

"Poll me," says Alex Fields.

"And me, too," says John White, "for this election is just beginnin'." The clerks polled them. They started votin'.

"Go after the Fraziers," says Brother Hankas.

"Too late now," says Doodle, "to go three miles and get people here and vote them in fifteen minutes! We just can't do it. Maybe we've already polled enough votes to beat them. We've polled ninety-eight. Sall's Pa, old Dad, ain't voted yet. Said he's waitin' to see if we needed his vote before he cast it."

Brother Hankas rode up to the hills. "Men and women," he says, "this is a damned dirty trick to play on us from Clay Creek. You low-life Laymores. I'll tell you what I'll do. If we win this election, Ike Laymore, you ride this Jack. If you win this election, I'll do anything you say."

"You can ride Amos Laymore then," says Ike Laymore, "the best man that's ever walked on these grounds."

"It's a go," says Brother Hankas, bitin' his lips. "I'll take him on if the Laymores win this election."

It was just before the polls closed. The Laymores run up and voted fast as they could, Brother Hankas watchin' the clock. He set right there on the Jack. The Jack was foamin' at the mouth and drippin' with sweat and foam from the belly and the hocks.

"I guess they got us," says Kemp Hedd from Clay Creek. "We thought we had them. Guess John won't get the school. Melvina will get it. They are a tricky bunch. Can't uptrip them!"

"Poll's closed," says Brother Hankas.

"A tied vote," says Ike Laymore, "we got ninety-eight votes."

"Tell you what I'll do with you," says Brother Hankas, "if I can ride Amos Laymore, make him say he's a rid man and my Jack throws you—then will you give us the election?

"What do you say, men and women?" said Ike Laymore.

"Yes," they shouted.

"What does my side say?" said Brother Hankas.

"Take them, Hankas," said Doodle. "Get them with your teeth, Hankas! Get them all for me, Hankas. Here's my knife."

When Eif Pratt saw Doodle's knife he pulled his, Jonas Hill pulled his pistol. Men started takin' out their knives.

"Wait a minute," says Brother Hankas. "Let's throw all our guns and pistols, knives and blackjacks here in a pile and do this thing fair. No use shootin' it out or cuttin' now. Let's go on and see who wins. It's all up to me if my side wins. Come on and let's do it fair."

The men throw their knives in a pile. One man throws a razor in the pile. They throw their pistols in the pile. They throw in enough pistols and knives to fight a battle between Clay Creek and the rest of Beech Grove.

"Now guard the heap, boys," says Ike Laymore, "while I ride the Jack and Amos rides Hankas Hinton."

"Hankas is too stiff," says Doodle. "Why, I rode old Hankas the night we went out to the Reeves pond froggin'. A man that's cut timber all his life is too stiff for anything."

I knowed what it took to make the Jack throw Ike. So I just walked up behind the schoolhouse where the cockleburrs grow and got three nice burrs. I sauntered off back toward the Jack. I got up close to him and Hankas was holdin' his nose. I fingered around the saddle a little bit as unconcerned like I was straightenin' it up for Ike. I slipped the burrs under the blanket.

Well, you'd died to have seen Ike leap in the saddle. Old Bill just doubled up with him. He leaped from the earth like a stuck hog! When he fell, he fell on Ike.

"Believe to my soul and God he's broke my leg," hollered Ike. "My God, take him off! Take him off!"

The Jack was squealin' louder than these little sawmill engines blow, and kickin' faster than a fan belt. Hankas run down and got him up. Got him off of Ike.

"I lost," says Ike. "God, that's a mean Jack. Mean as

a striped tail-snake. If he's mine I'd kill him or I'd conquer him. Nothin' like this can conquer the Laymores."

"Only the Hintons," says Brother Hankas. "Come on out here, Amos Laymore! Let's tangle! What kind of holts do we use?"

"Any kind," said Amos. "A break-neck if you want to."

"Don't need it," said Brother Hankas, as he made a wild leap at Amos. I wanted to turn my head. It was too late. Amos just piled Brother Hankas. Nose was bleedin' and his lips busted.

"Enough?" says Amos.

"Ain't begun yet," says Brother Hankas.

Brother Hankas just crawled down to Amos' feet. Amos stood back with his arms folded and laughed. He laughed loud as a cow coughs up a grass seed or a green apple. Then Brother Hankas just leaped up like a squirrel and grabbed him by the ear with his teeth. Of all the hollerin' you ever heard in your life—cryin' and beggin', and Brother Hankas just hangin' on with them old snaggled teeth of hissen!

"All over," says Amos. "Take the election! I've lost my ear!" Brother Hankas spit out Amos's ear.

"We got the election, ain't we, boys?" said Brother Hankas.

"Yes," they shouted, and made a run for their guns and knives. But the fightin' was over. People made for their buggies and horses and express wagons, jolt wagons and surreys. They unhitched their horses from the fences. The sun was goin' down. The day was over.

The lollin' drunk men still lay on the daisies. They were holdin' them down and not pushin' them up yet. Men wobbled past. Doodle was drunk and hollerin' around. He had his knife out shavin' the hairs off his arm. The election was over. Clay Creek winned for the first time in fifty years. John had the school.

My Brother Erric

You don't know us. We're the Pratt family. And we live on Smith Branch in Greenwood County. You've never heard of Greenwood County and you've never heard of Smith Branch. Funny about Smith Branch. There's not a Smith family living on Smith Branch. I guess this creek which is nine miles long was named for the Smith families—and there must have been many—that settled this creek about one hundred and fifty years ago when our part of America was very young.

Now there are many Pratt families on Smith Branch. I think Smith Branch should be changed to Pratt Branch. But I don't have power to do the changing. I do know the nine Pratt families living on Smith Branch in Greenwood County have eighty-one votes. And votes count in

Greenwood County. Votes have power. And we Pratts have a voice due to our numbers. But this is not what I'm about to tell you.

What I'm about to tell you about is my brother Erric. There are nine children in our family. And brother Erric is the only one of my brothers and sisters who has sticky fingers. Brother Erric is bad about picking up things in stores and in public places. Wherever there are loose things and with no one looking, Brother Erric might pick them up. He really likes to possess things. He likes to fill his pockets. And if his pockets can't hold what he picks up he is brazen enough to carry them in a shopping bag —a paper one, of course, or even in his arms.

Of course, we are on food stamps. All the Pratt families on Smith Branch are on food stamps. The land we possess—the poor hillside acres—won't produce enough food to feed us. And why should we try—why should we till the barren slopes and work our daylights out when we can get it free. It doesn't make good sense to work digging on hillsides to get our rations when we can get them free. And the Pratts are not as foolish as people might think. Why shouldn't we get it free if we can?

Receiving food stamps and all the other free benefits we're entitled to doesn't give my brother Erric the right to have sticky fingers. Now, sticky fingers is something everybody in these parts is against. The old saying here is, and according to the courts, if you kill a man—say in self defense—you go free, but if you steal two dollars worth of anything you go to the pen for a year and a day. If you even steal a chicken, you're a goner.

Once brother Erric stole a hen and rooster off a chicken roost tree by using a warm board which he put under them so they wouldn't make any noise. Brother Erric is smart that way in getting things. The warm board on a cold night was very pleasant to chickens. But our Pa knew old John McLean and he paid him five times what the chickens were worth. And Pa got brother Erric's thievery quieted down.

Then, when John Bently slept nights in his country store to catch the one or ones who had been breaking and entering he caught my brother Erric. Brother Erric had climbed up the outside wall, had gone through an attic window and had come down into the store. He caught brother Erric, who didn't go to the cash register but who was going for the candy. But all the same he caught brother Erric, and Pa begged John Bently to say nothing about it. He paid this time one hundred dollars to get brother Erric out of this scrape.

"Erric, why do you have sticky fingers?" Pa asked him. "You're the only one of my nine youngins who has sticky fingers. I know we're on food stamps which is a way of life in these parts—but to have sticky fingers and to steal—this is not like our people. You are an oddling amongst us. I never thought I'd raise a youngin with sticky fingers!"

But Pa *had* raised a youngin with sticky fingers among us. And this plagued my five brothers and three sisters. We were sure that brother Erric might do a big job in Blakesburg, Greenwood's county-seat town, or in some other town larger than Blakesburg. We worried about our brother Erric. Pa and Mom worried about him too since he was an oddling among us. I guess every family that has nine children there is an oddling among them.

Once, I heard Pa talking to Mom: "I think we're in for trouble. I believe Erric will cause it. He has eight sticky fingers and two sticky thumbs. Poor boy can't keep from picking up anything around him. If he'd be out where boys were playing marbles, he'd end up with half their marbles in his pockets. I don't know what makes him like that. His Pa and Ma never stole—and never did any of his people on his Pa's or Ma's side of his family."

Well, I guess brother Erric's big chance did come. He was in Blakesburg, our county-seat town, where he'd gone to see a Saturday-night movie. My poor brother Erric, who had the sticky fingers, was sort of a loner. One thing about him though, he liked good clothes, and even if he did have sticky fingers, he was a neat dresser. He liked a nice suit, a pretty shirt, nice necktie, hat, shoes and socks. As I've said he liked good clothes and he was the fancy dresser among his brothers.

And to tell you more about my brother with the sticky fingers, I think he is the most handsome of my brothers. He is six two, slender, with blue hawk eyes, a sharp pointed nose and tight lips. He is the type of man a young woman looks at twice when he walks by her along the street. Why should the most handsome of us Pratt brothers be the one with the sticky fingers?

One Saturday night while he was in Blakesburg to see a movie, he did a most unusual thing. He didn't get to the movie. Brother Erric observed a store building that was under repair. Brother Erric always watched store buildings where there were nice clothes. Of course, he first looked in at the windows where the lights were on—showing men's and women's clothing. And this happened to be at the McFadden Clothing Store.

This was at a time when McFadden's were repairing their store building. I suppose brother Erric, who was never, or even now, slow in his thinking, looked this store over. Whether he tried to open the door or not, after observing the nice men's clothing in the windows, I do not know. But brother Erric, being our brother with the sticky fingers, found a way to enter.

With this McFadden store under repair, brother Erric looked up where they were repairing the roof. So he climbed up the scaffolding and he went down into the store. He didn't have to open the door to enter. He went down into the store through the roof. And when he entered McFadden's store he had his pickings. He got himself one of the choicest young man's suits. He got himself underwear, handkerchiefs, nine shirts and six pairs of shoes. He fitted himself into a new hat. He gathered unto himself clothes to last him for a year.

But my dear handsome brother Erric made a mistake. He had turned on all the lights in the store and owner Jim McFadden was out strolling on one of his Blakesburg evening walks. He happened to walk by his store. When he observed the thief inside he called the Blakesburg night policeman, Stubby Fetters.

He entered the building and caught my poor brother

Erric. He really wasn't too hard to catch. He was really gullible. Really he was an easy thief—a harmless and pleasant thief—one who liked nice clothes and nice things. But brother Erric was a great catch for night patrolman Stubby Fetters. That very night Erric was taken to the Blakesburg jail. Poor boy! He was caught with all the clothes he'd taken from the store. He was caught red-handed. This time there was no escape. And it didn't look like there could be any escape.

Now my father had got brother Erric out of all his episodes, out of all his troubles before this big one. We, his brothers and sisters, had helped too—because we had actually prayed for our brother—because we had always been one for all and all for one. But, now brother Erric was in big-time thievery. He had really done it. We couldn't help him. He had been caught red-handed. And at our home we wept for our brother. Mom cried herself sick. There was no escape this time. The sharp eyes and the sharp teeth of the law had our brother Erric, and he was in the cooler.

Now, from the sharp eyes of the law we thought—really we knew—there was no escape. Our poor brother Erric at last was caught in the act. He had to confess his guilt. And he would be sentenced. He would no longer be a part of our family. And this would be something. Not to have our brother, one of the nine in our family. We had been close. One for all and all for one. Brother Erric in the Blakesburg jail.

"Erric is gone this time," Pa said. "We've tried to raise him right."

And my mother wept more. Strange but the oddling in a family the mother and father love more than the other children. Mom, I think, thought more of Erric than any of her nine children or anybody on earth. Pa favored him too over all the rest of us. But now, our brother Erric was faced with the sharp teeth of the law. There could be no other way. He was caught in Blakesburg's finest store—stealing the clothes which he liked.

There was no hope for my brother. Pa couldn't get him out of this one. My brother Erric in jail. My father had to go his bond to get him out of jail and get him home. He could do this. His bond wasn't big—twenty-five hundred. Our farm was worth more than this.

Now, let me tell you the end of this story. Erric came home—not with the clothing he had stolen but he came home to us. We welcomed him with open arms. He was back with us—our brother. We knew Erric was guilty. And we thought he'd go to the penitentiary. Poor boy! Our brother! He'd be the first of our family ever to go to prison.

Well, we got our brother a lawyer. He was appointed by the state for us. As I've said we don't have money and we live on food stamps. Really the state keeps our family and all the Pratts on Smith Branch. But we do have eighty-one votes in our family. Eighty-one votes is more than money in our county and state. Eighty-one votes is powerful. Eighty-one votes is wealth.

Let me tell you what happened in our higher court. Pa didn't think brother Erric had a chance—not one in our family thought he had a chance.

But here is what happened in the "higher courts." You know the higher courts. I think the higher courts, whatever they may be—are wonderful. Yes, when our prosecuting attorney, Jackson Keeney, said: "Erric Pratt didn't open the door—he didn't break and enter as you have him charged here. He climbed up the wall and went down and entered this store. Under the real sharp eye of the law you don't really have a case against this man. I am throwing this out of the high court." And throw it out he did. Brother Erric wasn't even tried.

Now this is what makes me proud of America. I am proud of the sharp eyes of the law. Right here was an important decision. That my brother Erric didn't open the door to McFadden Clothing Store—but, instead, he climbed up the wall of the store—up the carpenter's scaffolding and went down into the store from the roof. He really didn't break and enter—but he went up and over and down the wall. So, by doing this he evaded the sharp eyes of the law. Wasn't this the smart thing? To evade the sharp eyes of the law? But with Mom's prayers and ours, Brother Erric was lucky. So thank Heaven for the sharp eyes of the law of America. Thank Heaven that my brother Erric came clear of all charges.

And thank Heaven that my brother Erric is the most important of all the nine children in our family. He is really best known of all my sisters and brothers. Because he got a lot of publicity about entering the McFadden Clothing Store. He was the first and only one of us ever to get a picture in the papers. Think of this! My brother with the sticky fingers is the best known of all of us. He is a free man and his fingers can stick again. Maybe, his fingers will stick again and maybe they won't. It's not for me to say. I can only hope they won't. But I don't really know. But I will say he has been a lucky young man.

The Judge Takes a Holiday

The first time I ever saw the Judge was in the courthouse.
I went there to hear a trial. It was the time they tried
Leander Baisley's boy over that Spriggs girl and made 'im
marry 'er. I went there with my man Dave. Th' whole
house was crowded. Plenty o' wimmen there. I'm a-tellin'
you that trial had to come out like it did. Jist a-better had
a shotgun weddin' in the first place like th' Judge said,
and not be draggin' sich little matters into court. It
wasn't th' trial so much as it was th' way th' Judge
handled it.

I punched my man Dave in the ribs and I says: "Look
at th' Judge, won't you? He knows his business, don't
he? Jist once in a while he has to turn to that big law
book and show 'em somethin' when he tells 'em. Th'

Judge is a deep man." I could tell Dave didn't like the way I bragged on the Judge.

Dave says: "Yes, if you want to call 'im a deep man. Plays poker and bets on race horses. Drinks more whiskey than any five men in this courthouse. He's a dangerous man and not a deep man. I belong to his party, but I'll never vote fer 'im!"

Dave was just jealous. I could tell. My Dave, so little, like a scrubby white oak on a old poor bank. My Dave, with a little store a-sellin' baskets o' grub and a lot of 'em on credit until th' farmers sold their tobacco crops. W'y he didn't have the color in his face th' Judge had. I thought th' Judge was th' best-lookin' man I ever saw from th' first time I ever laid my eyes on 'im. Great big handsome man—face red as a beet sliced in two soon as it's pulled out'n the garden. Great big blue eyes behind a big pair of black-rimmed specks! And th' finest pair o' legs you ever saw on a man in Kentucky. Great long legs, and th' way they'd step. It's th' way th' Judge carries himself. Just like a thoroughbred Kentucky Bluegrass horse. He jist reaches out with his long legs and paws in the dirt—I love th' way th' Judge walks. Not some old shriveled-up Judge walkin' with a cane. Wears them tight-fittin', pin-striped, gray-worsted pants. I could tell from th' first time I ever saw th' Judge that he was th' man atter my own heart.

I went home that night with Dave. Back to th' same little old farm. Back to th' same little old place with a store beside the road. I just couldn't be contented. I couldn't go back to raisin' chickens fer th' store and helpin' Dave. Dave was so little, with his little hands and feet and his little wrinkled-up face. Th' Judge was so big and handsome. Color was in his face. He had big soft hands. He wore his shoes all shined like a lookin' glass. The way he walked. W'y, he was worth a million dollars jist fer a woman to look at.

I heard he was married. But that didn't make no difference. He was my dream man. You know besides wimmen havin' husbands, lots o' 'em have dream men. Th' Judge was my dream man. He was th' Lantern County judge. He didn't haf to run no store like Dave to make a livin'. He made his livin' with his head and books.

I said to Dave: "Why don't you clean up like the Judge? Why don't you grow a foot taller and get some color in your face? Why don't your hands and feet grow some more?"

Dave said: "That's crazy of you to talk like that. I'm too old to grow. A man can't grow no more atter he's forty."

Then I said: "Why don't you clean up then and wear white shirts and big striped neckties? Why don't you get you some tight-legged, gray-worsted suits with pinstripes runnin' down th' legs? Why don't you smoke big cigars and be somebody? Why don't you look like Judge Whittlecomb?"

Dave jist turned all kins o' colors before he could get th' words out'n his mouth: "Damn the Judge to hell no-how! You like him right now better than you do me! If I got as much of th' people's tax money as he's a-gettin' fer settin' up there on my tail and doin' nothin', then I

235

could wear white shirts and big ties and pin-legged pants too! I could have my shoes made to order and shined 'till you could see yourself in 'em. I could be somebody!"

I never said anything more to Dave about th' Judge. I took th' crates o' eggs to town and Dave stayed in th' store. It was on Saturday. I had some things to get in town fer th' store. I driv th' mules to town. I wondered if I'd make a good-lookin' wife fer th' Judge. I wondered if he even dreamed that his second wife was bringin' a express-wagon load o' eggs to town. I jist had to stop th' express wagon before I got to town and put a little powder on my nose and a little rose-bloom on my cheeks.

I didn't any more than get in town until I saw th' Judge. He went in th' drugstore. I hitched th' mules up to a telephone pole. I made it my business to go in th' drugstore. I wanted to get in before he got out. I'd get a cone of ice cream or a box of face powder. Jist somethin' so I could see th' Judge. When I walked in th' Judge jist turned and looked me over. He turned away from his cigars. Th' man ast me what I wanted and I says: "A box of face powder, please. Th' very best you got." I could tell th' Judge liked my looks. A woman can tell by th' way a man stares. And when a man leaves his ter-backer for a woman! Well, he's a goner.

I turned to th' Judge and says: "Good mornin', Judge Whittlecomb."

The Judge says: "Good mornin', lady." He tipped his soft gray hat and jist smiles. And I guess I smiled too while I was waitin' fer th' box o' powder.

I says: "You don't know me. I'm Bertha Stone—Dave Stone's wife. We's in to hear th' trial th' other day when you spoke of a shotgun weddin' . . . W'y, I thought I'd die a laughin'. I thought you handled that trial so well. I told Dave, I did."

"Oh, that's you," said the Judge. He put a big cigar to his mouth and lit it with a big fancy lighter. Struck the fire with his hands.

And I says: "Judge, you're awfully young to have th' big job you have. You are a deep man."

The Judge jist acted a little bashful. I got the box o' powder and paid th' druggist a quarter fer it. I started to walk out'n th' store. Th' Judge stepped out, too. Th' smoke was rollin' from his big cigar. Oh, but he was a monstrous big man. I was up beside of 'im now. I tell you I felt thrilled. Th' Judge was my love. Poor old Dave back there a-slavin' his life away with th' chickens and the store! Here I was in town with th' Judge. I jist felt sorry fer little Dave. I couldn't love 'im. If he was th' only man left in this world and we's put out on an island together, I couldn't love 'im. Th' Judge was my love.

I couldn't help it if he was a married man. In this life I feel like among th' wimmen it's grab and take. You jist get th' other woman's man afore she gets yourn. Lord, how I would have traded her my Dave fer th' Judge—this woman th' Judge was tied to. I'd never seen 'er. I didn't want to see 'er. I hated 'er!

"It's a purty day, Mrs. Stone," says th' Judge.

And I says: "Yes, it's a mighty purty day, Judge." I started walkin' down toward th' express wagon. Th' Judge just walked along beside o' me. I says: "Are you runnin' again, Judge?"

He says: "Yes, I guess I'll run again."

I says: "I'm fer you. I'll vote fer you and I'll get you all the voters I can. I'll get out and work fer you."

The Judge says: "You must be a mighty good wife to Dave Stone."

I says: "I'd make some man a good wife. But I don't make Dave Stone a good wife. I don't love him, Judge. But here I am talkin' to you like this and the first day I ever talked to you."

"That's all right," says the Judge. "A lot of us have our troubles. I have troubles myself."

When he said he had troubles my face began to color. I thought: "There might be a chance fer me. I'm goin' to tell 'im that I love 'im." Then I thought: "I'd better wait a minute and let 'im lead up to it." All th' time we's gettin' nearer th' express wagon. I says: "Don't you love your wife, Judge?"

And he says: "Oh, in a way I do. But I could love deeper. I don't love 'er like I ought to love 'er."

I jist had to say it. My heart ached so. I says: "Judge, th' first time I saw you in that courthouse, I fell in love with you. I made my man Dave mad th' way I talked. He got jealous o' you. I told him you was th' finest-lookin' man I ever saw. I guess I said the wrong thing to 'im. I ast 'im why he didn't grow some more and get as big as you. Then I ast 'im to dress like you and smoke big cigars like you smoke. Dave got so mad at me he nearly died. And he said a lot of things about you, Judge, that I'm not tellin' you. You jist watch Dave. He's little but he's mighty. He's a dangerous man."

"That's funny," says th' Judge, "I felt that way about

you soon as you come into that drugstore over there. I felt like you'd been the true love o' my life that I had missed. All of my young days come back to me. I could see th' girls go past. And among all of them . . . I saw you . . . jist a little younger than you are now but not any more beautiful. . . . Jist how old are you?"

"Judge, I'll tell you the truth," I says, "I'm thirty-four years old. I don't have no children. Not that I don't want 'em. Dave says he wants 'em, too. But we jist don't have 'em. We've got a little old dog we call our boy . . . a little old, long-haired, poodle dog."

We stopped by th' wagon now. I wasn't ashamed to let th' Judge know about me drivin' th' express-wagon load of eggs to town. I had found out the Judge was jist a good old family man. The Judge says to me: "I don't have any children in my home either. I want 'em. Polly says she wants 'em. But we jist don't have 'em. Jist th' two of us. It's a funny thing that you two are like that and we are that way."

Th' Judge puffed on his cigar. I'll never forget how sweet that cigar smoke smelled and the thousands of dreams that drifted away before my eyes on them big blue clouds o' smoke. I could see th' Judge as my husband. I could see a cozy little house with rose vines above the gatepost. I could see our little curly-headed girl playin' on th' grass. I could see myself goin' down th' street with th' Judge a-holdin' my hand and me so proud o' 'im!

"I'm goin' up on Shelf's Fork for a holiday next Monday," says th' Judge, "and you can come up there

239

some way. Leave Dave at home. I'll leave Polly at home. I'll tell her I'm on a fishin' trip with a bunch o' men. I'll be at th' Big Camp, right by th' Deep Hole in Shelf's Fork. You know where that is. I'll be in that little house down to th' left, on th' bank of th' crick. That's where you'll find me."

"I'll be right there," I says. "I'll be there some way. But if Dave finds me up there with you, he'll kill both of us."

"I'm not afraid of Dave," says th' Judge. "I'll handle Dave. He sells whiskey, don't he? And don't Tim Snider make th' whiskey fer him? Puts it in th' baskets of groceries Dave sends out. Dave will be my best friend before this thing is over. I've bought Dave Stone's 'groceries'!"

Th' Judge jist smiled and puffed on th' short stub o' his cigar. I jist stood and watched him walk down the street. Jist th' way he carried himself, so big and strong and powerful . . . so well-dressed . . . what woman wouldn't want th' Judge? He was my man. Jist to stand and watch 'im paw on th' street like a racehorse! And to think I had a chance of gettin' th' Judge!

I took th' eggs to th' produce house to ship to Cincinnati. Boys unloaded 'em fer me. I jist set on th' express-wagon seat with th' checklines in my hands and looked off into space. I would see th' judge Monday mornin' on his holiday. It sounded like a dream to me. I took th' express-wagon home and walked in th' store. I handed Dave th' money for th' eggs. Dave says to me: "Honey, what makes you so happy?"

I says: "Do I act like I'm happy?"

Dave says: "Of course you do."

I says: "Oh, I saw th' Judge."

I laughed real big so Dave wouldn't believe me.

"Ah," he says, "quit that a-kiddin' me!"

And he started laughin' too. Dave laughed and I laughed.

I pretended Dave was Judge Whittlecomb. I made myself believe I was in th' little dream house with roses above th' door and roses above th' archway over th' gate. I pretended our dog Old Bob was a little girl with ribbons on 'er hair. My whole life had changed. I was a happy woman. It had jist worked out like a dream.

Dave was so happy all day Sunday because I was happy. I walked with Dave back over th' farm. We planned this and that fer next year. Dave was th' happiest I'd ever seen him because I was so happy. He'd say: "Yes, my lovey-dovey . . . yes, my darlin'. You can have this. You can have that." I jist pretended Dave was th' Judge all th' time . . . I'd find myself jist floatin' like a cloud when I'd think of th' Judge. I'd find myself fightin' Polly, th' Judge's wife. I'd never seen her, I thought she was a big ugly-lookin' cow. I jist didn't want to see her. I was walkin' with th' Judge. He was my husband and I was his wife.

Monday mornin' Dave went back to salt the cows. He left me to stay in th' store fer 'im while he was gone. When Dave came back he didn't find me there. I got th' mules and hitched 'em to th' express wagon. I'm tellin' you I turned th' curves on two wheels. I whopped th' mules right up th' road and crossed the bridge into Bolt's

Run, th' little town where Polly was. Then, I headed right up Shelf's Fork to th' Camp, that little camp house by th' old divin' tree, right by th' deep hole. I jist left a streak of dust behind me fer fourteen miles. When I got there my mules was wet with sweat. I never saw so many people there. I thought jist th' Judge would be there. But to tell you th' truth I didn't care. Th' Judge was mine. He loved me and I loved 'im.

Here stood th' Judge in front of his cabin smokin' a big cigar and watchin' the boys dive off th' tree. When a boy hit th' water belly-buster, th' Judge would jist haw-haw and laugh. He says to me: "Honey, you got here, didn't you? I knowed you'd do it. Here is our little house all fixed up inside. Go in and see how you'll like it."

I went in th' house. It wasn't th' dream house I'd planned, but it was all right fer me and th' Judge. I says to him: "Judge, don't you think I'll make you a good wife?"

He says: "I know that, darlin'. You don't even haf to ast me that. You are goin' to be my wife, too. I'm not gettin' you up here jist fer a good time. I'm gettin' you up here to put th' question to you about how we are goin' to manage this thing. We've got to get married."

I says: "I don't know, Judge. You're the Law. You ought to know more about it than I do, honey. I'll take your advice any old time."

I jist left my mules out by th' house hitched to a syca-more. They's glad to stand and rest. I went to rollin' up my sleeves and gettin' dinner fer th' Judge. Jist to have 'im beside me smokin' them big sweet-smellin' cigars! A man with his high place in life and him so young. I says: "Honey, how did you get to be judge and you so young?"

He says: "W'y, I never went to college. I studied at home at night when th' other boys were runnin' and kickin' up their heels. Now their heels is in my hands. I've got my reward fer all my hard work. I'm a self-made man. I've worked fer what I've got. You got to work fer all you get in this old world. And I'm right now workin' on how to get you fer my wife so we'll be seen respectfully by th' eyes of th' law."

When I put dinner on th' table you ought to a-seen th' way th' Judge et. He'd say: "W'y these are th' best biscuits I ever tasted. Jist melt in your mouth. You are sure a good cook. And this coffee . . . ah, it is wonderful! I love it."

I says: "Honey, I love to cook fer you. I'd get up at any time durin' th' night and make you a biler o' black coffee. I'd make you good biscuits and cook you ham fer breakfast and fry you eggs. I'd jist love to do it and to keep th' house fer you."

Atter dinner I cleaned th' dishes and swept th' floor. Th' Judge set by th' table and smoked his cigars. Th' room was filled with smoke. I was so happy. I'd never been so happy in my life. I kept watchin' people out around th' swimmin' hole stare in at us. I saw a lot of people who traded at our store. It didn't matter to me if they all saw us. Who were they? They'd be glad to be in my shoes! Th' wimmen out there in that crowd would trade their husbands in a minute fer a man good-lookin' as th' Judge. He was the dream man o' many wimmen.

Th' people out there a-starin' in at us was th' old Gullets, Scymores, Blazes and Thombs! Jist a whole crowd of 'em! It was no skin off'n their shanks because I was with th' Judge. Girls out there tryin' to peep in our little house. I jist politely closed th' door!

Atter I got th' dishes washed and wiped and th' floor cleaned w'y I went over and set down on th' Judge's lap. He was through smokin' now. He put his arms around me and kissed me. I tell you it was Heaven to me. I was never so thrilled in all my life. I says to th' Judge: "Judge, I've never knowed what love was before. I've jist heard about it! This is my first true love, though I've been married to Dave fer fifteen years."

Th' Judge jist smiled. He run his middle finger and his index finger down across my nose. He helt his thumb betwixt these fingers. Then he says: "Look, I got your nose!" Jist as playful as a kitten. I was there all cuddled in his arms like a cat in th' egg basket.

I says: "You leave my nose alone, darlin'."

He jist kissed my face and kissed it.

I says: "Judge, this is th' real love. Young people are too silly to love. Love comes in the thirties . . . th' real love! I've never knowed love before. I jist knowed what they called 'puppy love.' Judge, don't you think love comes with th' thirties?"

"I do," says th' Judge, and he kissed me again and again.

Jist to think, a week ago th' Judge was in the courthouse sendin' moonshiners to th' pen. Now I was in his arms. He was woolin' me like a kitten.

Th' Judge tickled me under th' chin and told me th' awfulest thing about a woman dyin' and her picture comin' out on her tombstone atter five years because her husband married again. I says to th' Judge; "Sugar, if I was to die and some woman was to get you, my likeness would come out on my tombstone, too."

Th' Judge tickled my chin again. He kissed me and said: "Little Bo-Peep . . . lost her sheep . . ."

He didn't get to say any more. There was th' awfulest rap on our door. It flung open, and there stood Dave.

"I've caught you this time!" he yells. "Oh, so happy, huh! Guessed you come out here to see that scoundrel. Bring 'im out'n there. I want to see th' color of his liver!"

Dave pulled a long blue gun. I screamed; "Oh, Dave you can't do that!"

"Never mind," says th' Judge. "He's not goin' to do anything. He knows he'll hang before tomorrow night if he does! Oh yes, Davy, my boy, jist go on and shoot me! Remember, I'm in love with your wife—I'm going to marry 'er!"

"You . . ." says Dave. His eyes got as big with surprise as goose eggs. Dave must a-thought I was jist out with th' Judge. When he found out I was goin' to marry 'im it was somethin' different.

"You know, Dave, Bertha don't love you—she loves me! And I love her. Now I get your wife and you take mine if you want her. Polly'll make you a good wife. If you don't do this, I'll send you to the pen! You know I can do it. How long have you been peddlin' that moonshine whiskey out in grub baskets? How many baskets o'

32 VOTES BEFORE BREAKFAST

your grub have I had? When you go to th' pen, Bertha
can get a divorce then. The law will jist give 'er one. I'll
get 'er any way! Now you listen to reason, Dave, don't
be foolish. Put that damned old gun up. I've seen so
many I'm tired o' lookin' at 'em."

"You want my wife, do you, Judge?"

"Yes, I want your Bertha," says th' Judge.

"You got everything else you want. I guess you'll get
'er. You got me. If it warn't fer wastin' two shells, I'd
blow your livers into eternity."

I was scared to death. Little Dave lookin' in at th'
door. He was shakin' like a leaf in the wind with that big
gun in his hand. His eyes sparkled fire like a cat's eyes
atter dark. Th' Judge standin' by th' table in our little
room jist as brave as a lion lookin' right at his gun. His
face was flushed so red it looked like th' blood would pop
out any minute. It made me love 'im more. Two men
standin' face to face, and a gun ready is enough to scare
a woman! I didn't mind. I was ready to die with th' Judge.

"Get 'em damned old mules and express wagon,"
says th' Judge, "and get back to your store where you
belong! Go tell my wife if you want to. It will jist save
me from doin' it."

Dave says: "I'll haf to let you have 'er, Judge. I'd
ruther you'd take 'er and me know about it as to have
you slippin' around like this. I don't want this goin' on
under my nose. I ain't goin' to have it!"

Th' Judge says: "Nothin's goin' on under your nose er
behind your back that wouldn't go on before that face o'
yours."

"You can have 'er," says Dave. Poor little old Dave, I felt sorry fer 'im. He put the gun in its holster. He went out and unhitched th' mules. He got in th' express wagon and rid off. One of the Gullets rid his horse back. I knowed they was th' ones that went back and told Dave I was here with th' Judge. They don't belong to th' Judge's party. They fit 'im in all th' elections. If th' Judge has th' chance he'll make it go hard with th' Gullets! I was glad Dave was gone.

"Well, what are we goin' to do now," I says to th' Judge. "We are into it to our necks. This will be told all over Lantern County. Dave will go tell Polly. She'll start suin' fer a divorce on grounds o' neglect or desertion. Are we goin' to stay in our little dream house, honey?"

"That's jist what we are goin' to do, honey, until court starts. Then I must go back to town. I've got a lot of gun-totin' charges, shotgun weddin' cases and a lot of moonshine-whiskey charges. I'm in love fer th' first time in my life and haf to work. Wish all my life was a honeymoon here with you, honey! Jist out here on Shelf's Fork where we can hear th' whippoorwills and th' frogs."

And then th' Judge jist naturally put his arms round me again.

We jist lived in our dream house. It was little, but we made out. Soon I saw Polly th' first time. She was with Dave. They were runnin' around together. It was causin' a lot of talk. No wonder th' Judge warn't satisfied with Polly. W'y Polly couldn't a-driv th' mules to town with the express wagon loaded with eggs. She's like a piece of glass ready to break. I says to th' Judge: "Honey, I may not have enough education to be your wife and be respectable talkin' among th' other wimmen, but I'll make you a better wife than her. Men do look at me twice yet when I pass 'em."

Th' Judge says: "Polly's in love with Dave. She jist suits him. With th' education she's got, she can be a lot of help to Dave in th' store. It'll work out a trade yet. I won't haf to send Dave to th' pen."

I felt sorry for Dave. Dave thought he loved me. But I heard about 'im first goin' once a week to see Polly. Then I heard he went twice a week to see her. Then Carrie Gullet told me he was goin' every night to see her. The Gullets know everything. Jist ast a Gullet and you get the news.

I lived in the camp house with th' Judge waitin' fer 'im to get possession of his own house. Th' Judge says: "I'll get possession real soon, honey. Jist be patient."

I says: "That don't worry me a bit, honey! I could live in a hog pen with you and be happy. I couldn't live in a mansion with Dave. It would kill me. I lost fifteen years o' my life livin' with the wrong man."

Th' Judge says: "I had the wrong woman, too. I was livin' with th' wrong woman fer seventeen years."

August passed by. Th' falltime come and th' leaves turned brown. Th' Judge would go out and bring in big loads o' birds and rabbits. Th' Judge is a big hunter. I tell you, life was Heaven to me in th' little camp house by th' swimmin' hole on Shelf's Fork. We jist kept waitin' fer possession of his house and fer Polly and Dave to marry.

It warn't a bit o' trouble in th' world. It jist worked out wonderful. Of course a lot of th' wimmen started talkin' around. That's to be expected. They stuck their long necks over th' yard palin's and gossiped about us. We's the talk o' Lantern County fer a year. Then it all died down, jist like a fire atter it burns th' wood. Th' Judge went right on with his work.

You see, th' Judge presided when I got my divorce from Dave. He presided when he got his own divorce, too. We jist wanted our divorces, and we got 'em. Nobody objected to it. We all knowed what we wanted. We got it. Th' Judge and I jumped th' broom th' next day. I was dressed fit to kill.

Three days later Polly and Dave got hitched. Didn't have th' decency to wait a respectable time at all. Well, I hope Dave is as happy with her as I am with th' Judge, but I jist don't see how he ever can be.

Law in Poppie's Vest Pocket

When the doorbell rang, Poppie and I were in the living room. He was resting in his favorite chair with his feet propped high. He was enjoying his expensive cigar and was blowing smoke rings toward the ceiling. When the doorbell rang the second time, I got up and opened the door.

"I'm Sergeant John Diller of the state police," said a man who was tall and blond. He was straight as a ramrod and about twenty-five. His blue eyes twinkled and his lips were tight. "Is this where Rosalee Littleton lives?"

"Sure she lives here," I stammered. I felt a heat wave go over me. I almost choked when I tried to talk. "What's wrong?"

I looked back at Poppie and he was rising straight from his chair without the support of his big hands on its arms.

"The Law, huh," he grumbled. "What does the Law want?"

"I have a date with Rosalee is all," he said.

"That's what you think," Poppie said, walking over. "Sergeant John Diller, your name sounds familiar! Didn't you arrest my daughter?" Poppie puffed on his cigar and sent a cloud of light-gray smoke to the high ceiling. "I believe you're that State Policeman I heard her talkin' about."

"Yes, we met under unusual circumstances," he admitted. He tried to smile as Poppie focused his small black eyes on him. "She ran a stoplight and I arrested her."

"But she didn't pay a fine," Poppie said as he blew another cloud of smoke.

"She beat the case," Sergeant Diller said softly.

"I'll say she beat it," Poppie said, blowing another cloud of smoke to the ceiling. "I carry an awful lot of law in my vest pocket."

Sergeant Diller looked strangely at my father.

"I can't understand my daughter havin' a date with the Law," Poppie said, trembling until I thought his cigar would fall from his hand. "What is this all about?"

"John, I'm sorry to be late," Rosalee said. "I wasn't quite ready when you came. But I suppose you've been well received."

251

"Yes, very well," he said, smiling. Then he looked up at Poppie's rugged six-foot-four frame, but he didn't smile. "I'm not too early, am I?"

"Rosalee, where are you going with this man?" Poppie asked. "Didn't this man arrest you? Didn't he even try to get you fined in the judge's court?"

"But I must admit the sergeant was right," she said, turning quickly to Poppie. "I did run a stoplight and that was wrong. I didn't pay a fine and that was wrong, too. I'm goin' to the show with John."

Rosalee was beautiful standing there beside John Diller. But she didn't come up to his shoulder and her black hair and dark eyes contrasted with his blond hair and blue eyes. When John Diller looked into my sister's eyes I could see a new light come to his. And I knew our father hated every man who had anything to do with the Law. And he hated the Law for reasons of his own.

"Well, Rosalee, if you must go with a policeman, all right. But remember," he said, shaking his long cigar wildly with gray ashes falling on the floor, "it's not with my consent and pleasure. I'm not sending you to the finest woman's college in this country to educate you for a policeman's wife!"

"Mr. Littleton, speaking of a college education—I have one," Sergeant Diller said, looking seriously at Poppie. "I have a degree from the state university. I worked my way through."

"Then, what are you doin' in them rags?" Poppie shouted. He looked Sergeant Diller's uniform over from the braid on the shoulders to the tassel on the hat and black stripes up the seams of his pants.

"I'm proud of this uniform, Mr. Littleton," Sergeant Diller said. "To me it represents the emblem of service to the people of this state. I feel that I can do as much good as . . ."

"That's enough," Poppie interrupted as he turned to go. "I know a little about the Law too."

Rosalee and Sergeant Diller walked quietly down the steps.

Poppie walked over to his big favorite rocker where he dropped down in it. I followed him and picked up the afternoon paper.

"That beats all," he said as he laid his cigar on the tray. "A man who's had as many run-ins with the Law as I've had and then my only daughter goes out with a policeman! A graduate of the state university, huh? I'll see! He's feedin' Rosalee a line! I'll check on him!"

"Poppie, our Kentucky state police are the best trained in America," I said. "They are second to English bobbies!"

"How do you know, Adger?" he asked.

"I read that in this paper not more than a month ago," I said.

"That paper feeds the people bunk," Poppie shouted. "Adger, I'm a practical man. You know my business. It's not what a lot of people call the right kind. I've been in it twenty years. I've been a success too. If I'm not a success, how could we live in the best residential district in Auckland?"

Poppie pulled another expensive cigar from his inside coat pocket. He struck a match with his thumb and lit his cigar.

"If Rosalee lived back on Greasy Ridge in Darter County, a ridge five miles long with two houses and no roads leading to it, I wonder if Sergeant Diller would want to date 'er?" He asked me, as he sent a cloud of smoke from his fresh cigar. "Would he climb Greasy Ridge through the redbrush, broom sedge and saw briars to see her? If we lived back there and he did this, I'd call it love. But I don't believe he would. He's afraid of tearin' his pretty uniform. Well, he got his eyes opened when he saw where we live. Maybe he doesn't know the business I'm in.

"I belong to some good organizations in this town and I give a lot to charity," he said, fingering in his vest pocket for a match. "If that sergeant had ideas about me, he'll have to forget them. I can beat him on any fine points of law."

"He's not after you, Poppie," I said. "He came to see Rosalee. I could see a love light in his eyes! Don't you get suspicious because he is the Law."

"Well, sooner or later," Poppie said, puffing smoke clouds from his cigar, "he'll learn about my business. He'll know, too, that I own my business lock, stock and barrel and that I made the pit and the arena with these two big hands. And when a man builds his business the hard way, he's not goin' to let a college graduate in his fine police uniform that we taxpayers pay for come in and tear it down!"

"But if he loves Rosalee . . ."

"Say, that's an idea," he said with a big grin. "If a man loves a woman, he'll bend over backwards. I could get chummy with the sergeant. I could treat him like I treat you. I b eve he might cooperate."

Poppie got up from his soft rocker and walked the floor. Then, he sat down again. He was a worried man. When he walked the floor, he was worried. He wouldn't go to bed until Rosalee came home. We heard the car park outside; we heard laughter and whispers. When they walked up the steps there was whispers. When they walked up the steps there was that last minute of silence before Rosalee came in.

"Well, how was your policeman?" Poppie asked trying to smile.

"Very, very nice," she said smiling. "I'm sorry you weren't nicer!"

"I couldn't be to him," he said. "What would your mother think of this man?"

"She'd love him," Rosalee said. "She'd approve."

"Rosalee, if you must go with 'im, bring him in and let me talk with 'im," Poppie said, trying to smile. "I'd like to know more about him. I know he's the Law."

"You're a wonderful father," Rosalee said, running over to Poppie. She tiptoed over and put her arms around his neck. "He's a policeman with high ideals! He's wonderful!"

Rosalee was smiling when she went up to her room. I'd never seen her so happy. And I remember before she went to college how Poppie approved of her going with Bill

255

Bennington who worked for us. When Bill came to see Rosalee, Poppie talked to him more than Rosalee. She never smiled when she was dating Bill. After she finished high school and went to college she forgot Bill. After three years in college she'd come home, ran a red light and was having dates with the state policeman who had arrested her.

"You know, Poppie, you had just as well invite John here," Rosalee said at the breakfast table. "There's no use to mention Bill again!"

"This can't be serious between you and that policeman?" Poppie said.

"I'm in love with him," she said. "I knew it the minute he gave me that ticket. It was love at first sight."

"Has he proposed marriage to you?" Poppie asked, his face coloring.

"No, but he will," she replied.

"But, what about my business?" Poppie said. "You know what it is!"

"You've handled everything else, Poppie," I said. "Can't you handle Sergeant Diller?"

"I might offer him a partnership in the business," he said. "If he doesn't want that, I'll find him something to do besides being a policeman. He can't make enough to keep you on his small salary."

"I'll live on his small salary and have peace of mind!" she said, rising from the table. "I've had enough insults in my lifetime over your business."

Sergeant Diller came three times a week to see Rosalee. Then we knew her romance with him was serious. Poppie got real chummy with John. One evening when he was in his rocker with his feet propped upon the footstool, smoking a cigar, John said something that pleased him.

"Mr. Littleton, since you and I are going to know each other for a long time, if I should ever have to arrest you, it will be embarrassing," he said. "But, if you break the law, I'll see that we take your trial to one of the lower courts. You won't be fined five hundred dollars and costs as you have been fined in County Judge Burton's court. It's always cost you a lot to get a new trial and beat the case. I'll be easy on you."

Poppie laughed and blew a cloud of smoke.

"Now you're talkin' right, John. You're welcome here in my house!"

"I know I am," John said, smiling at Rosalee.

"We can get along, John," Poppie said. "When there's anything I can do for you, let me know!"

While Rosalee and John kept on dating, Poppie and I continued with our business. There was much talk in Auckland about Rosalee's dating John Diller. There was talk over Auckland how Poppie had John Diller in his vest pocket. John Diller had been sent to Auckland by the state to assist the law in cleaning up the town. Our business was one of the biggest items on the list. There was talk all over the state that since Poppie was "big time" he had the state police and the city Law all in his little vest pocket. Because our business went on from Saturday night until Sunday morning over each weekend.

Spring had come and gone, and, now, part of the summer had gone. August had always been one of our best months since so many people were on vacation and everybody was loaded with money and ready for an exciting weekend.

This Saturday evening wasn't any different from any other Saturday evening that had come and gone over the years that were now faded memories of the past. We left our palatial home in the swank Auckland residential district. Poppie sat at the wheel of the car which was so long it needed a swivel in the middle so it could turn the corners. He had a big cigar in his mouth and he drove leisurely along over the Auckland streets he loves so well. He was very careful about stoplights.

"I never ran a stoplight in my life," he told me. "I've always been careful not to break the law in that respect. And, Adger, I've always paid my bills. I suppose you could call your father an honest man, even if his business has not been approved by the Law."

Poppie drove to the outskirts where he turned left on the Sadner Road and followed the Sadner River for a couple of miles. Here he turned left again on a narrow graveled road. There wasn't a house up this deep dark valley because Poppie had bought the land so we could keep our arena at a safe distance. He had always said the pit was explosive and should be a safe distance from homes.

"When a man's got a business he should always be there early," Poppie said, getting out of the car and knocking the ash from his long cigar with his index finger. "He should welcome the customers. Remember that, Adger! When I'm gone and you take over, remember how to carry on. That's why I've taught you from the bottom up. I know you don't like to dry-pick the roosters when they're killed. I know you don't have to do it. It's not been the five cents you get for pickin' each one! It's good training. It's the hard way. It's from the bottom up. You must learn every part of this business."

I didn't like to dry-pick the roosters, still warm, spurred to death and the warm blood still oozing from them and sometimes the last breath not gone. I didn't know whether or not I was going to like the business well enough to stay with it. But I didn't tell my father my thoughts. I was in high school, too, and I was thinking about something else. I'd had a lot of things said to me by my classmates and the people in town about my father and the business we were in. I didn't like these things that had been said to me. My classmates were jealous of my good clothes and my driving our big car to school. But I was nice to them. I spent on them the nickels I got for dry-picking spurred cocks so they would be my friends.

Poppie walked out and examined the pit which was down in the center of the arena. Our customers could sit down next to the pit or up higher to watch the fights. We had everything we needed to make us independent of the outside world, even to our own electric plant down between these two high hills.

"When I built this place I didn't tie up to the outside world with an electric wire or a telephone," Poppie said boastingly. "I bought plenty of space with no outside connections but a sweet little graveled road running to it. And I built the road, too. You know, Adger, it's a money-maker, and we are tax free!"

Then Poppie laughed a big booming laugh at his own words.

"Tax free," he repeated. "How could we pay taxes if we wanted to?"

The first car that pulled up was a car as large as ours with an Ohio license tag. It was John Schultz from Cleveland, who was a regular customer with built-in coops in the trunk. These coops were filled with Allen Roundheads, all full of fight. Poppie greeted his old friend, John, while each blew cigar smoke with their words. Doon Smathers from Burlington, West Virginia, was the second to arrive in his familiar expensive car with built-in coops filled with Doms. They looked like the domestic Plymouth Rocks, but they were no kin to domestic breeds when it came to fighting. They were big, tough fighters.

Dave Rowan drove up from Lyton, Tennessee, in a special make of car said to be more expensive than Poppie's. He was a professional in our business who went for high stakes. He believed in the Allen Roundheads because, he had once told Poppie, he liked their ability to shuffle and maneuver. He often told Poppie how he liked a chicken that would fly high. As more stars came into the August sky, cars trailed over our winding gravel road, all bringing fighting gamecocks, restless in their built-in coops and raring to go. A line of cars almost touching were coming up our private lane.

"What a crowd there'll be tonight, Adger," Poppie said. "Switch on the lights and get the tickets ready!"

Poppie couldn't greet the old customers and meet the new ones fast enough. Only a few didn't bring their fighting gamecocks. They came to lay money from their fat pocketbooks on the dotted line when other men fought their chickens. We had never had a crowd like this one, and still they kept coming.

"The arena will be filled tonight," Poppie whispered in my ear. "We'll be goin' strong until Monday morning! It might be a 'ten-grand' weekend. We've never gone that high, but it's not impossible in this business."

Poppie was in high spirits as old friends mixed and mingled and new faces showed up introducing themselves. There were a few drunks, but only one real sloppy drunk. Our customers unloaded their roosters while Poppie sold tickets at five bucks per head and I punched two holes in each ticket.

When Dave Rowan's helper put the gaffs on a big Warhorse and John Schultz put the gaffs on his Allen Roundhead, Poppie's judges, Bill Bennington, Dick Sloas and Percy Preston, checked each to see that everything was in order. The fight was on. The two gentlemen, John and Dave, each bet a grand on his fighting gamecock. Bets ran high all over the arena on both the Warhorse and the Allen Roundhead. And the seats were filled except for a few places on the top row that were the fartherest away from the pit. Poppie, big and commanding with a cigar in his mouth and his thumbs behind his suspenders, stood up close to the pit.

The fighting warriors faced each other. Then, the first power lick and the feathers flew. John's Roundhead maneuvered and shifted to meet Dave's Warhorse. Like a jet's taking off, the Roundhead went high and the Warhorse was floored but rose again and was waiting for his antagonist when he dropped back down in the pit. There were eager faces, and the few drunks hollered and shouted. The sloppy drunk said a cute thing about fighting Poppie in the pit as he went around punching our customers' tickets again. Everybody laughed at his antics. He punched Bill Bennington's ticket since Poppie required his helpers to have them same as our customers. Poppie had a ticket and I had one. He even punched Poppie's ticket four times. He punched my ticket three times. He attracted a lot of attention from the fight until Poppie had to call him down in a nice way. Poppie liked fun as well as anybody but he didn't like to see a drunk clown make a fool of himself and everybody else.

He had just got down in time for everybody to see the Roundhead's gaff spur the big Warhorse. Now, it was Poppie's job. He grabbed the Warhorse, put his head in his mouth and sucked the blood from his neck where he was gaffed and spat it on the ground. Then, he put the rooster's head into his big mouth again and blew wind into his neck. People didn't take any chances for he worked fast. Everybody, especially Dave Rowan, was pleased with Poppie's fast work. Then Poppie threw him back into the pit and the fight was on. What a fight! The Warhorse caught the Roundhead through the eye as he started to fly high, and the gaff went through his head. No use for Poppie to blow breath into a spurred rooster this time. The Roundhead was finished. He flopped a few times in the pit while the Warhorse stood up and crowed. Then the Warhorse walked a circle with his wings down and fell over dead. He was a fighter to the last.

John walked over and paid his bet to Dave. Gentlemen in business honor their bets. Betting was done in our arena by a man's word of honor. If the man was not enough of a gentleman to honor his bet, Poppie bounced him from the arena.

The sloppy drunk got up again. He wanted to punch more tickets and Poppie had to put him in his place.

"All right, John Stonaker," Doon Smathers said, "five grand on my Dom."

"I accept your challenge," John said.

These men were the big guns in the cockfighting world. No sooner said than the helpers were fitting gaffs on the roosters' spurs and the judges were seeing that everything was done in decency and order. Doon's Dom and John's Roundhead were put into the pit. The big Dom challenged and the royal battle was on. The sloppy drunk got up again, a short, barrel-chested man with watery-blue eyes, loose lips and a long pointed nose, and he wanted to sprout feathers and fight Doon in the pit. Then he leaned on Dick Sloas and started punching his ticket four or five times. Another spindly drunk put his arms around Percy Preston. He asked Percy to butt heads with him.

"Spirit of fightin' has got me, pal," he said to Percy. "See fightin' and I want to butt like the old ram did me when I's a boy."

That was funny and everybody laughed while the

feathers flew from the big husky Dom and the lanky Roundhead. Then the sloppy drunk came over clipping at the wind. He pulled Dick Sloas' ticket from his hatband and started punching it full of holes.

"Sit down there before I bounce you," Poppie warned him. "I can't go a sloppy drunk! I'm tellin' you my last time to sit down and behave before I pile-drive you!"

"Sloppy drunk, huh, and you don't like me," he moaned to Poppie. "Hit me, huh, with a fist big as a maul? Don't you hurt me, you big Jack on the Beanstalk!"

Poppie shoved him back in his vacant seat in the front row.

"Sit there," Poppie warned just as the Roundhead gapped the Dom.

Poppie grabbed the Dom and tried to blow breath into him.

"It's all over," he said, throwing the Dom to me. "Pick 'im in a hurry."

When I had dry-picked a half dozen, I always drove back to Cantrell and sold them at a low figure to a little restaurant where they ground them into chicken salad.

After I'd dry-picked the two roosters, I took them to my friend, Hewlett Armsworth, for chicken salad. Hewlett told me he was needing roosters for salad and to get some to him in a hurry. When I returned, the betting was something between Alvin Pennix's Dom and Seldon Cates' Warhorse. Each owner almost fought the other over his breed of fighting gamecocks. Each rivaled the other equal to the roosters. One never made a challenge the other didn't accept. This fight was fast and furious. First one gamecock was knocked out of the pit and then the other. The gamecocks seemed to sense the rivalry of their owners.

"There's goin' to be a raid here at twelve o'clock," said the sloppy drunk, rising. "There's goin' to be a raid at twelve! Whoopee!" He said something else but the laughter drowned his words. He was really a funny one.

"Who's goin' to make the raid?" someone shouted from up in the arena after the laughter had subsided.

"I am," he shouted.

The laughter was louder than before. The sound went up toward the stars and died on the August night wind.

"What time is it?" a man asked from the front row of seats.

The sloppy drunk stood looking at his watch.

"Twelve o'clock, and the raid's on," he shouted.

He pulled his coat back and showed his state-police badge.

The tall drunk sobered up and pulled his badge too. Men pulled badges where they were seated all over the arena before they went into action.

"It's a real raid," Seldon Cates shouted.

He jumped into the pit and grabbed his battered Warhorse. Alvin Pennix joined him and grabbed his Dom. They tried to make it to the gate. Poppie knew now it was a real raid, and he tried to save his customers. The whole place was thrown into wild confusion as the state police arrested and handcuffed Poppie. They arrested Bill Bennington, Percy Preston, Dick Sloas and me. They arrested all with tickets punched more than twice. Many of our customers were lucky enough to ram the gate before the police could block it. Many went over the high wall to the ground from the top seat of the arena. I never heard such gunning of motors down our lane.

"That scoundrel! Where is he?" Poppie shouted. "That John Diller! Is he here, too?"

Poppie and I scanned the score of state police but John Diller was not among them.

"He has a date with Rosalee tonight," I shouted to Poppie above the din of this confusion. "John's not in on this."

"There's something funny about it," Poppie yelled, spitting out a chunk of cigar.

"Listen, Mr. Littleton, if you behave and cooperate with us, this time it will be light with you," said the policeman who had been the sloppy drunk. "If it happens again, it will go hard with you."

"Yeah, a couple of grand, and a big weekend ruined," Poppie sighed as John Schultz tried to dive under a bale of hay.

A policeman got John and marched him to the door. "Now, get goin'," he told John.

"Thank you, thank you," said John Schultz.

The police turned all Poppie's customers loose this time but warned if they were ever caught again what the consequences might be.

Monday we were tried in Squire Albert Mennix's court and Poppie was fined only ten dollars. My case was dropped because I was a minor. Bill, Percy and Alvin, a nephew of Squire Mennix, were turned loose too.

"Not bad fellows at all," Poppie said, chewing shakily on his cigar as we drove home.

"What's ten dollars? It's a joke, Adger! Much better than a couple of grand and the trouble of getting it appealed and beating the rap. This is a cheaper way out."

Rosalee was embarrassed when she saw our names in the paper. Poppie's ten-dollar fine caused much gossip. People whispered he really had the Law in his pocket.

"It's a good thing you were not in on that raid," Poppie said to John Diller. "I couldn't have felt as friendly to you as I do now if you had been a part of it."

"I was home in bed when it happened," John said. "Rosalee and I had been to the theatre. But she and I were here before eleven. I was in my room shortly after."

"Poppie, let me tell you the good news," Rosalee said. "John and I are going to be married. I'll not go back to college."

"Well, maybe you don't need a college education," he sighed, trying to smile. "I thought you wanted a college education. I've tried to give you the best. What do you plan to do, John, after you marry Rosalee?"

"I plan to go on being a policeman," he replied.

"I can make you a better offer," Poppie said. "More money and a more exciting life!"

"I guess I'll stick to the state police," he answered casually. "I feel we need honest officials in all our levels of law enforcement!"

Poppie looked at John and laughed louder than the sloppy drunk had laughed in our arena.

"Let me congratulate you, Rosalee," he said half-heartedly, pulling her close to him with his big arm around her. "And you too, John!"

"We're to be married next month," she said.

"All right, if he's the man you love and you're the girl he loves," Poppie told them. "Just be sure you love one another."

One week before Rosalee and John's wedding two men came to see us. Poppie was slow at first to invite them in. But they invited themselves in. Each took a long surprised look at our furniture when he entered our living room.

"Mr. Littleton," said the soft-spoken man wearing glasses and a gray business suit, "I believe you owe us $200,000. We've come to talk this over."

"Owe you two hundred grand?" Poppie shouted. "Are you kiddin'? I don't owe anybody anything! Who are you? Are you trying to frame me?"

"No, we're not trying to frame you," said the taller, pale-faced man with a hatchet face and squint black eyes. "We're with the State Department of Revenue and you owe us this for amusement tax."

"Amusement tax," Poppie almost screamed. "On what?"

"You've been fighting gamecocks for twenty-one years, eight months and two weeks and you've never paid any tax on your gate receipts," said the soft-spoken man.

"But how do you know how much I owe you?" Poppie asked.

"You'll have to prove that you don't owe us this much," he said. "Can you do it?"

"You'll have to prove that I owe you," Poppie shouted.

"No, I won't for you've already pled guilty when you were fined ten dollars in Squire Mennix's court," he said. "You paid this fine after pleading guilty. This was published in the *Auckland Daily Independent*. I have the clipping here."

He pulled a copy of the paper from his briefcase.

"This is not in Judge Burton's court," said the taller man. "You can't appeal a fine under twenty dollars in this state, Mr. Littleton."

"I'll get the best lawyer in this state," Poppie shouted and pounded the soft rocking-chair arm with his big fist. "I won't be hoodwinked by all this petty trickery!"

"All right, we want you to get the best attorney," said the soft-spoken man. "We are both attorneys and know the law."

Then, we sat in silence in our living room while Poppie looked threateningly at them like he was going to bounce them from the room.

"We'd better be going," said the soft-spoken man.

The two men got up from their chairs.

"Just a minute," Poppie spoke in a more subdued tone as he arose too. "Rosalee, my daughter, is marrying Sgt. John Diller of the state police. They are to be married next month. Can't you hold this trial up and keep it out of the papers until after her wedding?"

The two men looked at each other.

"Yes, we can grant you that favor, Mr. Littleton," said the taller man.

Then, they bade us good day and left the house quietly.

"Now, this is really something," Poppie said as he walked toward his chair. "But I'll wait to see if John gets a promotion. If he does, he's had something to do with this."

Poppie fumbled nervously in his pockets for another cigar.

"Adger, I feel awful shaky inside," he said trying to smile. "I'm a ruined man. I have been tops in my business in this state. But I built my business on a weak foundation."

He lit a cigar and dropped wearily into his chair. He sat with his feet propped upon his footstool and blew smoke rings toward the ceiling. He stared at each ring vacantly while it disintegrated in the stuffy air.

The Voting Goodlaws

I had turned through the voting lists of eligible and registered voters of the eighteen precincts of Lantern County.
I had at my fingertips the name of every man and woman
in our party who hadn't voted. This was my job every
election day. And as long as our Greenough party stayed
in power in Lantern County, my reward for getting everybody out to vote was the job of road foreman over all the
county roads. It was a nice job. And it was something I
loved to work for. But our Greenough party could easily
lose to the Dinwiddie party, since we had only a hundred
more registered votes than they had. No one knew better
than I that if we stayed in power we had to vote every
Greenough vote we could and challenge to beat hell the
legality of some of the Dinwiddie votes. If we lost an
election, it meant my job.

Not one of the Goodlaw brothers had showed up to vote yet, so I was mighty proud when Bill Goodlaw walked in.

"Bill, how much medicine will it take to put you right?" I asked.

"About a pint, Oscar," he said.

I walked back into the closet where we kept brooms, mops, paper towels and, on election days, nerve medicine. I fetched old Bill a pint of medicine.

Bill fondled the bottle like a child fondles a stick of candy. "That looks like good medicine!"

"We've got two hours before the polls close," I said. "But you'd better get down to No. 1 and vote!"

"Okay, fellow," he said. "I'll step in here a minute and take my medicine. Then I'll be off."

Now that Lantern County had voted dry, Bill was afraid to take his medicine where he might be seen by someone that would later be called before the grand jury. But when he came back out of the Greenough party's consultation room, leaving the empty medicine bottle behind him, he was licking his lips and his eyes were brighter and his beet-red face was more alive.

"Ready to vote, Oscar," he said. "I'll go down to No. 1 and vote and be right back."

When Bill Goodlaw walked down the courthouse steps, Eif Madden, who always drives a car for us on election day to pick up the boys after they get their medicine and take them to the right precinct, picked him up and gunned his car toward No. 1. I knew when Eif Madden got a voter he took him there and brought him back.

There was one voter I didn't have to worry about any more.

But time was rapidly passing and there wasn't any way to recall time. After the polls closed, I knew the Dinwiddies would see to it that we Greenoughs didn't do any more voting.

Al, Lus and Chester Goodlaw, I thought. When will they get here? Only Bill has come to vote. Just an hour and a half before the polls close. If we lose these votes it might mean we lose the election. That would mean my job. Their votes might mean the extra points that win the game.

I checked my lists again. Lus Goodlaw had not voted in No. 2. Al and Chester had not voted in Precinct No. 3. For when they voted, I marked their names out like I had done Bill Goodlaw's name the minute he stepped inside Eif Madden's car. I knew he was a voted man. He'd vote because he loved to vote and Eif Madden would see that he did vote.

When I was still looking over the lists, I saw out my window a boy of fifteen or sixteen riding a mule down Main Street at full gallop. He rode onto the courthouse yard, tied the panting mule to a low-hanging limb of a maple shade and rushed up the courthouse steps.

"Mr. Kimble," he said, getting his breath hard. "Daddy won't be here to vote. I've come to tell you so you won't be expectin' 'im!"

"Whose boy are you?" I asked.

"Al Goodlaw's," he said.

"What happened to Al?"

273

"He dressed up in his good clothes for election day and went to the barn to saddle and bridle the mule and the mule didn't know him and kicked Daddy on the shin-bone right above the ankle and broke the bone square off."

"Where is your daddy?" We can carry him to the polls on a stretcher, I thought. We kept a couple of stretchers for that purpose.

"Oh, the bone was out of Daddy's leg," his son said. "And the doctor came and then rushed back and got the ambulance and they've taken Daddy to the Lantern County Hospital. Had to get 'im there in a hurry. He was sufferin' something awful."

"Gee, that's bad news," I said. "I hate to hear that."

Hate to lose his vote too, I thought.

"You know Daddy never missed a vote in his life since the year he was old enough to vote," his son said.

"Yes, I know."

"I must hurry home," the boy said. "Daddy'll be smarter next time than to dress up so his mule won't know 'im."

Al's son rushed from my office and down the steps. I watched him as he ran across the courthouse yard, un-snapped the bridle rein from the low-hanging maple limb, mounted and was off again down Main Street.

Al and Bill Goodlaw, I thought. They look alike. And they both stutter. Many people mistake one for the other.

Just then, as luck would have it, Eif Madden brought Bill back to the courthouse.

"I've got bad news for us, Bill," I said. "Mule kicked

your brother Al and broke his leg right above the ankle and he's in Lantern County Hospital and won't be here to vote."

"Who told you that?"

"His son rode a mule in here and told me," I said. "He's just left the office."

"Gee, that's too bad," Bill said.

"You know it takes that extra point to win sometimes," I said.

"That's right."

"Lus and Chester haven't come either."

"That's bad," Bill said. "Chester lives in the flat country in Ohio. But he promised me faithful he'd be back here to vote."

"I didn't know he'd moved."

"Yep, he went to better farmin' land. He's been comin' back to Lantern County and votin' two years."

"I didn't know that," I said. "We've never purged him from the register."

"You be damned sure you don't purge 'im," Bill said. "If you do, there'll be trouble. You know Chester loves to vote."

"Say, Bill, come to think of it, you and Al look alike," I said. "You both stutter, both are about the same size and have the same complexions. Don't you think you might vote for Al?"

"Well, I don't see why I can't," Bill said. "All of us boys own a farm together and we put our money together and pay the grocery bills and the clothing bills. We lived that way all our lives until old Chester pulled out because his wife got a little mad at my wife and decided she didn't like our partnership arrangement. But we've never voted for one another before."

"Al's in the hospital sufferin' with a broken leg, but I know he's hurt more because he'll lose his vote," I said.

"Just a little more nerve medicine," Bill said.

I got Bill another pint from the supply room and Bill stepped into the consultation room. In three minutes he passed back through my office and ran stiff legged down the courthouse steps. His face was beaming with happiness. He made for Eif Madden's car.

"Take me to No. 3 in a hurry, Eif," Bill said.

Eif gunned the car. He turned the corner onto Main Street on two wheels and sped down Main Street like a bullet.

If it will only work, I thought.

Then Lus Goodlaw came into my office with his hat in his hand.

"Lus, where have you been?" I asked. "I've looked and looked for you! I wondered if you were comin'!"

"I've had to help take Al to the hospital," he said. "Al's in bad shape with that broken leg. We sent Tommie, Al's oldest boy, to tell you."

"He told me," I said as I went after nerve medicine for Lus.

"Gee, Oscar," Lus said, "election day is a great day. And I'm sorry all this trouble had to happen to us today. Medicine!" He beamed as he shook the bottle and watched the beading contents.

"Step right in the old Greenough consultation room, Lus," I said, "and take your medicine where no snoopers will see you. Remember grand jury will convene next month. Then get to No. 2 in a hurry."

I suddenly realized Eif Madden had taken Bill to No. 3 and I didn't have a car to take Lus to No. 2. But by the time Lus had taken his medicine, I had thought of something.

"Lus, here's an extra bottle of medicine for you. Just don't pull it from your pocket where anybody will see it."

"Oscar, don't worry," he said. "It won't be in my pocket long."

"Say, Lus," I said, "old Chester's not goin' to make it here from Ohio in time to vote. You look like him. Both the same size and neither one of you stutter and spit when you talk like Bill and Al do. You vote in No. 2 and Chester votes in No. 3. Reckon you could drive my car and go first to No. 2 and vote and then drive over to No. 3?"

"Don't see why I couldn't," Lus said agreeable. "I hate to see old Chester lose his vote."

"Bill told me he'd lived two years in Ohio, but we've never purged him from the list."

"And you'd better be damned sure you don't," Lus said. "Old Chester has an awful temper. He's mighty fractious at times. We used to share everything together until he married Dellie Cluggish. She didn't like the way we had always lived, putting our money together and paying the bills and taxes. She didn't like our putting our cattle together and selling them and letting the money all be in all our names at the bank. She didn't like our owning Pa's farm together and never dividing it. That's why Chester pulled out and left us. Dellie's got a powerful influence over Chester. I guess it's safe to vote for 'im. That's one thing we've never done for one another before."

"You'd better move along, Lus," I said. "Not more than thirty minutes before the polls close!"

I gave Lus the key to my car. I pointed to where it was parked by the curb across the street.

"Get in and go in a hurry, Lus," I said. "You have to work to do it. Do it."

"And do it, I will," Lus said. "Poor old Chester won't lose his vote."

"We can't let him lose it," I said. "If you share living together then it is nothin' but right you share voting."

"You're right, Oscar," Lus said as he hopped down the steps like a sparrow.

I watched him get in my car and gun it down the street like a bullet from a rifle toward No. 2, his legal voting place.

Well, it's over, I thought to myself. All four votes of the Goodlaw brothers have been accounted for.

And while sitting in my office waiting for them to return from the polls, I thought about how hard it used to be, when I first started checking the voting lists and bossing the county road jobs, to untangle the Goodlaw brothers. I couldn't understand why they voted at three different precincts until I visited their six-hundred-acre farm. The center of this farm lay where precincts 1, 2 and 3 joined. This was one of the oldest farms in Lantern County and the Goodlaw family was one of the oldest families. Bill Goodlaw lived on the section of the farm that lay in Precinct No. 1. Lus lived on the section that lay in Precinct No. 2. And Chester and Al lived beyond the high hill that split the farm in two. And this section was in Precinct No. 3. Because it was so confusing, and since they shared crops, store accounts, whiskey bills and clothing accounts together, since they owned everything together and had their bank account so each could check on it when he wished, we had tried to put the farm in Precinct No. 1. But we couldn't do it. The Dinwiddies stopped us. And now for the first time it had worked to our advantage.

Everything works out for the best, I thought, as I watched Eif Madden drive up and let Bill out.

"Did it work, Bill?" I asked him the first thing.

"Slick as a ribbon," he said. "I hear Al got his leg broke after he had voted. It's okay. Don't worry."

"That's wonderful," I said.

"Sure is," Bill said. "I'm glad you thought of it, I feel better now. Al got to vote."

While Bill stood there, Tom Peters and Fiddus Layne dropped into my office and asked for some extra nerve medicine. They told me the election would be close. But that wasn't anything new. All of us knew it would be close; it had always been close.

Then Lus drove back, parked my car and came to the office.

"How did it work, Lus?" I asked him before he had time to say a word.

"Boy, you're smart," he said. "Everybody down at Precinct No. 3 called me Chester and asked me how I was gettin' along with my brothers. They didn't even know Chester had moved to Ohio!"

"Did I hear somebody speakin' my name?" Chester Goodlaw said as he came into my office with Dellie hanging onto his arm, just as Tom Peters and Fiddus Layne walked out with their medicine bottles showing in their hip pockets.

"Sure you did, Chester," I stammered. "Where have you been?"

"We've been tryin' like hell to get here in time to vote," Chester said.

"How much time do we have?" Dellie asked.

My hand was shaking so I could hardly reach my watch pocket. Finally I pulled my watch out and I said, "Twenty minutes left."

"That's time enough," Dellie said.

"Yep, plenty of time," Chester said.

I looked at Bill and Bill looked at Lus. Lus looked at me. His face was redder than a turkey's snout. His lips trembled.

Why did this have to happen? I thought.

"How about a little medicine, Oscar?" Chester said. "Like in the days of old! Boys, it's wonderful to get back to old Lantern County to vote!"

"Chester, you right sure you need some medicine?" I asked, for I could tell Chester already had had enough.

"You damned tooten," he said. "It wouldn't be like comin' home to vote unless I got my medicine. That's all I've ever asked. Just my medicine. Have to have it, Oscar!"

"You tell 'im, Lus," I said.

"Tell Chester what?" Dellie asked.

"About the votin'."

"Chester," Lus apologized, "we didn't think you were goin' to get here and I voted for you. See, we look alike and we don't stutter and spit when we talk like Al and Bill! I did it. I got by with it!"

"You voted for me, Lus?" Chester said. "Didn't you know I'd be here? Two blowouts and one flat and here I am in time to vote! And I'm goin' to vote or somebody will be hurt!"

"But Chester," I said.

"Don't Chester me, Oscar!" Chester broke in before I had time to speak my thoughts.

"We're goin' to vote," Dellie chimed in. "Why do you think we've come one hundred and ninety miles? We're goin' to vote!"

"But we used to share everything together," Lus spoke softly as he watched Chester's face redden like a mad turkey gobbler's snout. "We shared about everything together!"

"But each other's wives," Chester shouted, "and we didn't vote for one another! By God," he yelled as he poked a thick index finger under Lus's nose, "I am goin' to vote or I'll expose what has been done! I'll make you squeal! I'll vote or I'll make everybody squeal! I'll ruin you, Oscar! Goddamned if I don't!"

"See, Chester," Dellie said, as she hugged closer to him, "I used to tell you about this partnership business and how you and me got the worst end of it! Now you see," she cooed softly, "I was right. See, Lus has even voted in your place, stole your God-given right while we've burnt gasoline and tires speeding to get here. See! I told you long ago!"

"You can keep your damned medicine, Oscar," Chester shouted. "But I'm goin' to vote before time runs out! Hear me! I'm goin' to vote! I'll get you all into it! I'm goin' to old No. 3 and I'm goin' to vote the straight Greenough ticket!"

"But, Chester," Lus said, "just a minute. Let us explain!"

"Take it easy, Chester," Bill said. "I had to vote for Al today. Mule kicked him and broke his leg as he started to the polls!"

"I won't let you explain and I won't take it easy," Chester said. "Don't care how many Goodlaws the mule kicked. I'm goin' to vote. Or, I'll be goddamned if you all won't be sorry!"

"We'll go vote together," Dellie said. "Let's go Chester!"

"Just a minute," I said. "I've got an idea."

And I ran over to my desk and picked up the eligible voting list of Precinct No. 3.

"You'd better have an idea," Chester said. "And you'd better work fast. We've only got minutes."

"Here it is," I said. "Nelse Goodlaw."

"But he's dead," Lus said. "Died last May."

"He's only a second cousin," Bill said.

"He's not been purged," I said. "His name is still here."

"Then I'm Nelse Goodlaw!" Chester said.

"That's right," I said.

"If it doesn't work," Chester said, "everybody will be exposed and somebody will be hurt!"

This is the only chance, I thought, as I grabbed two bottles of medicine and put them in my pockets.

"Let's go in my car," I said. "Let's hurry. I'll get you there!"

Lus, Bill, Chester and Dellie went out before me and I closed and fastened the door to lock up the medicine. We rushed to the car. We got inside and I gunned the motor and we were off for No. 3.

Hope and pray it will work, I repeated silently to myself, for I knew Chester Goodlaw was a mean man when he was riled. I knew we had plenty of trouble on our hands.

If it wasn't for Dellie egging him on, I thought. But she gets to vote. That's another vote. That little extra point might win the game.

A thousand thoughts ran through my brain in the three minutes it took me to drive to Precinct No. 3. And soon as we arrived Chester and Dellie rushed inside the schoolhouse to vote. And I hurried over to a window and put my ear against the crack to hear how it would all come out.

"Hello, Chester Goodlaw," Mortie Webster, a good old Greenough election officer, greeted him. "What are you doin' back here?"

We're gone, I thought. The jig is up.

"Mortie, as long as I've known you," Chester said, "won't the time ever come when you'll stop gettin' me confused with Chester Goodlaw? I'm Nelse Goodlaw."

"Nelse Goodlaw," said Vinton Salyers, a Dinwiddie

election officer. "Nelse Goodlaw. Nelse Goodlaw. Something about him, I don't remember!"

"Remember what?" Chester said.

"I'm sorry, Nelse, I mistook you for Chester," Mortie said. "Chester voted about an hour ago."

"That's right," Vinton Salyers said. "For a minute I was all mixed up and confused."

"That's all right," Chester said. "All of us get confused sooner or later. But," he said, pointing a big rough index finger at Vinton, "you'd better say you're sorry!"

Chester, Mortie and Vinton laughed at the joke and Chester went behind the sheet to vote.

"Now, I'm Mrs. Chester Goodlaw," Dellie said.

"Honest, this is really confusin'," Vinton said.

"Well, I'm certainly goin' to vote," Dellie said. "Check your register and see if I've voted."

"You have not, Mrs. Goodlaw," Mortie said. "Check it there, Vinton!"

"No, she hasn't but Chester has," he said. "But Goodlaws always get me confused," he laughed. "They look so much alike. I can't tell 'em apart. I just know a Goodlaw when I see one!"

"Maybe you do," Chester laughed as he came from under the sheet and Dellie went in.

Lucky damn, I thought, as I put my hands in my pockets and held the bottles of nerve medicine to give Chester soon as he came from the schoolhouse. For the game had ended with our getting the extra point that might come in handy when the scores of both teams were tallied.

Love and the Law

The August stars blinked brightly in the blue morning sky when we left the Tibert Turnpike for Leatherwood Run. We had eight more miles to drive to reach the Big Woods, eleven hundred acres of virgin timber where squirrels were plentiful. We would get there early, for dawn was not breaking. Finn had hunted in the Big Woods before. He knew the groves of hickories where the squirrels went for their breakfasts.

It was a nice ride in our topless car. The morning wind was good to breathe down deep into our lungs. We heard above the low moan of the motor the hoots of an owl high on a Leatherwood hill. We drove along the creek and then we reached the narrow, sandy road again. The road was first in the creek and out again, all the way from Tibert Turnpike to the Big Woods. If a rain came, enough to make Leatherwood Run rise, we would have to wait until the water went down. Finn had been caught this way once. He drowned his motor in the creek because he tried to drive out too soon.

"Look at that, won't you," Finn said, breaking our silence as we left the creek water for the sandy road. "Automobile tracks. Somebody ahead of us!"

"I thought we'd be the first to the Big Woods," I said.

"We'll get a mess of squirrels," Finn laughed. "Plenty of squirrels in the Big Woods for them, too!"

Finn was usually peeved when somebody got ahead of us. But this morning it was different. We'd had a good morning. It was the kind of morning that he loved. Set the alarm clock for three. Get up when the alarm went off. Fry eggs and bacon and make a pot of coffee. Eat a good breakfast and get ready and be on the road by four. That's the way we'd done this morning. We had driven thirty miles across Blake County to Leatherwood Run. We were at the mouth of Leatherwood Run by five o'clock. That was plenty early. Somebody had to be ambitious to beat us.

I wasn't ambitious about hunting. I never cared to hunt for squirrels. And I certainly didn't like to get up at three in the morning from a soft bed to go thirty-eight miles to shoot squirrels. Finn was surprised when I volunteered to go to the Big Woods with him. But there was a reason behind this. Mom had asked me to do it.

"When Finn goes squirrel huntin' from now on, you go with him," Mom told me. "We don't want anything to happen in this family. I'm afraid there'll be trouble. It may be the kind of trouble we don't want."

This was after Lottie Bascom, a neighbor and once a friend to my brother Finn, had got himself appointed constable to arrest Finn for hunting without license. One morning in August after squirrel season had begun, Finn went to hunt on our farm. When Finn got to the hickory grove on Seaton Ridge, Lottie Bascom was there waiting for him.

"Consider yourself under arrest, Finn Powderjay," Lottie Bascom said. "I know you don't have a hunting license. You never bought a hunting license in your life."

"Show me your license," Finn said.

"Here's what I'll show you," Lottie said.

He showed Finn his badge.

"I've got you," Lottie said. "I've wanted you a long time. Now I have you."

"Don't lay hands on me, Lottie," Finn warned him as they stood under the hickory tree in the early-morning hour. "You know why you want to arrest me. Don't you touch me."

Both young men stood under the tree holding their guns as if they were ready to use them.

"I'll take you dead or alive," Bascom said as he leveled his double barrel on Finn. "Drop your gun before I shoot!"

Finn dropped his gun. Bascom was so sure he would have trouble arresting Finn, he had brought handcuffs. He handcuffed Finn, marched him in front around the long ridge road to Blakesburg. He took Finn handcuffed through the town where he had gone to high school. Lottie marched Finn before Judge Watt Burton. Finn pleaded guilty and was fined seventeen dollars and costs.

This was not all. Lottie Bascom knew Finn was too stubborn to buy a license now. And how Lottie knew Finn had changed his hunting ground we will never know unless some other Plum Grove hunter had reported him.

In the quietness of that morning when Finn was listening for green hickory-nut hulls to fall from a tall hickory, he heard footsteps in the distance. Finn looked in the direction of the sound, and Lottie was about a hundred yards away slipping toward him. Finn started to run. Lottie shot at Finn, peppering him with number-five shot. Lottie chased Finn three miles. He would shoot at Finn. Finn would stop long enough to shoot at Lottie. They shot all the shells they had at each other. Mom and I saw Finn take the last shot at Lottie. It was just below our house. Lottie jumped high in the air for the shot stung him. He didn't come all the way to our house after Finn. He knew better. But it was after this that Mom asked me to hunt with Finn. She begged Finn not to hunt at all. But Finn wouldn't quit squirrel hunting because his one-time friend had turned to be his bitterest enemy. Everybody at Plum Grove knew why this had happened.

Lottie and Finn had both fallen in love with Myrtle Edwards. Lottie would date her one night and Finn would date her the next. The rivalry grew until Finn and Lottie were no longer friends. They had stopped hunting together. And one Sunday, Finn and Lottie both went home with Myrtle from Sunday School. Slender, six-feet-four, blond-headed and blue-eyed Finn walked on one side of Myrtle Edwards. Big, square-shouldered, two-hundred-and-twenty-pound, black-headed Lottie Bascom walked on the other side. Slender, little golden-haired Myrtle Edwards walked between them. Each man talked to her for himself, trying to win her favor. This was the Plum Grove custom when two men loved the same girl. Everybody at Plum Grove wondered who would win Myrtle's love when Finn and Lottie left the church with her. Many followed to see who would go inside the house after they got to her home. They knew one would be turned back. They saw Finn go inside with her and Lottie walk away with his head down.

Finn had for several seasons nailed up more squirrel tails than any other young hunter. He had always surpassed Lottie Bascom. Young Plum Grove hunters who were unable to nail up as many squirrel tails as Finn were sympathetic toward Lottie. These young hunters hunted without license too, but Lottie had not arrested them.

This buying a license to hunt was something new. The young hunters at Plum Grove couldn't understand why they should be compelled to buy licenses. Their ancestors before them had hunted in the freedom of the clean wind, in the quiet, deep hollows by the clear, winding streams and by the Sandy River, in the deep giant forests without license. And the young Plum Grove men had hunted on each other's farms without hunting licenses in friendliness and good spirit. Lottie Bascom's arresting Finn had been the first time anything had ever happened to one of the young hunters.

When we reached the forks of Leatherwood Run, Finn stopped the car.

"I want to see which way the car ahead of us went," he said.

For there were two roads now. One went up the Left Fork of Leatherwood Run and the other went up the Right Fork. There were old log roads that trailed off into the deep dark woods. For the stars had left the morning sky and the dawn was breaking. We saw by our headlights where the car ahead of us had gone up the Right Fork of Leatherwood Run.

"Then, we'll go up the Left Fork," Finn said. "They've left us the good hickory groves. More squirrels up Left Fork."

Finn was pleased. We got back in the car and drove about a half mile up the narrow-gauged valley. Though it was early morning, the hollow was so deep and dark, and the branches of the giant trees overlapped above us, that it was like driving through a long green tunnel. We pulled off our shoes and left them in the car. We got our guns and took up the steep hillside that lay between the Left and Right forks of Leatherwood Run.

"On top of this point we'll find the hickory trees," Finn whispered.

"But the other hunters are over on the other side," I whispered. "We might run into 'em!"

"Let 'em be there!" Finn said softly. "We're as good a hunters as they are!"

When we reached the top of the high point that lay between the forks of this long valley, nearly every tree was a hickory. And beneath each tree the ground was covered with the shells of green hickory nuts.

Finn is right, I thought. He knows where the squirrels are.

"You sit under these trees and wait for 'em to come," Finn whispered. "They'll be here in a few minutes. I'll go down on the end of the point. We won't hunt too close."

I sat under a tall hickory tree and waited. I watched Finn go down the point among the hickory trees and out of sight. Once while I was waiting for the squirrels to come to the hickory trees, a big one came hopping over the ground toward the tree where I was sitting. But when he saw me he ran around a tree and then over the point. I had scared him away. But I thought more would come. For thirty minutes I sat waiting. Then, I figured the squirrel that had seen me had told the others. So I walked up the point in the opposite direction to the way Finn had gone. I found a big hickory with bushels of nut shreds beneath it.

I looked up the tree to see if I could see to the top. When I did this, little fine particles of green hickory nuts hit me in the eyes. I dropped my gun beside me. I sat down and tried to get the fine shreds of hickory-nut hulls from my eyes. I pulled on my eyelashes to make the eyes well up with tears to wash away these particles. While on the far end of the point I heard Finn's gun. He shot twice. Then I heard him shoot again, then twice more. Before I had gotten the particles from my eyes, I had heard him shoot fourteen times. I wondered why I hadn't heard the other hunters shooting.

Then, I picked up my gun and was getting ready to

find the squirrel that had thrown the hickory-nut hulls into my eyes, when I heard a familiar voice.

"Finn Powderjay, consider yourself under arrest!"

"So you've followed me here," Finn said.

"I'll follow you to the ends of the earth to get you."

It was Lottie's familiar voice.

I ran fast as I could to the car. I put my gun under the seat and my feet into my shoes. I ran back in the direction of Finn and Lottie.

"You've got me," I heard Finn say before I reached them. "You don't have to handcuff me. I'll go with you! Let me keep my squirrels."

"Sure, sure, you can keep your squirrels," Lottie said. "They are good evidence."

While Finn and Lottie quarreled I ran under the grove of green hickories down the point and over toward the forks of the creek. I didn't listen to their words. I hurried to get there before something happened. When I reached them, Lottie had handcuffed Finn. Johnnie Little was holding his gun.

"He's got me, Shan," Finn said. "Can't even come to the Big Woods and hunt in peace!"

"This is awful," I said.

"Shut up or I'll arrest you too," Lottie said, looking to see if I had a gun.

"What evidence will you have that I've been hunting?" I said.

"Then what are you doin' out here?" Lottie questioned me.

"How did you know Finn and I were comin' to the Big Woods, Lottie?" I asked.

"I told my friend, Johnnie Little," Finn said. "That's how Lottie knew. Johnnie had never been able to put up as many squirrel tails on his smokehouse door as I have. Have you, Johnnie?"

"That's not the reason," Johnnie said.

"Then what is the reason?" Finn asked. "I've got eleven more tails to go on my smokehouse door even if I am arrested."

"Your squirrels are my squirrels," Lottie said. "They'll be confiscated. Let's get goin' to my car."

"You bring our car, Shan," Finn said.

"Give me the keys," I said.

"Get it out of my pocket," Finn said. "I can't get it with these handcuffs on."

Lottie thought Finn meant for him to get the key.

"Keep your hand out of my pocket before I kick you," Finn shouted.

I got the key from Finn's pocket. I watched him walk down the hill in front while Johnnie and Lottie walked behind. Johnnie carried three shotguns, and Lottie carried Finn's eleven squirrels. It hurt me to see them do Finn this way. This would be another fine for Pa to pay. This would be a bigger fine, too. I knew Pa would go see Zack Bascom, Lottie's father over what had happened this time and there would be plenty of trouble. I knew the Plum Grove boys, fellows like Johnnie Little, would do some laughing, and Lottie would be their hero.

I walked slowly down the steep slope to the car. I could understand why Finn was sore at Lottie. I was sore at him too. I didn't like the way he was fighting back at Finn over Myrtle Edwards. I could hear the Plum

Grove boys laughing as I got into our car. I finally turned the car and started driving slowly down the green tunnel the way we had come two hours before. The sun was up now but not even a faint ray penetrated the roof of green leaves over this narrow-gauged valley.

When I drove down where Left and Right forks of Leatherwood Run united, Lottie and Johnnie were standing there with their prisoner waiting for me.

"What's the matter?" I asked.

"Three flat tires," Lottie said. "Both rears and my spare. Funny, how I got three flats in two hours! You got a pump?"

"I told you once we didn't have a pump," Finn said.

"But I wouldn't believe you," Lottie said, angrily.

"We don't have a pump," I said. "Come on, I can drive you to Blakesburg."

"Get in the back seat," Lottie ordered Finn.

"Don't get rough with me," Finn said.

Lottie opened the door and Finn got in the back seat. Lottie climbed in beside him. Johnnie Little sat beside me.

"Hate to leave my car out here," Lottie sighed as we started down Leatherwood Run.

"Serves you right," Finn laughed. "You followed me all the way out here. You've hunted all your life without license. Now, you've arrested me twice. But once," Finn chuckled, "you didn't get me. You picked a handful of number-five shots from your hide, didn't you?"

"I didn't pick any more shots from my hide than you did," Lottie told him.

I hit all the mudholes and ruts I could on our way to
Blakesburg. I wanted to give Johnnie and Lottie a ride
they'd always remember. All the way to Blakesburg
Lottie and Finn quarreled. Once Lottie told him he'd
never vote for Judge Burton again if he didn't fine Finn
one hundred dollars and costs.

Then, I threatened to put Lottie out of the car.

"Don't put 'im out, Shan," Finn begged. "I don't want
to walk handcuffed all the way to Blakesburg."

I drove on but I was hot under the collar over the way
Lottie was treating Finn. It was enough to make one's
blood boil to have a brother treated the way Lottie was
treating him. It was a quarter past eleven when I drove
to the courthouse yard in Blakesburg. When we got out
of the car, several of the old men who sat on the courthouse square and whittled for the longest shavings got
up from their seats to see what was going on.

"Mick Powderjay's boy handcuffed," said one of the
old men.

"What's he done?" one asked, angrily.

"Huntin' without license," Johnnie Little said. "It's
his second offense."

"You shut up," I said to Johnnie. "You know the real
reason. He took Lottie's girl!"

Then, the old men laughed and stuck their knives into
the soft pine boards. They knew what it was to win the
favor of a girl.

"Let's go listen to what Judge Burton says," said the
one with a gray mustache. "Might be interestin'."

When the old men followed us up the courthouse steps,

other people standing up and down the main street of Blakesburg started walking toward the courthouse. When we reached Judge Burton's office, the courthouse corridor was filled with old, middle-aged and young men, women and children. They were all trying to follow us into the judge's office.

"What's the trouble, boys?" Judge Burton asked, looking up from his desk over his spectacles.

Then the people began to crowd inside Judge Burton's office.

"Judge, I caught Finn Powderjay in the Big Woods hunting without license," Lottie said. "This is the second offense."

"Guilty or not guilty?" Judge Burton asked.

"Not guilty, Your Honor," Finn replied.

The crowd of onlookers were stunned. They looked at each other. They looked at Finn standing handcuffed before the judge. And they looked at Judge Watt Burton. I was shocked when Finn said he wasn't guilty.

"I'll set the date of your trial for September 16th," Judge Burton said, as he pushed his spectacles up on his nose. "Now I'll have you . . ."

"Don't bother about setting a date for my trial," Finn interrupted the judge. "Get me out of these handcuffs so I can show you . . ."

"No, no, Your Honor," Lottie interrupted. "He wants to fight. And as I have told you before, he's a dangerous . . ."

"Take the handcuffs off 'im, Warden Bascom," Judge Burton broke in. "He's not goin' to do anything!"

"Yes, I'm goin' to do something, Judge," Finn said, after Lottie took the handcuffs from his hands.

Finn put his hand into his pocket and came up with his billfold. He fingered inside his billfold.

"Here, Your Honor," he said, "look at this!"

The old men started laughing and whispering to each other. Smiles spread across the women's faces.

"It's your hunting license," Judge Burton said. "But why didn't you show it to Warden Bascom in the Big Woods?"

"He didn't ask to see my license," Finn said. "He slipped up and leveled his double-barrel on me and shouted: 'Consider yourself under arrest.' Then he handcuffed me."

"Did you do that, Constable Bascom?" Judge Burton asked. "Did you arrest this man like that?"

"Yes, Your Honor," Lottie admitted, while everybody in Judge Burton's office looked strangely at each other.

"Why did you do it?" Judge Burton asked. "Do you have a grudge against this man?"

"Ask me, Your Honor," I said. "I can tell you the whole story."

"I believe he let the air out of three of my tires," Lottie said. "My car is up the Right Fork of Leatherwood Run, thirty-eight miles from nowhere! And the sky looks like rain."

"Can you prove I let the air out of your tires?" Finn asked.

"You're dismissed, Finn Powderjay," Judge Burton said. "You may go."

"Give me my squirrels, Lottie," Finn said.

Then Finn gave six of his squirrels to Judge Burton, but he kept their tails.

When Finn and I left Judge Burton's office, the crowd followed. Lottie Bascom and Johnnie Little got up from their chairs to go too.

"No, no, fellows," Judge Burton said. "I dismissed Finn Powderjay. You fellows wait. I'm not through with you. When a man is wearing a badge of law and . . ."

That's all we heard. We were out in the corridor of the courthouse with the excited spectators. Loud voices and laughter and the thick courthouse walls muffled the sound of Judge Burton's words.

Sweetbird for Sheriff

Sweetbird is in the garden wearin' a straw hat. He is hoein' beans with a long-handle, gooseneck hoe. I look over the garden palin's and watch him cut the crabgrass. Sweetbird is as tall and thin as a hay pole, and has only one good eye. His arms are long and danglin' and his feet are large as small guitars. His knees are bowed like the curved handholds on our cutter-plow handles.

While he works, Sweetbird whistles a tune I've never heard before. I watch his elbows work in and out like a rooster's feet when he scratches for new worms to feed his hens. I watch Sweetbird turn his good eye toward the bean vines. Then he reaches down and pulls the crabgrass from the bean roots. Sweetbird fights his work. Now he stops whistlin' and begins to sing:

"I married me another, the devil's grandmother, oh, I wish I was single again, again, again, oh, I wish I was single again."

A rooster redbird sings in the apple tree above Sweetbird. This apple tree is white with blooms.

"Stop that singin'," Sweetbird says, turnin' his good eye up to the redbird. "You're not on the right tune and you bother me while I work. When a damn redbird hits a sour note . . ."

Sweetbird picks up a dry clod at his feet and throws it at the bird. The clod hits in front of me and I start walkin' down the county road. Sweetbird turns his good eye toward me. "Sorry," he says. "I didn't mean to hit you. I was just throwin' at that bird. It's got me vexed so I can't work. I'm trying to hoe my bean patch before the storm gets here."

"That's all right," I tell him. "You didn't hit me, Sweetbird. I must hurry to the store and get a sack of flour before the storm blows in. I don't want it to get wet and lumpy for I want good seldoms for my breakfast."

"Why do you call biscuits *seldoms?*" he asks.

"We seldom have 'em," I say.

"Elect me for sheriff," he says. "You'll have better times. You can call 'em biscuits then. You belong to the Right Party, don't you?"

"Sure do," I tell him.

"I'm goin' to be the Right Party high sheriff of Greenwood County."

"I didn't know you was runnin' for sheriff."

"Well, I am," he tells me. "I'm goin' to work as hard to get this office as I work to hoe these beans before that storm gets here. After I get to be sheriff, I'll clean up all the giggle water in Greenwood County. You know them Winthrops over on Deer Creek make giggle water by the truckload. The Winthrops belong to our party. But I'll dry up their giggle-water fountains when I get to be sheriff. Watch me dry 'em up!"

The bird in the apple tree sings: "Wet spring! Wet spring! Wet spring!"

"Damn you, shut up!" Sweetbird says. He picks up another clod and throws it up among the white blossoms. The clod bursts into sand. It streams down among the short green leaves and white blossoms like brown raindrops. The bird flies across the road to a willow tree.

"I must be gettin' on to your pappie's store," I tell Sweetbird.

Sweetbird bends over like the crook in a cutter-plow handle and goes to diggin'. He has spent too much time talkin' to me and throwin' clods at the rooster redbird.

I walk on up the dusty road under a shady roof of dark, thin-bellied clouds. But the air is filled with apple blossoms and is good to breathe.

Sweetbird's father, Spider Anderson, runs the store. He is a little skinny man with legs like a spider. His thin face is light brown, the color of a peeled hickory nut, and his hands are the right size to cut cloth with a pair of scissors. He has blue veins runnin' up and down his arms like green sour vines around a hickory tree. I can almost see the blood in his veins. When he talks he grunts like a pig. He squeals a little like a hungry pig when he is in a hurry.

"How are you, Jasper?"

"All right," I says.

"How's your pappie and all the folks? All gettin' along well?"

"Well as common," I says. "How's all your folks?"

"Well as common, too," he tells me.

"I come over to get a sack of flour," I says. "Pappie wants it on tick till he sells some starvation poles."

"All right," says Spider. "Your pappie's a good man and his pappie before him was, too. He traded with my pappie. Wonder if you and Sweetbird will make the same kind of men?"

Spider gives me the flour and looks over the black rims of his glasses into my eyes. He brushes his hands on his pants legs. Then he turns and walks behind the counter.

"I don't know what kind of a man I'll be," I say to Spider as he charges my sack of flour in the big book.

"But you'll belong to the Right Party, won't you?" Spider says as he puts his pencil behind his ear.

"Guess so," I tell him.

"No guess to it," he says squealin' like a pig. "Your pappie's pappie, old Iser Forshee, sleepin' up there on Lonesome hill, was the strongest Right Party man that ever snorted wind into his nostrils. Your own pappie is a strong one, too. He never bolted the ticket in his life. He's voted it straight. You tell your pappie that my boy, Sweetbird, is runnin' for high sheriff."

"I'll tell him," I says.

I put the sack across my shoulder and leave the store. I hurry back down the road to where Sweetbird is still diggin' in the garden. I watch him bend over, pick up another clod and turn his good eye toward the apple tree. He throws the clod into the tree.

"Shoo, damn you! Shoo!" says Sweetbird.

The rooster redbird flies across the road and alights on a poplar limb. Then Sweetbird grabs his hoe, bends over and begins to dig again.

When I get home, my pappie is hoein' the potatoes near our barn. He is hoein' fast, trying to beat the storm.

"Pappie," I says, "did you know Sweetbird is runnin' for high sheriff of Greenwood County?"

"His belongin' to the Right Party is all that will save him," Pappie says. "He is a scatterbrain. He's no good, but he is on my ticket and I'll have to vote for 'im. Who will be his deputies? Did Spider say?"

"No, he didn't."

"I hope Sweetbird will select good deputies."

"Sweetbird told me he's goin' to dry up all the giggle-water fountains in Greenwood County," I tell Pappie. "He said he would get the Winthrops. He said he was goin' to clean Greenwood County as clean as he was cleanin' the weeds from his garden."

"Winthrops' giggle-water fountains have been spoutin' since before Sweetbird was born," Pappie says. "They've been makin' and sellin'. His crazy talk will hurt him over there on Deer Creek. That's all Right Party county. Dave Rister is the only Wrong Party vote over there. Dave's got a jack and they get him out every night of the election and put old Dave on his back with a lot of signs and make him ride him up and down Deer Creek."

Bert Whalen walks down the road and stops.

"Menus," he says to Pappie, "did you know that Sweetbird Anderson is runnin' for high sheriff this time? Mort Denby is one of his deputies and Oscar Black is the other. The Oscar Black that lives on Beauty Ridge—not the Oscar Black of Flat Holler."

"I heard Sweetbird was runnin' for sheriff," says Pappie, leanin' on his hoe handle. "I didn't know who his deputies would be. I'm glad he's got good deputies. Sweetbird is a high-tempered, scatterbrained boy. He's not the man old Spider is. Spider raised him with a silver spoon in his mouth. That won't do, boys! It won't do!"

On Saturday mornin' Pappie and I take our mule and spring wagon and start to the store. We go to get meal, sugar and coffee. We take a basket of eggs, eight fryin'-size pullets and six young roosters to trade to Spider. We drive the spring wagon down the Sandy road and over the hill to Spider Anderson's store. When we drive in sight of the store, we see many men gathered around with their horses tied to the hitchin' posts. Men wallow on the grass and pull up sprigs of it and talk.

"What's gone wrong down there?" Pappie asks.

"I wouldn't know," I say.

"More folks there than usual," he says. "Somethin'

must be wrong. Someone in Spider's family might have been called by the Master to his reward in the Great Beyond."

We drive up to the store and Pappie hooks the bridle reins over a palin'. We get our eggs and produce and go inside the store.

"Did you hear about Sweetbird?" Jim Acres says to Pappie.

"No. What's happened?"

"Sweetbird was down there pullin' weeds outten the beans a while ago," Jim says faster than the spring wind flutters the poplar leaves, "and somethin' struck his leg. He thought it was a sand briar first. So he went out and carried back a load of bean sticks. He started to put a bean stick down and somethin' struck 'im again. He lifted his hand up and a big rusty copperhead was hangin' on. This made Sweetbird mad and he choked it loose and beat it to death with a bean stick. He didn't leave a piece of it. He beat it into the dust. He got his blood hot. He was out of his head in two minutes atter he got to the house. It took four men to hold him in bed a little while ago. They cut the finger and his pappie, Spider, sucked the blood and did a lot of spittin'."

"That's very bad news about Sweetbird," Pappie says. "I've allus wondered how he lost his eye."

"Throwin' rocks at birds," says Jim. "He never liked to let a bird sing when he was singin'. He says a bird can't keep a tune when it sings. One day he throwed a rock up in a tree at a mockin' bird and the rock came back and knocked his eye out."

305

"He's too high strung," Pappie tells Jim.

"And he's runnin' for high sheriff on the Right Party ticket," says Jim. "He's bound to be elected now. It's too late for anybody else to file. We've allus had a Right Party man for high sheriff in Greenwood County."

"I ain't so sure about it this time," says Tub Winthrop.

Spider Anderson walks in at the side door. "What did you say in my store?" he says. "Tub, I heard what you said."

"Spider, I'll say it again for you," Tub says. "I'm not sure we'll have a Right Party high sheriff this time. I'll say it louder if you want me to. Your boy had done said he'd dry up the giggle-water fountains on Deer Creek. He said he'd clean the Winthrops out over there if he was elected. I'm goin' to do my best to see he ain't elected. I'm goin' to bolt the ticket. Deer Creek will bolt the ticket if your boy gets well enough to run. We're goin' to make our giggle water over there and sell it. Ain't we bought our sugar, yeast and molasses offen you? Then you turn against us. We're Right Party men, too. We are goin' to vote for the Wrong Party this time. We are goin' to have the first Wrong Party high sheriff in Greenwood County."

"Get out of my store! Get out!" Spider squalls. "You ain't no Right Party man! You're a traitor! See this vest pocket? What my boy, Sweetbird, needs in Greenwood County is right here in this old vest pocket."

"Yes, but you ain't got Deer Creek," Tub says as he goes through the door.

"A split in the party, sure as the good Lord made

306

little green apples," Wes Stableton says and shakes his head like an addled rooster.

"Can't tell where this thing is goin' to end, boys," says Mort Taylor. "We might be over there stealin' that old jack out and decoratin' 'im up for the first Wrong Party victory since Abraham Lincoln!"

"You can't tell about Deer Creek," says Wes. "There's a tribe of Winthrops and they've married into the Goings and Preston families. They'll all go solid against Sweetbird. Sweetbird talks too much when he's in his right mind. Old Spider here in the store workin' and thinkin' the Right Party will win! There's an awful lot of hard feelin's stirred up when Sweetbird said he'd dry up the fountains."

We wait until Spider gets our coffee, sugar and meal. We sell our eggs and young chickens and pay on our account.

"What is the balance, Spider?" says Pappie.

"Just a minute," says Spider. "You owe me $9.32."

"Store count's too much," Pappie says. "I'll cut it down when the taters and corn come in. I'll soon be findin' some wild honey. I'll get it paid in full then."

"That's all right, Menus," says Spider, "you can have anythin' more you want. Come or send atter it."

We walk across the yard where men are wallowin' on the grass.

"Just as old Tub said," we hear Jim Sinnet say, "if Sweetbird's elected high sheriff of Greenwood County he will try to stop our makin' giggle water on Deer Creek. He's liable to have us in the Greenwood County jail. I've always voted for the straight Right Party ticket. But I'll scratch the Right Party ticket this time if Sweetbird Anderson gets well of that copperhead bite and stays on the Right Party ticket!"

"I will, too," says John Hammons. "It's just as old Tub says. It's dangerous to elect a man like Sweetbird for high sheriff. If he fights us like he did that copperhead and the little birds that sing in the apple trees, we'd as well move from Deer Creek, leave our homes and farms and go someplace else. We'll all land in the Greenwood County jail. I belong to the Right Party and Pap and Grandpa did too. They'll rise from their graves on Lonesome Hill when I scratch the Right Party. But they'll have to rise up for I won't vote for Sweetbird. I'll vote agin 'im."

"Who's runnin' on the Wrong Party ticket for high sheriff?" Pappie asks.

"Felix Hall is runnin' and his deputies are Ham Johnson and Roscoe Stone," says Sam Conley. "They are good men. I belong to the Right Party and I'm sayin' this, too. I know all three men; they will make good sheriffs. Greenwood County needs two parties anyway. When we git a man for sheriff like Sweetbird, I'm ready for a change."

It is the first Saturday in July and I walk down to Spider Anderson's store. The grass along the road is wilted and the wind sweeps up little clouds of yellow dust. The dust settles on the devil-shoestring vines that crawl along the worm rail fence beside the road. It is very hot.

I walk onto the dry, parched grass in front of the store

where men are wallowin' on the hot grass while they talk about Sweetbird and the election. They talk and pluck the dry stems and chew them.

"Yes, Sweetbird is some better."

"He lost his finger where that snake grabbed him the second time."

"I hear a place rotted outten the calf of his leg where it bit him the first time."

"A copperhead bite is pizen to a man's flesh!"

"It would a been better for our Right Party if that snake bite had laid Sweetbird up until after the election. He's got the Winthrops sore and they're as thick as sassafras sprouts over on Deer Creek."

"It's awful hard to elect a Wrong Party candidate here. It won't surprise me to see Sweetbird carry Greenwood County by a big majority."

"It will surprise me and I've been all over Greenwood County. I've heard the people talk. Our people get more for gallons of giggle water than for bushels of corn. They don't like what Sweetbird said about his dryin' up the fountains. Everywhere I go, I hear people talkin' about what Tub Winthrop said. 'A fellow that will beat a copperhead to pieces with a bean stick because it hit him twice and throw rocks at the little birds because they sing is a dangerous man to put over the people.'"

"Boys, I can tell how this election is goin'! Felix will be elected."

I ask for my mail and Spider gives me a catalog. That's all the mail I get. The store is filled with people sellin' eggs and buyin' groceries.

"How's my son, Sweetbird, runnin'?" Spider asks me.

"All right, I 'spect," I says to Spider.

"He'll be Greenwood County's next sheriff," Spider says. "You can't beat a Right Party man in Greenwood County. Sweetbird is a Right Party man. And old Tub Winthrop is fightin' 'im. Tub's already split the party. And he's tellin' I sold 'im sugar, yeast and molasses and meal to make giggle water. He's put this scandal out on me. Damn the Winthrops!"

"How is Sweetbird now? Pappie told me to ask."

"You tell Menus he's some better. He's pale from the pizen yet and he lost a finger. He lost some flesh from the calf of his leg, too. But Sweetbird will be able to stir a little the last of this month."

I take the catalog and start home. Sunflower blossoms bend their wilted stems in John Nye's garden. Wilted corn blades sag like spider webs in the morning dew.

When Pappie goes down to vote I go with him. At the Deer Creek schoolhouse I see men gathered in little groups. Sweetbird is with one group. He talks to a man and waves his hands high in the air. Then Sweetbird goes to another group and talks to a man. Then he runs over to another man and catches him by the shoulder and talks to him.

"There'll be one elected on the Wrong Party ticket this time," I hear a strange man say. "Sweetbird had the wrong talk about our fountains."

Men walk into the schoolhouse in single file to vote. They come out one by one, gather, and stand and talk. They talk with their hands. I wonder what they are talkin' about. I would like to be old enough to vote.

"Well," says Spider, as he walks across the dry, brown grass, "a little sprinkle of rain. That's a sign the Wrong Party is gettin' some votes. It will be just a warnin' though. You'll see by tomorrow when the vote is counted. Greenwood County don't go but one way here. I'll ride that jack of Dave Rister's from the mouth of Deer Creek to the head if Sweetbird isn't elected high sheriff of Greenwood County. I feel certain about my son's bein' elected. I feel like we got it in our pockets!"

"I'm afraid, Spider, you'll ride that jack," says Mort Hailey. "If all our Right Party men win, I'll ride the jack. You know I am a Right Party man and I vote the Right Party ticket. Sweetbird and Tub have split the Right Party. Sweetbird told all over this county he was goin' to jail the Winthrops for makin' giggle water. That talk won't do on Deer Creek."

"We'll see who rides the jack by eleven o'clock tomorrow."

"The election is over," says Pappie. "See the sellouts takin' flour home on express wagons."

We see the election officers haulin' the ballot boxes in a T-model to Blakesburg, county seat of Greenwood County. They will guard the boxes tonight and start countin' votes in the mornin' by nine. By ten we can tell how the election goes if we don't have a lot of shootin'.

Pappie and I ride twenty miles to Blakesburg in our express wagon. It is Wednesday mornin' and a great day in Greenwood County. We will soon know who our high sheriff will be. We stay in the courthouse yard and watch them post the votes on a blackboard fast as they

count them. All of Greenwood County's races are goin'
Right Party but the sheriff's race. It is a close vote. Tub
is standin' near us. Sweetbird and Spider are standin'
with a group of their friends around them. This is what
happened after Deer Creek was counted:

	Sweetbird Anderson: Right Party	Felix Hall: Wrong Party
Buzzard Roost	275	273
Plum Fork	193	194
Hillman's Mill	65	66
Iron Hill	360	379
Steam Furnace	268	250
Rock Hill	105	100
Smith	358	208
Centerview	79	56
East View	208	150
Oak Hill	101	99
Logan Cross Roads	307	286
Deer Creek	11	508
Total	2330	2569

There is nothin' for Sweetbird and Spider to say.
Sweetbird kicks the courthouse dust with his shoe. Tub
Winthrop stands across from him.

"Spider, how'll you like to ride Dave Rister's jack
from the mouth to the head of Deer Creek?" Tub says.
"Deer Creek is the land of the Winthrops and you'll ride
Dave's jack right past my house. This is one election when
poor old Dave won't have to ride his own jack."

"The first time since Lincoln," says Spider, "Greenwood County has elected a Wrong Party candidate. The Right Party dead will rise from their graves on Lonesome Hill when I ride Dave Rister's jack."

"Your ridin' Dave's jack will be a show worth the dead's risin' up from their graves to see," Tub says. "We'll be standin' by the road to watch you pass. You can't allus hold the people in your vest pocket."

32 Votes before Breakfast

Mr. Silas Devers was the man that hired me. He was the man that made all the plans. Even before daylight that morning, when we were getting ready to start with Al Caney, Mr. Devers got out a map. He had me to hold the flashlight while he went over the map. It was a map of Blake County. And he had little blue, red and black pencil marks running all over the map. While he ran his big forefinger over these lines, I couldn't help but watch 'im. He went from one voting precinct to another. I knew all the precincts because I'd worked in many elections before. But never before had I worked in an election when we got up at three o'clock in the morning and were on the road before four o'clock. I knew something was in the wind. As Mr. Devers looked over the map, when his forefinger went to a voting precinct, he stopped and held his finger there while he checked in a notebook with his other hand and read some directions. He had a lot of stuff written down I could hardly read. But I did make out a different name for each precinct.

It took Mr. Devers several minutes to go over his map and read his notes. But that wasn't none of my business. I was working for my party, the Greenough party, and I was a-gettin' paid besides. A ten-spot for the use of your car on election day isn't to be sneezed at. But Al Caney just sat there in the back seat of the car and rolled his quid of terbacker around in his jaw and I didn't see how he could do it that early in the morning before he'd had his breakfast. But he did. He didn't do any talking when Mr. Devers was goin' over the map. He didn't even try to look on. Sometimes he rubbed his big bony hand over his beardy face to wipe a sliver of brown ambeer from his lip. Al Caney just didn't seem to mind what was goin' on. I wondered if he didn't have an understandin' with Mr. Devers same as I had. But what stumped me was, I thought I could remember when Al Caney was a Dinwiddie. I knew all the other Caneys were Dinwiddies. I didn't exactly understand what he was doin' with us. But I would soon find out.

"It's a close election this time, boys," Mr. Devers said, as he took a last look at the map, folded it carefully, stuck it in his coat pocket and settled down in his seat. "We gotta start, Dave."

"Okay, Mr. Devers," I said, as I started the motor and turned on my lights.

Mr. Devers turned off his flashlight and stuck it in his pocket. Then he climbed in the front seat.

"Which way, Mr. Devers?"

"To the Blackoak precinct first," he said.

"But Mr. Devers," I said, "that's on the other side of Blake County!"

"Never mind where it is, Dave," he said. "You're getting paid and you must listen to reason."

"Okay," I said.

"Step on it," he said. "We want to be there by six. Want to be the first ones there when the polls open!"

I stepped on the gas. I went down the road like a bat out o' hell. There was not a light in any of the windows. Everybody must've been asleep. And I cut the curves from one side of the road to the other. I drove so fast I almost scared myself. But Mr. Devers didn't mind. He was so big that he took up most of the front seat beside me, and when I hit a chughole, the watch chain across his vest gave a little tinkle like a sheep bell. And Al Caney sat in the back seat, never saying a word, chewin' his quid and spittin' out the window.

"While the Dinwiddies sleep, we work," Mr. Devers said, and then he laughed like a big-throated bullfrog.

"I'm gittin' hungry, Silas," Al Caney said, as he rolled his quid with his tongue from his mouth onto his hand and threw it from the car. "I've not had any breakfast, you know!"

"I've not had any either," Mr. Devers said. "We've got to make Blackoak first. Then we'll talk about breakfast."

"It's chewin' that green burley twist that's making him

hungry, I thought. But I didn't say what I thought since it wasn't any of my business.

Al Caney groaned and complained with his stomach, and said he was about half sick.

"I'll fix all that half-sickness, Al," Mr. Devers said. "Just wait till we git to Blackoak. I know what you need. Our party'll have it on hand!"

Just before we got to Blackoak, Mr. Devers got out his notebook and looked at the name again.

"Remember, Al, your name is Casper Higgins, and you live on Sand Suck, if anybody questions you," Mr. Devers instructed Al. "Can you remember?"

"Sure can," Al Caney said.

When we drove up to the Blackoak school, there was a light in the windows. The polls had opened. But I didn't see a crowd hangin' on the outside like we always saw in Blake County on election days.

"My name's Casper Higgins and I live on Sand Suck," All Caney said when he got out of the car.

"That's right, Al," Mr. Devers said, as he rolled out like a big barrel.

Just to see what happened, I got out and went in too.

"We don't vote here," Mr. Devers told one of the election judges. "We're bringin' a man here to vote."

"Name, please?" one of the women clerks asked.

"Casper Higgins," Al said.

"Casper Higgins?" the clerk repeated. "Ain't he dead?"

"Dead! Am I dead?" Al asked. "I hope to tell you I'm alive! Isn't my name on the record?"

"It's been marked out," she said.

"Mark it back in," Al said. "I'm goin' to vote! How dare you mark it out!"

"Well, if he's not dead," one of the judges said, "he's entitled to a vote same as any taxpayer!"

See, we had two Greenough judges at each precinct, and the Dinwiddies had one. Our county judge was a Greenough, and he appointed the election judges.

"You see I'm not dead," Al complained, as if he were mad as a wet hen.

"Let 'im vote," the second judge said.

Mr. Devers seemed pleased. I saw him wink at one of the judges as Al went into the booth, a place surrounded by bed sheets, to vote.

Just as soon as Al had voted, we hurried out the Blackoak schoolhouse and were on our way.

"You did fine, Al," Mr. Devers said, reaching him two brand-new, one-dollar bills. "Smooth talk."

"But about my breakfast, Silas?" Al complained, rubbing his stomach. "Peers like I have a hard time gettin' my breath when I get hungry!"

"We'll take care of that at Plum Forks," Mr. Devers said. "Sorry I fergot to get you somethin' back there!"

"To Plum Forks next, Mr. Devers?" I said.

"That's right," he said. "Step on the gas."

I wondered how we's goin' to get any breakfast for we were goin' up Lambert River where there wasn't even a country store.

Before we got to Plum Forks, Mr. Devers looked at his paper and the map.

"You're Columbus Mitchell, Al," Mr. Devers said. "And you live on Hoods Run!"

"Okay, Silas," Al said. "I can remember that all right. I ust to know old Columbus!"

"Name, please," the woman asked Al.

"Columbus Mitchell," Al said.

"Columbus Mitchell," she spoke politely. "W'y I thought he'd passed on."

"Nope, right here he is," Al said, grinning and showing his front discolored teeth. "I'm here to vote!"

I saw Mr. Devers wink at one of the judges.

"Oh, yes, Columbus," the judge said. "Go on and vote!"

One of the judges looked puzzled when Al went back to vote.

Mr. Devers was mighty pleased when Al walked from behind the sheet.

"Say, you couldn't spare us a little nip, could you, Bill?" Mr. Devers asked the judge that he'd winked at a minute before. "We've not had any breakfast!"

"Shore," he said, and he got up from his chair while the other judges and clerks watched us.

He walked beside us to the doorsteps, talking in low whispers to Mr. Devers. Then he slipped Mr. Devers a big bottle that he pulled from behind his coat lining where I heard more bottles rattle.

When we got back to the car Mr. Devers took a swig first, and then he passed the bottle to me, and I nipped because I didn't like too much on an empty stomach, and then he passed the bottle to Al. I was glad he let me nip before he did Al, because Al's mouth looked like the mouth of a deserted coal mine propped up with decayed posts.

"Now, Dave," Mr. Devers spoke in a big way, "I'll let you in on the plan! We want to get all the precincts on Lambert River by eleven. Then we'll come down Sutton River and get all the precincts by three this afternoon. In the next three hours we can finish all the precincts in Blakesburg and down Big River!"

"You mean we're goin' to take in all thirty-two precincts?" I asked.

"That's what we're a-goin' to do," he said.

"Impossible," I said.

I could tell by the way Mr. Devers puffed up, I'd said the wrong thing.

"Oh, I guess we can make it if they don't ask Al too many questions," I said. "I mean if they don't hold us too long questionin' Al . . ."

"Never mind that, Dave," Mr. Devers said. "You leave it to me! I've got that all fixed up!"

Before we reached Farewell precinct, Mr. Devers consulted his map and notebook.

"Who am I now, Silas?" Al asked.

"Buck Stump," Mr. Devers said, "And you live on Dry Ridge."

I never knew a Buck Stump, but I knew a lot of Stumps lived on Dry Ridge. I'd fox-hunted with 'em. That was the home of the Stumps. Mr. Devers had fixed his notebook and map all right.

"Buck Stump," the clerk said, "I thought he was run away from here for stealin' chickens!"

"I never stole a chicken in my life," Al said, looking hard at the woman. "How dare you say that!"

But one of the judges tried to smooth it out for the woman.

"It must have been another Buck Stump," he said. "You know there's more Buck Stumps on that Dry Ridge. There's Old Buck, Little Buck, Red Buck, Black Buck, White Buck, and Zeke's Buck, and Cy's Buck . . . and a lot more I can't think of now."

Everybody laughed while the judges let Al go behind the sheet.

Al seemed awfully hurt when he returned from voting. The clerk who had made the mistake tried to apologize and be nice to him, but he refused all apologies. He got out as soon as he could, and we followed him.

"Well done, Al," Mr. Devers said. "Smooth talk."

"But ye forget something, Silas?" Al said.

"Breakfast, ah breakfast," Mr. Devers said. "We shall have that, Al!"

"No, it's not that," Al said. "I'm not a bit hungry now!"

"Oh, oh, yes, I did forget, didn't I?" Mr. Devers said, as he went down in his pocket for a roll of greenbacks bigger than the calf of my leg. He shelled off four new one-dollar bills for Al.

I didn't say anything. But I thought a lot. Here I was driving my car over this rough road and was only gettin' ten bucks. And just to think if Al did make all the precincts, it would be sixty-four dollars for him! There wasn't anything fair about it. But I wouldn't say anything. I'd wait until the end of the day! Somebody'd have to make things right.

321

Al voted at Wolf Pen as Lonnie Ailster, who was a Dinwiddie. The clerk said Lonnie was working in St. Louis. Al told her he'd never worked in St. Louis, that he'd never seen the place. Well, the judge that Mr. Devers winked at apologized for the clerk to make her feel better after she'd made the mistake. At Grassy, Al voted as Duff Anderson, and the clerk didn't question him, but congratulated him on coming back to his wife after disappearing for five years. At Riverbend, Al voted for Alvin Miller, a Greenough who was away cutting corn in Ohio.

"See, the farther out you get among the hills, the easier it is," Mr. Devers said. "Hardly anybody around Riverbend ever sees Al Miller. Hardly anybody knows 'im. See what I mean!"

"Yes, I see," I said.

But I said that just to be nice to Mr. Devers. I knew he could make that one little mistake.

But we went to the eleven precincts up Lambert River by eleven-thirty. Just thirty minutes behind schedule. Al voted at Kenton for Tim Wurts, a Greenough, who worked away in the West Virginia coal mines. He voted in Woodland for Tom Snyder, who had been sent to the pen in Atlanta for making moonshine several years ago. The clerks didn't question his registration or his identity, for they were so glad to see him back with his family. At Threeprong he voted for Hugh Gullet. He was questioned by the clerk, who said she was sure that Hugh Gullet had moved away.

"Moved away," Al said. "I've never moved away. How did that get started?"

And a friendly judge said he hadn't moved away, and he apologized for the clerk's mistake.

At Whetstone, he voted for Brice Tremble, a "lifelong" Dinwiddie. One of the judges said Al didn't look like Brice. But Al said he was Brice, and two of the judges let him vote. We wondered what the real Brice would say when he got to the polls. But Mr. Devers said he wouldn't get to the polls until late in the afternoon. Said he was over on Sand Suck where he'd been cutting timber and wouldn't spend a whole day for the election. At the Head-of-Lambert precinct, the last one up the river in Blake County, Al voted for John And-Seven-Eights Smith, a "lifelong" Dinwiddie, who was down on Willow Run running a sawmill. John's father had given him the middle name to distinguish him from so many John Smiths living in the Head-of-Lambert precinct.

When we finished with this precinct, Al had twenty-two pretty one-dollar bills stuffed down in his overall pockets. I thought plenty, but I still didn't say anything. For we'd just driven away from Head-of-Lambert precinct, on our way over the ridge toward Sutton River, when Al took some sort of a fainting spell. Maybe it was because he'd made all this money, and maybe it was because he'd chawed green twist so early in the morning, and on top of that drank some bad hooch. It had given me somethin' like the blind billiards. I could tell Mr. Devers didn't act the same, but he hadn't drank near as much as Al.

Maybe it was just as well it happened as we were about to reach the big hill that separated the two rivers. For

323

we wouldn't have wanted anybody around. There'd been a lot of people hanging around the polls who heard the argument when Al went in and said he was John And-Seven-Eights Smith. And now if Al got sick on us, and the real John And-Seven-Eights Smith did get back from the sawmill, we'd be in bad shape. But we opened the car door when Al passed out, and we carried him up on the bank by the side of the road and fanned 'im for a spell. When he came to, his face was whiter than any sheet we'd seen around the booths.

"Pay no attention to me, boys," Al spoke with little short gasps of breath. "I'm havin' trouble gettin' my wind!"

But I was glad when Al stumbled back to the car.

"Reckon he's all right?" I asked Mr. Devers. "Suppose we can make the fourteen precincts on Sutton River?"

"What are you talkin' about?" Mr. Devers asked me. "You know Al can make it all right. We're goin' to stop at the Porter Store on North Fork as we go down," he talked on, "and get some cheese under our belts. We're a little behind, but we can make all thirty-two precincts! That'll be a record, won't it?"

"Guess it will," I said, thinking about how a few men had been able to vote in five or six precincts in one day, but that I'd never heard in my life of one making eleven precincts before. We already had a record.

We stopped at the store and got cheese, brown sugar, sardines and crackers. We did most of our eating in the car, and Mr. Devers and I did most of the eating.

"Don't be douncy, Al," Mr. Devers warned. "We've

324

got a lot to do. You've got a lot more dollars to earn. Thirty-two votes may win this election! So, eat, my good friend!"

"Grub don't taste right," Al said.

Al only took a few bites, then he washed it down from the long-neck bottle he stuck in the cavern that was his mouth until his whiskers and mustache hid the bottle-neck. He gurgled and gurgled, and his Adam's apple ran up and down his neck like a tree frog. And after he'd washed the cheese and crackers down his gullet, he bit off more green burly from his twist. Then I saw a little color come back to his face.

"We'll take these precincts as they come, boys," Mr. Devers said, when he reached sight of the Sutton River.

At Blue Licks, Al voted for Lewis MacKenzie; at Hoptown, for Marcus Overton; and at Argill for Tom Kidwell. At Honeyville, he voted for Cief Hampton; at Centerview, for Tom Cromwell; at Enoch's Chapel, for Eif Fannin; and at Five Rivers, for Larry Watkin. At Twin Forks, Al voted for Milford Kilgore, a Dinwiddie, who had gone to a funeral. At Three Mile, he voted for Jim Welch; and at John's Run, for Jack Pruitt.

But at Pee-Pee-Dee, Mr. Devers turned pale as a mush-room when Al gave his name as Mart Spencer, and one of the clerks asked, "When did you get back from the pen?"

"I'm not the Mart that stabbed your brother," Al said. "I'm not even akin to 'im. I just happen to live among those Spencers."

The clerk was pleased. So were the judges. Al voted.

At Willow Grove, Al voted for Gus Powers; at Lundsford, for Demp Bush; and at Putt-Off Ford, for Hawk Seymore.

"Twenty-five precincts, and fifty dollars," Mr. Devers said, giving Al another two new one-dollar bills. "Seven more to go!"

Boy, that burnt me up. Here Al had made fifty bucks. A Dinwiddie by blood and belief had taken that much from our party, and I got a measly ten-spot! But I still kept my mouth shet. I knew Al had been through a lot too. He'd been twenty-five different men. And he'd had several faintin' spells in the back of the car. He'd been complaining about his stomach, and once or twice he said his ticker was flutterin' like a mockingbird's wings.

"We're comin' to Blakesburg No. 1," Mr. Devers said, "where we'll all get our legal and lawful votes! That'll make twenty-eight votes for the Greenoughs from us this mornin'!"

Mr. Devers had the look of victory on his face after we'd voted at Blakesburg No. 1.

"When we get to Blakesburg No. 2, you're goin' to be Rev. Spencer Hix that ust to hold the big revivals under the tent," Mr. Devers said.

"Did you hear me, Al?" Mr. Devers asked, since Al hadn't answered.

"Yep, I hear you," Al groaned. "I'm Reverend Hix in Blakesburg No. 2."

"Right," Mr. Devers said, as I brought my car to a stop.

I never saw so many people around at any of the voting places. They were swarming around Link Bratton's vacant-store building like bees around a hive.

We walked inside and Al had to stand in line to vote.

"Name, please?" the woman clerk asked Al.

"Reverend Hix," Al said. "I've voted twenty-eight times for the Greenoughs, and I aim to vote again!"

"What Reverend Hix?" she asked, looking Al in the eye.

"The Rev. Spencer Hix that used to hold the tent meetings," Al shouted.

"Sure, this is Reverend Hix," Mr. Devers said, as he looked at a Greenough clerk and winked.

"No, you're not Reverend Hix," the clerk said. "I go to his church. I heard him preach last Sunday. Against the Greenoughs too! No, you're not Rev. Spencer Hix! I know you're not! This is fraud!"

"I know I am," Al shouted. "And I'll show you that I am! I'll show you, I'll vote."

"Al Caney," Mr. Devers said, but it was too late.

Al started to dive behind the sheet when a big man grabbed him. Then the election judge caught Al around the legs. And down on the floor went all three men while more ran in to help.

"That thing's not Reverend Hix," a big woman shouted, and raised her green parasol above her head to hit Al. "I'll brain 'im," she screamed.

But Mr. Devers, who'd kept out of the tussle, ran up and caught her parasol.

"That awful man!" another woman shouted. "Thinks he's Reverend Hix! He must be drunk or crazy!"

Soon the voting place was filled with men and women.
They knew Reverend Hix. They belonged to his church.

I never saw such a mad scramble in my life! Al Caney
was screaming that he was the Rev. Spencer Hix. Women
and men were trying to get to him while he fought with
the men on the floor.

"He's drunk," one man said. "Let's have 'im arrested!"

"He's off in the head," another shouted. "Reverend Hix
just voted a few minutes ago!"

"Who brought 'im in here?" a big beardy-faced man
asked.

"That's the fellar," said a tall bean-pole man with
scattered beard on his face, as he pointed to Mr. Devers.

"Yes, that's the man," said a woman, who was in the
voting line. "That's the man over there!"

"Something strange goin' on here," said the big beardy-
faced man, "and I'll see what it is. Can't do Reverend
Hix like this! Look, this man, Al, has passed out. He's
drunk!"

Mr. Devers must have jumped fifteen feet out at the
door. I was a few steps behind him, but I couldn't run
like he did. I didn't know any man could run fast as Mr.
Devers. It looked like he was takin' steps on the wind.
For his feet were up in the air working like pistons. If
they ever hit the ground, it was so fast I couldn't see 'em.

"Here's my car, Mr. Devers," I screamed, but he was
so excited he didn't hear me.

He ran to some stranger's car with about two dozen
women and a dozen men after him. They were yelling
and screaming! And Mr. Devers opened the door of the

wrong car and got in. He thought it was mine. But I couldn't go after him. I had to save my own skin. They weren't after me yet.

"He's in Reverend Hix's car," a woman shouted. "We've got him!"

When I turned on the switch and started the motor in a hurry, I looked toward Reverend Hix's car, and I saw Mr. Devers trying to get him to drive on like he'd been doin' me. But Reverend Hix sat under the steering wheel and laughed while the mob of voters surrounded the car.

I gunned into the highway, and I was off like a flash of lightning cutting the night. I never looked back. I knew I'd keep on goin' as long as my ten Greenough dollars lasted.

Peace and the Right Party

Our boss, Big Jim MacRowan, was six feet tall, with shoulders broad as a corncrib door. His arms were like knotty saplings and his fists like hammers. He could carry white-oak crossties all day and never tire. He was a man of action and everything had to be his way. He feared no man in Greenwood County or among the Kentucky hills. Each morning after he'd finished breakfast he stood up at the head of the table and pounded his chest with his big fists and boasted that he could whip his weight in wildcats.

This particular morning Big Jim's wind-tanned face was redder than usual. "Next time our road's blocked," he declared, "I'm goin' to swear out a warrant for Old John Meadows. There's a law in this state against blockin'

330

a road. I'll sure use that law on Old John if he don't behave himself."

Jim got behind the steering wheel of his heavy lumber
truck, and Little Tom Adams, his number-one helper,
got in beside him. Little Tom watched the road for wire,
rocks and logs. We often called him Babyhawk because
his thin-pointed nose was hooked like a hawk's beak. And
his hawk eyes could see a wire stretched across the road
in the morning mists better than any of our eyes. Alf
Rister and I climbed upon the big load of ninety-six
green crossties, and Big Jim started the truck down the
mountain road toward Blakesburg.

"A penny for your thoughts, Bobby," Alf said to me
as we rode along on top the crossties. "Are you still day-
dreamin' about that Meadows gal?"

"You're right, Alf," I said. "I think about Subrina all
the time. Never an hour when I'm awake I don't think
of her. And I even dream about her too!"

When we reached the boundary of Big Jim's timber
land, we heard Babyhawk yell: "Watch out, Big Jim!
Wire!" Big Jim slammed on the brakes so suddenly Alf
and I had to grab the binding chain that held the crossties on the truck.

Big Jim and Babyhawk jumped out as mad as two disturbed hornets. Big Jim pulled a pair of heavy pliers from
his pocket and snipped the four strands of wire in a new
fence stretched across the road. Babyhawk threw each
strand back over the bank.

"More of Old John Meadows' spite work," Big Jim
said, putting the snips back in his pocket. "He's sore be-

cause I outbid him when Rance Leffard put this land up for sale. Now he's tryin' to fence me in."

The more Big Jim thought about John Meadows the madder he became. Now he turned to me and shook his thick finger at me. "Bobby Love," he said, "I'm goin' to fight Old John to a finish. My men have got to be loyal to me. So don't let me catch you sneakin' off to spark that Meadows gal."

"You don't have to fret about that, Big Jim," I said, feeling unhappier than ever. "John Meadows says I'm on your side and won't let me step foot inside his house. Said he'd pepper me with that shotgun of his if I came around any more."

"Every man that works for me had better be on my side," he said, his face flushed red as a ripe sourwood leaf. "If I ever hear of you goin' to see his gal again, I'll fire you and take the rest of the debt you owe me out of your hide. I'm doin' you a favor, Bobby. When you are older and married to some nice woman you'll never get through thankin' me for keepin' you away from Old John's gal. They're a bad lot, those Meadows."

I thought about the new blue Sunday suit and the shiny yellow shoes I'd bought, just to look nice when I sparked Subrina. I thought how I'd borrowed the money from Big Jim to buy them, promising to work it out. Now I couldn't spark Subrina at all. I was caught right in the middle between these two ornery old men. For a minute I wished they would both drop dead.

Big Jim and Babyhawk got back in the truck, and we started off toward Blakesburg again. By the time we got to Blakesburg and unloaded our ties, it was almost noon.

Then we followed Big Jim to Charlie Denton's office.

"Charlie," Big Jim said to the tall, lean, young-looking county attorney: "That John Meadows is blockin' my road. He's mad at me because I bought the Rance Leffard land that lays beyond his farm. The road he's blockin' is an old county road I reopened. He can't block it, can he? John Meadows is a dangerous man."

"Because both you and John belong to the Right Party and worked to elect me, I'd like to keep this trouble out of court," Charlie said.

"Why don't you go and see Old Amos Bodie? He is a father to all of us in the Right Party in Greenwood County. He always has kept the peace among us. He believes in peace and the Right Party."

"I'm willin', Charlie," Big Jim replied instantly. "But will Old John go see 'im too?"

"I'll see that he does," Charlie said. "Tomorrow afternoon at about two you be at Old Amos Bodie's. I'll drive out and see John this afternoon. Let's have peace in the party. Election is coming up this November. We don't want trouble in our party."

"This suits me," Big Jim said. "I don't want to split our party, and besides I'm a peace-lovin' man."

The next morning we drove to the sawmill and loaded. Big Jim was in a hurry to get to Blakesburg and be back in time to meet John Meadows at Amos Bodie's. We were on our way when Babyhawk let out a war whoop: "Rocks!"

Big Jim shoved the brake so suddenly Alf and I just had time to grab the binding chain.

"This is something," Big Jim said when he got out and

looked at the rocks that had been rolled down from the cliffs. "If John Meadows stays in the Right Party, I want out. If he goes to Heaven, I want to go to Hell. I never want to be where that man is."

Alf and I threw our handspikes on the ground, and then we got down and went to work. We lifted and pushed the rocks over the bank into the creek to clear the road. Big Jim mopped his brow with his red bandanna, and we went back on the truck again.

Big Jim stepped on the gas, and when we got to Blakesburg he ordered Alf and me to carry single instead of double on the heavy crossties.

"Let's hurry, boys, and unload," he said. "We want to be at Old Amos Bodie's at two as we promised. I've got plenty to tell Old Amos about this man."

That afternoon Big Jim drove his truck down the Threeprong Valley road and parked at the mouth of Little Greenbrier. We couldn't drive clear to Amos Bodie's, for there was only a path to his cabin. We followed Big Jim up the path. I didn't want to go to be a witness against John Meadows. And I didn't want to cross Big Jim MacRowan. I just wanted to stay out of it. I thought how pretty and sweet Subrina was. I wanted to see her again. I really wanted peace.

When we got there, John Meadows was waiting. Amos Bodie greeted us by our first names in his soft feeble old voice. He was sitting in a rocking chair under an apple tree that was white with blossoms. His long white hair rested on his clean, faded-blue shirt. His white beard almost reached his lap. Both hair and beard were as white as the blossoms on the apple tree. Amos Bodie had lived in this cabin alone as far back as any of the old people could remember. He was our prophet, and he always had settled disputes in the Right Party. He didn't know how old he was, for he was born before the state started keeping birth records. He believed he might be young enough to be in his nineties.

Old Amos asked Big Jim to stand before him and tell his story. Big Jim explained how the road he was using across John Meadows' farm had been a county road for more than thirty years. Then he told how John had tried to close the road so he couldn't haul his crossties to Blakesburg and how he found wire stretched across and big rocks in the road. He told Old Amos Bodie it was spitework because he had bought the seven hundred acres of timberland John Meadows had wanted. Big Jim wanted us as witnesses, but Old Amos told him he wouldn't need us. When I heard this, I gave a sigh of relief—John Meadows never would have forgiven me if I had testified against him.

After Big Jim had told his story, John Meadows, six feet six, slender as a sapling, tough as a white oak and as stubborn as a clinging wild grapevine, stood up before Old Amos. He said he was born in Threeprong Valley and had lived in the same house and on the same land all his life, and the road that Big Jim MacRowan was using was once a county road but had been closed years ago. He explained that there was another road down Big Greenbrier to the Tiber road Big Jim could use, and it was only a couple of miles longer that way. He said since his farm lay on both sides of the old county road he had a right to fence it in. Then he accused Big Jim of cutting wires and letting his cattle out, and he said he had to roll rocks down from the cliffs to stop him.

After the two men had told their stories, Old Amos said: "Big Jim MacRowan, you have no right to trespass on John Meadows. That road has not been used for years. Take the Big Greenbrier road to Blakesburg with your crossties. Let us have peace in the party."

Big Jim's chest swelled like a bullfrog's throat and his eyes glinted. I could tell he had been taken by surprise when Old Amos ruled against him. "I'll be damned if I take the Big Greenbrier Road," he swore. "I've got a right to use the shorter road. I ain't givin' an inch, even if it splits the Right Party down the middle."

Old Amos' wrinkled features hardened and his long white beard seemed to quiver. "There's evil in your heart, Big Jim MacRowan," he said. "Cast it out before you start a feud in the Right Party."

Big Jim spit on the ground, turned his back on Old Amos and walked away. Alf and Babyhawk followed right on his heels. I waited a moment, hoping that John Meadows would speak to me, but he stood there looking right through me, so I trailed Big Jim down the mountain path feeling more miserable than ever.

The big trouble started the next afternoon when we were making a second trip to Blakesburg. As we took the turn around a steep cliff, just this side of John Meadow's hill pasture, the truck jolted to a stop, and Big Jim jumped out of the cab, his face redder than a ripe tomato. A barrier of heavy log bars had been built right across the road.

Big Jim tried to lift one of the logs, but it wouldn't

budge. He pulled his bandanna from his hip pocket and mopped his brow. "We'll fix old John for this," he said. "Fetch the ax, Babyhawk, and Bobby and Alf you climb down here and help me."

Babyhawk chopped the three bars in two so he and Big Jim could carry one end of one half and Alf and I could carry the other. We carried the six halves out of the road.

"This is the last straw!" Big Jim shouted when we dropped the last bar. "I'm goin' to put John Meadows in jail if it's the last thing I do."

After we'd gone to Blakesburg and unloaded, Big Jim went to young Charlie Denton's office and got a warrant for John Meadows for blocking a county highway still used by the public.

"I'll spend every cent I've made to jail that scoundrel," Big Jim said. "You watch me. I'll put him behind bars!"

A month later court convened, and John Meadows was tried. A jury found him guilty, and he was fined one hundred dollars and jailed for thirty days.

"That jail sentence will do him good," Big Jim told us at his supper table as he lit his cigar. "The fine won't amount to much, but that thirty days behind the bars will make a new man of Old John. We'll have peace while he's in jail! I'll bet when he gets out he'll behave like a man!" Then Big Jim reared back, patted his full stomach with his big hands and said: "Two hundred forty-five pounds of man!" He laughed at his own words and blew smoke rings toward the unpapered shanty ceiling.

The first day John was out of jail he walked out into

his meadow with a shotgun across his shoulder. His meadow bordered the road we were driving over from Blakesburg. John aimed at a crow flying over, fired, and the crow fell from the air and hit on top of the cab. I peeped from behind and watched Big Jim grip the steering wheel and step on the gas. He wasn't laughing now, and his face was pale as frosted crabgrass. We went around the curves bumping the banks until we reached the shanty. When he got out he was shaking like the willow leaves in a spring wind.

"Old John's a good shot," he said. "I believe he'd about as soon shoot a man as look at him. I've always said he's a dangerous man, but he's more dangerous than I thought. I thought that thirty days in jail would do him good. It's made him worse."

The Court had given John Meadows the right to fence on both sides of the road but warned him not to put a fence back across the road. When we returned from Blakesburg one late afternoon, there were rows of peeled locust posts set on both sides of the road. Big Jim's truck hitched on a post and tore a plank off the bed. Then he got out and measured the width of the road. It was ten feet between the posts.

"Your truckbed is too wide, Big Jim," I said. "The state only allows you an eight-foot-and-two-inch bed. I've told you this all the time. You've been crowdin' other cars off the narrow roads, too."

"Now the truth comes out," Big Jim shouted at me, shaking with anger. "You're on Old John's side. You're still hankerin' for that gal of his. That's the kind of loyalty you give me—me, who took you in when you didn't have a place to sleep."

"I've worked hard for everything I got out of you," I said. "Subrina and I aren't to blame for the fight you and Old John got into."

"You better not let me catch you sneakin' over to the Meadows while you're still workin' for me," Big Jim threatened. "I'll fire you and then I'll whip the daylights out of you. And I'll take those fine clothes you're so proud of. Remember, you still owe me money."

"Leave him be," Alf Rister spoke up. "All Bobby said was that your truck bed is too wide—and that's a fact."

Big Jim simmered down, for a while anyway. But that night when we sat down to supper in his shanty, he got to talking about John Meadows again. He just couldn't think of anything else. "No, that jail sentence didn't help Old John any," he grumbled. "Guess there's only one thing that'll do him any good. Only one thing will stop him. I've got a good single-barrel shotgun and plenty of shells with number-three shot. He needs a good sprinklin' —one that will burn him right good."

After we had finished supper, Alf and I went outside to carry in a load of wood. We left Babyhawk and Big Jim still sitting at the table smoking.

"Do you believe Big Jim will sprinkle Old John?" Alf asked me.

"He's just talkin'," I told Alf. "I don't believe he means it. He knows Old John is handy with a shotgun and might do some sprinklin' too."

"Man, I'd hate to be sprinkled with number-three shot

339

at close range," Alf said. "I'm afraid of a shotgun ever since we played the shotgun game over on Leatherwood. We used to go huntin' and if we couldn't find any rabbits, we'd get about a hundred yards away and shoot at one another. I've been burned until I couldn't sit down. We did this for fun! What will happen when men like Big Jim and Old John shoot at one another?"

"Don't worry, Alf," I said. "Old men like to brag. They like to bluff."

"I hope you're right," Alf said as we started back with our wood, "but I've never seen anyone hate like Big Jim hates John Meadows. It's sure tough on you—caught right in the middle."

"I know it," I said. "But he can't keep me from loving Subrina. She's waitin' for me. Just wait 'till I get Big Jim paid off."

"What will you do then?" he asked me.

"You just wait and see," I said. "I'll grab my clothes and take off like a bee-stung pup. I love Subrina Meadows so much it hurts me, Alf!"

At five next morning Alf and I were dressed and ready for breakfast and work. Big Jim didn't act his natural self at the breakfast table. He'd always told a few jokes to start everybody off in a good humor for the day. But this morning he didn't have much to say as we sat around the table eating bacon, eggs and biscuits and drinking our hot coffee. He didn't stand up and beat his chest and say he could whip his weight in wildcats.

After breakfast we drove down to the sawmill to load. Big Jim gave his sawmill boss, Shin Allen, instructions for the day. He had but few words to say to Shin or to any of us. After we'd loaded, he drove back and stopped at the shanty. He got out and went in, and when he came out he had his single-barrel, twelve-gauge shotgun and his big hand filled with shells.

"Boys, I've always kept my powder dry," Big Jim said. "Number-three shot will stop that scoundrel if he starts anything when we tear the posts out. They must come out. I'm not goin' to make a new truck bed."

"Big Jim, don't have any trouble if you can help it," Babyhawk said. "A shotgun is a dangerous weapon. I was trespassin' once and got sprinkled with one! It set me on fire. I almost never stopped runnin'!"

"I won't have any trouble if I can help it," he said. "You know I'm a law-abidin' and a peace-lovin' man."

Babyhawk helped him lay the heavy drag chain on the cab floor of the truck. They got back in and we started down the road. Big Jim drove to where the posts were set, and here we stopped. Babyhawk got out and fastened the chain to a post and then to the truck. Big Jim stepped on the accelerator and pulled the post out.

"Stop tearin' out my posts!" John Meadows shouted as he came running across the meadow. "You've got no right to do that!"

John Meadows had his single-barrel shotgun across his shoulder.

When Babyhawk saw John coming, he dropped the chain he was wrapping around the second post. He took off as fast as his legs would carry him up among the cliffs. Big Jim stepped down from the cab with his shotgun. He didn't wait for John Meadows to come all the way. He leaped the Threeprong Creek, climbed the bank and walked toward John.

"Let's go, Bobby," Alf shouted. "I told you! I don't want to see anybody sprinkled with shot. Maybe get his eyes put out!"

Alf was running with his cap in his hand and I was at his heels. We ran a safe distance before we stopped to look back.

"It looks bad," Alf sighed. "They're gettin' too close to one another!"

"Maybe they're bluffin'," I said.

Alf's face was pale and his lips trembled.

Big, square-shouldered Jim MacRowan and long John Meadows were still going toward each other, holding their single-barrel, twelve-gauge shotguns ready for action. When Big Jim raised his gun to his shoulder, John came up with his. Both guns cracked about the same time and long puffs of black smoke spit from the barrels. Both men jumped back a little when the shot spattered around their legs. Then John turned to reload and caught Big Jim's second shot in his seat. He leaped up, turned and fired just in time to hit Big Jim in the same place. Big Jim jumped a foot off the ground and slapped his hand on the spot. Both fired the third shot just as Subrina and her mother, Myrtle, came running across the meadow.

"They're not over seventy yards apart," Alf stammered. "Looks like they'd fall. I wonder what's holdin' 'em up!"

"Stop it, Big Jim," I yelled. "Don't shoot again!"

My heart pounded. I looked for both men to drop but neither went down.

"Get off my property," John panted as he pulled another shell from his pocket.

"Don't shoot again, Daddy," Subrina screamed.

Then Big Jim turned and limped toward the truck. Babyhawk started scooting down from the cliffs, and Alf started back toward the truck. I leaped the creek and started running toward Subrina and her father.

"Go to 'im, you low-lifed copperhead," Jim Mac-Rowan shouted. "Now I know whose side you're on!"

He raised his shotgun to his shoulder, aimed at me and fired. The shots fell like a gentle rain. They didn't even burn me—I was too far away.

Subrina was holding onto her father when I came up.

"Are you hurt, John?" I asked him.

"Burnin' on my chest and stomach," he sighed painfully. "And that load I got behind is settin' me on fire. Old Jim must have used high-powered shells on me. Maybe his gun is full choked. Mine is only half. I must be set on fire more than he is!"

"Let's get to Blakesburg before they do," I said. "Let's see the county attorney first and the doctor second. Let's get the Right Party and the Law on our side."

"Oh, Bobby," Subrina said, weeping. "I'm glad you're with us."

Subrina took her father by one arm while her mother held on to the other to help him to the truck. There were little dots of blood on John's neck, and it was soaking through his shirt in little spots and oozing through the seat of his overalls.

"I know how you stand now, Bobby," John said when we reached his truck. "Now is when we need you."

343

We helped John into the cab, but he couldn't sit down. He stood in the cab leaning over Myrtle who was taking on something awful. Subrina sat next to me and she was crying too. I gunned the truck down the lane to the Threeprong Valley Road for I saw Big Jim's truck coming with Babyhawk at the wheel.

"We've got the lead on 'em," John said. "Try to hold onto the lead! They're right behind us! We must see young Charlie first!"

"Their truck is loaded and ours is empty," I said. "They won't pass!"

By the time we reached the top of Red Hot Hill, Big Jim's truck had fallen far behind. The steam was boiling up like white smoke from our radiator when we pulled up to the courthouse in Blakesburg. Young Charlie Denton, the county attorney, had just walked up to the steps to begin his day's work.

"I tried to tell you, Young Charlie, when you prosecuted me and sent me to jail, that this Jim MacRowan is a dangerous man," John called. "We sprinkled one another this mornin'. He came right over on my land after me with a shotgun. I'm hit all over, stingin' and burnin' somethin' awful."

John was stiff when we took him out of the truck. When he walked he shuffled his feet; as we went up the courthouse steps to Young Charlie's office, Myrtle got on one side and I got on the other to help him.

"You need a doctor first," Young Charlie said as he looked at John.

"He's pale from the loss of blood," Myrtle said. "Look

344

how red this handkerchief is! I wiped all this from his neck!"

"I need you first and a doctor second," John told him. "Jim MacRowan is comin' here too and he's right behind us!"

"I'll call a doctor," Young Charlie said. "While he examines you my secretary will take your story."

"I've got my witnesses right here," John told him. "Bobby Love here has worked for that feller over a year. He can tell you how even Amos Bodie couldn't do anything with Big Jim."

"I know that," Young Charlie said. "Old Amos told me all about him. He told me Big Jim would tear our Right Party apart unless we stopped him."

"I saw it with my own eyes," Subrina said. "I saw him shoot Daddy three times!"

"He shot John right on our premises," Myrtle cried. "We used to have peace. We didn't know what trouble was until that man moved to Threeprong Valley. We've had trouble ever since he moved there!"

"Besides, he's about to tear up the Right Party," John grunted painfully.

The county attorney was talking into the telephone. "Sheriff Atkinson," he said, "Big Jim MacRowan shot John Meadows and wounded him badly a little while ago. Shot him three times and his hide is a sieve. MacRowan is on his way to Blakesburg with a truckload of crossties. Be sure to get the shotgun he used on John Meadows. We'll need it at the trial. Arrest everybody on the truck."

Dr. Norris arrived with Emma Bolton, the county nurse, and soon they picked nearly an ounce of shot from John's chest, neck and seat. John told his whole story to County Attorney Charlie Denton. Young Charlie's secretary took down every word John said. Then she took down our statements as witnesses.

Just as we were finishing, Sheriff Will Atkinson walked in pistol butts sticking from a holster on each hip. 'Attorney, we got your men in jail," the sheriff said. "We got three men and we've got the shotgun for evidence over in my office."

"You didn't jail Alf, did you?" I said.

"Alf who?" Sheriff Atkinson asked.

"Alf Rister," I said. "He didn't have anything to do with all this trouble!"

"Which one is Alf?" he asked.

"The young man with the white hair and the ferret-colored eyes," I said. "He never tried to hurt anybody in his life."

"Jailed him too," Sheriff Atkinson said. "Whose side are you on, anyway?"

"John Meadows' side, of course!" I said as I looked at Subrina. She never looked prettier to me. Her big blue eyes were filled with tears. The long lashes above them looked like ferns shading a pool of misty mountain water. Her lips were as soft and pink as pawpaw blossoms in early April.

"Bobby Love will be my key witness when this trial comes up," John said. "We'll put MacRowan in jail this time!"

346

"Big Jim belongs in jail and that's where I'm going to send him," Young Charlie said. "He's caused a lot of ill will in the Right Party. We've got to take him out of circulation."

A smile spread over John's face. When we left the office he shuffled his feet across the floor. He rested a hand on each hip and bent over to keep from bumping his head as he went under the door.

"Tobacco season is comin' on and you won't be able to work," Myrtle sighed. "This is awful."

"Dr. Norris told me I'd be improved in three weeks," John grunted as we walked down the steps.

"I don't have a job," I said. "I lost my job this mornin'. And I don't have a home."

"You have a job now," John said. "You can go home with us right now. I know how you stand. I'm thankful to the Right Party and my friends."

We walked slowly with John toward the truck. Subrina's face was beaming when she looked at me. The tear mists were gone from her eyes. I had never been so happy in my life.

ACKNOWLEDGMENTS

"A Little Piece of Striped Candy-colored String" was first published in *Southwest Review*. Copyright © 1968 by Southern Methodist University Press. "As the People Choose" originally appeared in *Esquire* magazine in the October, 1940, issue and was later reprinted in the Jesse Stuart short-story collection *Men of the Mountains*. "Uncle Felix and the Party Emblem" is reprinted from the *Georgia Review*, © 1966 by the University of Georgia. "The Election" is reprinted from *Prairie Schooner* by permission. Copyright © 1939 by the University of Nebraska Press. "The Judge Takes a Holiday" appeared in the February, 1939, issue of *American Mercury*, Box 1306, Torrance, California, and is reprinted by permission. "Law in Poppie's Vest Pocket" was first published in *New Little Man* in January, 1959. "Love beyond the Law" is reprinted with permission from *Country Gentleman* © 1948 by The Curtis Publishing Company. "The Voting Goodlaws" was first published in *Southwest Review*. Copyright © 1948 by Southern Methodist University Press. "Love and the Law" is reprinted from *Georgia Review*, © 1955

348

by the University of Georgia. "Sweetbird for Sheriff" is reprinted by permission of *Esquire* magazine © 1956 by Esquire, Inc. "32 votes before Breakfast" originally appeared in *Esquire* magazine in the July, 1947, issue and was later included in the Jesse Stuart short-story collection *Clearing in the Sky*. "Peace and the Right Party" is reprinted by permission of *New Letters,* copyright holder for *The University of Kansas City Review*. Permission of the author has also been obtained for reprinting all of the above-named material.

About the Author

For his thirty-fifth published book (not counting his first venture, which he had privately printed in an edition so limited that any one of the nine copies still in existence is worth $1,000), Jesse Stuart has chosen to bring together a collection of short stories which make it perfectly clear that political connivance and skullduggery are as old as the Kentucky hills. It is here that the stories take place; the politicians are as autochthonous as the land and the author. Stuart seldom goes far from the land of his birth when he's looking for a subject about which to write a story or a poem or a novel, though his travels have taken him all over the world.